Swept Away

GWYNNE FORSTER

Swept Away

ARABESQUE®

Recycling programs
for this product may
not exist in your area.

SWEPT AWAY

An Arabesque novel published by Kimani Press/May 2009.

First published by BET Books, LLC in 2000.

ISBN-13: 978-0-373-83159-3
ISBN-10: 0-373-83159-5

www.kimanipress.com

Printed in U.S.A.

To my husband who loves me and whom I love;
to the memory of my father who gave me my first
lesson in the meaning and power of a man's love;
and to my stepson who is so much like them both.

Chapter 1

Veronica Overton walked with prideful steps into the executive ladies' room on the fifth and top floor of the building that housed the agency, Child Placement and Assistance—CPAA—that she headed as executive director. In the three years that she'd been its chief, she'd developed the agency into a driving force on Baltimore's notoriously depressed and blighted west side. When she went home to her co-op town house in upper-middle-class Owings Mills, just outside Baltimore proper each night, she could pride herself in the knowledge that she'd made it; she'd accomplished what millions strove to do. She'd reached the top of her profession before her thirty-third year, and by bringing integrity to everything she did, she'd won the respect and admiration of everyone who knew or knew about her. Veronica reached the entrance to the ladies' lounge and stopped short.

"What do you know about that?" she heard a woman ask. "Her Highness, Lady Veronica, is flat on her backside. The invincible Miss Overton. Not even the governor can get her out of this one."

Veronica recognized Mary Ann's voice when she said, "Why're you so happy about it? I think it's a reflection on all of us. Somebody slipped up somewhere."

"Yeah," came the voice of Astrid Moore, the woman who had competed with Veronica for the position of executive director, "but Her Highness is the one who'll burn for it. That man means business."

Veronica rubbed her arms to relieve the sensation of burrs and thorns attacking her skin. Forgetting that the women thought themselves alone, she startled Astrid with a hand on her shoulder.

"What are you talking about? What's happened that I don't know about?"

Astrid's glistening white teeth sparkled against her smooth dark skin. "You didn't know? Schyler Henderson just held a news conference. Seems Natasha Wynn is missing from the foster home we placed her in, and he's suing CPAA for negligence."

Veronica couldn't help bristling at the accusation, even as apprehension raced like blood through her body. "Negligence? He's out of his mind. Some children run away from their own parents."

"Yes," Mary Ann said, stepping over to Veronica's side in an unspoken gesture of support. "But Mr. Henderson said the home in which we placed Natasha is an unsuitable environment. You know what that means."

"Do I ever!" Veronica wrinkled her nose against the sweet, sickening perfume that Astrid sprayed around her neck and ears. "Thanks for your loyalty, Astrid. Be sure I won't forget it. Not ever," she added with pointed sarcasm.

She inspected her light brown skin, combed her black, artificially straight hair, refreshed the lipstick that matched her dusty-rose raw-silk dress and walked out of the room head high and shoulders straight. People said she walked regally, but she felt anything but regal right then. A blast from Schyler Henderson and his Advocates for the Child (AFTC) people could topple her, destroy all that she'd done and sink her into professional disgrace.

She welcomed the sharp mid-March air that greeted her when she stepped out of the CPAA building. Winter had hung around longer than usual, and she tugged her street-length black shearling coat closer to her body. At the corner, she bought some roasted chestnuts from Franco, who told her proudly that he'd sent three children through college on what he made selling them. She believed him. Over twelve years, chestnuts at ten for a dollar fifty could have bought him a mansion.

The twenty-minute train ride home gave her just the time she needed to unwind after a hard day and to begin thinking of her other life. Her choral society, work with the shelters and her plan to help juveniles achieve more respect in their neighborhoods. She wanted to form them into groups of volunteers who would assist people in emergencies. As she entered the two-story brown brick structure, she couldn't help feeling a sense of pride. It was hers, and she didn't owe one penny on it.

After a light supper, she sipped ginger ale and watched the evening news. The Henderson man was everywhere, and his commanding presence and mesmerizing charisma seemed to have worked their magic on the reporters. Not one of them questioned his accusations; not one pointed out her contribution to the people in the area she served. Sickened by the media's readiness to put her on trial, she flipped off the TV and set about planning her defense.

The next morning she sat in her office with her deputy, Enid Dupree, discussing the agency's options. Enid didn't believe they had the resources or the proof to combat AFTC. "Veronica, you know Henderson is formidable when he makes a case against you. Look at the way he managed that case against the boys' club."

Veronica sat forward. She'd forgotten that case. "But this agency is not culpable."

Enid shrugged. "Doesn't have to be. He believes in his soul that we've destroyed Natasha Wynn, and if you didn't have anything more to go on than the evidence he cited to the press, you'd say he's right."

"I know he's a heavyweight. Everybody around here knows about him and his crusades, but people say he's honorable."

"Somebody's feeding him half-truths. I'd bet my new face on it."

Veronica's shoulders shook with her laughter. "You paid eight thousand dollars for *that* face. You mean you're that sure we've got a stool pigeon in here?"

"You heard what he said at his news conference. He sounded as if he'd been reading our files."

"Then he should have read the truth. That foster home has had a perfect record." She gritted her teeth. "You wouldn't believe how I'd like to get my hands on that man."

Enid's new face bloomed into a lusty female grin. "Me, too. Lord knows I would, and I wouldn't be taking my hands off him anytime soon. Believe me, I'd—"

Veronica could hardly believe what she heard. Enid never talked about men unless discussing them professionally. "Wait a minute. Are you saying—?"

Enid didn't bother to show any embarrassment at having raved about a man. "Haven't you met the guy? If he doesn't send your blood rushing the wrong way, you haven't got any. I'm fifty-four, but just looking at that man from a distance of twenty feet made me pray."

"Pray?"

"Yes, honey. If I hadn't prayed for self-control, I'd have gone straight up to him and said or done something stupid."

Thank God it wouldn't be a jury trial, and with luck, the judge would be a forty-year-old ladies' man. "I've seen him on TV, but I never got the impression that he was irresistible."

"Same here, but Mr. Henderson in person is an all 'nother cut of cloth. Those eyes! And, Lord, that million dollar charisma. Whew!"

Veronica leaned back in her chair, picked up a pencil, twirled it, put it down and shuffled some of the papers on her desk. Restless and impatient. "All right. I get it. That only means I've got work to do and plenty of it. He's used to getting his way, no doubt."

Laughter spilled out of the woman sitting beside her desk. "If he told me what his 'way' was, I'd see that he got it."

At Veronica's icy stare, Enid threw up her hands. "Just kidding. Just kidding. See you later."

Veronica watched her leave. She trusted Enid, but she didn't care to do battle with a male heartthrob. Competence she could handle, but she didn't relish being the generator for a man's ego trip. She read and reread the information in Natasha's file. The agency hadn't made a single mistake with the girl. Who knew why an eleven-year-old would run away. A sudden chill stole into her. A child wouldn't run away from a warm, loving and happy home, would she? If indeed that was what had happened. Lord forbid Natasha had been a victim of foul play.

She mused over the problem and, on impulse, asked her secretary for Schyler Henderson's phone number. She couldn't plan if she didn't know precisely what the charges were.

"Schyler Henderson. Good morning."

His warm, caressing tones gave her a mental picture of a perfectly proportioned male lying supine on a bed of dewy grass with a warm breeze kissing his bare skin. She reined in her thoughts.

"Hello, Mr. Henderson. This is Veronica Overton."

"What may I do for you, Ms. Overton?"

So he didn't engage in small talk. She held the receiver away and stared at it. She respected professionalism. She told him she'd learned of his charges through the media.

"It seems to me that if you were seriously concerned about our placement practices, you would at least have spoken with me before you made your public grandstand."

"I considered it, but since I didn't know you or how you operated, I decided against it."

"Well, I want you to know that I had no idea Natasha wasn't in that home until one of my staff told me about your press conference."

"Ms. Overton, that home is unsuitable. The child has disappeared, and no amount of discussion will change that. The only way we'll stop this...these tragedies is nip them at the source."

"That home has served more than a dozen children over the years without one unpleasant incident. Furthermore, my agency has an impeccable record, and we provide the only service of its kind to West Baltimore. If you destroy us, what can you put in our place?"

"I'm not out to destroy your agency. We need it; you and that agency have been a good thing for this community. But we must protect and preserve every child, every little life, Ms. Overton. No mistake is tolerable. My aim is to make sure that our children get the best possible service. From the information available to me, it appears that Natasha Wynn didn't get that so, much as I'd rather not move against you, I have to do what I believe is right."

Schyler hung up, got the file and read it through again, assuring himself that he hadn't misrepresented the woman or her agency. Still, an uneasy feeling settled in him. He'd never met her, but he knew her reputation and he was loathe to sully it. Women, and especially African-American women, had a hard enough time getting executive jobs and receiving the support they needed after they got them. He didn't want to knock her down, but when he remembered his own travails in first one foster home and then another, he had to stay his course for the child's sake. He called the district attorney's office to lodge his complaint.

Brian Atwood answered the phone. "Man, Overton has a spotless record. You asking me to dethrone that icon?"

Schyler sat down, put his feet on his desk, crossed his ankles and leaned back in his swivel chair. "I know who she is, and I don't want to hurt her, but it's my job to act when a child is endangered." He could imagine that he'd worried Brian, the coward of their college class.

"I hope you know what you're doing, man. She's rock solid."

Fishing with Brian could be fun, but working with him tried his patience. "*Was* rock solid. I'm sending the file over by messenger."

"Okay," Brian said, a tad slowly, Schyler thought. "I'll get back to you."

Three hours later, Schyler lifted the receiver hoping his caller was not Veronica Overton and breathed deeply in relief when he heard Brian's voice. "What do you think?"

Brian didn't hesitate. "I'll check this out and if I find cause, I'll bring charges."

A week later, AFTC's charges against Veronica's agency were aired in Family Court.

Schyler strode into court, certain of his grounds but unhappy about the damage he might inflict on a woman of commanding stature and singular achievement. She had rescued Child Placement and Assistance from irrelevancy and made it a force in the community. He knew about her, had heard her on radio and seen her on television, but he'd never met her. A half-smile settled around his mouth. She always sounded so correct, perfect, like Miss Betts, his fourth-grade teacher. He hadn't liked Miss Betts, he recalled, because she never gave him credit for what he did. Sometimes, he wished she could see him now. He'd grin at her and show her his thumbs up sign, the way he always did when she was mean to him. He laughed to himself, because he knew he was procrastinating. Much as he hated it, he had to present this case.

He walked away from his side of the aisle, greeted an acquaintance and shook hands with him, still postponing the inevitable. Then he sat at the table provided for him and looked across the narrow aisle that separated him from Veronica Overton, intending to bow graciously, and did a double take. Right straight to the marrow of his bones. An arrow with his name on it. She'd looked at him and his heart had taken off and sped unerringly to her. *Get ahold of yourself, man.* This spelled trouble, because she'd reacted to him as surely as he had to her. Quickly, he focused his attention on the papers in front of him. She'd been looking at him again and had diverted her gaze when he caught her at it. He ran his fingers through the thick black wavy hair that disputed the purity of his African heritage. Now, what was that all about?

Veronica glanced up just as the tall, distinguished-looking man entered the far side of the chamber. Schyler Henderson. A giant of a man. At least six feet five inches tall, though trim as an athlete. She'd never realized he was so tall and, for reasons she refused to examine, imagined that he'd dwarf her five feet ten inches. Not that she wouldn't like it; she enjoyed being with a man who made her feel soft and feminine. She settled her gaze on him. She wouldn't say he was a knockout, but… He looked at someone in front of her, smiled, and long strides brought him to within a few feet of where she sat. His smile claimed his whole face as he shook hands with the man before going to the table reserved for him and sitting down.

The bottom dropped out of her belly, and she knew what Enid meant about blood flowing backward. She stared at his back while something leaped within her, quickening her insides. She couldn't move her gaze from him. He sat alone, without a lawyer, leaning back, as relaxed as a marathon runner at the end of a race. She brought herself under control and *breathed.* Lord, she'd never seen such eyes.

The judge called the proceedings to order, and Brian Atwood read the charges. She marveled at her ability to sit quietly through it. Her agency's lawyer refuted the charges, and she strummed her fingers on her knee. Such a waste of time and money. It hadn't occurred to her that Schyler would be the one to argue on behalf of Advocates for the Child. She bristled at the assurance with which he read the brief he'd written as a friend of the court.

"No matter what CPAA's reputation is, it cannot be allowed to endanger our children. The tragedy of Natasha Wynn has sullied the commendable reputation that this agency established during the previous three years. But saving a hundred children does not excuse the loss of one."

Angry at him as Veronica was, he fascinated her. And thrilled her. She watched, spellbound, as he strolled from one end of the bench to the other, a consummate actor.

He spread his hands as though helpless. "Of course, Your Honor, we can pat them on the back and say, *now you be good little boys and girls and don't do this anymore.* Sure, and we could be right back here a month, two, three or a year from now with another tragedy." He looked over at her and smiled. "We wouldn't want that, Your Honor." To her surprise, he called her to the stand.

Veronica took the stand. "Thank you for the opportunity to speak on my behalf, Mr. Henderson. Not many of us can claim to have achieved perfection in every aspect of our lives as you so obviously have, so you'll forgive me if I don't blow my own horn and let the agency's record speak for itself."

She could see that she'd stung him, but he was only momentarily nonplussed. "When we're dealing with people's lives, we'd better be perfect," he replied, his tone gentle and his manner respectful.

She refused to allow him the last word. "Since you know that, Mr. Henderson, I'd think you'd have gotten your facts straight before you took an action that could destroy *my* life."

A look of distress flashed across his countenance, and she got a sense that he regretted the entire affair, but he quickly replaced it with an expression of confidence and asked the judge for a ruling against CPAA.

The judge, apparently having heard enough, announced that he'd render a decision within ten days and dismissed them.

Veronica marched out of the chamber, head high, without a glance in Schyler's direction. He'd had the temerity to accuse her agency. She couldn't think of any torture good enough for him. As the crisp March air hit her face, enlivening her skin, invigorating her, his long shadow paired with hers, and she didn't doubt that he'd maneuvered it so that they'd leave the building together.

She didn't look at him. Deliberately. She didn't want any of his magnetism, though it seemed to radiate from him even when she wasn't looking at him. "I'm surprised you'd care for my company, Mr. Henderson. It taxes my credulity to think you'd allow yourself to be seen with such an irresponsible person as me, a menace to the well-being of Baltimore's children. Sure you haven't mistaken me for someone else?"

He took a deep breath and let it out slowly. "This isn't personal, Ms. Overton. I've admired your work, but this tragedy requires restitution."

She stopped walking and looked up at him. "And you don't care who pays. Is that it? You don't even know that there is a tragedy. She's missing, but for all you know she could be safe. Where there's no body, there's no murder; any detective will tell you that. Make a name for yourself at somebody else's expense, please."

He faced her, towering over her, either unable or not caring to hide the sensual awareness making itself known through the prisms of his remarkable gray eyes. "I'm not a crusader, Ms. Overton. I'm trying to protect children because they can't do that for themselves. I'd never set out to hurt you. You... you're..." He looked into the distance, protecting his thoughts, and when he looked back at her, she couldn't mistake the compassion his eyes conveyed for anything but what it was. He *did* dislike hurting her.

He stared down at her, his gaze unfathomable. A half-smile formed around his sensuous mouth. Then he winked. "See you next week." And he was gone.

Schyler's steps slowed when he approached the restaurant where he'd told Brian they could meet for lunch, as his mind grappled with the enigma that was Veronica Overton. Once there, he ordered a hamburger with french fries, coleslaw and a dill pickle, and a chocolate sundae for dessert.

"Aren't you hungry?" Brian asked, as he watched Schyler pick at his food.

"I don't know. I just don't feel that spurt of adrenaline, that excitement that I usually get on a case. I don't feel like making the kill. Maybe I ought to turn this job over to somebody else and stick to engineering."

"This doesn't surprise me. It's a real bummer. The woman's standing in the community didn't happen accidentally. She had to work her tail off for it, man. You're going to make yourself a bunch of enemies."

"I know, but I can't help it. When I became head of Advocates for the Child, I took an oath to pursue vigorously every case in which a child had been put at risk. It's my job, and I have to do it, but I…" He rubbed his forehead. "You don't know how I hate the thought of jeopardizing that woman's career."

"Well fasten your seat belt, man. I've got some news for you."

"Yeah?"

"Those foster parents have separated. I got it when I called my office just before you walked in here. You can't lose this one."

"Separated after twenty-three years? What about?"

"Seems she's tired of doing everything in the house while he comes home at night, buries his face in a book or newspaper and cultivates his mind. She's mad as hell and she's not taking it anymore."

Brian's laughter grated on his ears. He didn't find it amusing. "That doesn't make it a bad home for a child."

"Does if they argued about it a lot."

Schyler nodded. "If the man's such a lost cause, how'd she stand him for twenty-three years?" He finished his chocolate sundae. "Gotta go, man. See you in court."

He hailed a taxi to his office at Branch Signal Corporation, where he worked as chief of electrical design. An engineer by profession, he'd gotten a law degree so that he could help underprivileged people, particularly children, who otherwise wouldn't get competent counseling. He didn't charge for his services to AFTC, and although he represented the foundation, he didn't practice law.

He went to his drafting table and began working on a method of tapping electric energy in summer when it was cheapest and storing it for use in winter when it became more expensive. He was too disconcerted to work. Something…everything about that case bothered him. He walked over to the window and looked down at the crowds scurrying along Calvert Street like ants after sugar. He'd gotten one good look at her, and she'd poleaxed him. In all his thirty-six years, no woman had done to him what she did without trying. He wondered how he'd had the presence of mind not to stare at her. He lifted his left shoulder in a quick shrug. She wasn't immune to him either. But he suspected she had the strength to put aside whatever she felt, to ignore it and him. Too bad. He'd give anything if he'd met her in more favorable circumstances.

Veronica walked into Enid's office without knocking, something she never did with any of her employees. Allowing a person privacy was essential to good relations. She dropped into the chair nearest the door and, in a gesture uncharacteristic of her, folded her hands and dropped them into her lap.

"For goodness sake," Enid exclaimed, "what happened? Don't tell me he…he… Good Lord, I knew I shouldn't have let you talk me out of going to that trial with you."

Enid got up from her desk and walked over to her boss. "What? Did the judge rule against us?"

How could Veronica tell a woman who was her subordinate what Schyler Henderson had done to her? That her common sense didn't function when she was close to him? That he was the Greek God Apollo incarnate? Well, maybe he wasn't, but what difference did it make? If he had invited her to lunch, she would probably have gone with him.

"Did he?" she heard Enid ask in a voice that had become plaintive.

She straightened up. "No. No. It's not that. His Honor decided to make us wait ten more days." She rose from the chair, patted Enid on her arm and left. In her own office, she prowled around for a few minutes; then she shook her body as if divesting her clothes of chaff and her shoes of loose soil. On top of that sex-charged aura, he was a gentleman. He'd indicted the agency, but he hadn't said a word against her personally. And he'd been sorry, almost apologetic about that. *He's a man I could spend a lot of time with and be happy doing it. If only I'd met him in more favorable circumstances.* But she hadn't, and she'd better stop thinking about him.

Before the week's end, however, Veronica's thoughts of Schyler were not filled with longing for him. Natasha Wynn had been apprehended, wan and emaciated while stealing food in a supermarket, and AFTC had indicted her as the head of the agency.

Enraged, she phoned Schyler. "What's the meaning of this? Are you trying to destroy me? Why are you persecuting me?"

His long silence only served to heighten her annoyance. Finally he gave her an answer different from what she would have expected, all things considered.

"Ms. Overton, I am not your attorney, but I will give you

some good advice. Please don't appeal to my good nature. I have one, yes. But I place my responsibilities above my personal feelings."

Her bottom lip dropped. She held the phone away and stared at the receiver. Talk about *chutzpah!* "Your personal feelings? Where do they come in?"

He let her have another pause. "You're old enough to know the answer to that question. If you'll excuse me, I'll see you in court next Monday. And be prepared, because I'm duty bound to get a conviction in this case, though I may have come to hate the thought, and I'm warning you that you're in trouble."

"Wait a minute. I don't know the answer to that question, and if you do, I wish you'd let me in on it."

He expelled a long breath, and she imagined that he closed his eyes and prayed for patience. "I tell myself the truth," he said, "even if I don't mention it to anybody but me. You were right there with me when it happened, so you know what I'm talking about. But don't let that lull you into complacency about this court case."

So he acknowledged the electricity between them, felt it and would still do what he regarded as the noble thing. If she hadn't been facing the fight of her life, she'd admire him for it.

"One doesn't expect protection from one's avowed executioner. Better look closely at your motives, Mr. Henderson. See you in court."

She hung up, her nerves rioting through her flesh, making a mockery of her cool manner. The case against CPAA hadn't been settled, and now AFTC had indicted *her.* That indictment was a death knell that filled her head with dislike for Schyler Henderson. Yet, his eyes, his smile, his masculine bearing raised havoc with her feminine soul. The moist telltale of desire dampened her pores, and her heart stampeded like horses charging out of a corral. She dropped her head into her hands as her warring emotions pitted her against herself.

* * *

The day of decision arrived, but before the judge ruled on the case against CPAA, Schyler presented to the judge his agency's case against Veronica *herself*. Once more, she refused to answer questions but, instead, challenged Schyler and AFTC.

"My record is my defense. The whole of Baltimore, Maryland, knows what I've contributed to this community. Whose sins are you demanding that I pay for?"

Schyler knew that the effect of the blow she'd landed had to be mirrored in his face, telling her that she'd touched a nerve.

"I'm not being personal, so would you please try to resist it?" he said, deciding against a return thrust.

She countered his every point, fencing as skillfully as Errol Flynn or the great Olympians of the past. And he wanted her to destroy his arguments, prayed that she would, though he did nothing to help her. After she'd been on the stand for about an hour, Schyler conferred with the district attorney, who then asked the judge for a bench consultation, saying he wanted to withdraw the charges, that he could not aptly substantiate them.

Schyler knew without doubt that only once before in his life had he experienced such an overwhelming sense of relief. He'd finally lost a case, but he couldn't be happier. AFTC would make certain that Natasha Wynn received all the support she needed, but her two weeks of pain on the streets of Baltimore had taught her and all concerned a lesson. Him, too, and maybe he'd needed it. He went out to face the reporters who crowded around him, their bulbs flashing and notepads bobbing in the air as they shouted for his attention. He was the man of the moment.

Over their heads, he saw Veronica walk out undisturbed. A fierce pain gnawed at his belly; her wings had been clipped, and he and AFTC had engineered it. Their intentions had been good, but as his father had told him dozens of times, the highway to hell was paved with good intentions. He watched her for as long as he could see her, her head high and chin up, and fought the urge to wade through that sea of reporters and take her into his arms.

Veronica made her way back to the office, called a staff meeting, gave them the outcome of the trial, packed her briefcase and left. Several blocks from the train station, at the corner of Reisterstown Road and Bock Avenue, she crossed the street to where she knew she'd find Jenny with her shopping cart full of useless things.

"You here early today, Ronnie." Jenny claimed the gap between her front teeth made it impossible for her to say "Veronica." "Ain't a bit like you. You not sick, I hope."

In spirit, maybe. "I'm all right, Jenny. Thanks. I have a few things to do at home."

Jenny squinted at the sun and sucked in her cheeks. "I been sitting here every day it didn't rain for the last almost two years, and this the first time you ever had anything to do at home. Well, I ain't much to offer help, but ifn' you need any prayers, you just let me know." She rolled her eyes skyward. "He don't always answer mine for me, but when I prays for other people, he do."

Veronica pressed a few bills into Jenny's hand. "Thanks, friend. I'll take all the prayers I can get."

"I sure do thank you, Ronnie. I know I'll get something to eat every evening, 'cause somebody from Mica's Restaurant across the way always brings me some fried lake trout and cornbread and collards. What you give me, I uses to buy soap, toothpaste, aspirins and things like that. I could use another blanket this winter."

"I'll make sure you get one. If you'd just go see that social worker, we might be able to get you a place to stay."

She'd given up hope of getting Jenny off the street. What had begun as a solution to the loss of her apartment had become a matter of psychological dysfunction. Jenny no longer seemed to want a home; she had become inured to her hardships and accepted them as her way of life.

"Yes ma'am. I'm goin' down to the shelter and get cleaned up, and I'm goin' to see her. Yes ma'am, I sure am."

Veronica waved her goodbye and struck out for the train station.

At home, Veronica watched Schyler on the local news channel, transfixed by the smooth manner in which he made it seem as though all parties to the litigation had won. *Won?* She'd had the carpet yanked from under her. She flipped off the television and took out her knitting, hoping to settle her nerves with the rhythmic movements of her fingers, and at the same time, to make some headway on the two dozen mittens and caps that she gave every Christmas to children at the homeless shelter. Schyler's hazel eyes winked at her and refused to be banished from her mind's eye. Reluctantly, she answered the telephone, hoping that the caller wasn't from the media.

"Hello."

"Veronica, I just saw Schyler Henderson's press conference," her stepfather said. "I hope the man will leave you in peace now. He can say what a great agency you're running, but if he thought so, why did he do this to you? I feel like calling him and giving him a piece of my mind."

She couldn't help smiling. Sam Overton never failed to support her. Time and again he'd proved his boundless faith in her, and she loved him without reservation. "He was trying to make amends as best he could. I can't deny that the case has done some damage, but the agency will survive, because nothing exists that can replace it."

"All right, but what about all those awards the city and state have given to you and to the agency? They can forget about what you've done for that city?" She could imagine him snapping his fingers when he said, "Just like that? It's sickening."

"Don't worry, Papa, I'll be fine."

"Then what're you doing home this time of day? I couldn't believe it when Enid told me you'd gone home."

"Best place to clean out my mind. I was in no mood to console the sixty-seven employees who'd be drifting into my office for assurance that they still had jobs. How's Mama?"

"Pretty good today. She's asleep right now. Don't worry, Veronica. As long as you do your best, you can hold your head up. You're competent. Nobody can take that from you."

"Thanks, Papa, but right now I don't have much enthusiasm for service to the public."

"It'll come back. Looks like we've both met our Hendersons."

"What do you mean?"

"Long story, child. There was one in my life once, and he won, too. But only for a little while. So chin up."

"Thanks, Papa. Love you. Give Mama a hug."

"You know I will. Talk to you later."

She went back to her knitting, more tranquil now, musing over her stepfather's comment that he, too, had met his Henderson. But if she knew Sam Overton, he'd said as much on the subject as he ever would. She searched for a solution to foster care but couldn't think of a workable alternative. Still, something had to be done. Restless, she put her knitting aside, went to the Steinway grand in her living room and began to practice a song that her choral group had chosen for its next performance. But after half an hour she gave it up, went out on her back porch and sat there, looking at the ripening of spring, trying to count her blessings.

Schyler had been home twenty minutes when the phone rang. He lifted the receiver, knowing instinctively that the caller was his father.

"You didn't call to let me know how the case went," Richard Henderson said to his son. Not accusing; he didn't do that. He merely stated the facts.

"I didn't have anything to rejoice about. I lost, but I'm not sorry."

He could imagine that his father, knowing how he hated to lose even the most trite argument, raised his antennae.

"Why not?"

"Instead of answering my question, she asked me if I wasn't demanding that she pay for someone else's sins. Dad, that thing cut me to the quick. Maybe I was. I…I just don't know."

"Don't punish yourself for nothing, Son. You said the case had merit. You questioning your judgment?"

"Yeah. I don't know. The case against the agency made more sense than the one against her." He rubbed the back of his neck. "For the life of me, I don't know why I went after her like that…like a lion after a gazelle. She…she's…"

"I see. You liked her. You more than liked her, you bent over backward not to let your feelings get in the way, and you think you overdid it. Right?"

Arrow-straight as always, Richard couldn't have put it plainer. Schyler rubbed his square chin and released a breath of frustration. "Something like that but, well, that's history now. Our paths won't cross again unless we meet at a conference, a fund-raiser or a civic meeting."

He rubbed his chin, reflecting on what could have been. Too bad. Rotten, lousy timing. This woman had gotten to him in ways that he couldn't have imagined. And right then, he didn't want to examine his feelings, a mélange of almost everything a man could feel for a woman. Almost. Something remained that he'd never given to any woman. But if he got to know her…

"Would it help to call her and tell her you're sorry, or maybe that you're glad things worked out as they did?"

He didn't believe in putting Band-Aids on life-threatening wounds. He'd take his medicine. "I don't think that'll help, but you're right. I ought to do something to restore her status in the public's eyes. I'll call a news conference. That's how it got started."

His father's low growl of a laugh had always comforted him in an odd way. "You going to eat crow?" Richard asked when he finally stopped laughing.

Schyler didn't catch anything amusing. "Don't like the stuff. No way. I'll fix it, though."

Veronica flicked on the television in her office, leaned against her desk and watched Schyler tell the press that his complaints against CPAA and Veronica were not substantiated and reminded them that the case had been thrown out of court. When hours passed and not a single reporter had telephoned to get her reaction to the press conference Schyler had called to exonerate her, she knew the damage to her and the agency exceeded what she'd imagined. She was no longer good news copy, and she said as much to her deputy.

Enid tried without success to camouflage her disheartened mood. "When a man drops an egg, he thinks his only problem is cleaning up the mess. Does he stop to deal with the fact that there is no longer an egg?"

It surprised her that she didn't want to hear him vilified. "Don't you think he tried to repair the damage?"

Enid sucked air through her teeth hard and long. "Not in my opinion. He should have come right out and said he made a mistake in bringing the charges, that he was wrong and next time he'd see to it that his assistants did a better job of getting the facts."

Visions of his eyes glistening with heat for her flashed through Veronica's mind, and she remembered his words: *"You were right there with me."* He'd wanted her and hadn't tried to hide it, and he had known that she reciprocated what he felt.

Veronica leaned back in her chair, folded her hands behind her head, crossed her knees and pondered Enid's attack on Schyler. She thought for a few minutes before answering. "You're forgetting that the girl was missing, he didn't know where she was and, when she surfaced on a charge of stealing food she was a shell of her former self. His crime was in caring too much."

Enid rolled her eyes skyward, crossed and uncrossed her ankles. "If you say so. I don't know what we're going to do, though. Fund-raising's going to be a problem."

"Don't worry. I'll think of something. Right now, I need a change of scenery."

Chapter 2

At home later that day, she walked around her elegant town house. She picked up a paperweight and stared at it. For the past five years she'd done nothing but work. CPAA had been her whole world. She thought of what she'd done with her life and what she hadn't done. As a child, she'd had such promise, gifted in music and art. But she'd chosen the safe way, a career that would enable her to make a good living and help her parents. She'd done that. Renovated their home, refurnished it and eased their lives. But her dreams were still that, dreams. She'd never swum in the Pacific; stood before the Taj Mahal; skied on a mountain top; gazed at the Mona Lisa; flirted with a handsome Egyptian; and she'd never sung Billie Holiday songs in a jazz club.

She might have made a difference in the lives of a few people, but in the world? Not at all. And what could she show for her thirty-two years? A busted career. And the misfortune to have met, in a battle that had ruined her, the one man who had made her fantasize about love in his arms. A picture of herself in her high school cap and gown mocked her from the top of her piano. Oh, what hope and what naiveté. She'd had the world on a string then. But a decade and a half later, she still didn't have the nest, children and love that she craved, and she'd lived a life of adventure only in her dreams.

Her thoughts went back to her childhood, filled with love and her parents' caring. But it had encompassed only a few short years. Study and work were about all she had ever known: work for food and clothing; study for the scholarships that would take her to the next level. And when she finally reached the top, staying there had consumed all of her time and energy. She had never known a man's love, never enjoyed a carefree vacation, never spent hours chatting with friends. She hadn't lived, only worked and struggled. And what had it brought her? She wanted to taste life, to do the things about which she had always fantasized, and to shed her affected aura of ultraconservatism.

The next morning she called Enid to her office as soon as she got there. "Sit down and brace yourself. I'm taking leave from the agency. Then I'll decide whether to remain."

Enid's mouth opened wide in a wordless exclamation of horror, and Veronica could see that she'd shocked the woman.

"You're not serious! Veronica, don't do anything you'll be sorry for. Wait a few months until all this settles. I know you've—"

"I've spent the night thinking about it, and I need to get away from here, at least for a while."

Enid leaned forward, her suddenly sallow complexion a testament to her sorrow. "Is it Henderson? I know he's sorry, and I know he cares about what happened and about you, or he wouldn't have called that press conference and tried to make amends."

Veronica's heart fluttered wildly. Then, something sprang to life within her, like a jonquil popping through the earth in spring or a song leaping to life in her mind, but she controlled her response to it. "That was gracious of him. Maybe he cares, and maybe guilt drove him to do it. I don't know, and if I change my plan of action because of him, then what? I wish him well, but today is my last day in this office. I have three months of leave stored up, and I'm taking it. If I decide not to continue working here, I'll give notice." She called a staff meeting, locked her desk and left.

On her way home, she stopped by Jenny's corner and handed the woman an envelope of bills.

Jenny peered into the large brown envelope, closed it and looked at Veronica. "You hit the lottery, Ronnie, or is this the last time I ever gon' see you?"

A tinge of guilt struggled with the wave of sadness that overtook her. She hadn't thought of Jenny as a dependent but as someone she helped, a friend, even. Now she understood that the woman depended on her. She looked at Jenny's shopping cart of things that only she valued and fought back tears. She couldn't even invite her to a nearby restaurant for a cup of coffee because she wouldn't be allowed in with her "things."

Resigned, she forced a smile. "I'm taking a three-month leave, Jenny. If I get back before that, I'll drop by to see you. That little change in that envelope ought to keep you until I get back. I'd...I'd better run for my train."

Jenny put the envelope in her coat pocket and secured the pocket with two safety pins. "You know I thank you. You know it. I...I hope you finds what you lookin' for, Ronnie. Somethin's wrong sure as my name's Jenny, but you needn't worry none. Anybody with a heart big as yours is always gonna be blessed. I ain't even gonna worry 'bout you. Go on now, and get your train."

Veronica hesitated, saw the tears in Jenny's eyes, turned and rushed across the street. Jenny wouldn't want to be seen crying.

She spent the next day storing her valuables and securing her house. Then she packed her bags, put them in the foyer, stuffed a few things in a small suitcase and left for her parents' home in Pickett, North Carolina.

As she'd expected, her stepfather was not pleased about her plans. "How can you just walk away from what you devoted your entire adult life to? It bothers me seeing you this way, like you don't care what happens. Stay here with us for a while and get yourself together."

"I'm taking some leave I've got coming to me, Papa. When that's up, I'll have to make a final decision about the job."

"That's better, but don't walk away from it like you could get another one just because you asked for it."

She looked into her stepfather's sad eyes and knew that for the first time in her life she was going to ignore his advice, to disobey him, and she hurt—not for herself, but for the man who had sacrificed so much for her. But she drew a measure of contentment from her mother's words, telling her that she should always be true to herself.

"Your papa means well, and he's even right. But if you feel you have to find what's missing in your life, honey, do it now. Right now when you're free, when it won't affect anyone but you. Don't compromise on important things." Veronica noticed that she released a long, labored breath. "And always be sure of what you feel." She patted Veronica's hand. "I'll be so glad when spring comes."

After supper, Veronica sat alone on the back porch. As a child, she'd spent many lonely hours on the porch of their old house, knowing the world around her and dreaming of the universe that she had yet to discover. She'd known the approaching automobiles by the sound of their motors and the screech of their tires, knew the neighbor who chopped wood by the rhythmic noise of his ax, recognized every dog by its bark. She had loved the old porch and had given every splintered slab of wood its own name and its own story, had imagined them as ships that took her to special places. An only child, she'd spent most of her childhood alone while her parents worked at whatever jobs they could find. She glanced around at the lovely porch furniture, the yellow brick walls, and the yellow curtains that blew out of the kitchen windows. For the last four years, she had enabled her parents to live comfortably, and she would see that they always did, but she had to follow her dream. An early spring breeze whistled around her, and she tugged her woolen sweater closer, gazed up at the sky illumined with millions of stars and thought about Schyler. If only… A shudder passed through her. Too late for that.

The next morning she kissed her parents goodbye. "I'll be in Europe for a while, Papa. Write me in care of American Express."

She went back to Owings Mills, got the bags she'd left in her foyer and took a Swissair flight to Switzerland.

"I'm going to do everything I always wanted to do and see the things I've longed to see," she promised herself as her Swiss guide helped her strap on her ski boots.

"You've only had two lessons, and you've done pretty well, miss, but you're not skilled enough to go chasing down these mountains by yourself," Tomass, her German-Swiss guide cautioned her.

Emboldened by her early success and invigorated by the calm, crisp mountain air, she felt as if she could soar over the snow-covered peaks that surrounded her.

"I'll be careful, Tomass. Promise."

He finished lacing her boots and towered over her, reminding her of Schyler. "If you respect these mountains, they'll respect you. Some champion skiers have gotten careless or cocky and breathed their last breath right here."

They compromised. She bought another hour of his time, and they skied together, her cares falling away like discarded clothing as they flew with the wind at her back.

"We'd better call it quits," he said, two hours later. "Be sure to get a hot tub, because every bone you've got will be screaming." At the chalet she thanked him, returned the rented skis and set out for a hike across the lush, green valley.

Beauty as far as she could see. She hadn't known that the Alps, the grand mountain range of Europe that stretched from Italy through France and Switzerland to Austria, was of such imposing grandeur, so spectacular a feast for the eyes. She walked briskly, marveling at herself and the world around her, hardly able to believe she'd just skied on the Jungfraujoch, that rugged prize of the Swiss Alps that stood 11,333 feet at its peak and where skiers had challenged nature for over 850 years. At its foot nestled Grindelwald, arguably one of the most scenic places on earth. She gaped, spellbound, when her eyes first beheld it. Then she turned away from the awe-inspiring scene of snow-covered mountain, green valley and alpine roses that perfumed the air, wanting to banish the desire to have Schyler Henderson hold her hand as she stood there. She took a deep breath and quickened her strides through the meadow, enjoying a feeling of spiritual renewal.

Bewitched by the scenery, she lost track of time and place. Against the majestic white peaks, wildflowers of every color littered the fields, putting to shame the Ricola television advertisements.

"*Guten Tag, Fraulein.* Where you headed?"

She hadn't seen the man as she strolled along deep in thought. "Hello. Where'm I going? Well…nowhere special. I'm just walking."

The tall, blue-eyed blond gazed at her with frank appreciation of what he saw. "It gets dark early in these mountains. Where you staying? There's no lodging anywhere near here."

She noticed that he said it matter-of-fact-like, as though her situation were hopeless. "I'm staying at a hotel in Interlaken."

"*Interlaken?* You're at least a three-hour trek from there. You'd better come with me."

Go with this stranger? She didn't think so. She smiled her best I'm-in-charge smile. "Thanks, but I'll get there okay."

She didn't fool him. "By morning you could be covered with snow. You don't know these mountains, miss. You'd better come with me."

He started to walk away and tendrils of fear unfurled through every molecule of her body. Suppose he was right. "Wait. Where are you—?"

His piercing eyes, as blue as the clearest sky, didn't smile when he said, "Home. My parents will put you up. There's no moon tonight, so I have to get there before dark. Nothing to fear. So come."

He walked on, so she followed him, and followed, and followed until she thought her knees would crack.

"How…how much farther is it? I'm winded."

He pointed to a distant light, the only other sign of life for as far as she could see. "Another couple of kilometers or so. Come along now."

Another two miles. She stifled a groan and geared up her strength. When at last she stumbled into the two-story, unpainted chalet with its sloping roof and windows lined with boxes of blooming geraniums, she felt as if she hadn't an ounce of energy left.

"Papa," her rescuer told the older man who greeted them at the door, "she's lost, so she's staying the night."

Words were exchanged in German, and for a while she wondered if the old man would let her stay. But he smiled, shook hands with her, and switching to French, asked her name. When she told him, he welcomed her and called his wife, from whom she received another welcome. Veronica followed the woman up the rustic stairs to a cheerful room. She'd never seen so many handmade quilts, hand-embroidered sheets and pillowcases as were stacked on shelving in the room. She thanked the woman and dropped into the nearest chair.

"*Nous prendrons le dîner dans quelque minutes,*" the woman said, as though anyone who didn't speak German would speak French. "We eat in a few minutes." Veronica followed the woman to the bathroom, which was clearly the only one in the house, for a woman's shower cap hung on the same hook as a man's razor strop and razor. She hadn't known that men still used them. Glad for the chance to refresh herself, she did so as best she could. She went back to her room, and a short time later, heard a knock on her door.

"Miss Overton, we're ready to eat."

She opened the door, and he stared down at her. "My name is Kurt."

He left her standing there and headed down the stairs, giving her no choice but to follow. As soon as she got to a bookstore that carried English titles, she intended to read about the Swiss culture. Unless she was missing a beat, the status of Swiss women was not too high. In the dining room, whose centerpiece was an enormous stone fireplace over which hung a rifle, several oil-filled lanterns and a large, noisy cuckoo clock, Kurt's parents and a man she assumed was his brother sat at the table waiting for them. Kurt's father said grace, a long soulful-sounding supplication in German. Then he introduced her to his other son, Jon. The family ate without conversation of any kind, limited their words to requests for the meat, or the bread or whatever else was wanted. They drank wine with their dinner, but she declined, thinking it best to face the night with a clear head. After the meal, the woman of the house refused Veronica's offer to help clean up, but Veronica wasn't certain that she was expected to sit around the fire with the men.

Kurt's father lit his pipe and cleared his throat. "You understand French perfectly?" he asked her in French.

She told him she knew what was being said.

"Good," he replied in French, "my son Kurt needs a woman, and he likes you. Not many women want to live out here, because it's too harsh. But we have a good farm, and we live well. We want you to stay."

Her heart landed in the pit of her stomach. When she could close her mouth, she said the first words that came to her mind. "I wouldn't think of living with a man I wasn't married to."

Since the old man didn't understand English, Kurt replied. "I'd take you for my wife, if that's what you want."

Stunned, she felt as if her brain had shut down. He couldn't be serious. She looked at him. He meant what he'd said. They had already entered the twenty-first century, and this guy spoke of getting married as if that were the same as shelling a peanut. One thing was certain: she'd better not laugh.

"I'm sorry," she managed at last, "but I can't do that."

She couldn't believe the disappointment that registered on his face. "You're already married?"

"I'm not married, Kurt, but where I come from, we treat marriage differently. I'm sorry. Please thank your mother for the dinner." She asked to be excused and was glad she remembered how to say it in French.

Her nerves rioted throughout her body when she realized that Kurt was following her. She stopped at the top of the stairs and confronted him.

"Why are you following me up here, Kurt?"

"You won't marry me, and you will leave tomorrow morning. Will you at least spend the night with me?"

She'd have panicked if he hadn't spoken so gently, without belligerence.

"I don't believe in casual...er...sex, Kurt."

He studied her for a minute, and a look of pure pleasure settled on his face. "You needn't worry. I assure you there'll be nothing casual about it."

"I'm sorry."

He released a long breath. "I'm sorry, too. What time do you want to leave tomorrow morning? We eat breakfast at six-thirty."

She stifled a smile of relief because she didn't want to encourage him. "As soon after breakfast as possible. The hotel must have worried that I didn't get back there last night."

From his facial expression, you'd have thought he saw a Martian. "They don't care, as long as you or somebody pays the bill. We'll leave here at seven-thirty. If you don't mind riding in the truck, I'll drive you down to Interlaken."

"Thank you, Kurt. For…for everything."

He shrugged. "Maybe next time I'll get lucky."

Veronica walked into her room at the Hotel Europa in Interlaken, so-called because of its position between two lakes. Excited about her adventure but relieved that it had ended without mishap, she got the notebook she'd bought in the hotel's small store and began to write. Kurt hadn't interested her, but during their ride down the mountain and through a narrow pass to Interlaken, she'd developed compassion for him. Eligible though he was—and handsome, if your taste ran to his type—he couldn't find a woman he wanted who would agree to live with his family in the home whose foundation his great-grandfather had built and that he refused to leave. The worst of it, to Kurt's way of thinking, was that his brother couldn't marry until he did. She recorded the events of the previous two days and put the tablet aside.

Time to move on. She walked out on her tiny balcony and looked at Lake Thunersee nestled in the bosom of an endless flower-filled meadow beneath the Jungfraujoch Mountain on which she'd skied. Why couldn't she have shared it with Schyler? Here, in the most beautiful place she'd ever been, she was alone. She shrugged it off, as she'd always done, packed, paid her bill and took a taxi to the station. The taxi driver assured her that if the United States was full of women who looked like her, it must be paradise for a man. She took that with the proverbial grain of salt, not bothering to disabuse him of his assumption; she was already learning that it wasn't the place but the person who counted most.

Her hotel in Geneva faced the train station. She dropped

her bags inside her room door, went to the phone and called American Express.

"Yes, Miss Overton, we have a message for you. We don't open mail, so you'll have to pick it up here."

A feeling of dread stole over her, but she blew out a heavy breath, called Swissair and in four hours was on her way to Pickett. She was eating lunch on the plane before she remembered her mail at American Express. It didn't matter; Papa was the only person who knew her whereabouts, and as much as he hated to write letters, something had to be seriously wrong.

A week after her return home, she sat on the edge of her mother's bed and leaned forward so she could understand the muffled words. She couldn't make sense of them, except for the last.

"...find him. Find your father...please find him. Sorry."

Days later, the services over, she and her stepfather began adjusting to life without Esther Overton. Veronica hated to leave him, but he insisted that he'd be happy with his memories, because Esther would always be with him.

Shortly after her return to Baltimore, she made a luncheon date with Enid. She had to talk to someone other than her stepfather.

"If she told you to find your birth father, you'd better do that," Enid said. "She had a reason."

"But I grew up thinking he...he deserted us. She said so herself. I don't want to find him. I spent my whole life detesting him."

Enid was adamant. "Maybe she wanted to right a wrong. How do you know? If that's the last thing she said, you'd better do it. Get a private detective."

"I...I suppose you're right. Anyway, I promised her I'd do it. Uh... How's...uh...Mr. Henderson these days? Still rolling heads?"

Enid pushed her glasses up on her nose. Since she'd had

her face lifted, the bridge of her once prominent nose was considerably smaller, and her glasses no longer stayed in place. Veronica wished she'd get a pair that fit her nose.

"Mr. Henderson called several times just after you left. At first, he thought I was lying when I said I didn't know where you were and that you'd taken leave from the agency. Veronica, he was distressed. Have you two been together…I mean… Is anything going on with the two of you? His reaction wasn't what I'd expect of someone who only knew you casually."

Veronica shook her head, knowing that Enid's sharp eyes wouldn't miss her discomfort. "There's nothing between us, Enid."

"But there could be?"

"Better to say there could have been."

"My Lord! And he knows that, too, doesn't he?"

Veronica nodded. "So it seems. It's been good talking with you. Let's…let's see each other often. Okay? I've gotta run back down to Pickett and get what information I can about my birth father. Call you when I get back."

She passed Jenny's corner on the way to her train but didn't expect to see the woman on that rainy day.

Bright sunshine relieved the dreariness of her task as she sat in what had been her parents' bedroom shuffling through the papers she'd found in the bottom drawer of her mother's dresser. Tension gathered within her as she stared at the picture of a happy threesome—herself at about age two sitting on her birth father's lap and her mother smiling up at them. She stared at the likeness of the man her mother had begged her to find. Now she at least knew what he looked like, and she realized that she resembled him. She put the picture aside and searched further. Satisfied that she had enough information, she took out the few items she needed and closed the drawer. Her stepfather didn't seem to have touched anything in the room or to have slept in it since losing his wife.

She went back to Baltimore, hired a private detective and gave him the photo and other information about her father, including his status as a Vietnam veteran. Six weeks later, the detective informed her that he had found a man who acknowledged being her father and who offered as proof the birth dates of her and her mother and when and where he'd lived with them as a family.

"He lives with his adopted son in Tilghman, Maryland, on a little fishing peninsula. Has a great place a few steps from the Chesapeake Bay. Nice guy, too," the detective informed her.

Her hackles shot up, and she could feel her bottom lip struggling to stay in place. How dare he desert his own child and adopt someone else's? The bitter taste of bile formed on her tongue, and she couldn't wait for the chance to tell the man who sired her how she detested him.

"Something wrong?" the detective asked. "Not to worry, Miss Overton. He's an okay guy."

She took control of herself. "No. No. Everything's fine, and you've done a great job."

She jotted down the address and telephone number that the detective gave her, paid him and turned a new page of her life.

It wasn't a journey she'd ever thought she'd make, and she'd as soon not have to do it now, but she'd promised, and it couldn't be done except in person. A travel agent reserved a room for her in the town's only hotel. She rented a Taurus, packed enough for an overnight stay and set out for Tilghman. Ordinarily she tended to speed, but on that morning she lumbered along at forty miles an hour. Killing time, postponing the inevitable and annoying other drivers. She crossed the Chesapeake Bay Bridge, took Highway 50 toward Easton and turned into Route 32, which took her along a winding two-lane highway past the yacht haven known as St. Michaels. From there to Tilghman, she could see the bay on either side of the winding route, but with the sharp and frequent curves of the road, she didn't dare enjoy the view.

Tilghman's quaint quietness took her aback. What kind of man would content himself to live in such a remote place, in the middle of a body of water known to be wild in a storm? She checked into the little wood-frame two-story hotel, and it embarrassed her that the innkeeper witnessed her astonishment at the attractiveness of the room.

"It's lovely and bright," she said in an effort to make amends. She asked the woman whether she knew her birth father.

"Of course. Everybody in this place knows everybody else. It's walking distance, but you can drive if you want to. Keep on down the street 'til you see a traffic light, turn left and walk to the end of the road. That white brick house is the one you want. Take you about ten minutes walking."

She talked herself out of going immediately. After all, he might not be at home on a Saturday morning. She got her copy of the book, *Beyond Desire,* and her gaze fell on the scene in which Marcus Hickson succumbed for the first time to Amanda Ross Hickson's lure and kissed her in spite of himself. She didn't want to read about any other woman's passion in a man's arms, so she flung the book aside. She'd seen a restaurant next door, went in and ordered a crab cake, but her stomach churned in anticipation of the coming confrontation with her father, and she couldn't eat it.

"Quit procrastinating, girl," she admonished herself, got into her car and drove to 37 Waters Edge. She parked and looked out at the bay. Beauty in every direction in which she looked. Leaning back in the driver's seat, she contemplated the difference between her birth father's evident life style and the condition in which she'd grown up. The big white brick bungalow with its red shutters and sweeping and well-tended lawn was beautiful and, she knew, costly. She thought of her life on Cook's Road in Pickett, so named because so many of the women who lived there worked in private service as cooks. In the days of her youth, their house hadn't been painted, and they couldn't afford the seeds and tools with which to create a lovely lawn. Her stepfather had given them all that he could, had filled their lives with love, and had sacrificed so much in order that she could have a better life. She had never faulted him for their near-poverty. But when she looked at the wealth before her, she had to work hard at not hating the man she would soon meet.

She put the car in Park, got out and strolled up the winding walkway. She had to shake off the trepidation that almost made her turn back, but her fingers trembled nonetheless when she knocked on the door.

Chapter 3

Now who could that be? He put his felt-tipped pens in the holder he kept for that purpose, slipped his feet into his house shoes and took his time walking to the front door. He had to finish the design of his New Age cable TV channel descrambler before he went to bed that night, and he didn't welcome an intrusion. He knew his dad wouldn't go to the door, because he didn't let anything, especially unexpected visitors, interfere with his work. The brass knocker tapped several more times, less patiently than before. He opened the door.

He stared. Something akin to hot metal plowed through his belly, and an indefinable gut-rearing sensation winded him as if he'd just run a mile. She stared back at him.

"What are you doing here?" they asked each other in unison.

"I live here," he managed, groping for his sanity. Where had she come from and why was she here? But he didn't ask her, because he didn't trust his eyes.

"You…you live here?" She checked a piece of paper that she held in her left hand. "Is this 37 Waters Edge?"

A twinge of apprehension coursed through him. "Yes. This is number thirty-seven. Why are you here, Veronica?" His hope had already begun to dissolve into nothing, because he saw no affection in her manner, not so much as a smile. Rather, she seemed troubled, far more so than when they'd sparred in court. He didn't like the aura of unhappiness that seemed to settle over her.

"Why are you here, Veronica?"

Her deep breath and eyes that suddenly glistened with unshed tears rocked him, but he waited, trying to ignore the pain that suffused his body, for he realized at last who she was. And he knew she wasn't happy with what she'd discovered.

"I came to see Richard Henderson, my birth father. Don't tell me; I've already guessed. You're the son he adopted."

He didn't recognize his own voice, cracked and tired. "I'm Richard Henderson's son."

They stared at each other, stared for one poignant moment. As if she didn't want to be reminded of the fire that had burned between them, she dropped her gaze. At that, he opened the door wider and beckoned her to enter.

"You've rattled my whole foundation," he told her. "This takes some getting used to."

She didn't look at him but perused the foyer where they stood. "Tell me about it. Is my father home?"

Cue number two: she didn't intend to be friendly.

Veronica closed her eyes as though in fervent prayer. "Are you related to Richard Henderson?"

Schyler backed up a few steps, symbolically distancing himself from her. "Related?" he asked, shaking his head as though denying the possibility. "By blood, you mean?"

She nodded, afraid of his answer, vaguely aware of a sense of foreboding. She didn't want a relationship with Schyler

Henderson, did she? So why was she afraid he'd say yes? And even if her heart skipped and hopped at the sight of him, even if her blood boiled thinking of him, wasn't he the man who had self-righteously jimmied her world?

"Well?" she pressed him.

"Not to my knowledge," he finally said. "He took me in when I needed him, and I'd give my life for him." He closed the front door and began walking with her toward the rear of the house, but suddenly he stopped. "Why are you searching for him after all these years?"

His aura warmed her, but she didn't want to respond to Schyler's gentle but disconcerting charm and braced herself against it. "I promised my mother. The last words she said to me were 'Find your father.' Is he here?"

"Yes. But shouldn't you have called to let him know you'd be here this afternoon? I doubt a man's heart will stay a steady beat if he lays his gaze on a daughter he hasn't seen in thirty years—suddenly and without warning." His manner was gentle, but his voice stern, giving notice that he'd protect Richard Henderson from everything and everyone, including her.

He was right, but she'd acted partly on impulse. She'd also gotten the courage to do it and she didn't believe in procrastination. Besides, if she'd asked for an appointment and waited for his reply, she could have gotten cold feet. Or, she'd reasoned, he could have refused to see her.

"I had no guarantee that he'd agree to see me," she said, answering Schyler's mild reprimand. "After all, he deserted us."

His body stiffened, and the gray of his irises seemed to lighten as though glazed over with a coating of ice. She saw his jaw working and knew she'd angered him.

"I don't believe it!" he spat out. "If you came here to cause my father distress, don't fool yourself into thinking I'll stand for it. I *won't!*" He walked ahead of her. "My father's back here."

As they passed the dining room, her gaze took in the contemporary walnut furnishings and the crystal chandelier that dangled from the ceiling. She imagined that the beautiful carved breakfront contained fine linens, crystal, porcelain and silverware, and resentment of Richard Henderson threatened to choke off her breathing. She'd bet that chandelier cost more than her beloved stepfather made in months of grueling, back-breaking work.

She reflected on Schyler's admonishment of minutes earlier. "I've seen the lion close up when he roared loudest; he can no longer frighten me, Mr. Henderson."

She couldn't let the pain she saw in his eyes soften her attitude. He'd had her father's love; she hadn't. Yet, something in her hurt for him, and because of him. He put a half-smile on his face, but it never reached his eyes, and she had to grasp her shoulder bag with both hands to prevent herself from reaching out to him. He opened the door to what appeared to be a small solarium. Sunny and homey with white rattan furniture and numerous green plants.

"Who was that at the door, Son?"

Son, indeed! For the first time in thirty years, she heard the voice of the man who'd sired her. And in spite of herself, excitement and anticipation shot through her.

How gentle his voice, she thought, when Schyler answered his father, and how solicitous. "Brace yourself, Dad," he said, blocking her entrance to the room. "We knew she'd come sooner or later, and she's here." He stepped aside. "Come on in, Veronica."

"Veronica? *Veronica!*" As she walked in, Richard Henderson bounded up from his desk and started toward her. "*Veronica!*" He pronounced the name as if it were sacred to him. "I despaired of ever setting my eyes on you again."

He opened his arms to her, but she couldn't walk into them, couldn't make herself act the lie. She gave him as much as she could, extending her hand to him. After seconds during which tension crackled in the room and her blood pounded in her ears, he took her hand and held it, though only for a second.

He stepped back then, and she saw him as he was. Tall. Proud. Self-possessed. If she'd hurt him, he didn't show it. "If you're not glad to see me, Veronica, why have you come?"

She tried to shove aside the connection she'd instantly felt to him. An indefinable something that drew and held her, repositioning her center of gravity.

"I came because it was my mother's last request of me. I promised her I'd find you."

He gasped, held his head up and his flat belly seemed to jam itself against his backbone. He closed his eyes, large and almond shaped like hers. "Esther is dead? Your investigator didn't mention it. She's dead?"

She nodded, unwilling to believe the news would mean anything to him. "Just before my investigator located you."

From the corner of her eye, she saw Schyler move toward his father, but Richard walked over to the window, turned his back and gazed out. From the bend of his shoulders, she knew he'd gone there for privacy, to shield his emotions and to get a grip on them. She glanced at Schyler, but the dark expression that clouded his face as he gazed in the direction of his father gave her no comfort. She walked halfway to the window and paused, uncertain as to what to do. She thought she detected a quick, jerky movement of his shoulders as though a shudder had torn through him. But the man possessed dignity.

He turned and smiled at her. "At least you've come. I'd like us to get acquainted. Would you...would you...spend the night?"

She wasn't prepared for a love-in, not after years of resenting this man who had rejected her, only to welcome another man's child into his home and his heart.

"Thanks, but I'm staying at that little white, two-story hotel on Front Street. It doesn't seem to have a name," she told him, "and I'm leaving tomorrow morning."

Richard made a pyramid of his long fingers, propped up

his chin and scrutinized her. She had the feeling that he judged her and found her wanting. But what could he expect from the daughter he'd left thirty years earlier?

He gazed steadily into her eyes. "If Esther told you to find me, what did she want me—or you, for that matter—to know?"

She'd wondered about that but couldn't guess a convincing answer. "I...I don't know. She didn't get a chance to tell me."

He knocked his right fist into his left palm as she'd seen Schyler do while he tried to sway the judge against her. "I see. In that case, we'll have to spend enough time together to figure out what was left unsaid. *So stay for dinner.*"

A command if she'd ever heard one, and her good sense told her to obey it. She glanced at Schyler, who'd said nothing during her exchanges with his father. His guarded expression told her that she'd displeased him and that she was on her own.

"My housekeeper is usually here on Saturdays," Richard explained, "but she's at a church outing today. The food will be edible, though, because I cook about as well as anybody, and I've taught Schyler to do the same."

He shifted his glance to Schyler. "Son, why don't you show Veronica our little village while I get the meal together? We eat at six-thirty, Veronica."

"Well I—"

Schyler had her by the arm. She didn't think she'd find his fingerprints on her flesh, but he had certainly touched her with gentler fingers in the past.

"Finish your writing, Dad. There's plenty of time before dinner. I'll entertain her."

He ushered her into the living room and pointed to a brown leather recliner. "Make yourself comfortable."

Dark colors didn't do a thing for her, and her green suit would die against brown. Feeling wayward and, in a way, trapped, she ignored his suggestion and sat on the huge cream-colored sofa.

"Thanks, but I'll sit over here."

He stood several feet away looking at her. And saying nothing. She resisted crossing her knee, or swinging her foot, or pulling her hair. And she was damned if she'd rub her nose. When she could no longer stand this scrutiny, she blurted out, "Are you being rude deliberately?"

His shrug was slow, nonchalant. "If I were, you'd probably know it, considering what an expert you are at it."

She knew she deserved the reprimand, for she'd hurt Richard Henderson when she didn't return his warm greeting. But she couldn't explain it to Schyler, couldn't expose herself by telling him what her youth had been compared to his.

Instead, she defended herself. "I'm honest, Mr. Henderson, and I'm not good at pretense. I was as gracious as I could be."

He dug the toe of his house shoe into the broadloom carpet. "Yes. I suppose you were. But that's not saying much. Did you plan to hurt him? Did you come here to get revenge for something he doesn't seem to remember?"

She could feel her shoulders sag with a heavy weight that seemed to shroud her body. Weary in spirit. She knew it wasn't the kind of fatigue that a tub of hot water could soak away. It seeped into her marrow and nearly brought tears to her eyes.

"I don't know," she replied, trying honestly to understand her motive. "I don't believe I planned anything. This is a trial for you and for him, but what do you think this visit is doing to me? I looked at him, and for the first time, I saw myself. My eyes, hair, coloring, face and height. It's as though I didn't know myself until now. Don't you think this is a shock for me? That it hurts? No. You're too busy judging me. Both of you."

He stuffed his hands in the pockets of his trousers, sat down with his legs spread wide apart and gazed steadily at her. After what she figured was a full minute, he rested his left ankle on his right knee and leaned back in the chair.

"And how do you think I feel, Veronica? You've taken up permanent residence in my head. A woman who turned me around. A woman who detests my dad and with whom I've had a rough legal battle. A woman who probably blames me for having done my job as honestly and competently as I knew how. But the worst of it is the fire between us, a fire so hot not even our attitudes toward each other can put it out."

She jerked forward, ready to deny it, even as the woman in her yearned to touch him and to feel his hands hot on her flesh.

He waved a disparaging hand. "I don't need your agreement on this. I'm thirty-six years old, and I know when a woman is attracted to me. We both felt that…" He threw up his hands as if in surrender. "Chemistry or whatever the minute we met."

She opened her mouth to disown it and to accuse him of arrogance, but dancing lights suddenly twinkled in his eyes and a smile played loosely around his mouth, knocking her off balance. Her heart shimmied, frenzied, like a demon possessed, and in spite of herself, her hand clutched at her chest.

"Don't worry," he soothed, "the way things are going, I expect fate intends to keep a lot of distance between us. A pity, though. We could have danced one hell of a dance."

She leaned forward, disappointment chilling her to the bone, yet fascinated with his cool acceptance that he wanted what he wasn't likely to get or even to pursue. "How can you say that when we've never even tried to be friends?"

He flexed his shoulders in a quick shrug and strummed his fingers on the wide arm of the recliner. "Certain people can't begin with a friendship." Shivers coursed through her as desire blazed briefly in his gray-eyed gaze.

He shrugged again, seeming to downplay the importance of what he said and of what he'd felt. "With us…too many obstacles. Too many and too big when we met and even stronger ones now."

"Right. The main one being all that energy you expended trying to get me convicted of a crime I didn't commit."

He flinched, and a stricken expression flashed over his face. Then he laid back his shoulders and looked her in the eye. She had to hand it to him; the man ruled his emotions.

"Do you want to reopen that matter? The judge dismissed the case for lack of evidence, vindicating you. Let's bury it, shall we?"

She couldn't believe he'd said it. "Don't you realize you torpedoed my career? *Let's bury it,* you say." She snapped her finger. "Simple as that."

He leaned forward, his eyes beseeching her. "I'm not callous, Veronica. I just can't see the use of continuing the argument. If I've caused you any damage, you know I'm sorry, and I'll do anything I can to repair it."

She gave him the benefit of her sweetest smile. "A guy thing, huh? If you don't see a reason, there isn't one."

His gray eyes widened in surprise. "Good grief, is that the way I come across to you?"

Don't let him snow you, girl, she told herself, when crinkles appeared at the corners of his eyes. "Just cut it right out." She slammed her hand across her mouth when she realized she'd spoken those words aloud.

Caught out, she jumped to her feet. "I'll...I think I'll see what's going on in the kitchen." She didn't know why she'd said that; she didn't want to be alone with her father because she didn't know what to say to him.

Schyler saved her. "Uh-uh. Dad hates to have anybody in that kitchen with him when he's cooking."

She sat down. Trapped. She had to get out of there. Away from him and his mesmeric eyes and seductive smile. "In that case, I think I'll go for a walk. You must have something you'd rather be doing."

His teasing grin and the sparkles in his eyes couldn't be taken for anything but frank deviltry. "Not another single thing," he said and placed his right hand over his heart. "Just keeping you company, and it's my pleasure."

No sooner had he said it than Richard appeared in the door of the living room. "There you two are. I know you wanted to finish that descrambler, Son. So I appreciate your taking the time to get to know Veronica, because that's important to me."

As Richard looked from one to the other, Schyler put up his hands, palms out, in surrender. "Okay, so I lied. Truce?"

"I won't ask what that was about," Richard said and left them alone.

She didn't realize her demeanor had changed until Schyler frowned. "How can you dislike him so much when you don't even know him?" he asked her. "Is he kind, warm, gracious, honest and decent? Is he? Does he pay his debts, and does he help people who can't do for themselves? Does he? You can't answer, and that means you can't judge him."

She wanted to erase the pain reflected in his eyes, to hold him and... For a quick moment, her gaze went toward the ceiling. A father she'd been taught to despise inextricably tied to a man whose smile made her head swim and whose every gesture made her long for the feel of his arms hard around her. A man who made her dream dreams that kept her blushing for days. If she was being punished, she'd like to know what she'd done to deserve it. She wished her ambiguous feelings toward him would sort themselves out, that she could either despise Schyler Henderson and dismiss him from her life or let herself feel what her heart and body longed to experience. And while her conflicting feelings battled with each other, she searched for a gentle reply. Truthful, yet without the verbal tentacles that could pierce the heart.

"It's best not to pry, Schyler—if I may call you that. There's a well of hurt and misery that you apparently know nothing about. I don't know anything about it, either, only what I've been told, what I had drilled into me ever since I've known myself. You said you're not callous. Neither am I. Don't dig deep. It's enough that one of us carries the burden."

He reached across the three feet of space that separated them and grasped her hand. "Don't make that mistake, Veronica. All three of us feel the pain. Tell me why you've taken a three-month leave from CPAA and why you've hinted you might not return to your job."

She shared with him her reasons for downplaying the importance of a job that had consumed all of her energies, thought and passion for the previous five years. Her proving ground. The place where she'd taught herself that she could do whatever she set herself to do and do it well. Her chest went out and her shoulders back.

"I had to get away from there, to find myself. I'd done a lot of things, covered a lot of miles and garnered my share of laurels, but…" she faced him fully, wanting him to understand what she'd never told anyone "…but I'd never lived. Never wrestled with a relationship slipping through my fingers, never argued and gossiped with girlfriends, never opened my arms wide and let the breeze blow me wherever it would."

"Back up a minute," he said, and she had the impression that he was putting events into their proper perspective. "That case wasn't the only reason why you decided your office can get along without you for three months?? Is that what you're telling me?"

"Some of my reasoning was bound up with that, the fact that after so much acclaim, the community that I had served so selflessly could forget so quickly."

"What do you mean, people forgot?"

She waved a hand in disdain. "Not one reporter asked me for an interview when that case was closed in my favor."

His sharp whistle sliced through the room. "I never dreamed."

"It's okay now. I learned a lot from that."

"So you went to Europe. Then what?" he asked.

"I think I've done more living in the weeks since I left CPAA than in the previous thirty-two years and five months of my life."

He leaned toward her, an animated expression on his face, and squeezed her fingers. "You did something you always wanted to do?"

The mere memory of those few exhilarating days eased the harsh feelings that had beset her since she'd stepped across Richard Henderson's threshold.

She nodded eagerly. "Yes. Oh, yes. I skied the slopes of the Jungfraujoch, hiked alone through the mountain terrain, spent the night with hospitable strangers and got a proposal of marriage from their six-foot-four-inch tall, blond and handsome elder son. Every single second of it exhilarated me. Free. Almost a part of nature. I'll never forget it."

Schyler felt her fingers soft and warm in his hand. He'd held them for all of five minutes, and she'd let him. He focused on her words. "A proposal? You sure you're telling all of this?"

When had he last seen a woman wrinkle her nose in pure wickedness? He braced himself. Maybe she wasn't as strait-laced as he'd thought.

"All except…uh…his…er request after I turned him down."

"Wait a minute! Don't tell me…you—"

She interrupted him, snatching her hand from his as she did so. "You think I'm crazy? The man was a gentleman. He asked. I said no to that, too, and he didn't press me."

Schyler let himself breathe. "I would have been surprised if your answer had been different." He rubbed his chin, reflecting on some of his own temptations. "But when we're under stress—and you certainly were—we sometime behave out of character."

A softness seemed to envelop her. He wouldn't have associated shyness with her, but he sensed it in her changed demeanor and saw it in her lowered gaze. Long lashes, half an inch of them, hid her large, almond-shaped black eyes—so much like his father's—from him.

"Your eyes must be the most beautiful I've ever looked at. It's a wonder they don't get you into trouble. Every time you blink, it's as if you're flirting."

She managed to look at something beyond his back. "I've been told that."

Right then he made up his mind to get to know Veronica Overton. He'd seen her regal in her professional armor and arrogant with his father, but the woman before him at that moment was sweet and feminine. If he dug deeper… He stood and it seemed natural to reach for her hand. He did, and she grasped it.

"Come help me set the table for dinner. I can tell from the rattling in the kitchen that he'll have it ready in five or six minutes."

Being with her gave him a good feeling, he realized, but he didn't fool himself. No woman would ever be important to him unless she showed genuine affection for his father. He eyed her as they set the table, and he liked the way she went about it. Unhurried. Self-assured. She might well have been in her own home. At the thought, his belly tightened, and whispers of air skittered through the hairs on his forearms and the backs of his hands, teasing his nerves. Warning him. *No you don't, man,* he told himself. *Don't go there! Don't you even think it.* But an image of her in his home, belonging there, and filling it with warmth flitted through his mind.

He shook his head symbolically, getting his mind straight. "You could grow on a guy."

She whirled around, her face wreathed in the warmest smile he'd ever seen on her. "Think so?"

"Yeah. You think you could handle it?"

Now she *was* flirting with him. He walked over to the china cabinet where she stood twirling a linen napkin. She grinned at him. "No doubt about it. I can catch anything you can pitch."

He looked at her hands propped against her hips and couldn't help laughing. "Anytime you want a demonstration, be glad to oblige you. I like a woman with guts, and you've got plenty."

"Hmmm. You're pretty sure of yourself, aren't you?"

So she liked to challenge! Fine with him; he enjoyed a good jostle, and he saw in her a worthy opponent. "I'd better be. A tongue-tied lawyer and an insecure engineer might as well not leave home."

She worried her bottom lip. "Engineer?"

"Yeah. That's the other hat I wear."

He yielded to the temptation to pull the strands of hair dangling in front of her left ear lobe, tugging on them much as he would have on the rope of a bell. "I'm confident. Yes," he said recalling her comment. "You're not lacking self-confidence yourself." He watched her tuck the errant strands behind her ear and marveled at her ability to look over his shoulder at some object past him, but not into his eyes.

"A little boy in my second-grade class used to do that, pull my hair, I mean." She still didn't look at him.

He stepped closer to her. "If you don't look at me, I'll disappear. Is that what you think? You have to deal with me, Veronica, and I'm here to tell you it won't be child's play, either. Believe me!"

She looked at him, her long lashes sweeping up from her cheeks, and her expression was one of mild defiance. Figuring her out could be a full-time job. "I'm equal to the task, Schyler, so let's not waste time outdoing each other."

He had to force the smile, because he liked her too much. Or he would, if it wasn't for her attitude toward his father. Wanting her had never bothered him too much; he could deal with that. But to like a woman who heated your loins every time you looked at her… He let out a harsh breath. *Straighten out your head, man.*

She might like the truth, and she might not, but anything short of straight talk could take him where he didn't want to go.

"Look, Veronica," he said, pronouncing her name slowly to emphasize the importance of his words. "I've watched a lot of animals square off, but except for a mother guarding her young, they were never male and female. So don't count on a big fight between us to cool things off. It isn't going to happen."

Her hand went to that unruly hair hanging over her ear, and when she spun it around her index finger, he knew she was stalling for time. Thinking. She had plenty of patience with herself. Good. He liked that, so he waited.

"You know, Schyler," she said at last, "you've been talking out of both sides of your mouth. The right side says maybe, and the other yells, 'Don't even think it.' Doesn't matter, though, since I probably won't be around when you get it straightened out."

Her mocking tone set off the sparks that tripped his ego, but he reeled it in. He made it a point to control his reactions to such deliberate provocations as the one she'd just thrown at him. He was his own man, and if he accepted every gauntlet, he'd get bandied around like a hockey puck.

He smiled as best he could, though he knew it barely touched his lips. "I see you like to fence," he said, glad for the presence of mind not to say what he was thinking. "Remember that a clever swordsman knows his opponent's strengths and weaknesses before he agrees to duel."

"Well, I'm glad to see the two of you getting along," Richard said as he placed a platter of food on the dining room table, ending their game of taking each other's measure.

Schyler didn't want his father to think they'd come to terms, because they hadn't and probably never would. Only mutual passion united them, and they both had the strength to ignore that.

"We were setting the table, Dad."

Richard nodded slowly, as one trying to accept the inevitable. "I'll get the rice and salad. What do you want to drink, Veronica?"

Schyler couldn't help relaxing when she replied, "Water or white wine with club soda in it," because his father didn't hold "drinkerds," as he called them, in high regard.

Richard returned with the remainder of the meal and lit the huge, five-inch-thick candle that graced the center of the table. He sat between his daughter and his son and held out a hand to each of them. Schyler wondered if the hand Veronica held gave her the same sense of security and well-being that his father's hand had always given him.

Richard bowed his head. "Heavenly Father, we thank you for this food, and on this special occasion, we thank you for each other. I had decided, Lord, that you weren't listening to me all these years, but it seems that you were. It's not exactly as I had hoped and prayed it would be, but she's here with me. You've given us a second chance, an opportunity to erase the hurt and the pain of these thirty years. But with your help and me trying all I know how, I know I can't miss. I'm accepting this second chance for which I do thank you. Amen."

Schyler glanced first at his father, who was reaching for the dish of rice, and then at Veronica, who'd glued her gaze to their father. If they could get through the meal in peace, he'd be grateful.

"Have some rice," Richard said to Veronica, as though he ate with her every day. "You can't eat shish kebab without rice."

Schyler thought his heart had stopped beating. Would she accept the dish his father held out to her?

"Nobody has to beg me to eat rice," she said and held out her plate for him to serve her. "Saffron rice, at that. What kind of meat is it?"

He had to control his heavy release of breath or they would both know he'd feared her response.

Richard served her a large helping and laid two skewers of shish kebabs on it with pleasure so obvious that Schyler ached for him.

"It's lean, tender pork, slices of sage sausage, mushrooms, onions and green peppers. And I marinated the meat in my special sauce all day." He watched as she sampled it.

"Hmmm. This is fabulous." A smile of pure contentment

covered her face as she glanced up at her father. "I'm telling you, this is great."

Schyler said a silent prayer of thanks, and he could see the hope written on his father's face. He wanted to tell him that he shouldn't move too fast or hope for too much. But how could he prick that fragile balloon of optimism? Veronica's behavior was probably nothing more than good manners. The test was yet to come.

Veronica listened to the man she'd learned by age four to dislike say a prayer of thanks that he had been reunited with her, and she heard him express his hope and faith for a future in which she was a part. Her heart constricted at the sound of his words, and she'd never been more torn in her life. But when he passed her the rice, gazing into her eyes with a look that was part challenge and part prayer, he touched her deeply in an indefinable but life-giving spot. From the corner of her eye, she read on Schyler's face a dread, even a fear that she would refuse the food her father held out to her. *I've got decent manners, I'm hungry and I love rice,* she told herself, handing him her plate.

And she was glad she did. She saw Schyler take a deep breath, close his eyes and let the air pour out of him. And for a second, Richard raised his eyes skyward before looking at her with a smile of delight on his face.

"You're one terrific cook," she told him and meant it.

"I like to cook," he said, savoring morsels of meat and mush-rooms. "That's when I do my best thinking." He glanced at his watch. "Schyler, it's still light for another hour or so. Could you give her a tour of our little village? I'll have the kitchen cleaned by the time you get back, and we can have dessert."

Veronica looked at Schyler. "You don't clean up when he cooks?" She shook her head. "Shame. Shame."

Schyler's eyebrows shot up with such speed that she knew she'd suggested the unthinkable. "Me? Clean up after he cooks? You're joking. He cleans up his own mess, and when I cook, I do the same. Ready to go? The bay is spectacular about now."

She settled into the passenger seat of Schyler's cream-colored Buick Le Sabre, big and comfortable like the man who's driving it, she found herself thinking. He backed out of the garage and headed for Front Street, and all she could see as he drove through the little village were white buildings.

"Is there an ordinance in this town that requires all the buildings to be white?" she asked.

"I don't think so. This place is the bedrock of tradition, so it's probably just copycatting. I think I'll check that."

"I can't imagine growing up here, though I suspect it was more fun than where I lived, considering you've got the Chesapeake Bay at your doorstep."

So she intended to keep their conversation impersonal, did she? All right. He was known for his patience. "The Seafarers Museum is our biggest attraction. Back in the seventeenth and eighteenth centuries, this region was a pirate's playground. They came to replenish their supplies and to ply their contraband goods. Of course, there was a great deal of legal trade as well. Spanish galleons used to take refuge in the bay from those powerful Atlantic storms. So we have a phenomenal cache of treasures from ships that were sunk in these parts. Maybe I'll take you through the museum next time, but right now I want you to see the sunset over the bay." He turned the car south, swung down Waters Edge to the bay and parked at the edge of the beach.

He looked down at her feet. "At least you've got on low-heeled shoes."

He got out and headed around to her side of the car, but she opened the door before he reached it.

"Why didn't I know you'd do that?" he asked.

She favored him with her sweetest smile. "Simple. Because you're not omniscient. That's supposed to be the Lord's specialty."

He stopped, stuck his hands in his pants pockets, emphasizing his broad chest and flat belly, rocked back on his heels and did what could only be described as a slow burn.

"I get angry about twice every couple of years, Veronica, but you've nearly shoved me to it twice this day. Try not to give vent to your sharp tongue and remind yourself what it feels like to hurt." Before she could answer, he took her arm, walked along the narrow beach and paused. "Veronica Overton, the executive, is a far cry from the woman I'm looking at."

She didn't mind the comment; in a way, it was accurate. On the nose. "When I was that woman, I hadn't skied the slopes of the Jungfraujoch, and I hadn't hiked alone for miles over flower-strewn meadows in the lap of the Swiss Alps. Imagine being the only person for miles and miles around with God's blue sky, towering white snow-capped mountains and flowers of every color for company. Not a puff of wind, and air as fresh as new life. It was truly a rebirth. So you're right. I'm different, and I hope I stay that way. I'm not chasing fame or success, and I'm no longer hell-bent on becoming Secretary of Welfare. I don't even give a snap about any of it. I'm myself. Free. I mean *free!*"

His stare didn't make her uncomfortable, because she knew he was seeing her with new vision. "And you were yourself before," she heard him say under the edge of his breath. He turned toward the water and stopped as though frozen in time. "Look! Would you just look at that?"

She followed his gaze to the long red rays that streaked across the rolling water, fanning out from the huge red globe that moved slowly downward against a navy blue and gray sky. At her gasp, he moved closer to her, and for the first time, the feel of his arm around her waist sent powerful shivers of sensual awareness plowing through her. Helpless to prevent her tremors and realizing that he was well aware of her reaction to his touch, she made herself look at him to brazen it out, as if trembling for him were of no consequence.

But he denied her that avenue of escape. "Months ago, when you were the consummate executive, I as much as told you we'd have to deal with this. Don't count on its going away by itself and of its own accord. The chemistry between us is strong enough to cause an explosion, and nothing will make me believe you don't know that."

"I'm not going there right now, Schyler. That isn't something that bears discussion."

"Oh sure. If you talked about it, that would make it a fact," he said. "Well, discuss it or not, whatever hooks men and women has its claws in us." He laughed a deep tension releasing growl. "No point in worrying until it gets unruly."

She stepped out of his encircling warmth and walked along beside him swinging her arms. The sun dipped into the Chesapeake Bay, and she couldn't help reaching for him, clutching his sleeve.

"Schyler. That was… It was so beautiful. I don't think I ever saw anything to match it."

He took her hand and sat on a log that had rested in its spot so long that the elements had bleached it. "I love to sit here and look out at the bay. You should see it in the moonlight when the stars almost blanket the sky. I've spent hours thinking and dreaming right in this spot. Did you have a special spot where you fought your fears, dreamed dreams and plotted your future?"

Suddenly, she didn't want to share that part of his life with him, and she couldn't tell him about the times when her only toys were the stories she told herself. Not about the things and places she imagined when, as a small girl, she'd sat on the back porch of her parents' modest home and tried to count the stars. Not when she'd talked to the owl that hooted nearby and cried a child's pain when the bird didn't respond. Schyler had lived in luxury by comparison, a luxury that was rightfully hers. She pulled her hand from his and jumped up from his precious log.

"What is it? What's the matter, Veronica?"

"Nothing. It's… Nothing. I…have to go. That's all."

He stood, and she swung away from him, fearing his touch. As she moved, she felt her right leg come out from under her, but as quickly, he grabbed her, breaking her fall, and a burst of heat skittered through her body when she realized his fingers were splayed across her right breast. Warm. Delicious. Arousing. She wanted him to caress her, to… She needed him to tighten his hold on her and love her. His breathing deepened, and she heard him suck in air. He didn't move his hand, but he had to know it was there, where he wanted it to be. The thought kicked her pulse into overdrive and heat spiraled through her veins. Desire quickened her body and, as though he willed it, she raised her eyes and gazed into his—heated pools of blatant need, of hot undiluted want.

She should move, get out of his way. She had to…

"I'm not forcing you to stand here," he said, his voice low. Guttural.

She wanted to move, but he kept looking at her like that, making her belly churn until her body wanted him to…to…

"I've…I've got to—"

He didn't spare her. "If you don't want my mouth on you, say so. Right now."

She stared into his fiery eyes, glittering pools of unbridled desire, and told herself to run while she still owned herself. At her hesitance, he lowered his head, tightened his grip on her body and stroked her breast possessively, as if he owned it.

"Part your lips for me, take me in and get what you want."

She told herself not to open her mouth, but her disobedient tongue danced around its edges and dampened her lips. She heard him suck in his breath in anticipation.

"Schyler. I…I'm—"

His mouth came down on hers, and frissons of heat pelted her feminine center. Her arms went around him and tightened, and his tongue plunged into her mouth with an expertise that shocked her and sent her blood racing like a wildfire out of control. His hands roamed her body, stroking, teasing, possessing, seducing. Making her his own. Beads of perspiration dampened her forehead, her nerve ends curled like lamb's hair and the strength went out of her knees, but still he kissed her. She felt his lips tremble, but that didn't stop him. No longer caring about the consequences, she grasped the back of his head and sucked on his tongue, feasting on it, loving him, taking all he offered. She gave no thought to his pagan groan as his hand squeezed, pinched and caressed her breast; she only wanted, needed his loving. He wrapped her tightly to him, taking her will and her energy, and she slumped in his arms.

They held each other, silently, unable to move and unwilling to articulate what they truly felt.

At last she got breath enough and sense enough to speak. "Schyler, this is…we can't…I mean…Schyler, I don't know, I—"

"Shhh. I know I took it too far, but I needed the feel of you in my arms. Badly." He blew out a mass of air. "I didn't dream it could be like this."

He took her hand and started walking toward the car. "I hate to drop something that stirs me the way you do, but you're going to force me to let it go." He flexed his shoulders in a quick shrug. "And that may be for the best. But hell, it sticks in my craw like cracked glass."

She didn't attempt to coat the truth. "You're right. We have to let it go, because it spells nothing for us but misery."

He wanted more. "Will you admit, as I do, that under better circumstances, we…we…might have made memorable music together?"

She noticed that when he said it, he grinned as though savoring a delightful thought. And she knew she should be as honest as he, but no other man had exposed her naked need as he'd done, and she felt too vulnerable and finessed her reply.

"You're attractive in many ways, Schyler. I respond to that."

He laughed aloud. "I don't suppose I had a right to expect more. We'd better get back. Dad's got that chocolate soufflé ready by now."

She gulped. "Chocolate soufflé? He can make *that?*"

"Yeah," he said in a voice tinged with pride. "And does every time he cooks dinner."

Her eyes widened. "Why?"

His laughter wrapped around her like a blanket of contentment. "Veronica, I love chocolate. I would eat chocolate soup, chocolate bread, chocolate anything for as long as anybody would give it to me or I could get it for myself. Dad humors me. I expect he's tired of it. Every dessert cooked in that house has chocolate in it, and a lot of it."

She couldn't believe it. "He spoiled you."

They reached the car, and he opened the door for her. "Yes, he spoiled me. When he met me, I was almost ten years old and couldn't remember ever having heard the word love directed at me. He knew that."

There it was again, and it would always be there, looming like a gallows between them. Her joviality was gone.

"Dad's going to enjoy impressing you with his soufflé."

His words penetrated her conscious thought only vaguely. Growing up, she hadn't known chocolate soufflé existed and didn't get a taste of chocolate unless one of her schoolmates shared a piece of candy with her. Her mother and stepfather hadn't been able to afford the luxury of chocolate. But the man who'd given her the seed of life had lavished it on a child he didn't sire, catering to that child's need and whims. Bitterness simmered within her, rising like bile on her tongue, eating away the rapport she had achieved with Schyler and her father. The hurt came back with the strength of a gale-force storm, beating back the passion that Schyler had dragged from the very bowels of her being.

"I don't think so," she said, almost absentmindedly. "I'd

better be going. Be seeing you." She wanted to run, but controlled the urge and walked as rapidly as she could, leaving him standing there. She didn't look back. She couldn't.

Chapter 4

With his feet glued in their tracks, Schyler watched Veronica go. He could call her or with his longer legs he could catch her. He did neither. What good would it do? He just stood there. One minute she'd been locked to him body and soul, fire and spirit, giving him all the sweetness a man could want—her heat and passion and the promise of her body. No point in thinking about the pain that seared through him as she practically galloped out of sight. He'd had pain before, and he'd feel it again. That didn't bother him; he knew he could handle it. But when had a woman stood toe-to-toe with him, taking his passion and demanding that he take hers and give her more of himself in even greater measure? He wanted the ultimate experience with her. Even as he stood there in the dying daylight, everything in him down to the recesses of his loins wanted him to go after her and have her for his own. But he doubted he'd ever release himself within her. And maybe it was for the best; if he went that route, she'd own him, and from where he stood, he couldn't see a future for them.

He glared at the stars that mocked him with their hollow, twinkling promises. The water lapped loudly at the cove nearby, reminding him of his loneliness. He'd been hearing that same noise for twenty-six years, and for generations to come, his descendants—if he had any—would know its steady, sometimes soothing, sometimes disquieting rhythm. He'd wanted her to share it with him. He flexed his right shoulder in a quick shrug. A relationship with her was hopeless, had been from the minute he'd first looked into her wide, long-lashed eyes.

He knew now that the prospect of their being more than adversaries—in court or out—had just plummeted to nil. He had only to mention his father's name and her passion for him disappeared like smoke in a windstorm. And what could he do about it? He loved his father. He picked up a stone, sent it skipping across the water and headed back to his car. So what? He'd known plenty of disappointments. He shook his head as he unlocked the car. He wouldn't lie to himself. This one was a Goliath. She was in him, and he knew she'd stay there. But what the hell! It wouldn't kill him.

"Where's Veronica?" Richard asked him when he walked into the house.

He never lied to his father, and he wouldn't do it then. "I'm sorry, Dad. She decided not to come back."

Richard stared at him, obviously speechless. "Did you have an argument?"

He heard the dread in his father's voice and knew that he anticipated the truth. "No, we didn't."

"Then what happened?"

He had to tell him sometime, to let his father know the circumstances under which he'd first met Veronica, and he'd better do it right then. He sat in the brown leather recliner, leaned back and closed his eyes.

"Dad, I didn't meet Veronica for the first time this afternoon. I—"

Richard dropped into the nearest chair and leaned forward. "You knew her? And you never told me?"

"I knew her, yes, But I didn't know she was your daughter until I opened the front door for her this afternoon."

He described his acquaintance with Veronica, told his father about Veronica's extended leave from her high-profile job and of the part he'd played in it.

The right hand Richard raised when Schyler began to talk stayed where it was. Frozenlike. He parted his lips as if to speak but didn't make a sound, merely shook his head as though denying the possibility of what Schyler's words implied. Schyler wondered about his father's thoughts while the man he loved so dearly stared at him for long minutes. Without warning, he slumped in the chair.

Schyler lunged out of the recliner and rushed to his father. "You all right?"

"No, I'm not." The words struggled up from Richard's throat as if they'd had to pull themselves out of him. He sat up straight. "Did you…did you tell…is that all of it?"

He went back to the recliner and sat there. "I'm not sure you want to hear all of this, but if I tell you everything now, you'll know where you stand with her."

"Go ahead. I can take it."

Schyler ran the tips of his fingers back and forth against his chin. Pensive. He didn't like revealing his most private feelings to another man, not even if that man was his father. But his father deserved any truth that might comfort him.

"I fell for her hook, line and sinker the minute I laid eyes on her, and nothing that's happened since has abated it one iota."

He imagined his father's whistle could be heard half a block away. "And you went ahead with that case against her?"

"Worse. I brought the second suit two weeks later." He leaned back, locked his hands behind his head and closed his eyes. "She's a fighter. Man, does that woman have a set of guts. She's not afraid of anybody or anything. If those daggers she pitched at me while she was on that witness stand had been real, I'd be pushing up daisies this minute."

He could sense the tension easing out of his father when Richard laughed and admiration for his daughter flashed in his eyes.

"Gave you what for, did she?"

"You could say that."

Richard made a pyramid of his hands, bracing his index fingers against his chin. "The two of you were managing to be pleasant up to the time you left here, though I suppose that was for my sake. What happened out there on that beach?"

Schyler let out a long, heavy breath, sat forward and dropped his head in his hands. After a minute, he sat up and looked at his father. "Up to then, I'd never touched her. Out there, I did, and what we felt hit both of us like a volcanic eruption. Then…well, I got to talking about you, and…" He threw up his hands. "It's over before it started. At least as far as I'm concerned, that's the beginning and the end of it. It never stood a chance anyway."

Richard shook his head as if in wonder at the incredulity, the seeming otherworldliness of events that had governed his relationship with his daughter almost since her birth. He looked at the son who had filled his empty life and given him a reason for living. A reason to set goals and to work hard to achieve them. He had to find a way to communicate to Schyler the folly of giving up, of fooling yourself into believing you could do without anyone who could do without you, but he had to tread softly. Schyler was, after all, a grown man and proud of his independence.

"I see you've resigned yourself to living without her," he said, measuring his words as carefully as he could. "I did that once, and I've regretted it every day since. Not anymore. My daughter and I will come to terms. Good terms. I don't doubt it for a second. You think you're young, strong and invincible, that you're bigger than anything that can happen to you. But you wait until this thing starts eating away at your guts, slicing through your innards like acid, dulling your senses. Wait till every woman you look at—white, black, Asian or brown— looks just like her. You haven't been miserable, Son. You haven't hurt so badly you wanted to die. Just pray to God it all gets straightened out." He grasped mentally at the breath that seemed to have escaped his lungs. "Do you know where she lives?"

His flesh crawled. He'd never known how his father had suffered. He'd grown up wanting to be like him, to do everything his father did. He'd even chosen his father's profession of engineering. But he didn't want for himself what his father had just described. Yet, he didn't see how it could be avoided.

"I can easily find out where she lives," he said. "Tell me, do you know why she resents you?"

Richard massaged his forehead with the fingers of his left hand. "I can only guess that Esther concocted some trumped-up explanation for why we weren't together. And whatever she said didn't make me look good but covered up for her."

Schyler restrained the whistle pushing at his lips. "It must have been a pretty strong indictment."

"It had to be to cover up for... Maybe some day when it doesn't hurt any longer, I'll tell you all of it. But I can't stand to rehash it now."

"You mean... After so many years, you—"

Richard interrupted him. "Yes, it hurts. If I can bring Veronica into my life, that will help, but nothing will ever erase the..." He slapped both his knees with his palms. "The soufflé is first-class tonight. How about some?"

How could his father possibly smile after the gut-wrenching tale he'd just told? "You bet," Schyler said, trying to keep his voice light. "Don't you get tired of chocolate?"

Richard's grin eased over his face and settled in his eyes, eyes that now reminded Schyler of Veronica. "Me? Haven't you figured it out? You've forced so much of it on me that I've gotten where I have to have my daily chocolate fix."

They laughed, stood and walked arm in arm to the kitchen. Each faced a battle: Richard intended to win his. If he didn't, Schyler and Veronica wouldn't stand a chance. But Schyler had resigned himself to what he considered the hopelessness of a meaningful relationship with Veronica, and moved his mind on to other things.

As Veronica walked, her steps slowed and her energy seemed to dissipate. She leaned against a lamppost and tried to collect her wits. What had made her do it? Run from him like that? The hold Schyler had on her and the way he'd demonstrated it... No. She had to be honest with herself. That wasn't the reason. She'd met a man different from the one her mother had told her about. A man set in a very different mold. And she could have liked him. A lot, too. But for thirty years he'd been a monster, someone she detested, and she couldn't shove that aside or wash it away just because he cooked the best rice she'd ever tasted. She knew she'd wounded him when she didn't go back for his prized soufflé, and she'd hurt Schyler, too. Her spirit crumpled when she realized that she envied Schyler her father's love, his pampering and the status a successful father gave his children. She didn't like admitting it, because she'd always considered jealousy beneath her, believed it robbed a person of common sense and dignity. She pulled herself away from the post and walked on. Richard Henderson didn't add up. He was an enigma that she knew she'd never figure out without being around Schyler, and she couldn't risk that danger. She had no intention of letting herself become involved with Schyler.

She got in her car and realized she hadn't locked it. There was something to be said for a village the size of Tilghman, she mused, but she'd be leaving it come morning. Maybe for good.

* * *

Several days later she found herself in Baltimore, back in her old territory lunching with Enid.

"So tell me about this fling you had over in Europe. Meet any hunks?"

Veronica let her gaze roam around Wilma's Blue Moon Restaurant, reflecting on the hours she'd spent at that same table discussing CPAA's business with Enid and others of her staff and marveled that she didn't miss it.

She decided to tease Enid. "I didn't see anything but hunks. If you're looking for one who's different, go over and take your pick. Of course, you might have to take their ideas about women right along with them. I had a fling, but it was an affair with freedom, you might say. Me and Mother Nature all alone. It was incredible."

Enid cocked her head to one side. "Then why'd you come back so soon? If I'd been in your shoes, girl, the people in this town wouldn't know where I made my last tracks. They don't deserve you."

Months ago such a compliment would have pleased her, but now she shrugged it off. "That's behind me, Enid." She told her friend about her mother but nothing more.

"Seen Mr. Henderson since you've been back?"

Had she ever! "I knew you'd ask that. Anything new with him?" She hoped Enid wouldn't catch her evasion. "Who's he after now?"

Enid's dreamy-eyed expression brought a sheen of perspiration to Veronica's forearms. Was what she felt for Schyler merely the usual reaction of the average woman? His regular due?

"Girl, I wish he was after me," she heard Enid say.

She didn't want to watch Enid drool over Schyler Henderson. She sipped the last of her coffee, gave Enid and Wilma the tiny porcelain Swiss yodelers she'd bought for them in Interlaken and bade her friend goodbye.

"Let me know where you'll be, honey," Enid said.

Veronica wrote her name, address and phone number on a piece of paper. "In case it's been erased from your computer, here it is, but be careful who gets hold of it." She started off, turned back and hugged her friend. "See you."

Enid ducked her head, but Veronica had seen her tears. "Don't worry about me, Enid. I'll be all right. But there's so much I haven't done, seen and felt, things that I've dreamed of since childhood. Now may be my only chance to live fully. To the hilt. And I'm not letting it slip by. I'll stay in touch."

Enid nodded and walked away.

Veronica stopped in Kmart, bought a jumbo-size umbrella with a long handle and headed for the train to Owings Mills. When she reached the train station, she crossed Reisterstown Road and turned the corner.

"Ronnie! Ronnie! I knowed you'd come back. I just knowed it. I missed you a whole lot, Ronnie. People don't talk to me when they past here. I 'preciate every single penny people gives me. Lord knows I do. But you don't throw money at me like you was 'fraid to touch me, Ronnie. You comes to me and hands it to me and talks with me. While you was gone, weeks went by and nobody said a word to me lessen I went to buy something. And then they didn't say nothin' if they could help it."

The woman's anguish drifted through her like a throbbing ache, for she had never before heard Jenny complain or even show dissatisfaction with her predicament. Yet, she couldn't get Jenny to motivate herself enough to receive real assistance.

"You don't belong out here," she told her. "I told you I'd help you get a place if you'll only fill out that form I gave you."

"I'm gon' do that, Ronnie. Honest. I just dreads them slammin' them doors in my face."

Veronica stepped closer and patted Jenny's shoulder. "If you'll trust me, that won't happen. Here's something for you." She handed her the umbrella. "This will keep you dry, and it's good for shade, too."

Jenny's wide grin lit up her face. She grabbed the umbrella and ran her fingers up and down it, feeling it, caressing it. "So pretty, Ronnie. And it's new. Brand-new. Well, can you beat that? I don't know when I last had anything that hadn't been throwed away. Real new. Well, I declare."

Such a small thing, that umbrella. Jenny's pleasure in it humbled her. She folded some bills and handed them to the woman.

"Oh, no, Ronnie. You keep that." She patted her coat pocket, still secured with the two safety pins. "I still got some of what you gave me before you left. I'll let you know when I run out. You know I thank you, don't you, Ronnie?"

Veronica nodded. "See you next time, and you fill out that form."

"I hope you ain't out here in the middle of the day 'cause you sick or somethin'."

Veronica couldn't help smiling with pleasure at Jenny's concern for her. "Nothing like that. I'm on leave." She looked at her watch. "I have to get my train. Bye now."

"Bye and thanks. I'm gonna fill out the paper. You hear?"

Veronica walked into the town house that she'd worked so hard to get and in which she'd always taken such pride. Sunlight streamed through the living room's large bay window, its brilliance giving the room an added cheerfulness and an elegance that complimented her achievements and her personality. For a minute she let herself glory in it, but a few seconds later the picture of Jenny on the corner with her shopping cart of junk and her joyous acceptance of the one new thing she'd had in years undercut her pride in her home and her possessions.

Discomfited, she wandered through the house, flicked on the television to a Senate debate, sucked her teeth in disgust at the hypocritical posturing and shut if off. She turned on the radio, and a Mozart concerto flowed around her. Her favorite, but not on that morning. Schyler. Schyler. If only she didn't care. She walked into the kitchen and looked out of the window and at a blue jay flitting from limb to limb on her prized cherry tree. She couldn't help remembering the soul-searing trek over the meadow in the Swiss Alps.

Schyler. Schyler. She didn't want to go to the singing group that she loved; didn't feel like knitting the mittens and caps that she always created as Christmas gifts for homeless children; and she couldn't work up an interest in the state's foster care system. She wanted what she couldn't have. She wanted that wild, hot, unearthly feeling she'd gotten when he had her in his arms. If only she could feel his hands, his lips, his body... Oh Lord, what was wrong with her!

Without thinking, she did as she'd always done when she stood at a precipice and needed balance. She called her stepfather.

His voice blessed her with the solace that he'd always represented in her life. "I was hoping you'd call, Veronica. I don't like not knowing where you are."

"I'm home."

"Good. I know you're upset about your mama being gone and all that, but she's better off now, and we have to be glad for that."

"I'm handling it, Papa. What about you?"

"I'm doing fine. When are you going back to work? When I called Enid, she said you had three months' leave to use up. That doesn't make sense. You can lose a lot in three months, including your job."

She didn't want to distress him. He'd think she didn't appreciate her blessing. And besides, she wanted him to know she'd always be there to help him if he needed it. "I haven't had a vacation in years, Papa, and that trip to Europe just whetted my appetite."

He knew her so well that he probably suspected she wasn't telling all, but she knew he wouldn't pressure her to share a problem before she was ready. He had so many ways of communicating his love for her, and it came to her now in his softened voice and gentle concern.

"Well, get some rest, and you be careful roaming around all by yourself. Come see me when you can. I'll be praying for you."

She pushed back the threatening tears, though there was no sorrow in them. Just an overwhelming love. "Thanks, Papa. You know I will."

She waited for him to say goodbye, but he hadn't finished. "If you're running from something, girl, you might as well stand still and face it, cause it'll catch you anyway. I can testify to that. And if you're trying to find something, look inside yourself first. It's there, baby. You just need the courage to take it."

How had he read her so accurately? "I know, Papa. I know. Here's my cell phone number in case you lost it. You can reach me wherever I am in the country. Love you, Papa."

"You're my heart, Veronica. Always have been. Always will be."

Nothing had changed, but she felt a lot better. She phoned Hertz for a rental car, got out some maps and sat down to figure out where next to satisfy her wanderlust. The following morning she packed a few essentials along with her Buddy Guy, George Strait and Leontyne Price cassettes, her knitting bag, six cans of ginger ale and a supply of Butterfingers. She laughed at her taste in music. Blues, country and opera, not to mention the jazz and chamber music and other classical morsels that she wasn't taking along. She went back into the house and got a couple of Billie Holiday cassettes, in case she stayed away more than a few days and began to miss them. She looked at the beloved house that she once hated to leave for any reason, shook her head at the changes in her, got in the Mercury Cougar and headed for the Adirondack Mountains.

Dusk had begun to settle over the tiny hamlet of Indian Lake when she turned into Geandreau's Cabins, a group of furnished, red clapboard cabins on Highway 28 facing Adi-

rondack Lake. The brochure promised scenic beauty and only
nature for company, if one wanted that. Here and there, houses
predating the Revolutionary War proudly displayed their
plaques of authenticity and stood arrogantly, as it were, among
the youthful and less imposing school, church, tiny post office,
hardware store and Giant supermarket. What did the villages
do for entertainment or for intellectual stimulation? An eerie
quiet. Solitude.

She quickly learned that if she wanted that, she'd have to
insist on it. At supper in the nearby café, a stranger joined her
as soon she sat down.

"You're not from 'round here," the old man said. "Staying long?"

She remembered that she was in a small town, tried not to
show impatience and made herself smile. "A few days."

"Ain't much to do here 'cept swim and go canoeing. Fish
don't never bite no more; weeds suck up the oxygen in the lake."

Not according to her knowledge of chemistry; like all
other lakes, that one was nothing more than a combination
of oxygen and hydrogen. She let the old man have his wisdom. "That so?"

"Sure thing," he said. "If yer husband wants to go fishing,
I can take him down to the Indian Lake in the morning. They
bites down there. No charge. Just friendly. I likes the company."

She supposed if she lived in a tiny place like Indian Lake,
she'd be expected to have a husband. "I'm not married."

He peered at her as if to make sure his eyes hadn't fooled
him. "Where you from?"

She told him, and watched him shake his head, seemingly
in dismay. "No wonder. Them city fellows don't know a
woman when they sees one. You better get started. Raising
young'uns ain't easy when you get older. Takes more energy
than you got. Get yerself a good man 'fore you too old to find
one." He looked closely at her. "You got one, ain't you?"

What could she say? There was someone who could fill her

life with all it lacked, all she desired, but he was just another of her dreams.

"There is someone, but I have no hope for an enduring relationship with him."

The old man cocked an eyebrow and rubbed the gray stubble that grew from his jaw. "He ain't married or engaged, is he?"

She shook her head as the weight of her plight with Schyler and her father bore upon her and, for reasons she would never be able to explain, found herself telling that stranger the story of her life, omitting nothing. The bare truth as she had never even acknowledged to herself.

The old man looked down at the cold food on his plate, food he'd ignored while listening to her story. "Seems to me you're yer biggest problem. Don't pay to harbor hatred. You gotta forgive and forget, and believe me, you'll be a lot happier. And you better find out what yer mother wanted you to know, 'cause I'd bet me boat yer real daddy's a decent man. And as for Schyler—that's his name, ain't it—seems to me like the only thing between you and him is yer hard heart where his daddy is concerned. You think of these here things, gal, 'fore you find you ain't got nothin' but tragedy all 'round you. Go back home and deal with this thing."

The old man drained his cup of chicory-passing-for-coffee and pushed back his chair.

"Let me take your check," she said on impulse.

His smile, weary and forced, barely touched his face. "Thanks, but I oughta be taking *your* check. If God was listening when I told you the truth, maybe he'll consider I just atoned for *my* sin. Years ago I walked off and left my wife and children 'cause I couldn't stand seeing them suffer for what I couldn't give them. I regretted it later, though that didn't help me much. But I don't believe yer real daddy did that, 'cause he had money. You take care."

For a second she leaned back in the booth, taken aback by the man and his words and wondering if Providence had sent her a messenger. She didn't deserve responsibility for the mess that mired down their lives—hers, Schyler's and her father's. She'd learned that her birth father had walked out on her and her mother long before she could recite her nightly prayers. Schyler didn't believe it possible, and neither did the old stranger, who now knew far more about her than any other human being. She paid her check and walked out into the wet night air. Stillness all around her. Not even the wind rustled, and not a moving thing in sight. She stopped and looked around. Where was the old man, who'd left less than a minute earlier? She hadn't heard a car drive off. She shrugged, thankful for the peace that surrounded her.

As she neared the cabin, raindrops pelted her. Harder and harder, thicker and thicker they fell. She stopped, spread her arms and let the rain drench her. A symbolic catharsis. At last she went inside and closed the door, her hair knotted and her clothing sticking to her skin. She stared at herself in the bathroom mirror. Inspecting herself. But the burden of the old man's words still weighted her down.

She washed and dried her clothes in the washing machine and drier, showered and crawled into bed. Hours later, she uncoiled the sheet from her body, retrieved the light blanket from the floor, smoothed out the crumpled sheets and crawled back into bed. Still another hour passed, and she hadn't been able to conquer demon sleep. Desperate, ignoring her own caution and following her heart, she dialed Richard Henderson's phone number and prayed that Schyler would answer.

His voice illumined her being like the sudden glow of candlelight in a cell of darkness. "This is Schyler Henderson speaking."

She opened her mouth, but no words came, for she had nothing to say, only a need for his nearness.

"Hello." He spoke calmly, a patient greeting, as if he knew the caller needed courage.

"I...uh... Sorry, wrong—"

"*Veronica!* Don't. Don't hang up. Why did you call? Tell me. Do you...do you want to...to talk with me?"

What had happened to her composure? "I..." She couldn't lie. "I don't know why I called you, Schyler. I couldn't sleep, and I—"

"Veronica, if you need me, just say so. Wherever you are, I'll...I'll go there. Right now."

She pondered the urgency of his voice and tried to register the meaning of his words, but they didn't seem real. None of it did. "Thanks, but I'm in the Adirondack Mountains."

She could hear his silence screaming at her over a thousand miles of telephone wire. "When did you...? You just left here day before yesterday. Veronica, what's the matter? It's one...one-thirty in the morning. You called me because you need me. Can't you tell me?"

Just stay on the line and keep talking to me. Say anything, but talk to me. "I just felt if I could talk to you a little. I didn't know what I'd say. I... *Oh, Schyler! Have you ever felt that there was nobody else...anywhere?*" She wanted to bite her tongue the minute she heard the words escape her lips. She held her breath in anticipation of his answer.

"Have I...? *Veronica!* You wouldn't ask me that, if you didn't need me. Why do you think I was wide awake when you called? Tell me when you're going back to Baltimore and I'll be there waiting for you."

Talons of fear pricked her. Did she dare be alone with him? "I'm not sure I should have called you. Maybe this was a mistake."

His voice, low and husky, sent waves of warmth rolling through her, pushing aside her fear. "But you need me. I know it as surely as I know my name. There's unfinished business between us. After you left me on the beach, I figured that had to be the end, and I resigned myself to that. But it isn't over. Not for you. Not for me. I'm glad you called me. When will you be back?"

She wanted to see him, to be with him, and she supposed he knew it. Lying didn't make sense. "Day after tomorrow."

"Come back tomorrow. I need to see you, too. Will you do that?"

"I...I thought I'd..."

"There's no point in stalling. You'll still need me tomorrow, Veronica. I've told you before that we have to deal with this. We've no choice. Will you come back tomorrow?"

"I'll... All right. I'll be there tomorrow night around seven-thirty."

She could hear his release of breath and knew he'd been anxious. Then he said, "Don't worry yourself to death about what will or won't happen when we see each other. It can only get better. Sleep now. And drive carefully tomorrow." The silence stretched out, heavy with unspoken words and feelings. "I'm glad you called. Good night."

"Good night, Schyler."

She hung up, rolled over and accepted the fact that she felt better for having talked with him and for knowing she'd see him. He'd said she shouldn't fret about the imponderable. But what had she promised? And what did he expect?

Schyler walked into his office shortly after noon that Monday, threw his briefcase on a chair and got the telephone book. He had to call Enid Dupree and get Veronica's address, because he'd forgotten to ask her for it. He'd planned to stay at his father's place in Tilghman, where he wouldn't be disturbed, and work there until he finished his design for the descrambler, an instrument that would permit free access to TV cable stations. But she'd called him, needing him. And she'd called at a time when his head was full of her and his body screaming for her, demanding that she fulfill him. If she'd called him at almost two o'clock in the morning... She'd asked him if he'd ever had the feeling that there was no one else *anywhere,* but him. Too much pride, even in her distress, to tell him flat out that she was lonely, but it had been there in her voice, her attitude and in the time of night. Lonely? His body had answered for him, proclaiming its readiness.

He'd been crawling out of his mind when that phone rang, strung out, as his father's words telling him what it was like to love a woman he couldn't have roared in his head. *Had he been lonely?* The sound of her voice had pounded the pit of his belly, clawing at the intimate depth of him—down deep in him where he lived. He braced his right elbow on the desk and propped his head up with it. Had he been lonely? He'd known nothing but loneliness and rejection until he met his adoptive father, but those childhood experiences seemed like pinpricks now compared to the ache that ground in him when she walked off that beach. He had denied it to himself, but it had deepened with every passing minute. He dialed CPAA and asked for Enid Dupree.

"CPAA. Enid Dupree speaking. How may I help you?"

Hmmm. Good telephone manners. "Ms. Dupree, this is Schyler Henderson. Do you have Ms. Overton's address and phone number? I need to be at her place this evening, and I don't have it."

"Well, now let me see, Mr. Henderson. If she wanted you to have it, she'd give it to you, wouldn't she? How do I know you're not planning to rub salt in those wounds you've already inflicted on her?"

He looked at the red marks that the pressure of his fingers, balled into a tight fist, had left in the palm of his right hand and tried to relax. "I don't want to arouse media suspicion by getting the information at the courthouse, but I will if I have to. I told her I'd see her tonight, and short of breaking the law, I'll keep my word to her."

"I see. I'm not giving you her address unless I'm assured you're not going to damage her any further. Take that or leave it."

Tough, was she? He respected well-placed loyalty, and he

was glad Veronica had a friend in the woman. "I don't have any guilt about Veronica, Ms. Dupree, because I only did my job as I understood it."

"Hmmm. I see. All right."

He thanked her, jotted down the information and stuck it in his shirt pocket. He hadn't told his father about Veronica's call because he hadn't wanted to raise his hopes. And he was trying to keep his own feet on the ground; the real problem between Veronica and him hadn't changed since she'd walked away from him on that beach. He hung his Don't Disturb sign on his door, turned on his answering machine and got to work.

At seven-fifteen that evening, he parked across the street from 31 Comfort Road in Owings Mills. He didn't see a light in the town house, so he stayed in his car. He'd wait there all night, if he had to. Ten minutes later, a gunmetal Mercury Cougar parked in front of number thirty-one. After what seemed like an eternity, the trunk opened, and Veronica stepped out of the car. Getting to her was an all-powerful urge, but he had to restrain himself lest he frighten her in the gathering dusk.

He walked across the narrow street and called out to her as he approached. "Veronica."

She had leaned over the trunk and her head came up sharply. She whirled around. "Schyler!"

He raced to her with his arms open, and she sprinted to meet him. He had no words for that moment when her arms went around him and he folded her to his body. Her lips were there, raised to his. She parted them, and he tasted her breath and finally the heat of her mouth, and his world spun off its axis. She dived into him, holding nothing back, moaning her passion until desire threatened to strangle him. His heart beat out a rumba and when her body trembled, he dipped his tongue into the nectar of her mouth and kissed her with all the longing fermented in him. There, in the darkness, she moved against him, unmindful of their lack of privacy and, God help him, he felt a rush of blood and a swift tightening of his groin. He ordered his libido under control, folded her to him in a gentle embrace and tested his willpower.

He hugged her close and stroked her back, calming them both. Her soft, sweet woman's scent tantalized his nostrils, and he inhaled the feminine sweetness of her that seeped into him like a powerful elixir. When she put her head on his shoulder and seemed to burrow into him as though seeking warmth, he kissed her cheek and set her away from him.

"Let's get your things out of here and take them inside."

He locked the car, took her bags, and with one arm around her, walked with her to her front door. He wouldn't have believed she could be so nervous, but he sensed the tension in her and vowed to overlook it. This was a night for bonding, and he had no intention of pressuring her about anything.

Simple elegance. Just as he'd expected. Instead of the traditional mirror, a large reproduction of Doris Price's painting *On Stage,* an acrylic of a jazz combo in tribute to Miles Davis, hung above a beige marble fireplace. He dropped the bag on the floor and turned to her. Her wide eyes glittered with excitement, but her long, silky lashes immediately shielded them. He'd glimpsed exhilaration in them, but also vulnerableness. What she needed wasn't passion but tenderness, so he tempered his need. "You got any coffee?" he asked, not because he wanted any; he didn't, but he had to put her at ease. "I can make it; that long drive probably tired you out."

Her smile, signaling her understanding, told him he'd set the right tone for their first date. She led him to the modern kitchen and showed him the percolator and the coffee.

"Know how to operate a percolator?"

Thank God she grinned when she said it, or he'd have gotten the impression that she thought him stupid. "If I put myself to it, I may be able to manage the thing."

Her grin threatened to burst into a laugh. "You're sure, now?"

He tweaked her nose. "Mind your manners, gal. When women challenge me, I become a caveman. You wouldn't want to see that, would you?"

"Oh, I don't know," she said, her nerves obviously back in order. She stroked her arm, absentmindedly, almost as if she were somewhere else. "A good strong man can bring out the best in a woman. I mean…er…you know."

He had to laugh. "You're reckless. You know that?"

"Who me? I'm all bark and no bite. Look. You make the coffee while I change my shoes." She left, rather hurriedly, he thought.

Shoes, huh! He made the coffee and searched the kitchen for something edible. No luck. He found an advertisement for a Chinese restaurant, phoned the place and ordered some food.

"Do you mind my doing that?" he asked when she returned having replaced her jeans and shirt with a caftan, but wearing the same shoes.

"I sure don't. I didn't eat any lunch."

"You drove nonstop from Indian Lake?"

"Except once to get gas. If I hadn't, I'd still be on the road."

Don't assume anything, man. "Veronica, I'm getting some positive signals from you, but my gut instinct tells me not to follow up on them."

He'd swear her relief was palpable and knew at once that he'd better tread with care. Her response confirmed his judgment.

"You…you're right. We… Maybe if we just try to enjoy each other's company, to get acquainted—"

"That, too. But I'm not interested in pretense. Or small talk. Or banalities. I need to know what's happening to me. And to you, Veronica. And I want to start now."

He took her hand and walked with her to the sofa. "I know why you walked away from me on the beach after sharing that unbelievable kiss with me. And I know nothing has happened since to change your feelings about my dad. But I'm not here to talk about him, but about us. You called me. Do you understand why and have you accepted it?"

He lifted the lid of the crystal candy jar that rested on the table beside the sofa, unwrapped a mint and held it to her lips. She glanced up at him, smiled and parted her lips, and he thought he'd have died if he couldn't have hugged her.

He wrapped her in his arms and rocked her. "I don't know where we're headed, but something in me wants to go there. What about you?"

She snuggled closer. "I'm maybe overly cautious about most things, or I used to be, but I don't seem to be running this show. I surprised myself when I called you."

"What did you want to tell me?"

"I… Nothing. I just…I don't know."

It wasn't good enough. He'd said he wouldn't push her, but he couldn't accept that answer. "How did you feel after we talked?" He tipped up her chin so he could look into her eyes.

"Better. As if things were as they should be. I…I felt good."

Lousy timing. The sound of the door chimes reminded him that he'd ordered their dinner. He got up, paid the delivery man, brought plates, napkins and flatware from the kitchen, put them on the coffee table and served their food.

"You're handy around the house," she said.

"You betcha. There was only my dad and me, so I learned how to do everything." He winked at her. "I've got talents you can't even guess at."

Her tongue probed the center of her left cheek and her left eyebrow eased up. He couldn't help laughing. "Straighten out your mind, Veronica."

"You clean up yours," she shot back. "I was thinking how talented you are, and—"

His hand paused between the plate and his mouth. "Sure you were. And I'm president of the United States."

She tossed her head in pretended haughtiness. "Are you accusing me of fudging the truth?"

She slapped him playfully on the knee, and he liked that. He wanted her to get familiar with him, and he wanted her to enjoy doing it.

"Fudging the truth? Definitely not. You're nowhere near it. You assumed I had reference to my…er…manly attributes, now didn't you?"

She gave an exaggerated sigh and looked toward heaven, as though begging assistance. "What else? We're dealing with the nuts and bolts of the male mind here."

Laughter rolled out of him. He put down the fork, laid his head back against the sofa and guffawed, a roaring cleansing laugh.

"What's so funny?" she asked, clearly taken aback by his uproarious laughter.

When he could breathe more easily, he sat straight, picked up his fork and returned to his lobster. "I'm not going there, Veronica. No way. So don't press me on it."

She glared at him. "I thought we were going to share ourselves, to…uh—"

"Veronica, quit while you're ahead."

He hoped he hadn't annoyed her, and he'd begun to think he'd done just that, when suddenly the fork clattered in her plate and giggles poured out of her.

"See what I mean?" he needled. "I was about to decide you were slow on the uptake."

She took their plates and the remaining evidence of their meal to the kitchen and returned with a bottle of Pouilly-Fuissé and two wineglasses.

"Instead of giving me low marks for wit, you ought to compliment me on my clean mind."

"Yeah. They're harder to find than good wit these days." He ducked, figuring she might throw a punch or maybe that wine bottle at him for that transgression. Instead, she smiled and poured them each a glass of the white Burgundy wine and sat beside him.

Every time she raised those long lashes slowly and deliberately, she knocked the wind out of him. He waited for her sally, and she let him have it.

"You know, I've heard that some…er, people use their sharp tongue as a salve to soothe their frustrated libidos, but I don't suppose that would apply to you."

What a woman! His stare belied his admiration. "Down deep, you love danger. I wouldn't have believed it, and I expect you didn't know it. You want me to prove something to you? Just say when, because, sweetheart, I can hardly wait."

"Why is it that you can find a double meaning in everything I say? Is that a guy thing?"

Not now, man. Don't let her get you off the track. Ignore it. He raised his glass. "We can fight later. Thank you for being with me tonight."

Her hesitation before touching his glass with her own, and the unreadable expression she plastered on her face gave him a feeling of unease. Worse still, her smile didn't quite make it to her eyes.

"Am I losing you already?"

She shook her head, slowly as if in deep thought. "No matter how I feel, Schyler, I can't be sanguine about a relationship with you."

He didn't want to hear it. "Because of those court trials?" In his heart, he hoped that was the reason, but he feared otherwise.

She waved a hand in disdain. "You may have done me a favor with those court cases. The experience taught me an invaluable lesson about people and life. I don't hold that against you."

A sensation of dread threatened his joy at being with her. "Then it boils down to my dad. I love him, Veronica. I know it hurts you to hear it, but if it hadn't been for him, I'd have grown up as just so much human junk. Worthless in the eyes of society; the same society that shunted me from home to home, never caring how I fared, just getting me out of sight and mind. I can't pretend he isn't a part of my life, a part of *me*. Never mentioning him."

The long, labored breath she released told him that she, too, struggled with some kind of truth. "I'm trying to understand."

"What? Tell me."

He listened to her tale of an old man, a spiritlike being, who joined her for supper the night she'd called him. A man who'd insisted that she had to forgive.

"You told him about my father?"

She nodded. "I found myself telling him the story of my life, omitting nothing, from the time I knew myself. I, who have guarded my privacy as if it were a stack of gold bullion."

"Then, why?"

"I couldn't square what I'd done with the woman I think I am. Walking off from you that way and not going back to tell my father goodbye. I knew I'd hurt him, and you, too. I couldn't get it out of my mind."

"And now?"

"The same. The old man heaped a load of guilt on me, telling me that if I don't forgive and forget, I'll be the culprit *and* the loser. Thinking back, he could have been an angel. He led me straight to the story, and had one of his own to match it. I walked outside right behind him, but he was nowhere. Pretty nimble, I thought, for a man well past eighty years of age."

He'd digest that another time. "And when you called me, you'd been lying awake wrestling with it."

"The truth? That and more. I called because I needed you. I didn't know in what way, only that…that I did. I knew somehow that you would rid me of that terrible emptiness, that feeling that there was no one. I…"

Her voice seemed to fade, whether from weariness or pain, he didn't know. He slid an arm around her and drew her to him. "Don't ever hesitate to reach out to me. I'll always be there for you, no matter what."

She was digging herself into him, claiming what he'd never allowed any woman to have, not even the woman who briefly bore his name. She draped an arm across his chest and rested her head on his shoulder, and the sweetness of it sucked him ever deeper into her orbit. He inhaled her feminine scent, a delicate allure that he could have taken in forever. In spite of the tenderness he felt, desire stole over him, stabbing him all the way to his marrow. He had to get out of there.

"I'd better go, sweetheart. Walk me to the door."

She stared at him. "Why? What's the matter?"

He couldn't help it if her reluctance to have him leave her boosted his ego. What man would react otherwise? *Prudence, man. You know more about this business than she does.* "If I don't go now, I won't want to, and I don't think staying is indicated at this time."

She seemed to muse over that, looked steadily at him and must have read his feeling on his face, for she got up immediately.

"Right. Where do you live? Anywhere near here?"

He shook his head. "One-ninety Charles Street in Baltimore." He handed her two cards. "And here are all my phone numbers. When am I going to see you again?"

She studied him intently for a minute. "You think it's a good thing, us seeing each other, when we haven't settled anything?"

"What could we settle if we didn't see each other? Besides, we did settle something: we want each other, and we care about each other. Right?"

"I guess."

Left to her, she'd have him covering the same ground every time they spoke or saw each other. No way. "You guess, huh?"

The hell with intentions. He pulled her into his arms, held her head and possessed her mouth. It didn't surprise him that within seconds, she began aggressively to love him back. But he'd showed her the facts, and he couldn't risk full-blown desire.

He stepped back. "You guess?"

She ducked her head. "All right. You made your point. Now scat."

"Scat? What the devil is that?"

She opened the door, planted a kiss on his mouth and gave him a gentle shove. "See you tomorrow."

His pulse quickened, and for a moment he had a light-headed sensation. She wanted to see him tomorrow. "You bet. I'll call you around ten."

Chapter 5

Veronica fought her almost lifelong habit of getting out of bed at sunrise. Rays of early-morning sunlight filtered through the blinds, and she pulled the cover over her head and turned toward the wall. Not that she was sleepy; she wasn't, but thoughts of the previous evening with Schyler filled her mind and she couldn't help luxuriating in the memory, reliving his touches and the wonder of it all. She stretched her legs, moved her head from side to side, hugged herself and indulged in the sweet indolence of leisurely anticipation. The evening would find them together again. Would he take her in his arms in that tender way he'd done the night before? And this time, would she let herself go? She could hardly wait to see him. Eager for the evening, she sprang out of bed, dressed, ate a breakfast of tomato juice, scrambled eggs, biscuits, raspberry jam and coffee and wandered around the house.

Now what? She wasn't restless, she told herself, only impatient for the night. Too early to play the piano, as some of her neighbors might be enjoying their last hour of sleep. She could catch up on her knitting for homeless children, but somehow that didn't appeal to her. Once she'd never had enough time, she reflected, but now she had more than she could use. She got her garden gloves and tools, went out to her backyard and started digging around her plants. She stopped resisting thoughts of Schyler, of the way lights danced in his eyes when he laughed, almost changing their color, and the half-smile that seemed to move over only one side of his face. She leaned the spade against the fence and told herself to think of something else. But three hours later, as she transplanted marigolds, she admitted that he was not only in her mind but headed for her heart.

A few minutes before ten, she raced back into the house, washed her hands and waited for Schyler's call. Suddenly angry that she'd put herself in a position where she had nothing to do but wait on a man's telephone call, she added a linen jacket to her shirt and jeans and started for the door. If the phone had rung one minute later, she'd have been in the rented Mercury Cougar returning it to Hertz.

"Hello. This is Schyler."

As annoyed at herself as she was, her heart nonetheless became fast and unruly. She calmed herself. "Hi."

"I hope I didn't waken you."

"Of course not. I was on my way—" She stopped herself, but with his fast mind, she knew he'd picked up on it.

"Wait, here. Weren't you expecting me to call at ten o'clock?"

"Uh…sure. I just—"

"What changed since last night? If we're not on the same wavelength—"

She didn't want to tussle with him. "We'll see each other tonight as planned. Right?" Anxiety sent a sensation of pinpricks up and down her arms as his silence lengthened.

"If that's what you want."

She sat down and kicked off her shoes. "What about what you want?"

"All right. Suppose I pick you up at your house at about six-thirty. We'll get some dinner and...and take it from there."

Either he'd done a lot of thinking since he'd left her, or her foolish lapse had made him wary. "I'll be in Baltimore this afternoon, so I could meet you somewhere."

His silence seemed endless, and she knew he might easily tell her to skip it. She was ready to hang up when he said, "I'll be at my office in Branch Signal Corporation until five-thirty. If you still want us to be together, call me at five and tell me where to meet you."

"Okay."

"In the meantime, would you please be prepared to tell me what happened last night, when you encouraged me to expect at least a warm, loving greeting this morning?"

"I... Nothing happened. Not a thing."

"To your way of thinking, maybe. Talk with you at five."

Slowly she hung up. He wasn't going to let her play with him, and she'd better watch her words and actions. In truth, it made no sense to begin a romance with Schyler, but they teetered on the edge of that, and possibly something deeper and more all-consuming. No matter how they felt about each other, Richard Henderson stood between them, an impediment to any joy they could ever know. She threw the keys on her dresser and went to the piano. She'd return the car later.

Lost in the Chopin étude that she coaxed from the keys of her Baldwin piano, she barely heard the telephone ring and wouldn't have answered it if she hadn't thought Schyler might be the caller.

"Hello."

"Hi. What took you so long? I was about to hang up."

"Enid! How are you? What's up?"

"Long story. You free for lunch?"

"I can make myself free, but of course, it will be a sacrifice, in view of my pressing obligations."

A feeling of nostalgia crept over her at the sound of Enid's laughter. She'd already forgotten how Enid loved to laugh and did so at every opportunity.

"I've been hoping you'd get bored and take your job back. What time and where?"

They agreed to meet at Wilma's Blue Moon at one-thirty. Tough luck. She had to dress for the evening, so she settled for a black sleeveless silk dress and matching jacket, a long strand of white pearls, black shoes and bag. She wasn't crazy about herself in black, but it could take five hours of wear and still look decent when she met Schyler.

She left the car at Hertz and took a taxi to Wilma's. She'd developed an affection for Wilma and enjoyed a brief exchange with her before going to Enid's table.

Enid didn't look as if she'd had any good news recently. "Should I head out of here right now?" Veronica asked her after they'd greeted each other.

Enid sipped her white wine. "Well, it's not exactly jump-for-joy time, though I did meet someone."

Veronica read her menu and digested the dissatisfaction she detected in Enid's voice. She didn't think the new man could be responsible for Enid's gloomy expression. "Any butterflies doing the boogaloo in your tummy? What does he look like?"

"He's decent-looking, but the thing is his flawless body. Schwarzenegger, move over. And there's the rub. A strapping fifty-two-year-old man who can't leave the gym long enough to… You should see him."

Veronica stifled a laugh. "Shouldn't hurt your fingers one bit to slide over those hard male muscles."

Enid sucked her teeth and glanced toward heaven. "Pa…leeeze! My itchy fingers haven't had a chance to do that. When he does leave the gym, perfecting his body, he's too darned tired to…to use it for anything."

"Maybe a little flab around the middle is better. Tell him to take a hike."

She watched the look of incredulity move over Enid's face. "You should see the looks these young gals give me when I'm with him. I'm hoping some other men will wonder why he's with me and move in on him. I ought to get *something* for this eight-thousand-dollar face."

Veronica noticed that Enid pushed her salad around in her plate but barely touched it. Not a good sign; Enid was a hearty eater. So Mr. Perfect Body was not the reason Enid wanted to see her. She finished her sandwich of smoked salmon on pumpernickel bread and her endive salad, pushed back her plate and waited. But Enid continued to toy with her food.

Apprehension coursed through her. "What's going on, Enid? Something's eating at you, and it isn't that guy."

"No, it isn't. It's CPAA."

Veronica sat forward and gripped the edge of the table. "What about it?"

"Brace yourself. The police arrested a woman for backing the numbers, and guess where she lived."

"I don't think I want to know."

"She's Madge Williams's sister, and she'd been staying with Madge for the last seven months hiding out from the police. You know how many of our kids Madge has?"

Veronica let out a long and heavy breath. Lord, not again. "Three, and she's had them for five years."

"Right. Uh...did you...uh, see Schyler Henderson last night?"

"What? How did you find out about that?"

"He called me yesterday to get your address and phone number. I guess I gave him a hard time, until he explained why he wanted it."

"I saw him. What's he got to... Wait a minute—"

"You got it. He called me this morning about half an hour before I called you. Said he doesn't want a fiasco similar to the last one. He asked for all the information we had on

Madge Williams. You know, her record as a foster mother, where she goes to church, her husband's associates, things like that."

Veronica deepened her intakes of breath, fighting the weight that lodged in her chest. "Do you know when he learned about this…this woman's arrest?"

"Probably this morning, since the arrest was made last night. The story's in *The Maryland Journal*. Why? Anything happening between you and Schyler?"

"I don't know. We're drawn to each other, but…we're like birds in a windstorm; something batters us from every side. I doubt anything will come of it."

"From the looks of you, I suppose you're seeing him again tonight. I'm sorry about this latest mess—one more burden that we didn't earn. I just hope he doesn't decide to press charges. Of course there's one big problem—the caseworker certified every one of those seven months that the only people living in that house were Madge, her husband and those three kids."

"I know. It doesn't look well for the agency. I think you ought to have weekly conferences with the caseworkers as a group. I've suspected that some of them don't give full and candid reports."

"Good idea. Say, would you like to go to Deak's on Charles Street? I need to unwind sometime. Friday, if you don't have a date."

"Great. I love jazz. Let's be in touch around four o'clock Friday and firm it up."

Enid looked at her watch. "What'll you do from now till your date with Schyler?"

"I'm going to the library. I want to review the history of foster care in this state. Be in touch."

At four-thirty Veronica put her writing pad in her handbag, satisfied that she'd made some headway on her review of the foster care system. She dropped a coin in a pay phone and dialed Schyler's office number.

"Schyler Henderson speaking."

"Hello, Schyler. This is Veronica. Where would you like us to meet?"

"Hi. You're right on the minute. I feel like a good meal. Where are you right now?"

"At the public library."

"Stay there. I'll pick you up in twenty minutes."

She went outside and sat on the steps to wait. *We're right back where we were this morning,* she thought, as she fought rising irritation that she recognized had nothing to do with Schyler but with the time on her hands.

She watched him sprint up the steps, stood and waited for him. How would he greet her? He stopped inches from her and stared down into her face. She smiled, and as if that had been the cue he sought, he opened his arms and folded her to him.

"I wasn't sure of the welcome I'd get."

"Neither was I. Where're we going?"

He folded her hand in his and started walking down the steps. "Little Italy. Do you know La Tavola?"

Did she ever! "Oh, yes. It's my favorite Italian restaurant. You've got great taste."

He glanced down at her, and she loved the smile that crawled over his face. How'd he do that? "Was that ever in question, considering my taste in women?"

The weight that had burdened her chest since she'd gotten Enid's bad news seemed to vanish, and though she knew there'd be pain before they parted, she let herself relax and enjoy the sweet contentment that he spun around her. When they got to the car, which he'd parked a block away, he stopped.

"Veronica, call me old-fashioned, and maybe I am, but my Dad taught me from childhood that women deserve special treatment. I will ignore you and cater to your professional standing when we're in a business gathering, but I want to open this car door for you. Nobody will see you but me."

He looked around. "Just wanted to be sure I was telling the truth. Humor me, will you?"

Taken aback by his serious demeanor, she could only stare at him.

"And that goes for opening it when we get where we're going. Okay?"

"Uh…sure, if it's so important to you."

"It is."

He opened the door and assisted her into the car, and her mind went once more to the kind of man her birth father must be. Had he changed, or had her mother not realized what manner of man he was? A sense of unease crept into her, but she knew that to dwell on it was a sure way to spoil their evening.

La Tavola offered the perfect romantic nook with soft lights, white tablecloths and bouquets of flowers on widely separated tables. She followed the headwaiter to their table in a corner at the back wall and knew it was a prized spot when Schyler slipped the waiter a sizable bill.

"Break down tonight and have a glass of something," he urged. "I don't drink much either, but a fine Italian meal deserves the best wine."

"Whatever you order."

His eyebrow shot up. "Look here. I didn't mean that you should give away your inalienable right to say no to whatever I suggest."

She grinned. She couldn't help it. "Come now. You don't seriously believe that's a remote possibility."

"Well, the way things were going… You were so cooperative that I was getting nervous."

He ordered white wine, a Mondavi chardonnay, leaned back in his chair and let his gaze roam over her. "You're striking in black, and I wouldn't have thought it; I like dark women in warm colors. Shows what I know."

She watched the waiter pour their wine. "Thanks."

Thrills danced along her nerves when he winked at her, not once but twice, teasing. Promising. "Thanks for what?" he asked her. "The compliment? It's my pleasure to look at you. I was just stating a fact."

They gave their orders and sat gazing at each other, not speaking, as they waited for their food. His passion-filled eyes loaded her mind with all kinds of provocative images, and she welcomed the arrival of the meal when she could at last pull her gaze from him.

They'd been together nearly an hour and he hadn't mentioned CPAA. Maybe he wasn't planning a suit. Or maybe he thought she no longer had an interest in the place. She tried to push it out of her mind and enjoy her meal—and him.

She ate heartily, savoring the dessert, a luscious lemon tart, and he smiled his pleasure at her enjoyment.

"I go for a woman who has a hearty appetite and doesn't pick over the food. It doubles my pleasure in her company."

She folded her napkin and laid it beside her plate. "What if they get fat?"

He seemed to ponder his answer. "Was your mother short?" She shook her head. "Then that won't happen with you. Dad eats like it's a rare occurrence, and he's the same size he was the first time I saw him."

She leaned forward. "Where did you meet him?"

"In Baltimore. He was sitting on those white stone steps. Just sitting there. Almost dusk one evening in the spring. I waved at him, and he waved back. I remember fantasizing about him, because he was friendly, and I waved at a lot of people who ignored me. I made it a habit to pass there often and he always waved. One day, I stopped and talked with him, and he asked if I wanted to go with him to get some ice cream. That started it. *Ice cream?* He might as well have asked me if I wanted a million dollars. They had ice cream where I lived, but I didn't get any of it."

She shook her head. "We didn't have ice cream either."

Why had she brought up that subject? "Schyler, I don't think we'd better get on that right now."

Almost magically, a sheen of sadness covered his eyes. "Do you think we can possibly make it?"

She'd been thinking the same thing. "I've been asking myself that all day."

He ordered brandy for himself and a tawny port for her. "Can you tell me what happened this morning?"

"I...I didn't understand it until I was sitting on the library steps waiting for you. I was irritated—"

"What, this afternoon, you—"

"Hear me out. It had nothing to do with you. It was me. I got mad at myself because I didn't have anything to do but wait on a phone call. I got up at six o'clock this morning and didn't have one thing to occupy my time, only to wait for ten o'clock. I practically went nuts. So I found myself headed for the door on my way to return that rental car just as you called. It wasn't rational, so don't ask why."

"I see. You have to go back to work. Is that it?"

Her long fingers strummed the table. "I intend to, but I'm not ready yet."

As they left the restaurant, he took her hand. "There's a quiet bar around the corner. I need to talk with you."

A hole opened up in her stomach, but she pretended light-heartedness. "Why not? It's early yet." Better that than go to either his place or hers.

He chose a small, round marble-topped table in a far corner. "What would you like?"

Her manners appealed to him. She wanted club soda on shaved ice with a twist of lime. She didn't drink, and unlike some women he'd dated, was above ordering a cocktail and letting it sit untouched in front of her. He got her drink and the same for himself. There was something to be said for sobriety. He put their glasses on the table along with the cocktail napkins and a dish of nuts. When he sat down, his knees touched her, and she gave him a quick glance before diverting her gaze self-consciously. It never ceased to amaze him that so much electricity ricocheted between them. He'd never shared such powerful chemistry with any other woman.

He had to open the topic, and he had to do it gently. He reached across the little bistro-type table and took her left hand. "This…Veronica, this mystery has to be solved. If we don't get to the bottom of it, there can't be anything for you and me."

"You mean about my mother's request?"

"Right. Have you tried to figure out, going back over everything you remember from your childhood until now, what your mother had in mind?"

"It's even kept me awake many nights. I've just about concluded that she wanted to right a wrong. After all, she was dying. But whether she'd…uh…wronged me, or your dad, or he had something that belonged to me, I don't know. All things considered, her request did not make sense."

The pain of her denial stabbed at him. "You can't refer to my dad as your father, can you? It's a shame. He wants so badly for you to love him, to be his daughter."

She closed her eyes for a minute and rubbed her jaw, as though easing away anguish. He didn't rush her. At last, she looked at him, almost pleading. "I'm trying. Trying hard, because I know what's at stake. But I've always seen my stepfather as my father, and I love him every bit as much as you love your dad. I can't…and I won't, do anything to hurt him. Never."

"I understand that, and I appreciate it. Are you saying that if you reached out to my dad, you'd feel guilty as though you were betraying your stepfather?"

He felt her hand unsteady in his own and clasped it tighter. "It's so…so strange. I know he's my father," she said, "and if I hadn't been told that…these things about him, I'd like him a lot. But I don't seem to be able to get over that lifelong image I've had of him."

"There's a clue in it somewhere, and we've got to find it. My dad's been so sad since he learned your mother had died that I can't even bring up this subject. Can't you discuss it with your stepfather? Surely he'll have some ideas."

"I started to, but I can't. I haven't even told him she asked me to find my father or that I located him. I…maybe he'll think she wasn't happy with him after all and that she wanted your dad. I don't know how he'll take it. I'm scared I'll hurt him if I mention it."

He ran his fingers over his hair, took a deep breath and released a lot of air from his lungs. He'd never been so frustrated. "What a mess!"

He wondered if she knew her right hand strummed the table, as though practicing scales on the piano. He supposed she was impatient with the subject, but he had to pursue it.

"I know it's an awful muddle, Schyler, but I can't help it."

"I know that. Your allegiance is with your stepfather, just as mine is with my dad, and these are both strong ties."

He had to know, and he couldn't await the test of time to find out. "Do you feel an allegiance to me? Even a little bit?"

He liked the fact that she looked him in the eye and didn't hesitate. "I'll stand with you, Schyler, so long as you're in the right and I don't have to go against my stepfather. Even if you were wrong, I wouldn't voluntarily move against you. I'd never do anything to hurt you."

Her hand, still enfolded in his own, had become damp from the intensity of her emotion, and he knew she meant what she said.

"That's more than I'd hoped for," he said. "You'd support me in spite of the position I put you in with that business about Natasha Wynn?"

"It's hard for me to forgive. Always has been, but as I told you before, putting distance between me and that job has given me new life."

He studied her intently, trying with all his might to keep

his feelings for her out of his face. But he must not have succeeded, because he could see her answering passion.

Might as well go for broke. "Do you believe you can depend on me, that I'll never let you down no matter what?" he asked.

He didn't like her hesitation. She bit at her bottom lip. "Yes, I believe that, but only so long as your principles aren't in question." Suddenly, she seemed uncertain.

"Schyler, Enid told me about Madge Williams."

He knew she could tell that she'd surprised him. "When? The case broke open yesterday, and I only learned about it around noon today. I'm sorry it happened, especially now when we're trying to get to know each other."

"You're going to ask for an indictment." It wasn't a question; she knew he'd do it.

"Do I have a choice?"

"Knowing you, I don't suppose so. I'd like to ask Madge if she knew what was going on."

He reached for her other hand and now held both of them. "Don't do that. You could be accused of attempting to coach her, and that could be construed as obstruction of justice. Let your lawyer do that."

Her shoulders drooped. "You're right. Anyway, it doesn't matter; this will be the end of CPAA."

"Don't be so sure. I'm not making a public issue of it. I don't need to get my tail singed a second time. Besides, from what I've learned, Madge Williams's sister has a police record of dishonesty. Madge might not have known her sister was a fugitive. That would put her in the clear."

He leaned forward and searched her face. "Can you separate this man from the one who may have to bring charges against you?"

Her frown didn't reassure him, nor did the weariness that seemed to overcome her. "I'm not sure I can do that. Can you?"

He stood. "That's what worries me. I'd better take you home."

* * *

As he drove toward Owings Mills, he didn't feel like talking, and he suspected she didn't either, so he turned the radio on and found a program of golden oldies.

They rode without speaking for several more miles. He supposed that her fingers strumming on the dashboard to the rhythm of the music indicated that she knew a measure of contentment. He was glad for it. No matter the state of their relationship, he wanted her happiness.

We interrupt this broadcast for a special announcement. Northern Air flight 603 from West Palm Beach to Salisbury is missing in flight. We'll have more news later. Stay tuned to this station.

Schyler slowed down and pulled over to the sleeve. "Did he say Northern Air?"

"Yes. Flight 603. You know someone on that flight?"

"I don't believe this. Brace yourself. My dad is on that flight."

She sat forward, cupping her mouth with the palm of her right hand. "*What?* He can't be. How do you…I mean, who said so?"

He wrapped his arms around the steering wheel and laid his head on it. "It…it can't be. It just can't be. He called me at my office this afternoon complaining about the heat down there and gave me his itinerary."

Her voice came to him, thin and wavering. "Did you…did you write it down? Maybe you're mistaken about the number."

"I'm not. It's the same as the number on my license plate." He reached in the glove compartment, got his cell phone and dialed information for the airline's number. He dialed the airline. "It's no use. Everybody's calling that number."

He heard the fear in her voice. "I… We never got a chance to…to work out anything. Schyler, what are we going to do?"

He'd almost forgotten that she, too, would be in pain, that regardless of the past, she had some feelings for her father. He turned to her and saw her shoulders sag, as she shook her head, no doubt in disbelief. He folded her in his arms and rocked her while taking for himself what comfort he could.

"It's…there's nothing definite," she said at last. "Just pray he's safe."

He held her to him, needing the arms that she wrapped around his body. "Five hours ago, he was laughing and jesting with me, Veronica. And now…now, I—"

She tightened her arms around him. "Schyler, honey don't. Nothing's certain. Let's go back to your place and wait."

"I don't much feel like driving, but I suppose that's best in case anyone wants to reach me."

"I'll drive, if you want me to. This isn't happening. It…it just can't be."

We interrupt this program for a special announcement. His heart hit the pit of his stomach. *No word yet on that missing Northern Air flight 603. Stay tuned.*

He closed his eyes, took a long breath and let the air out of his lungs. "Thanks, but I can drive." He took the next exit, swung around and headed back to Baltimore. "You know, I always figured I'd take care of my dad in his old age, the way he looked after me when I was a kid. Not with money, because he won't need that. I wanted to care for him, with my family, surround him with his grandchildren to fill his late years with warmth, pleasure and companionship. I wanted him to know he'd never be lonely again the way he was when I met him. I…I can't believe he'll…perish in a wreck."

Her hand stroked his shoulder in a gesture of comfort. "I should be comforting you," he said. "I can imagine you're thinking all sorts of things right now."

"I'm just trying to remember that we don't know anything definite. I can't give up hope. He and I didn't come to terms, but I…I hadn't counted it out."

He parked in the garage beneath the apartment building in which he lived, took her hand and led her to his apartment. "I had envisaged a different reception for you on your first visit to my home."

A peculiar comfort flowed through him when she squeezed his fingers, communicating her solidarity with him. "We can have that reception another time, and it will be a fun time, too, because he's going to be all right. Safe," she said, as they entered his living room. "Why don't you turn on the television, and let's sit here and keep each other company?"

He was glad for her presence and told her so. "I'll get us a drink and something to snack on." He looked at her a long time. "You're pretty special."

Veronica sank into the corner of the soft leather sofa, emotional conflict warring within her. In spite of the legacy she'd been given of Richard Henderson and her hard feelings about him that strangled her relationship with Schyler, she could barely tolerate the anguish as she waited for word of his safety. She closed her eyes and leaned back as pain stabbed at her, pain for herself and for Schyler. Would she ever know the meaning of her mother's last words? She felt Schyler's warmth as he sat beside her and turned on the television.

"Pull off your shoes and get comfortable," he said. "We may have a long wait. I dialed the airline again, but it's still busy."

When she rested her head on his shoulder, he hooked his arm beneath her knees and brought them across his lap. "You'll be more comfortable this way."

She awakened in that position with her head against his shoulder and early morning sunlight streaking through the venetian blinds. She sat up. "Schyler? What... Any news?"

"I've dialed that number until it's permanently etched in my brain, but it's still busy."

"Maybe if you call Wayne Roundtree he can get some information from one of the wire services." She looked at the wine and chips on the coffee table. Untouched. "What time is it?"

He pushed back his shirtsleeve and looked at his Omega. "Seven-ten. Too early to call Wayne. I'll make some coffee."

She went to the window and looked out. Unseeing. Devastated. The ringing phone shattered the silence, and she collided with Schyler as they both raced toward it.

"I'll get it." His damp palm gripped her hand as he answered. "Schyler Henderson."

Fear furled up in her, siphoning off her breath when she heard his gasp. "What? Who *is* this? *Dad?* For God's sake, don't play with me, man. *Who is this?*" He stared at the receiver.

She caught it as he almost dropped it in its cradle. "Who is this?"

"This is Richard."

She would recognize that voice anywhere and anytime. "*Father!* Weren't you on that plane?"

"Veronica? Yes. I was. We made a forced landing in a little abandoned airport somewhere in North Carolina and sat there in the worst storm you ever saw. No food and no communication until the storm blew over about an hour ago. I'm glad you're with Schyler. Let me speak with him."

"I'm…I'm so glad you're all right."

She handed Schyler the phone and collapsed into the nearest chair, her heart racing at a frightening pace. She didn't hear what Schyler said and wasn't aware that he'd hung up until he lifted her from the chair and into his arms. She didn't know whether the tears that washed her face were his or hers, whether her joy was for him or her father. She only knew intense relief.

He hugged her to him. "I'll cook some breakfast and take you home."

But all of a sudden she had a need to be alone. "Thanks, but I'll take a taxi. You're as washed out as I am. Where was he calling from?"

"From the plane." He took a deep breath. "Whew. I don't

want another workout like that one." He started toward the kitchen, but she stopped him.

"Please don't cook for me. I can't eat yet. I'm too out of sorts. Could you call a taxi?"

He walked back to her. "All right. I understand how you feel." He called a taxi. "Thank you for being there for me. I don't like us separating like this. I... Will you have dinner with me this evening?"

She nodded. "What time?"

"I'll be at your place at a quarter of seven. Okay?"

He waited with her for the taxi. "See you this evening. Try to get some rest."

At home she showered, turned off the telephone and crawled into bed. Time would tell how the events of the previous night affected her relationship with her father.

Their evening together wasn't what she'd hoped it would be. They were not alone at their table, and both of them knew it. They knew as never before that the woman who loved Schyler would be a part of his father's life. And they knew, too, that she still hadn't accepted that. Even their efforts at humorous bantering fell flat. He held her hand as they left the restaurant, but joy in it eluded her. Their need for each other shouted aloud to them. Silent torture. Though he put his arm around her as they walked, he didn't suggest prolonging the evening.

He parked in front of her house and walked with her to her door. "I don't think I'd better come in." At her questioning look, he half laughed. "I'm not in a mood to practice self-denial tonight."

She didn't want him to leave without holding her just once, but she wasn't ready for a deeper intimacy with him, so she couldn't insist. Yet, she had to have something of him. Some warmth. Some sweetness.

She reached up to brush a kiss on his cheek, but he chose that moment to turn his head, and met her lips. Unprepared for the electricity that shot through her when his mouth touched hers, she didn't wait for his embrace but locked him to her, gripping him tightly in her arms.

"Veronica! Sweetheart…hold up…we can't… Oh, honey."

His arms tightened around her, and she felt the male in him jump out and claim her. He spread his legs apart and pulled her hips to him. Hot desire went arrow-straight to the seat of her passion, and she parted her lips, symbolically asking for all of him. His tongue plowed into her mouth, tantalizing her. Loving her. She heard her own moans and recognized her need for all of him. For his essence. Her only thought was the man who held her, and she burrowed into him, offering everything and demanding just as much.

Suddenly, he lifted her and set her away from him, chilling her in that hot July evening. "Baby, we…we can't do this till… Honey we have to settle a few things."

She reached out to him, needing the warmth of his loving arms, but he held her still.

"Veronica, I'm getting in deep here, and you are, too. I want to consummate what I feel for you. Do you hear me? I need to make love with you, but if I do that while all these other issues are looming like trapdoors, one of them will break us. As it is, we're hanging by thin threads over quicksand."

He was right, and she knew it. "Maybe we shouldn't see each other again until this latest case is settled."

He looked into the distance. "That's just it. We *have* to see each other—in juvenile court. And another thing, Veronica, I…can you go out to Tilghman with me this coming weekend? My dad would be so happy if you'd…if he could see you from time to time."

It was too soon. She hadn't come to terms with it. "I'm planning to go visit my stepfather next weekend."

He gazed down at her. "Have you already promised him?"

She couldn't lie. "It's time I went."

His expression chilled, and she knew she'd lost points with him. "Have you already forgotten? This morning we thought we'd lost him, and you hurt just as I did, but you still can't budge. You can't give him anything? Not even a…a pretty card telling him you're glad you met him or that you're happy he's all right?"

She realized she'd dropped her head and quickly raised it. "If it were possible, I'd call my mother on the carpet for this. I'm full of conflict right now, but I guess you'd say even that is an improvement. At least I now know he doesn't occupy an insignificant place in my life. I…I'll write him a note. But Schyler, I don't promise to do it tonight. I hope for your sake that he can handle this while I'm trying to find my way."

He let his left knuckle graze her right cheek. "I see. Thanks for your company this evening. I'll be in touch."

She watched, astounded, as he walked slowly down the steps, got in his car and didn't once look back.

Veronica sat on the edge of her bed and drained herself of tears. It wasn't worth it. She wasn't going to tear herself to pieces over him. She'd nearly fallen in love with him, but he was torn between his love for his dad and his feelings for her. And he was a man to whom loyalty was sacred. She knew if it came to that, he'd choose Richard Henderson. She, too, had to be true to herself and honest about her feelings. Not only for him, but especially for her father. And she needed time to accommodate herself to the realization that she did care about her father. She went to bed and sank into artificial sleep. He met her there and spent the night taunting her, grinning at her when she reached out to him, always remaining an arm's-reach away. She awoke the next morning exhausted.

For the next two days she worked on her assessment of the foster care system. Schyler hadn't called, and she doubted he would. She phoned Enid and told her about the project.

"I'm excited about this, Enid. Would you mind reading what I've written?"

"Sure thing. You can give it to me tomorrow night. Remember we said we were going to listen to some jazz."

"That's right, we did. How about meeting for supper at Louie's Bookstore Café and staying for the show."

"Sounds good to me. Seven-thirty?"

Veronica agreed.

"How's Mr. Perfect Body?" she asked Enid soon after they seated themselves at Louie's.

Enid rolled her eyes. "Still perfect, still exercising and still tired."

Veronica released a refreshing laugh. "Dump him, girl. He'll still be tired in the year 2010."

Enid sighed dramatically. "Tell me about it."

"At this part of the show," the maître d' announced, as Veronica and Enid sipped their after-dinner espresso coffee, "we invite audience participation. You guys don't have to be Frank Sinatra, Paul Robeson or Luther Vandross, and you ladies don't have to sing like Sarah Vaughn or Billie Holiday. When the mike gets to your table, just open up your pipes and sing. You could be the next Celine Dion or Brandy."

When the waiter brought the mike to their table, Enid waved it away, but Veronica told the band to play "Lover Man" in the key of G. Feeling as though she'd come home at last, she sang every verse, and as she finished the last chorus, it occurred to her that the waiter had taken the mike from the other customers after they'd sung only two or three lines. However, the applause and shouts of bravo when she'd finished settled the question.

"Good gracious, Veronica," Enid said in awe, "I never dreamed you could sing like that. You could've gotten rich as a jazz singer."

She knew she smiled from ear to ear, flush with a sense of

having accomplished something she'd longed to do. "Thanks, Enid, I'm glad you liked it."

No point in adding that she could sing anything, not just jazz. Minutes later, a waiter placed a silver champagne bucket containing ice and a bottle of Veuve Cliquot—one of the best champagnes France had to offer—on their table. The accompanying note read: "It's been forty-some years since I heard 'Lover Man' sung like that, not since Lady Day passed her prime. If you're looking for a job, call me."

She looked at the card—Jack McCrae. McCrae's Round Midnight—and gulped. The man owned the city's best club and one of the finest on the East Coast. She handed the card to Enid. Enid stared at it, turned it over, read the message and looked back at the name of its owner. Veronica read the astonishment in Enid's facial expression with amusement. If the woman knew how she loved to shoot pool, she'd probably flip backward. Straitlaced Ms. Overton was about to give the people of Lord Calvert's old palatinate a good shakeup. When she thought of it, not a lot had changed since the English king granted old George Calvert, the first lord Baltimore, feudal control over what became the city of Baltimore. In some respects, the ensuing 350 years hadn't seen as much progress as the pundits liked to boast.

Enid must have detected her determination, for she looked aghast and leaned across the table. "You aren't going to take this seriously are you? *You wouldn't.*"

Veronica felt better than she had in days. Hadn't singing jazz in a club, even for one night, been a dream of her youth? "Does night follow day?" she asked. "Just watch me, girl."

Enid's eyes widened to twice their normal size. "You're serious?"

A desire to dance gripped her, but she had to settle for a rejuvenating laugh. "You bet I am. I've dreamed of it for years. And imagine starting at the top."

Enid looked at Veronica as if she were seeing her for the first time. "Well, I'll be!"

Veronica wrote a note and gave it to the waiter, and when she left Louie's that night, she had McRae's word on a six-week stint in his club, Round Midnight. Let Enid stare at her, she didn't care. Enid could think what she liked.

"Something went wrong with you and Schyler," Enid said.

Veronica tossed her head, suggesting a nonchalance that she didn't feel. "Why do you say that?"

"Because I'm not stupid. You're not a reckless woman, and you're not impulsive."

Veronica allowed herself an elaborate shrug, and it occurred to her that she was developing too much skill at pretense.

"Not to worry, friend. I'll keep it between the lines. Trust me."

Enid stopped walking and propped her hands on her hips. "Seems like I'll have to. You get it together with Schyler before you do something you'll be sorry for."

"Like what? Singing professionally is an honored tradition."

Enid sighed, capitulating. "Well, if that's what floats your boat I guess you know what you're doing."

"I wish I did," Veronica murmured to herself as they separated.

The next day she phoned Rush Jordan, a jazz saxophonist and former college chum, and told him her news. Over the next few days, they put together a four-piece band—piano, guitar, tenor saxophone and bass fiddle—selected some songs and began rehearsals. She didn't tell her stepfather, so if she fell on her face, he'd never know.

"Did you ask her to come out this weekend?"

Schyler looked into the distance. It pained him to hear the note of anxiety in his father's voice. How could he explain without hurting him—and without lying?

"We have to keep our distance right now, Dad," Schyler

said, taking the easy way out. "I have another case against that agency."

Richard's face clouded in a frown. "You mean you'd put her through that...that hell again?"

Schyler moved from the door and walked from one end of the solarium to the other. "Do you think I want to? I'm going to do all I can to leave her out of it, but if the foster mother's lawyer calls Veronica to the stand, the prosecuting attorney will have to examine her."

"Can't you do something to prevent it?"

Schyler knew his father wanted to protect Veronica; he wanted to shield her, but it wasn't within his power.

"I'm only there as a friend of the court, and I can't question her except in exceptional circumstances. I don't have a license to practice; you know that."

"Yes I do, and I'll never forget those responsible for it, either."

He shrugged. No point in going over that ground. "That's behind me. I'm happy as an engineer."

But he knew Richard couldn't let it go; that he'd never be satisfied until Schyler was a full-fledged lawyer. Not because he needed to be, but because he'd earned it.

He'd been graduated from Howard University School of Law at the top of his class and passed the national bar exams on the first try. He understood his father's grief about the injustice. He hadn't accepted the ban either, but he refused to let that setback circumscribe his life.

"Do you think she'll spend some time with us when that case is over?"

What could he say? "I don't know, Dad. It's my gut feeling that she won't unless she has more to give you than last time. She's not hypocritical, and she's not good at pretense. She loves her stepfather, and...oh, heck, it's all so convoluted."

"Yeah. It's that all right, but I've waited thirty years, and I'm not giving up now. I won't try to pressure her, though, and don't you; she has to come to me of her own accord. And I have faith that she will."

Schyler rubbed the back of his neck. "I hope it's vindicated."

"It will be. How about you and her? Has she given you something to…to hope for?"

What a question! He flexed his right shoulder in a quick shrug as though the truth was irrelevant. "Hope? Every time I touch her. It's more like electricity between us than mere chemistry. But her resolve is strong. She's every bit as tenacious as you are."

"That so? You'd better back up. Don't give her credit for your stubbornness. *You're* the one who's set the conditions. If I know you, and I do, you've told her that if she can't love the two of us, it's no go. Otherwise, you'd be with her right now."

"She's wrong. I'd stake my life on your decency and integrity. Whatever her mother brought her up thinking about you was pure fiction."

"That's for me to deal with. Veronica is honest. *Train a child in the way it should go, and when it is old, it will not depart from it.* That's in the Bible, and you can bet on it. I need a chance to show her that whatever unfavorable thing she heard about me is untrue. Telling her isn't likely to help."

From where he stood, it was virtually hopeless. "I'll work on it."

"Listen, Son, you work on it for yourself; I'm still able to fight my own battles."

"I know that, Dad. I've always known it and respected it. But I'm in the middle of this, and as long as this cloud hangs over her, I can't free myself to—"

"You can't *let* yourself love her is what you refuse to acknowledge. I'd have thought you'd learned a lesson after what I told you of my life these past thirty years. Until I got you, I had nothing to live for. You're headed for the same tragic existence."

He let the wall take his weight. "Lord, I hope not. I try to see it her way, but…." He looked toward the ceiling and let out a harsh breath. "She's pretty special, but I don't see anything in the near future that's likely to bring us closer together."

"Try telling her you need her."

He couldn't help laughing. She'd told him that in so many words, and it had brought them closer. He shrugged. "Who knows? Something's got to give."

"You've got to wear slinky, beaded stuff," Jack McCrae insisted to Veronica. "None of those prim Chanel and Mary McFadden gowns. Get yourself a De la Renta. Today, everything is glitz."

"And today, women choose their own clothes," she shot back. "You asked me, Mr. McCrae. Remember? I was sitting at that table minding my business. I'll wear what I like or I won't sing."

She hadn't expected him to adopt a conciliatory tone, but he softened at once. "All right. All right. Wear jeans if you want to. With that voice of yours, when you open your mouth and start to sing, nobody's gonna care *what* you've got on. Besides, you're a knockout; you'll blow their minds."

She'd thought she'd be nervous singing in a place like Round Midnight, but when she heard the words "Five minutes to show time," her only thought was that another of her dreams would soon come true. Thoughts of Schyler and her stepfather tempered her exhilaration. She'd wanted to invite Schyler, and she knew he'd have come, but she couldn't bear to be with him, stick a vacant smile on her face and pretend there was nothing between them. Her stepfather would have been proud of her, but she hadn't told him because she didn't think it fair to interrupt his mourning. She sucked on an ice cube. She'd been told that Pavarotti did that, but her choral director counseled drinking hot liquids before singing. She took a last look at herself in the mirror. She'd worn her long, silk red sheath unadorned, put diamond studs in her ears and let her hair hang down on her shoulders. She liked the effect. A little conservative, perhaps, but appropriate for a woman who'd headed the city's largest and now most notorious social agency.

She strolled out on the stage to her band's arrangement of "Lover Man," bowed to the smattering of applause, nodded to the band and began to sing. After the first second or so, the only sound was that of her voice. Not a whisper. Not a glass clinked.

"Lover man, where can you be…ee," she sang as the song ended. The silence nearly split her eardrums, and then…the thunderous applause, the yelling and stomping. *Bravo, bravissimo* and *right on* assailed her ears.

She bowed and bowed until, overcome with emotion, she fled the stage and leaned against the nearest wall. The patrons yelled for her return, calling her name—Veronica! Veronica! Stunned by their response, she had to work hard at calming herself. Jack McCrae appeared, took her arm and escorted her back to the stage.

But the glory dimmed for her when she realized he had his arm tightly around her waist. From that second, it wasn't the patrons' adulation that struck her most forcibly but Jack McCrae's proprietary manner with her. His hand on her body. She plastered the smile on her face and got herself out of his arm. He'd made a public statement, and she'd made hers. If this was show business…

Chapter 6

Brian's telephone call did not surprise Schyler. A week was a long time in Brian's scheme of things, and his bent on taking action, any action, so long as his boss could see him working, was one reason why Brian would always be assistant something or other.

"You don't have to jump in there right now, buddy," Schyler said. "As far as we can tell, the only person guilty of anything is Beatrice Long. I questioned Madge Williams for nearly two hours. She's a decent woman with an unprincipled person for a sister."

"Look, man, the department can't afford to let this thing go unpublicized."

"No. But if you drag CPAA into it, you're going to lay an ostrich egg, because AFTC and I won't be with you."

"If I can get Veronica Overton on the stand, I'll have my case."

Tension gathered in his belly. "She's no longer there."

"But she was there when the crime was being committed."

"Suit yourself, but you're headed for a demotion if you go through with this. Your case won't stand up."

"So you're not with me on this one?"

"Definitely not, buddy. It's strictly a criminal case that has nothing to do with child welfare, and if you're smart, you'll treat it that way."

He hung up, called Enid, got the information he needed and wrote a brief for the court. Veronica was not going to be Brian Atwood's ladder to public acclaim.

Annoyed with Jack McCrae, Veronica slipped out of Round Midnight, called a private taxi and went home. She didn't have to sing at his club or anybody else's, and she'd quit Round Midnight if the man didn't give her some space. But oh, it had been one great moment in her life. Her ears replayed the applause and cheers as she sank into the taxi's soft leather seat and relived the moment when she knew she had triumphed. If only… Best not to think of Schyler right then.

She paid the driver and let herself into the house. Sitting on the edge of her bed, she pulled off her stockings, looked at the clock on the night table beside her bed and restrained herself. Midnight. If she called him, she'd spend the night with him in his bed or hers, no matter what either of them wanted. She got ready for bed, crawled in and started counting sheep.

Schyler arrived at his office early that morning, pried the lid off the plastic coffee cup and got his first caffeine of the day. Leaning back in his big tufted-leather chair, he put his feet on the desk and opened Wayne Roundtree's paper, *The Maryland Journal.*

What the…? He sat forward, lowered his feet to the floor and stared at the front page. It was her picture all right. He looked closer and saw her name beneath the photograph. "A new star shot across the horizon last night," the front page heading read. "Get thee to Round Midnight and treat thyself to the magical, soul-stirring and seductive voice of Veronica Overton. Nothing like it's been heard in this city in years," the story began.

He laid the paper on his desk, reached absentmindedly for his coffee and wet his lips with it. What on earth would she do next? He looked back at the headline and the picture of her, striking in a red evening gown, standing at that mike as if she'd done it all of her life. He didn't know what to make of it. Needing confirmation, or was it support, he wondered, laughing at himself, he dialed Wayne's private number to get the story firsthand.

"She was good, huh?" he asked Wayne, as his friend raved about her.

"Good? Man, she was fantastic. I'm going back tonight. Want to join me?"

He did not want to give Wayne the opportunity to read and analyze his emotions.

"Thanks, but I'll have to catch it another night."

He leaned back in his chair and closed his eyes. *What a woman!*

"Henderson speaking," he said after the phone had rung six times.

"Sorry to disturb you," Richard Henderson said, "but I just opened my copy of *The Maryland Journal,* and I thought I'd check with you to make sure I don't need glasses."

He'd forgotten that his father subscribed to that paper and was sorry he hadn't prepared him for the jolt. "Your eyesight is fine. I could hardly believe it myself. Wayne said he was there and that he didn't overstate either her performance or the reception she got."

"You weren't there?"

"We're not in touch these days, so there was no reason why she should have told me."

"I see. Well, she certainly looks beautiful in this red gown. Wish I could've been there."

"Yeah. Me, too."

* * *

Tuesday morning following her triumphant debut as a jazz singer, Veronica prowled around her house. Restless. Six o'clock Tuesday morning and nothing to do until her performance Thursday night. She got a cup of coffee, flipped on the television and sat down to kill some time. Almost immediately, the screen showed a dazzling picture of Crystal Caverns at Front Royal, Virginia. On an impulse, she called Hertz for a rental car, dressed, collected some maps at the gas station near her and at eight o'clock was on her way to the renowned caves.

As darkness fell, she headed home after an exhilarating day, still awed by the majesty of the myriad shapes and colors of the famous crystals. She glanced at the rearview mirror and tentacles of fear shot through her body. That green Oldsmobile had tailed her for miles, and the blue Cordova just ahead of her wouldn't let her pass. The night deepened and her anxiety increased. When the car ahead of her slowed down and the one behind her speeded up, she switched into the center lane so as not to be run off the highway, reached for her cell phone and dialed Schyler's cell number. She hoped he could get the number of the Virginia state troopers and telephone them.

"Richard Henderson speaking."

She was too nervous to be disappointed. "Father, this is Veronica. Is Schyler there? Please!" She hadn't meant to sound desperate, but she knew she did.

"No, he isn't, and he forgot his cell phone. What's the matter?"

She told him and swerved to the right lane as the car ahead of her veered toward center. "They're trying to…to drive me off the highway."

"Where are you?"

She wondered how he could sound so calm. "I-66W headed toward the Capitol Beltway."

"Have you passed the I-66 West exit?"

"Not yet."

She sensed his relief. "Good. Exit there and don't signal first or he'll follow you. Turn right when you get off the ramp and drive into that gas station. It's always open and it's attended. Get out, lock your car and take your car keys. Jess will be waiting out front for you. Just tell him you're my daughter."

"The exit's coming up now."

"Call me when you're inside the station, and stay there until one of the troopers shows up. Don't leave there alone. You understand?"

"Yes, sir. Thanks."

She exited onto the ramp, glanced quickly at her rearview mirror and saw that the Oldsmobile had followed her. *Lord, please let that gas station be open!* She breathed again when she saw the brightly lit station and the man who stood outside its door.

"You Veronica Overton?" he asked as she opened the car door.

She didn't think she'd ever known such relief. "Yes. I'm Richard Henderson's daughter."

He extended his hand. "I'm Jess. Your dad and mine fought together in Vietnam. You have to be careful driving these highways at night. Carjacking is getting pretty common. I called the troopers like your dad asked me, and one of them will be along soon and escort you to Washington. Those car thieves will have to find another victim."

Her shirt clung to her perspiration-dampened arms and back, and her car keys dropped to the pavement when her shaking fingers attempted to put them into her handbag.

Jess picked them up and handed them to her. "Settle down, now. You're out of danger. Come on inside, and I'll get you a cup of good strong coffee."

"Thank you, Jess." She sat on a high stool beside the soft drink dispenser. "I'd better call my father." She dialed Schyler's cell phone and Richard answered at once.

"I'm at the gas station with Jess, Father."

His relief sprang to her through the wires when he breathed, "Thank God." The words seemed to lunge out of him. "It's one of the longest twenty-three minutes I've ever lived."

How comfortable she felt talking with him. "It seemed even longer to me, Father. I don't know how to thank you."

"Don't. That's what fathers are for, to be there when their children need them. Get home safely, and don't forget me."

He's so consistently gentle and kind, she thought, more confused than ever about him. "I...I won't, Father. I won't."

The trooper followed her as far as the Capitol Beltway that skirted Washington. Forty-five minutes later, she walked into her house, drank a glass of milk and went to bed. Ordinarily, she would have put it down as a day she could have done without, if it hadn't been for the experience with her father. She was old enough to recognize the difference between pretense and sincerity. He'd been as worried for her as her stepfather would have been. And yet... Had first her mother and then she done him an injustice? Maybe she'd never know.

Friday night, one week later, Schyler's swift strides took him to his reserved, stage-side table at Round Midnight. The show's popularity was such that he'd had to wait a week for reservations.

The lights lowered, a spotlight shone at center stage, and she glided toward it in a strapless red gown that flared at the hips and reached the top of her shoes. Cheers, whistles and stomping nearly deafened him. She clasped the mike and smiled at her audience.

"Thank you," she said. "And thanks for coming out to be with me tonight. I'm going to...to..."

He heard the catch in her throat when she saw him. He didn't want to unnerve her, so he smiled and gave her the thumbs up sign. When her smile widened, he got his breath back. What a set of nerves she had, and that speedy recovery from a momentary lapse heightened his pride in her. Then she winked at him and his heart took off. She was in him as deeply as ever; no point in denying it. He took a sip of the water that a waiter had placed on his table, ordered bourbon and branch water and sat back to watch her.

"I'm changing the program a little tonight," she said. "Instead of opening with 'Lover Man,' I'd like to sing 'Something.'"

"No," someone yelled. "Ya gotta do 'Lover Man.'"

She laughed, thanked the man and told him, "I don't have the blues tonight, and I'm not wondering where lover man is. Maybe later."

He hoped that remark was meant for him. The words, "Something about the way he moves," poured from her lips, and she glanced at him, paused briefly and winked again, seducing him, shackling him. He thought her the picture of femininity as she sang to every man in the room, and he wanted to grab her away from that mike and keep her just for himself.

Her smooth, velvet tones washed over him, intoxicating him, snaring him in the honeyed web she spun. He gave in to it, relaxed and let her have her way with him, because he didn't doubt for a minute that she knew her effect on him, was aware that she victimized him. Still, he wasn't ready to succumb. Not yet.

When she finished the song amid thunderous applause and cheers, he stepped to the stage and handed her a white orchid. She reached for it, smiling as she did so, and he had to restrain his impulse to pull her off the stage and into his arms. Wayne hadn't overstated any of it; he could have listened to her sing forever. He sat down, called a waiter, wrote a note and sent it to her.

"Would you please sing 'Solitude'? S.H."

She read it and nodded slightly in his direction. From that, he surmised that she didn't encourage requests, but that she'd sing it for him. After her next number, her rich tones filled the room with Duke Ellington's great song. He didn't know why he'd asked for that one until he heard her sing it. Then he knew. He'd longed for her, had needed to see her, to be with her.

He couldn't continue to vacillate between his feelings for her and his loyalty to his father. He didn't think she'd change, so he had to come to terms with the prospect of changing or living his life without her. He gazed at her as she bowed, accepting the adulation of her fans, yet diffident, as if she didn't deserve their praise. *Attractive* didn't describe her. Something radiated from her, a something that grabbed him down deep.

The applause died away, she left the stage and the lights dimmed. He sat there fighting with himself. Go to her, get a polite thank you for the orchid and a rebuff if he asked for her company? He wrote on the back of his business card: "Dear Veronica, You are incredible. Wonderful. I wanted more. So much, much more. Schyler." He pushed the card under the door of her dressing room, shoved his hands into his pocket and headed for the elevator.

"You just get better every night, girl," Enid said. "I've heard you every night, and I've been trying to figure out why you didn't do this a long time ago. Girl, you can *sing!*"

Veronica slipped off her red satin slippers, brushed them with a towel and put them back in their box. "All you see is this crowd screaming and shouting after I do a number. What you don't take into account is that people are fickle, and I could come here one night next week and find the place half empty."

"They love you."

She caught herself as she was about to suck air through her teeth. Her mother had hated that. "I'm a fad. Next month, they'll be roaring for someone else."

Enid walked to the door, stooped and picked up a card, turned it over and stared at it. "Say, look here, will you? This is from Schyler Henderson." She handed Veronica the business card. "I didn't know he was in the audience. Did you?"

"Didn't you see him give me that orchid? No, I guess you couldn't with everybody standing. Yes, he was there."

Veronica had to control her fingers as they reached to snatch the card from Enid's hand. "Let me see."

She read the words, took a deep breath and let it go. So he wouldn't come to her dressing room. He had to know that she longed for his nearness, that she... She put the card in her handbag. Doggoned if she'd pine for him or any other man.

"What did he say? Is he waiting for you someplace?"

"He said I was incredible. Period. Let's get going. I'm starved."

The bottom fell out of her belly when she heard the knock. She was on the verge of inviting the caller to come in when she remembered Jack McCrae.

"Yes? Who is it?"

"You were great tonight, babe. How about supper in a few minutes?"

She had no intention of playing chess with the devil, and that's what an involvement with McCrae would amount to. "Sorry, Jack. I already have plans. Glad you liked the show. Good night." Maybe he'd eventually get the message. *If he doesn't and soon,* she promised herself, *I'm out of here.*

Schyler pushed the elevator button, locked his hands behind him and walked back and forth along the corridor, deep in thought. From the corner of his eye, he glimpsed a tall man wearing a white suit and red tie and stopped pacing. Perspiration dampened his palms. Jack McCrae. His hands balled into fists as he watched McCrae knock on the door of Veronica's dressing room. He couldn't make out what the man said, but he had the pleasure of seeing him leave with that door still closed. He stood in the middle of the corridor, legs wide apart, his nails still digging into his palms.

"Patrons are not allowed in this area," Jack said, walking toward Schyler, his distorted face proclaiming his anger.

Schyler let a mocking smile cover his own visage. "Is there any other entrance to Ms. Overton's dressing room?"

Flames of furor sprang into McCrae's eyes, and Schyler took pleasure in letting the man conclude whatever he liked.

"I said this is off-limits."

He walked to within three feet of the man. "I know the law, McCrae, and I hope you do, too. I don't see any signs that say no admittance. If you don't allow Ms. Overton to have guests, I suggest you tell her." Let him digest that! A bell signalled the elevator's arrival, and he left McCrae standing there.

His stomach lurched and churned when he thought of McCrae's possessiveness of Veronica. When he got to the street, he bought a bottle of Perrier at a nearby candy store, drained it and waited for his stomach to settle. In control once more, he got into his Buick, parked across the street from Round Midnight and waited. Finally, he could let himself relax. Veronica left with Enid Dupree, and he watched her as she walked, increasing the distance between them.

He drove home and looked around at the elegant emptiness of his life. Frustrated and dissatisfied, he got a shot of bourbon and went to bed. Hours later, still without sleep, he sat up. He could do one of two things: forget about her, if he could, or try to teach her to love his father. Of the two, he had a better chance of softening Veronica toward the man who had sired her.

He'd sat through each of her last seven shows. At each one, he'd requested that she sing "Solitude" and always, after hearing it, he'd stood and given her a white orchid. And after each show, he wrote the same message on his business card, pushed it under her door and walked away.

Saturday night, he shoved his card under Veronica's dressing room door, turned to leave and stopped. He had to see her, touch her. He walked back and knocked.

"Yes," came her soft voice. "Who is it?"

"Schyler Henderson. May I see you?"

He wasn't used to shivering in midsummer, not even in an

air-conditioned environment, but he felt as if the temperature dropped by forty degrees while he waited for an answer. He let out a long breath when he heard her lift the chain. The door opened, and she stood there smiling. Smiling at him.

"Hi. Come in."

He stepped through the door, and from the corner of his eye, he caught sight of McCrae headed in that direction. He closed the door and gazed down at Veronica.

"You…you're unbelievable. Just plain incredible. I don't have words to describe how I love to hear you sing."

Her smile glowed an unmistakable welcome, and something like tiny pinpricks darted up and down his spine.

"Thanks for your nightly note and especially for the orchids. I've put them all in that crystal bowl. Look."

She took his arm and walked with him to a table on which stood a lamp and a picture of someone he took to be her mother. Eight white orchids with pale yellow stigmas and golden pistils at their center floated atop the still liquid, like water lilies in a clear, virgin pond.

"I didn't know whether you liked them." He looked around the room. "Who sent you those?" he asked, pointing to a vase of American beauty roses.

He knew the answer when she shrugged. "Jack. He sends them every night."

He didn't succeed in stopping the frown that he knew she questioned. "He's very possessive of you."

She looked at him with wide brown eyes, half hidden by her sweeping lashes. "Yes. He is. But if you want to know why, you'll have to ask him, because I have no idea. Why haven't you knocked before?"

He contented himself with the knowledge that she didn't encourage McCrae's attention. "I knocked tonight because I'm tired of not being with you. I know I'm the one who opened this latest chasm between us, and I know it's still there. But I had to see you."

"I'm glad you're here. I've missed you. How... How's my father?"

He couldn't believe she'd asked. Was it an olive branch? He hoped so. He took her hand, reaching out in return. "Thank you for asking. He was a proud man when he saw that story and the picture of you on the front page of the paper. Oh, yes. He told me about your near mishap with those carjackers. I could see that he was happy I'd forgotten my cell phone and that he'd been the one to answer when you called. It meant everything to him that he was there for you when you needed him."

Her eyes widened, and he thought he detected in them signs of pleasure in what he'd told her. She confirmed it with her thanks. "It meant everything to me, too, and I'm glad he approved of my singing. When I started this, I didn't think anybody who knew me would find out about it, but Jack called in the press, and you know what they do."

It wasn't much, her reference to his dad as her father, but it was more than he'd hoped for. If only she would open her heart as well as her mind.

"May I see you home?"

"I need some food."

His grin must have showed her his pleasure, because her whole countenance glowed. She loved to eat, and he enjoyed watching her do it. Everything in him was clamoring for more of her, and he ached to hug her, but he couldn't risk it. He was too hungry.

"All right. We'll eat first. Say, where's Ms. Dupree?"

"She's got a cold, so you can be my chaperone tonight."

"Chaperone? Is that what she's doing here every night? Discouraging McCrae?" He knew he shouldn't have said it, because her temper wasn't reliable. But he had, and he couldn't take it back. He waited for her reaction.

Her glare wasn't unexpected, but he knew his eyebrow went up when she propped both hands at her sides and patted her right foot as though counting to ten.

"Schyler, you don't have to say every single word that gets to the tip of your tongue."

He flexed his right shoulder, admitting to no contest. "Can't argue with you there. Ready to go?"

Her hesitation lasted a little too long for his comfort, but he waited patiently, because he deserved her reprimand. He smiled in relief when at last she opened the door, doused the lights and took his arm. "If I don't eat, you may have to carry me."

"It'll be my pleasure."

Veronica reached for Schyler's hand as they walked out of the tiny bistro. He would know that she'd been longing to be with him, that in the weeks since they'd last been together she'd been on an emotional treadmill. She didn't know what he wanted now or what he would demand as terms for closer, more intimate ties. And, Lord help her, she didn't know how far she'd go in order to be with him. But she knew she'd be honest, so she released his hand, lest she promise more than she could give.

As he drove to Owings Mills, she slid down in the bucket seat, rested her head against its soft leather upholstery and closed her eyes. Drinking in the peace, the heaven of just being with him.

"Sleepy?" His voice seeped into her, calming, soothing like the skilled fingers of a master masseuse.

"No. Just relaxing."

The car stopped, and she sat up. "We couldn't be in Owings Mills so soon. I know you're a speed demon, but this would be a record, even for you."

"It's a beautiful night, and I'm not ready to call it quits. Let's walk around Mills pond for a bit. I spent many a night here during those years when I used to run away from foster homes." He walked with her to a bench and sat there with her.

"You slept out here in…in the open…at night?"

"On this very bench. My foster parents usually had children of their own, and they made a difference between their own children and me. I didn't get the hugs and kisses or the second helping of cake or the ice cream. Clothes, food and a place to stay, but not love. I hated being treated differently from the others."

"But didn't you tell your caseworker?"

"Sure, but I guess I couldn't explain how I felt. I used to see my dad sitting on his white stone steps every evening when I came from school, and I wondered about him and started speaking to him. He always smiled and spoke to me. He was so friendly. One day I stopped and asked him why he didn't go in his house, and he said he lived alone and liked to watch the people pass. After that I stopped and talked every day, and he seemed glad to see me. I couldn't wait for school to let out."

"Are you saying he sat out there because he was lonely?"

"That's what I learned later. I told him about myself, and one day he asked me if I wanted to walk with him down to the corner and get some ice cream." His voice darkened with tones of nostalgia, and she had to lean close in order to understand his words. "I ate it so fast that he asked if I wanted another cone and bought me a double one. I guess that's when I began to love him. He made me stop running away, took me to the social agency and explained to them that I wasn't bad, just unhappy. After about a year, he managed to adopt me. He was divorced, and I begged him to get married so I'd have a mother. He said he'd do anything for me except that, because his heart didn't have room for another woman. Until now, I didn't understand that."

Her heart ached for him. Never to have known a mother's love. How could she begrudge him the love that her father gave him? Her fingers wrapped around his and gently squeezed.

"Oh, Schyler, I'm…I guess I've been thinking too much about myself. Comparing my life as a youth with yours and blaming my father for giving you the comforts that he denied me. I don't know what the truth is; I just know that I'm glad for your sake that you found him."

"And yet, you can't open your heart to him. Do you at least understand why he's so...why I love my dad the way I do?"

"Yes. Yes, I do. And I can understand how you may be torn between us."

He rested his right ankle on his left knee and leaned back against the bench, almost as if he were alone. "I'm not torn, Veronica, because I know myself well enough to know that I'll never sacrifice him for anybody or anything, no matter how much I suffer for it. And I can't watch you hurt him."

"I'd respect you far less if you were different."

He stood. "Let's walk." When they reached a bronze statue of someone named Owings that stood darkened by time and the ravishment of the elements, he let it support his back, wrapped his arms around her and held her.

"I couldn't resist this any longer. You'll say I give you mixed signals, but where you're concerned, my head and my heart are constantly at war. I need you, Veronica."

"And I need you. But this...the power of this thing between us terrifies me sometimes. I'm scared to get in any deeper, because you can walk away, and I know it."

He held her closer, and she let his shoulder give her head a resting place. "You can walk away too, and you've done it," he reminded her.

Her body began to make its demands, and she attempted to move away from him, but he held her close. "Don't deny me this moment. Let me enjoy holding you in my arms. Come and spend the weekend with us. It's wonderful on the bay this time of year. If not the weekend, then one day?"

"Schyler, I care for you, and I don't want to do anything that hurts you. I don't want to hurt my father either, but I need time to come to grips with my feelings. Can you be patient? Your dad is not the only thing that stands between us. It's getting late."

"At least you've arrived at the point where you don't want to hurt him. That's something!" As they stood at the edge of the pond, their reflections gazed back at them. We don't look like happy lovers, she thought, as she felt his arm ease around her. They walked back to his car arm in arm, and she felt cheated. She wanted from him everything that a man could give a woman, but his price was high, and she couldn't meet it. At least, not yet.

He parked in front of 31 Comfort Road and walked with her to her door. "I'll call you tomorrow."

She realized she wasn't in a mood to settle for a cool goodnight and stepped into him so quickly that his arms opened to her before he had a chance to rationalize his way out of it. She let the palm of her right hand stroke his cheek. Emboldened by his hard male response, she raised herself on tiptoe and brushed his lips with her own.

"Veronica, you don't know what you're doing."

"I know I need you to hold me and…and, oh, Schyler." Her parted lips moved against his own as though of their own volition. "You can't just walk off without—"

A sweet and terrible hunger stirred in her as he unleashed his passion, tantalizing her with his driving tongue. His big hands found their way over her back, her hips, her arms and finally his fingers rolled over her left breast. Blood roared in her head as his tongue, his lips and his hands possessed her.

"Schyler, please. Honey, can't you… Can't we—"

"This is the way it could be for us, if we could get those cobwebs and skeletons out of our lives. When we give ourselves to each other, I don't want us to be trapped by misgivings, hatred and suspicions. You're all I want in a woman. If we spend this night together, it will probably be our only one. I want more for us. I cheated myself once, and I refuse to do that again."

She leaned against her front door, rubbing her upper arms

in frustration. "Does that mean we aren't going to see each other again?"

His half-laugh struck her as cynical, though she knew he hadn't meant it to be. "We can't flounder like this, Veronica. We either have to move forward or drop it. Let's try to be friends for now. You said you wanted time to come to grips with having your father in your life. I'll try to be patient, but not forever. I can't allow myself to be torn up indefinitely."

She cupped his face with her hands. "Don't burn any bridges." She'd never begged a man for a kiss. Never had to. But she hadn't loved a man before, either. "Kiss good-night?"

He locked her in his arms, fastened his lips to hers and sent soft currents of peace throughout her body as he cherished her with an exquisite gentleness that she'd never before experienced in him or any man.

"I want you to remember this. I'll always be there for you, no matter where, when or what. Call you at ten. Good night, sweetheart." He didn't wait for her response, and she watched him until he drove away.

Would their evenings always end at the top of her front steps? She didn't belabor the question, as she walked in and closed the door. What was the use? She couldn't act the lie, and he had the mental toughness, iron will and self-control of a Hercules. But she wasn't ready for him to go out of her life, and her will, she decided, would be as strong as his.

Certain that she'd hear Schyler's voice, she picked up the receiver after the phone's first ring.

"You spent one hell of a long time telling that fellow good night."

"What? Who is this?"

"Jack. What is that guy to you?"

She stared at the phone as if it were an enemy and considered dropping it into its cradle.

"Well?"

She didn't want to break with him right then, because the

club filled her time, but she would. "That isn't your business, Jack. I work for you, and you pay me. My private life is no concern of yours."

"You're very independent."

She could almost feel his anger burning her breath through the telephone wires, but she refused to let him intimidate her. "And I intend to stay that way. I like singing at Round Midnight, but I don't have to. I don't even feel the need to."

"I could make it impossible for you to sing anywhere else in this city."

"I suppose you could try, but you'd waste your time. If I had wanted to sing professionally, I'd have been doing it years ago. I could quit right now and never miss it. So what'll it be? I sing and you mind your business, or Round Midnight is history for me as of this minute?"

"You can't leave; you're still under contract, and besides, I don't want you to leave. My patrons would murder me. You don't have time even for a cup of coffee with me, but—"

"Jack, did you think I had no private life, clout and no connections in Baltimore just because you read that Enid Dupree is acting director of CPAA? There is someone. I'm sorry."

"If he isn't there with you right now, he's not worth much."

She twirled the telephone cord around her right index finger, kicked off her shoes and wiggled her toes, relaxing them. "If you knew who he was, those words wouldn't have entered your head. So what is it? Do I sing Thursday night or not?"

"You sing. A contract is a contract."

She looked toward heaven and let out a deep sigh, no longer annoyed with him. "Ever heard of sexual harassment? What'll it be?"

"All right. All right. Babe, you're beautiful and special in so many ways. If that guy slips up, turn around. There isn't anything I have that I wouldn't give you."

"Good…" A thought occurred to her. How had he known how long she'd been with Schyler? "Where are you right now, Jack?"

"You don't want to know, babe. Good night."

He seemed to have backed off, but knowing his personality, she didn't trust it. If she looked out her front window, she'd probably see him driving away. No. He wasn't a man who inspired her trust.

She completed her ablutions, put on her red teddy, her favorite nightdress, and crawled into her bed. But as soon as she lay down, she began to toss and roll, and she knew that daylight would find her without sleep. She got up, strolled over to her desk, put on her favorite Ray Charles CD and tried to make peace with her roving mind. Her gaze fell on the issue of *The Maryland Journal* that reported her first performance at Round Midnight. She picked it up and gazed at her likeness sheathed in red silk. What had her father seen when he looked at it, and had his pride been in that picture or in Wayne Roundtree's review? She should have let him know about her opening, and not only him but her stepfather and Schyler. But she hadn't expected success and certainly not a front page review in any newspaper—just six weeks of a childhood dream come true.

Write him a note. Just three words, but write him, her conscience nagged. She sat down, fighting with herself and with her natural inclination to do what was right. She picked up a sheet of notepaper and a pen. But what would she tell her father that wouldn't hurt him more than no note at all? She could thank him again for rescuing her from those car thieves.

Do the right thing, she told herself. *It's your credo, isn't it?* Ray Charles finished singing and still her pen remained poised above the writing paper, her mind lodged in the past. Then she flipped on the radio and Merle Haggard began to sing "Mama's Hungry Eyes," and she dropped her head in her hands and let the tears pour. Her mother wouldn't be pleased, because whatever she had wanted in that last request hadn't come to pass. She'd better pull herself together. After a few minutes, she wrote. "Dear Father, Schyler told me of your

pleasure in my successful opening as a jazz singer. Thank you
for your good wishes, and also for saving me from what could
have been a dangerous encounter. All good things. Veronica."

She addressed an envelope, put the note in it, sealed the
letter and placed it beside her door keys. Then she switched
off the radio and turned out the lights, singing as she did so.
A lightness, almost akin to giddiness, overcame her, putting
an extra spring in her step, and she went to bed and to sleep.

Veronica rolled over, looked at the clock on her night table
and received a shock. Nine-fifty. She hadn't slept that soundly
since losing her mother, and never beyond six on a working
day. She checked the clock. It was Monday, no doubt about
that. She answered the phone after the first ring.

"Hello."

"How'd you make out without me Saturday night?" Enid
asked. "Say, don't tell me you were asleep. You're getting used
to that easy life."

She stifled a yawn. "No untoward incidents. How're you
feeling?"

"Fair. I'm at work. Have you had any information about
the Madge Williams case?"

Veronica sat up, fully awake. "Not a thing. Why?"

"The prosecuting attorney, our old friend Brian Atwood,
brought suit, and the agency trial began this morning."

She jumped up and paced the floor for as far as the telephone
cord would reach. "For goodness sake, what happened?"

"The judge read a brief written by a friend of the court and
ruled that neither Madge, CPAA nor anyone associated with
it is culpable."

She let the bed take her 147 pounds. "Friend of the court?
Who could that be? I mean, who'd care enough to do such a
fabulous job as that?"

"I thought you'd guess."

She ran her hand through her hair. "You thought I'd…

Wait a minute. Are you saying Schyler... Uh. Uh. He brought the suit, didn't he?"

"Atwood brought suit. Schyler wrote the brief."

"You got your facts straight?"

"Right. So be sure and thank him."

Thank him? She'd hug the breath out of him. "Any idea why he did it?"

"Brian wanted some notoriety for himself, but Schyler investigated. Strictly professional. Believe me."

"Well, I'll be. He didn't even mention it to me."

She brushed her teeth, got her caffeine fix, sat down at her desk and called Schyler's cell phone number. She figured that if he'd been in court that morning, he hadn't made it back to his office.

"Schyler Henderson."

She took a deep breath and plunged in. "Hi. It's me, Veronica."

"Veronica? What's up. I was just about to call you. Are you okay?"

"Schyler, Enid just called me. Did you write that brief?"

"I...uh... It was the decent thing to do. I started this raid on CPAA, not to mention on you, and I intend to monitor it. I wouldn't have thought this town had so many flesh eaters. It's over. For you, CPAA and, unfortunately, for Brian, I suspect."

"I don't know how to thank you for this, Schyler, but you know what's in my heart."

His voice deepened and took on a sensuous tone. "I had the facts, and I knew Brian would disregard them. You don't owe me any thanks, but I wouldn't mind knowing what's in your heart."

She figured she'd better ignore that, because he didn't want the truth. "Saturday night after you left, I kept a promise to you, I—"

"You wrote my dad?"

"What? Are you a mind reader?"

"Then you did?"

"Yes. It's just a line or two, but...well I wrote it."

"At least you've taken a step. I...thank you. He'll be happy. I know he will. Stay at it, sweetheart. I'll meet you halfway, and I don't doubt that he'll do the same."

"I'm doing my best."

"I don't mean to quiz you, but could I have seen McCrae driving toward your house as I was leaving Saturday night?"

"It's possible. He called me as soon as you drove away."

"If he's a problem, just let me know."

"Schyler, I can take care of him. I've told him to mind his business or get another singer. He likes money, and I'm a good draw, so I don't expect him to make another move on me."

"I'm glad to hear it. But if he does, I'll teach him a lesson."

Chapter 7

Schyler wondered what was behind it. Veronica was too honest to pretend, but she'd written that note. He had to take her at face value, accept her gesture toward his father and not eat himself up peeping around edges and through cracks trying to second-guess her. Trouble with it was that with that one act, she'd tightened her grip on him, had drawn him so much closer to her. He ran along Tilghman's white beach enjoying the sand beneath his bare toes and the gray, red and blue circus of the early morning sky as it greeted the coming of the sun. He stopped to wait for Caesar, his golden retriever, who had discovered something of interest. The dog did as he pleased, because he'd never been scolded and trusted Schyler and Richard's love.

"Come on, Caesar, we've got to get back home."

The two frolicked for a few minutes, mostly to please Caesar, but instead of his usual enjoyment of it, nostalgia for a family and children with whom he could enjoy the wonders of nature darkened his spirits.

He disliked being in Baltimore on summer weekends, but he'd forgotten a design he'd planned to complete while in Tilghman, so he dressed, drank a glass of grapefruit juice, ate some cereal and put a leash on Caesar.

"Caesar and I are going to my office, Dad. I should be back in a couple of hours."

"Pick up a logarithmic scale ruler for me, will you? I had a couple of them on my desk, but I can't find either one."

Schyler looked down at Caesar. "Shame on you. I'll bet you've got thousands of dollars worth of stuff stashed away."

He hadn't planned to be in his office five minutes, but the red light flashed on his answering machine, and he sat down.

Wayne wanted a date for them to go fishing, Enid Dupree wanted him to call her; and Veronica hadn't wanted anything except to say hello. He dialed her number, and his usual patience deserted him while he waited for her to answer.

When he heard her voice, the thumping in his chest took him by surprise. He knew she had a piece of him, but he hadn't thought she could send him into a spin with the mere sound of her voice. It bore watching.

"Schyler. You called me?"

"Yes. I'm planning a party to celebrate my closing at Round Midnight next week. It's been great, but I'm ready to move on. I'm closing on Friday night, and the party would be Saturday night. Can you come?"

"Wouldn't miss it. When did you decide to do this? On the machine you said you just called to say hi. Thanks for the invitation to the party, but I confess I got a bigger bang out of thinking you just wanted to talk to me."

"You're a genius at pressing your case. If you're as good an engineer, you're an ace."

"Thanks. Can we see each other tomorrow night? I have to finish a design this weekend, and I'd better do that before I see you."

"I'd planned to catch up on my knitting tomorrow, but yes, I'd love it."

"Knitting? You could spend a day doing that?"

"I need to. I knit for the homeless, and I'm behind in my quota."

"You're some woman. Are you inviting McCrae to your party?"

"Can I not?"

"Damned straight. But suit yourself. I just hope he's found something to do with his hands that doesn't involve you."

Her laughter curled around him like a lover in the grip of passion. "He's not crazy."

"You don't have to be crazy to act the fool."

"He won't if you're there. Besides, I don't encourage him. What will we do tomorrow night?"

"Anything you like. I'm great at the movies."

In his mind's eye, he saw the grin spread over her face and her lashes sweep down the way they did when she was amused. Her laughter teased him into a frivolous mood, and he couldn't believe it when she said, "What do you do in the movies other than watch the screen, relive your adolescence?"

"Well," he stalled, "that, too. I had a pretty good reputation as a movie-house tease by the time I finished high school. Pride wouldn't let me go the limit. Nowadays, I can afford conveniences that make it unnecessary. Uh… That's what you meant? Right?"

"No, that isn't what I meant. I thought you were referring to 'making out,' you know…petting. Your gang must have been pretty wild."

He propped his feet up on his desk, leaned back in his chair and smothered a laugh. "I never thought so. What did yours do?"

"We…uh… We held hands. After all, movies and gossip were the only entertainment. The movie changed every two weeks, but the gossip changed minute by minute, depending on who was telling what, and we kids didn't risk being the latest topic. You really taking me to a movie?"

He wanted to ask her where she'd lived as a child, but she'd change the subject if she thought he was prying. "Yeah. If I can find one that'll either make you weep or fill you full of sentiment, guaranteeing I'll have you in my arms for an hour and a half."

"We don't have to go to the movies for that. Just open them when I'm close by."

"Veronica, be careful what you joke about. I'm a man who believes in making people live up to their notices, and I've got a fistful of yours. You with me?"

"I'd love to see a movie with you, but don't think I was joking; I'd never been more serious. Just open your arms, and I'll walk straight into them."

Suddenly irritated that she seemed so sure of him, he growled, "You talk like that when you're twenty-five miles away, but don't try me when I can get my hands on you."

She was baiting him, he realized, and in spite of himself, heat simmered in his loins. "Nobody can fire me if I don't finish this design today, so you back off or I'll be there in twenty minutes, and my arms will be open wide."

"Oh, come on. Can't you stand a little honesty? I let you open doors for me because you insist, and I love the courtesies you extend to me, but I'm entitled to tell you what I want. You reserve that right, don't you? Well so do I."

He sucked in his breath and took control of his mind. "Sweetheart, if you knew what was on my mind, what I want from you, you'd stagger under the weight of it."

"I've never staggered in my life. See you tomorrow. What time?"

"How's six o'clock?"

"Perfect. Here's a kiss."

He heard the sound of a kiss and wondered what she'd do next. "Behave yourself," he said. "See you tomorrow."

He hung up. Stunned. She'd asked for time to resolve her feelings about her father, but she'd pressured him to ignore his promise to do that. He shook his head. *Woman, thy name is enigma.* He found his design, put that and one of his logarithmic scale rulers in his briefcase and patted Caesar's head.

"Let's go, boy."

She'd shaken him up all right. She'd just had a shower, patted herself dry and soothed a delicately scented lotion all over her body. Then he called, and she'd let it all hang out. He'd probably make her eat her words, but she didn't care. It had never occurred to her that catting with a man could be so much fun. She put on a shirt and a pair of slacks and telephoned Enid.

"You said you crochet. If you're not busy this morning, drive out here and help me make these caps and mittens for the homeless kids. Gosh, I'm so far behind. How about it?"

"I don't have any yarn."

"I've got plenty. I'll treat you to homemade pancakes, country sausage and maple syrup."

"Okay. Be there in an hour."

By one-thirty they'd finished several pieces. Veronica put on her Leontyne Price arias and got lemonade for them both. "I'm giving a party when I leave Round Midnight, and I'm in a quandary. Should I invite Jack?"

Enid paused in the act of swallowing her lemonade. "Will Schyler Henderson be here?"

"I hope so. I invited him."

"Then quit while you're ahead. McCrae's after you like a bear after salmon, and you can't accuse him of sexual harassment on the job, because you won't be working for him any longer."

Veronica infused her voice with an air of mystery. "Suppose I invite Wayne Roundtree. Nobody would act up in front of the publisher of *The Maryland Journal.*"

Enid's eyes sparked with mischief. "Girl, you're kidding.

Guys like McCrae thrive on publicity. Any kind. They don't care. Don't say I didn't warn you."

Veronica pulled on the hair that hung over her left eye and twisted it around her left index finger. "I'll have to think about this some more. How's Mr. Body Perfect?"

Enid lifted her right shoulder in an elaborate shrug. "Still exercising and still washboard perfect. I gave him the boot and he had the nerve to ask me why."

"What'd you tell him?"

"Trust me, Veronica. You don't want to know. Anyhow, one goes and another comes."

"Who is it this time?"

"He's solid, but he's seven years younger than I am, and I told him so. When he said that didn't matter, I told him about my eight thousand dollar face-lift, and he just laughed at me. He says unless I'm a criminal, I'm stuck with him. Oh, and he doesn't hang out in gyms."

"I hope it works for you, Enid."

"You hope. I'm praying." Her tone softened and took on a wistful timbre. "I like him, Veronica. I flipped over him the minute I saw him. What's happening with you and Schyler?"

"We're in touch, not as close as I'd like, but something is happening. I'm just not sure what. Let's do this again when you have time."

"I'd love it. Think about lunch one day next week."

They said goodbye, and with a satisfied feeling of having accomplished something important, Veronica put away the knitting and crocheting and began preparing for her Saturday night show.

Schyler turned off Highway 50 into Highway 33 and stopped at the vegetable stand. Dolf Tilden had raised and educated his children, built his family home and supported his parents from the proceeds of that stand. A smile appeared on his time-ravished face when he saw Schyler.

"Want your reglah, or you shoppin' today? I think yer pa already got his supplies yistiddy."

Old man Tilden was the only person he'd ever heard pronounce yesterday as *yistiddy.* "Then I'll just have my regular. About four pounds, please."

He bade the man goodbye and headed home. The odor of Italian tomato sauce met him at the front door, and he thought for the nth time how lucky he'd been to find Richard Henderson.

"Smells good. Here, I brought you something."

Richard's grin began to surface before he reached for the bag. "You must be old man Tilden's best customer for these nuts. I'll never eat my lunch with these things around. Thanks. Sure you don't want some?"

"I think I'll wait for whatever you're cooking. Anyway, boiled peanuts are just as fattening as roasted ones. You may not gain weight, but I will."

Richard shelled one, popped it into his mouth and savored it. "Suit yourself. You won't catch me begging you to eat any." He put the bag on the kitchen table, went to the stove and stirred his sauce. "I got a note from Veronica this morning. Would you believe that?"

Schyler kept his voice neutral, as if they weren't discussing anything important. "What'd she say?"

Richard stopped stirring, shelled another boiled peanut and put it in his mouth. "Nothing much. I think she was thanking me for standing in for you the other night when she called for help and for being proud of her debut as a jazz singer—I guess you told her about that. And maybe she was letting me know she was glad I'm alive. No, she just wrote a couple of lines, but...well, she wrote them. It's something I'll treasure."

"Try not to put too much hope in it, and let's not worry about it."

"My faith won't let me worry, Son, and you shouldn't either. Bit by bit, you'll see a change. Seen her lately?"

"I just spoke with her."

Richard walked over to him, an expression of anxiety on his face. "Do you get along? Do you believe... Can you hope for a good relationship?"

He didn't want to mislead his father, because he knew himself, and he knew his feelings about the matter hadn't altered, though he meant to do what he could to sway her. "We get along, Dad, and don't worry about our feelings for each other. Nothing ephemeral about them; they're here to stay."

"Both of you?"

"Both of us. Don't let that sauce burn."

Richard cocked an eye and looked at Schyler. "I am tending the sauce. You two feel like this, and still your relationship is at a standstill. Is that right?"

"Uh, more or less."

"Schyler, one day this stubbornness of yours is going to cause you a lot of trouble. Veronica and I will come to terms with each other. You take care of your own relationship with her."

In spite of himself, Schyler reached for a handful of boiled peanuts and began eating them. Richard laughed. "I see I'm right. You've got your price, and you're not budging from it. What if she refuses to tolerate that?"

Schyler straddled a straight-back kitchen chair and rested his chin on his folded arms. "I used to worry that I didn't look like you. You know, I prayed myself half-crazy wanting to look like you, walk, talk and do everything like you. But when I look at Veronica, the image of you, your exact eyes, even smiling exactly as you do, I'm glad my prayers didn't get answered. It would have been awful if she and I looked just alike."

Richard poured the tomato sauce over a pan of eggplant parmesan and put the pan in the oven. "All right, if you don't want to talk about it anymore." He grinned, and Schyler realized that his father had a new kind of happiness. "She does look like me, doesn't she?"

"Yeah. You'd have a hard time convincing anybody that she wasn't your daughter."

Richard's hand lay gently on his shoulder, and it didn't surprise him when his father said, "She means a lot to me. She's my child, and I love her, but no one will ever take your place in my life or in here." He pointed to his heart. "And don't you let yourself forget that for one second. You hear me?"

He patted the hand that rested on his shoulder. "I couldn't forget. Not ever. And I know she won't take my place. I just want her to assume her own rightful role in your life."

"Well get busy. I want some grandchildren."

No more than he wanted him to have them. "Come on, let's eat. I'd better get to work."

Richard took the pan out of the oven and looked at Schyler. "Yeah, finish that design. I want you to inspect that lighthouse for me. And I want Veronica's address."

Schyler's head jerked up. "What for?"

"Better relations, Son. Better relations."

Veronica hadn't seen Schyler dressed casually. Indeed, she hadn't convinced herself that he'd consider going anywhere without a jacket and tie. But you didn't dress up to go to the movies, did you? She settled on an ankle-length white linen skirt with a side slit to the knee and a yellow-and-white striped jersey overblouse that reached her hip. If he came dressed, she'd get the matching jacket and put on some high-heeled shoes. If he came casual, she'd put on a pair of flats and go as she was. She breathed easily when he appeared in a red collared T-shirt and white linen pants.

"Hi. You look good enough to eat," he said and brushed her lips with a quick kiss. "Want to see *Shakespeare In Love?* Or would you rather see something that'll scare you senseless?"

"Shakespeare. No contest."

He grinned down at her. "That won't give you an excuse to hold on to me."

"You still think I need an excuse? I've come a long way, baby, as the saying goes."

How could he switch from humorous to serious in a second, she wondered. His expression reminded her of the minister of her parents' church when he got on the subject of sinners at the angry gates of hell.

"What's the matter, Schyler?"

"Thinking how much you've changed. You aren't the same woman I saw for the first time in Judge Greene's courtroom. You're younger, more alive and...and more full of fire. You've come further than you probably realize."

They ate a light supper of quiche and salad at a little restaurant on Calvert Street and took their seats seconds before the movie began. He held her and as she watched the movie, she moved closer to him, living the love that unfolded before her eyes. She hadn't known she cried until his fingers brushed the tears from her cheeks.

"Do you always cry in the movies?" he asked as they left the theater.

She wanted to hide in the shelter of his shoulder to avoid his scrutiny, his knowing gaze. "I don't remember ever having done that before. It...somehow, it touched me."

"You have a gentle, loving nature. I'm not—"

"You mean I'm a pushover?"

He seemed surprised. "Not you, lady. Never."

His laughter, dusty and warm, made her want to curl up in him. His eyes sparkled, his white teeth flashed against his light tan complexion and he radiated something that she needed.

Caught up in his charm, his body's inviting scent and his merriment, she blurted out, "I could stay right here with you forever."

His mood darkened, and it didn't surprise her, for she was getting used to his mercurial personality. "I could stay with you forever, too, and not just right here." He put his arm around her and began walking toward his car. "How do you think this will end?"

She slowed her steps, and he had to stop walking. "I'd give a lot to know. I'm scared to guess."

He pressed her. "How do you want it to end?"

Her temper threatened to surface when she realized what he was asking, and she tried to control the rising irritation. "I want it to end the same way you do. I don't want to wake up one day and see my life scattered around me like a pile of rotted debris. I want a home, a man who loves me and children to love and nurture. How the devil do you think I want it to end?" She broke away from him and began to run, but he caught her in a few quick steps.

"Veronica. Veronica, stop it. Honey, please don't cry." He had her tight in his arms, but she couldn't stop the tears that cascaded down her cheeks. "I wouldn't hurt you for anything on earth. You're precious to me."

They'd reached his car, and he stood with her beside it, holding her and calming her with gentle strokes.

"I'm sorry. I don't know what's wrong with me. It's not like me to…to cry like that. I hope I haven't ruined your evening."

"You haven't done anything to apologize for, and if you can't let me see your pain as well as your elegance, your talent, your competence and your happiness, I'm not worth much to you. I want to know and experience the whole woman."

"I try to be honest in my relations with people, Schyler. What you see is what you get."

"Yes. And that's the rub. I'm not going in tonight, because we're both vulnerable, and what we need isn't comfort. We need to make love as an expression of our feelings for each other, but I haven't yet turned that corner." He looked steadily at her, letting his long fingers caress his chin as he appeared to muse over something. "Ever been in a lighthouse?"

"No. Why?"

"Would you like to go with me one Sunday soon and spend the day there with me?"

"I'd love it."

"We'll have to leave around six in the morning." She nodded. "But we'll see each other before then. I enjoyed the evening."

She made herself smile. "Me, too. We'll be together at my party Saturday night, won't we?"

"Right. I almost forgot about that." His lips brushed hers in a soft, quick kiss, and she watched him bounce down the steps, whistling softly.

Don't think about it, he told himself repeatedly as he drove home. Half an hour later, he parked in the garage beneath the apartment building in which he lived and summoned the elevator. With luck, he'd get into his place without seeing anyone he knew. He'd never been so washed out in his life. He pulled off his shirt as soon as he closed the door, hung it on his left shoulder and rummaged in the refrigerator until he found a bottle of ginger ale. He counted eleven bottles of club soda. The contents of his refrigerator were just as lopsided as his life.

He stepped out on his ninth-floor balcony that overlooked a park, a green oasis in the midst of concrete clutter, propped himself against the railing and took a swig of ginger ale. He had to deal with it, but he'd rather take another bar exam than face the dilemma that tortured both of them. Veronica's near hysteria couldn't be lightly dismissed, and no matter that she'd smoothed it over, he was at the root of it. A woman didn't say those words to a man with tears shimmering in her eyes unless he'd precipitated them. She'd never know how close he'd come to crying with her.

He'd known that she cared for him, that they both cared, but he hadn't considered the intensity of his own feelings, or that she was as capable as he of putting up a good face and pretending it didn't mean as much as it did. Shivers coursed through him as he pictured his father's life of longing for the one woman he'd loved. But how in the name of saints was he supposed to divide himself between Veronica and his dad and be loyal to both of them? He looked up at the sky, serene and stately with its still-bright moon and blanket of stars and stopped himself before he shook his fist. It was becoming unbearable.

Veronica inspected the hot hors d'oeuvres, the bar and the array of food set out in the kitchen. She'd gotten the best caterer she could find, and he hadn't let her down. Decorations on the dining room table included twenty-inch-high, white beeswax candles in silver candlesticks, ribboned nosegays of tea roses and a horn of plenty from which spilled fresh strawberries, plums, apples, fragrant peaches, blackberries, green grapes and sprigs of peppermint. For the meal, she'd ordered a ham, platters of grilled jumbo shrimp, Dauphin potatoes, skewered sticks of chicken satay, buttermilk biscuits and a mixed green salad. Cheesecake, cookies and vanilla ice cream would round it out.

She dressed in the red silk evening sheath she'd worn the first night at the club, brushed her hair down below her shoulders and fastened a pair of sparkling rhinestones to her ears. She applied Fendi perfume where it counted most, lowered the foyer and living room lights and smiled, satisfied with the effect, just as the doorbell rang. She crossed her fingers and headed for the door. With any luck, it wouldn't be Jack McCrae.

She'd never seen Enid look so beautiful or so feminine. "Hi, you're the first. Come on in and tell me what you think."

"Veronica Overton, this is Madison Wright."

Enid hadn't exaggerated in her description of him. "I'm glad to meet you, Veronica. Thanks for inviting me."

"I'm glad you're here." And she was, because it meant she wouldn't be in the house with Jack McCrae if he arrived early and only the waiters for protection. "Get comfortable. I have to answer the door." The next big party she gave, she'd hire somebody to greet her guests. She'd be a wreck from opening the door forty times in one evening.

The whistle shot from her lips before she could control it.

Schyler Henderson in a white worsted suit and yellow tie that set off his wavy black hair and gray eyes would tempt good girls to go bad. She told him as much.

His grin sent butterflies flitting all through her. "I haven't lured you off course. *Yet.*"

She laughed at his emphasis, because he'd had plenty of unused opportunities to seduce her. "Enid and her significant other are here, come on in."

After she let in half a dozen more guests, Schyler said, "Leave the door unlocked, and don't wear yourself out. Am I to expect McCrae?"

She nodded. "I couldn't convince myself of a plausible reason not to invite him."

Schyler stared into her eyes. "Are you with me this evening?"

"I'm with you."

He put an arm around her shoulder. "Then forget about McCrae."

But Jack wasn't so easily overlooked. He arrived half an hour before the party was scheduled to terminate, and she knew he'd planned to remain after every other guest left. She took Schyler's hand and walked over to greet Jack, who wore his trademark white suit and red tie. No one in that room would know what it cost her not to giggle. Schyler had worn a white suit deliberately to deprive Jack of the chance to stand out among the other men present.

"Mr. McCrae, have you met Schyler Henderson?"

His lip curled into a snarl. "I wasn't aware that you were doubling up on your dates this evening, Veronica. That's for kids."

"What gave you that idea, Jack? Mr. Henderson is my date for this and other evenings."

His glare told her more about him than she'd learned in the eight weeks she'd known him. "Why did you invite me then?"

She felt Schyler's arm around her shoulder, and she hoped Jack would take the hint. "I told you I was celebrating the end of my successful run at Round Midnight. Wouldn't I have been rude if I had neglected to invite you?"

"Say Jack, Schyler, anything for Monday's front page?"

She glanced over her shoulder at Wayne Roundtree and knew a sense of relief. "Wayne, I didn't know you'd gotten here yet. Who is—"

"Meet my wife, Leah."

Tall and uncommonly good-looking, Veronica decided about Wayne's wife. "Welcome, Leah. I thought I'd been told your name was Banks."

Laughter erupted from Wayne and Schyler, and Wayne's wife gave him the bad eye. "I agreed to be called Leah until after our marriage ceremony just to please my loving husband, and trust me, honey, this man is in trouble. Leah is not a name I care for."

Veronica liked the woman at once. "Okay. Banks it is."

"We don't have any news for you, Wayne. At least not yet," Schyler said. "But stick around. Never can tell."

"How's it going, Jack?" Wayne asked, in an obvious attempt to pull the man into the conversation.

"Downhill. Fast." He fixed a steely gaze on Veronica. "See you around." With that, he walked out.

"What got into him?" Wayne asked.

Banks waved her right hand in a gesture of dismissal. "Pa…leeze. Schyler's what got into him. If I ever saw a case of jealousy, that was it. The man is blistering with hatred."

"Don't let my wife set you off, Veronica. She says what she thinks."

"Not to worry, brother," Schyler said. "They're kindred souls. Veronica doesn't bother to bite her tongue either."

Gradually the crowd thinned. Veronica went from room to room in search of Enid and found her on the balcony with Madison's arms tight around her. She turned to go back inside and bumped into Schyler.

"I've been waiting all night for this," he said and opened

his arms to her. She hesitated, glancing over her shoulder at the loving couple, but he tightened his grasp around her waist, tipped up her chin and smiled. "You said I only have to open my arms, remember?"

Her hands reached for the back of his neck, and strange, exotic sensations wound through her as, for the first time, his hands stroked her bare flesh. She attempted to move away, to hide her reaction, but he held her.

"You haven't kissed me, and I need some sugar, sweetheart."

She parted her lips and gave herself over to the electrifying shock of his mouth on hers, but when his tongue found its home within her mouth, a whimper of submission escaped her, and he set her away from him.

"I'd better go. I don't dare find myself here after everybody else leaves."

In a fast recovery, she raised both eyebrows. "Oh no. Go drink some more club soda or…or something. I'm not having these people think I gave a big party and didn't even have a date. As soon as the last one leaves, I'll push you out the door."

Her heartbeat accelerated when he stuck both hands in his pants pockets, emphasizing his masculinity, looked her in the eye and didn't smile. "And what will you do if I decide I don't want to go out of that door?"

Momentarily stunned, she could only gaze at him. A mistake, she realized, when suddenly he seemed to have captivated her senses. His wonderful gray eyes had become pools of fiery desire, and his male scent, his heat slammed into her. *Lord, don't let him touch me,* she silently prayed, as the hot man in him hooked her as surely as a harpoon ever captured a whale.

"You would never do anything against my will," she said, confident in her assessment of him.

He continued to gaze at her, but she couldn't tell whether he was sending a message or looking for one. He took his right hand out of his pants pocket and brushed her cheek with the back of his hand. "You're right about that, but before you get overconfident, remember what just happened. I can make my will your will, but I don't intend to seduce you deliberately, and you're not going to seduce me. Whatever happens between you and me will be something that we each enter into with our eyes open, because it's what we each want. So, like I said, I'd better go. I have my limits, honey. Tell Enid good-night. Oh, and tell her to stick with that guy; he's a good man."

She walked with him to the door. He opened it, gave her nose an affectionate pinch and left. She wasn't sure what to make of it, of him, and of their relationship. Richard Henderson. Always Richard Henderson looming over them, a shadow even at darkest night. What had he thought of her note? She busied herself with her remaining guest, but her mind roamed elsewhere. With Schyler and with her father. A resolution had to be found, because she didn't see how she could let Schyler drop out of her life. And he would if she couldn't bring herself to embrace his dad. With his tenacious will, she knew he could do anything he set for himself. Enid and Madison were the last guests to leave. Veronica hugged Enid and whispered Schyler's message in her ear.

"I'll call you," Enid promised.

Madison hoped they could make a regular foursome, and she welcomed the idea, though she suspected Schyler would prefer their going it alone.

"Now that I have all my evenings free, we can arrange something," she told them.

Alone at last and her house in pristine order, thanks to the caterer, she kicked off her shoes, got out of her dress, put on her Buddy Guy CD and began writing herself a letter. She captioned it, "How I hope to spend the rest of my life." An hour later, she looked at what she'd written and shuddered. Not a hope in heaven. She turned off Buddy Guy's blues and went to bed.

* * *

The following Sunday morning, Schyler rang Veronica's doorbell at precisely six o'clock. He knew she'd be ready, but he hadn't expected her to have a picnic basket in hand.

"I brought along my CD radio, too," she said, after reaching up and brushing a quick kiss on his mouth. Quick or not, her kisses always sent lightning sparks shooting through him.

He told himself to knock it off, that he had a whole day with her ahead of him. "Don't you have a sweater? We'll be on the water, and it may be cool." She pointed to the leather tote beside the door. "Okay, let's get started. We've got a good two and a half hours' drive ahead of us."

Shortly after eight-thirty he parked at Kinnicock on the Virginia peninsula and rented a motorboat. "Who's going to navigate this thing?" she asked.

He let her see his slow, thorough appraisal as he arched an eyebrow. "Ms. Overton, I grew up on the Chesapeake Bay. Remember? Sail or motor, it's all the same to me."

She shook her head. "Somehow, I never associated you with the outdoors."

"I guess we've both had our surprises, because I sure as hell never thought I'd hear you sing in a nightclub. It's about ten minutes from here." He checked the boat, helped her in and headed for Rock Island.

"My dad engineered the redesign of this lighthouse for a client who bought it from the local preservation society and had it renovated as a vacation home. The client's a painter, and I expect we'll be seeing a lot of his seascapes."

"Is that what your dad does?" He didn't miss the surprise reflected in her voice.

"Yeah. I thought you knew he's an engineer, a distinguished one, too. You should see his portfolio—some of the finest structures in this part of the country. He asked me to inspect the builder's work, because he knows he can trust me to find any problem."

"So he's an architectural engineer, and you're an…a what?"

"An electrical engineer, but I make a good building inspector, because I studied architecture. It was required."

He docked the boat, tied it to the hitching post and helped her out. Her delight in their surroundings pleased him, and he was glad he'd brought her.

"Do you know I've never even thought about lighthouses. Are there many of them in use?"

He took her into the keeper's quarters and set the picnic basket on the old oak table. "I'd say there're probably a hundred along the east coast alone, though many are in disrepair. I expect they're all automated now and don't have resident keepers."

She walked to the window and looked out at the Atlantic Ocean all around her. "This is idyllic. The world is somewhere else. Imagine living here all the time."

"It wasn't so idyllic to those keepers who had to defend themselves against hurricanes, pirates, Indians and the British army."

"No, I don't suppose it was. Have they been around that long?"

"Sure thing. Dad said the first in this country was built in 1716 in Maine. It's the famous Boston Light on Brewster Island in the Boston Harbor. We could go see it sometime if you'd like, because it's still there and still in use, though it was rebuilt after the British destroyed it in 1776 during the Revolutionary War."

He watched her prowl around the room, inspecting every nook of it, the walls and all the furnishings. "I could stay here for a while. I really could." She whirled around. "Any of these outside the United States? Maybe I'll go lighthouse hunting."

He hoped the idea wouldn't take hold, because most lighthouses were situated on dangerous outposts. "The concept can be traced back to the ancient Egyptians, but the English built the first real lighthouse in Plymouth, England, back in 1698, I believe. They've been springing up ever since."

"What are you going to do while we're here? Can I watch?"

"Sure. I'll inspect the plumbing and wiring. This one has a water purification system that has to be checked, too. I can't possibly do it all today; I may have to come out and spend a couple of days."

"If nobody lives in them, how do they operate?"

He liked her mind, her frank curiosity. "Most use electricity, and some use atomic power. There's one on the Chesapeake Bay, the Baltimore lighthouse, I think it's called, that was the first to convert to atomic power...somewhere in the mid-sixties, I'm told."

He slid under the kitchen sink. "Could you hold this flashlight for me?"

Lying flat on his back, he looked up at her leaning over him and told himself to straighten out his mind, but when he gazed up at her, it was too late. She stared down at him, open as a book, until the heat in him threatened to explode.

"Veronica, sweetheart, move and let me slide out of here."

He watched her tongue rim her lips and bit back an oath. She had to be the most sensual woman he'd ever met.

"I...uh. Go ahead and finish that. You have to work. I'll fix us some lunch."

By noon he'd checked the plumbing and made notes of what he'd found. Nothing that he couldn't fix himself the next time he came out. When he inspected the wiring, he'd have to check out the tower and the stairs leading to it. He walked out on the grassy slope where Veronica sat with their lunch spread out on a red-and-white-checkered cloth.

"I'm hungry enough to eat a whale. What'd you bring?"

"Ham and biscuits, fruit, cheese and fudge-covered brownies."

He hunkered beside her and looked at the food. "You made these brownies?"

"Sure. Why?"

"Do you know I'm a chocolate freak? I have never had

enough chocolate. Dad's forgotten how to make a dessert that isn't chocolate. This is wonderful."

He reached for one, and she slapped his hand. "Yes, I knew you loved chocolate, because you told me. But first, you eat something nourishing."

He looked at her and quickly diverted his gaze. She warmed him all over as surely as the sun warmed the earth. She handed him a ham and biscuit sandwich, and he bit into it.

"Hmmm. This is good. Another talent. You're loaded with them. Tell me. You're not singing any longer. When will you go back to CPAA?"

She let a lot of time pass before she spoke. "I don't want the kind of life I had. I don't think I could handle that corseted existence. The sameness day in and day out, and the constant striving for the next goal, the next accolade. I want to know I'm doing a good job and not have to worry about the ladder of success. Besides, I've given that job the best of my youth, and look what I got for it."

"You'll never know how sorry I am for my part in that."

She shrugged, held a small bunch of grapes over her upturned mouth and bit off one. Did she know how sexy that was? He shook his head as if to clear it.

"I really regret that, Veronica."

"You did what you believed was right. My quarrel is with the people who so quickly forgot what I'd done for their community, but I'm not bitter. That calamity showed me my true self, and I wouldn't exchange that for anything. You know, I've thought numerous times that you'd be a great lawyer. Why are you an engineer and not an attorney?"

"As a child I wanted to know everything my dad did in his work and how he did it, and he delighted in explaining things to me. I became fascinated with design and the discovery of new and different ways of doing things. So I got an engineering degree."

"But in that courtroom...I'd have sworn you were a lawyer."

"I am a lawyer. I..." He didn't feel like reliving that pain, but something in him wanted her to know everything about him. He fell back on the grass, stretched out, locked his hands behind his head and closed his eyes.

"I was married for a little over two years. My wife prevailed on me to join her father's engineering firm, and to please her, I left a job I loved and joined him, reluctantly, you can be sure. He built an industrial vacuum cleaner and offered a three-hundred-dollar, three-year-service contract at the point of sale. Those companies that didn't buy the service contract needed an expensive service within three months. Those that bought it never needed a service. The service contractors got wise and reported him. When my father-in-law was indicted, he accused me, and my wife, who was his accountant, sided with him. I spent three years in jail for fraud."

He opened his eyes and saw that she stood over him, obviously baffled. But he had to finish it, to let her know who he was and the burden he carried every day.

"When I got out, I divorced my wife, went back to Branch Signal Corporation, told them my side of the story and got my old job back. I'm still there. I studied law so I'd be able to help other innocent people trapped as I was."

"Then why don't you practice? I don't believe you didn't pass the bar."

"I passed it, but until then, I didn't know that a stint in jail meant I couldn't practice. I got my engineering job back, but I still don't have the respect of my peers in engineering that I previously had. I enjoy status and respect at Branch Signal, but I don't know what would happen if I left there and needed a job."

She sat down beside him and took his hands from behind his head. "I don't have the professional clout I used to command either, and I haven't been wronged as you have, but I'm going to say this anyway. I know I have to put my life in order, but you must do the same. You could help so many people, because you're honest, and you believe in what's right. You were wronged, and you have to clear your name."

He stared at her. "You don't have any proof that I wasn't guilty."

"Oh yes I have. You would no more defraud anyone than a saint would. I'd stake my life on your honesty."

He had to hold her, to fold her to him and cherish her. She went into his opened arms, lying above him with her head on his shoulder. The words that he would have spoken hung in his throat, and he nearly choked on his breath. How had he been so fortunate as to find the woman he held in his arms?

"Thank you." He couldn't say more. No other words would come.

"I want you to clear your name. Somewhere there is information that will prove your innocence. I'm with you all the way. Do you hear me, Schyler? I'm with you."

He held her closer, needing to be one with her, to merge his soul with hers. "Don't think I haven't burned to do it, but I don't see how I can put my dad through it again. The whole incident nearly killed him. He knew I hadn't done it, and he couldn't help me. I told him I had to clear my name, and he said if I didn't succeed, filling the newspapers with it again would damage me more than it did the first time."

She rolled off him and sat up. "How can he…he can't ask you not to…to reopen it. You're innocent."

He pulled her back into his arms. "He didn't ask that. He's just not sure it's wise."

"Well, I'm sure, and you have to do it. Look at you! Honorable. Exemplary, if a man ever was."

He kissed the corner of her mouth and hugged her to him. She was right. He had to do it, and she'd stick with him whether or not he succeeded. The breeze swept over them, gentle, fresh and warm, and he cradled her between his legs and let himself accept her loving comfort. He knew she'd one day lead him to his inner self, that part of him that he'd never discovered, and he banked his desire and let himself know the soothing comfort of unqualified love.

"All right," he said. "It's what I want to do, what I've needed to do for so long. I'm going for it. I listened to you. Now, I want you to return the favor. Think about what you sacrificed to get where you are, how much you're capable of contributing and consider returning to your profession. You've had a long enough vacation. And I think you should ask your stepfather if he can give you any clues as to why your mother wanted you to find your birth father. Will you do that? It's no more difficult than what you've asked me to do."

"All...all right. I...I will."

It didn't surprise him that she hesitated, because he knew she'd keep her word. He rolled her off him. "I'd better check that wiring so we can leave before the tide changes. We can do the rest another time. You with me?"

She nodded. "I'm with you."

Chapter 8

Veronica stared at the envelope, fully aware that its contents would probably alter the course of her life. Needing fortification, she made a fresh pot of coffee, went out on her porch in the early morning sun and sat down to read the first letter she'd ever received from her father.

"Veronica, my dear daughter," she read. "You can never know my delight in receiving your note. I understood that your aim was to be courteous, but I am also aware that you needn't have written me, and I thank you. It gave me pleasure that I cannot express, knowing I could help you when you needed me and that you let me help you. I took pride in your successful debut as a singer and in that spectacular review. To share in your glory, even at a distance, gave me much joy. And you can't know how glad I am that you were with Schyler in those hours when you both thought I might have been lost. Knowing you are there for each other will always be a comfort to me. I hope the time will come when you'll feel up to telling me something of Esther. I need desperately to know how she lived and died. And I want to know more about you. Much more. Call, or write, if only a postcard. I'll be happy to hear from you. Love, Your father."

She read it a second and then a third time. Finally she read between the lines, picking up what he hadn't said, listening to his restraint, sensing his effort not to let her feel pressured. The part about her mother puzzled her. If he'd been interested in them and how they'd lived, would he have left or, having left, wouldn't he have stayed in touch with them? She put the letter in her incoming mailbox among the missives to be answered later, correspondence about which she hadn't made up her mind. She knew she couldn't ignore it, and she didn't want to ignore it.

Several days later, she still hadn't come to terms with her time with Schyler at the lighthouse. His revelations had stunned her. What strength he had in refusing to allow his circumstances to beat him down! First the foster homes of his youth, and after all he'd overcome, the degradation of a jail term that he didn't deserve. And for the first time, he'd needed her. She'd felt it because, for once, he hadn't tried to hide it. At her party, he'd been possessive, eager for everyone present to know he was with her, but he'd promised nothing and hadn't asked for anything. At the lighthouse, though, something different, sweet and binding, had crept into their relationship. But if she couldn't make peace with her father, did he, could he care enough to accept her?

She dialed her stepfather, hoping to ward off an approaching morose mood. "Hi, Papa. You must have had your hand on the phone. How are you?"

"Doing pretty good. Thought I'd do a little dusting. You've got me living so comfortably that I'm bored half the time. I'm thinking about doing some work over at the church before that building starts to crumble. Maybe about three days a week."

She didn't like the sound of it, but she didn't like his being in that house alone seven days and nights a week either. "What would you be doing?"

"Well the structure needs some supports, and that's the least I can do."

Her eyes widened. First time she'd heard of that. "You can do that?"

"Yep. And I'm going to. When you coming to see me?"

"Soon as the weather improves. Pickett's a wet furnace this time of year."

"You air-conditioned the house, and I can sleep, but don't dare go outside before evening."

She told him about her stint as a jazz singer. "What do you think of that, Papa? The patrons just raved about my singing."

"You always had a sweet voice. Next time, let me know, and I'll come see you."

"I enjoyed it while I was doing it, but I'm going to do some thinking about my career now."

She could almost feel his relief. "I'm glad to hear you say that, because it's your true calling. You were always concerned about everybody but yourself, and especially about people in trouble."

She told him she'd call again in a few days and hung up. But as soon as she dropped the phone into its cradle, she remembered her promise to Schyler. Her conscience failed her when she decided not to call him back for fear of upsetting him. Yet she knew she'd have to tell him about her mother's last request and that she couldn't postpone it much longer.

In another week, she'd have to return to work at CPAA, and she wasn't ready to do that.

She answered the phone.

"Girl, you sure weren't expecting me," Enid said. "That wasn't a hello, that was a come here. I take it you're just fine."

"On the button. What about you? Or maybe I should ask about Madison if I want to know how things are with you."

"He's wonderful, that's how he is, which is why I'm calling. He wants you and Schyler to have dinner with us one evening."

"Uh... Sure, but who's cooking? Not you, I hope."

"Me? Don't make jokes. I could burn water. We'll be over at his place. He's got a cook, and I mean he's a cook."

"When? I'll check with Schyler. If you don't mind telling me, what does Madison do?"

"He's a corporate lawyer, a member of Barnes, Powell and Wright. He wants you there seven-thirty Friday night. Thirty-nine-ten Charles Street, penthouse. Now to my other reason for calling. You got one more week of leave, but the board voted to give you another six weeks, because I told them I thought you needed more time. They want you to come back."

"Thanks, friend, but I don't think that's fair to you. You've done the job for almost three months."

"If you don't come back then, they'll look for someone else. I'm a great deputy, but I'm not as versatile nor as good at this as you."

"All right. I'll think it over. Hope to see you Friday."

She put her father's letter aside. Better concentrate on that report on foster homes. She looked around her office, at her books, the carvings and other mementoes she'd bought at a Kwanzaa fair. They'd look better against a white wall. She reached for the phone to call her painter and thought better of it. She hated the smell of paint. She could finish making the dress she'd started months before she left CPAA. Or maybe she should try to answer her father's letter. No, she couldn't... Not yet. It deserved more than a casual answer. She got her garden gloves, put on a wide straw hat and headed for her garden in the back of the house. She stood there, looking at the plants that begged to be thinned, the weeds suffocating her rosebushes and the irises that arrogantly claimed more than their share of space. She threw up her hands, left the trowel, gloves and hat on the porch, went to her bedroom and telephoned Schyler.

Calm settled over her when she heard his voice, strong, husky and masculine. "Hello. Schyler Henderson speaking."

She hesitated, wanting more of his soothing tones. "Hello, Schyler. This is Veronica."

"Veronica? What a pleasant surprise. What's up?"

She could use Madison's dinner invitation as an excuse, but that wouldn't be honest. "Nothing special. I'm kinda out of sorts, and I figured a few minutes with you would be good for whatever it is that I can't get a handle on. Am I interrupting your work?"

"Yes, but I'm glad you called. Do you... Do you need me?"

She imagined that he'd leaned back in his chair and gotten comfortable. "Need you? I don't know. I didn't stop to analyze the urge to talk with you. Did your dad tell you he wrote me? I read the letter a lot of times, and I've got more questions now than I ever had."

"Are you going to answer it?"

"Of course, but I have to give it a lot of thought first. I talked with my stepfather this morning, but...Schyler, I didn't ask him. I think I'm scared to upset him, or maybe I just don't want to know the truth."

"But will you ask him?"

"Whatever I tell you I'll do, count on it."

"I need to see you, if just for a few minutes."

"Schyler, be careful. You haven't moved from your position, and I haven't...haven't slain those demons that you demand I kill. Don't... Don't make me...love you, Schyler."

"Listen, sweetheart, I don't think either one of us was ever in command of this ship. It's pretty late for caution. When can we be together?"

"Madison wants us over at his place for dinner Friday."

"Sounds good to me. Dressed how?"

"I'll give you the details later. Any progress with your case?"

"When you called, I'd been checking around to see if I can locate a reliable contact with access to my former father-in-law's firm. I need some records. I've got a couple of leads, and if they pan out, I'll be on the way. Could you meet me for lunch maybe?"

"When?"

"One-thirty."

She looked at her watch, thought about the many things she had to do and agreed.

"Great. Wilma's Blue Moon."

She hung up, phoned Enid, got the information she needed as to the time and dress code for the dinner and raced to the bathroom.

Schyler greeted Wilma, followed the waiter to a corner table and took a seat facing the door. He wanted to see her when she entered the room. He'd turned a corner Sunday at that lighthouse. For years, he'd stored up his pain, churned with regret about what might have been and put on a good face for everybody, including his dad, while it ate him up inside. She had believed in him unequivocally and had given him love. The perfect love of unqualified acceptance. She entered in long strides, her wide yellow skirt sweeping the air as she turned the corner, stopped and searched the room. He rose and strode to her.

When she saw him, she smiled, and his heart played leapfrog in his chest. He couldn't get to her fast enough.

"Hi."

Her breathless drawl had the sexiest sound. He stopped before her and let his eyes feast on her warm brown face and her beautiful eyes. Everything about her pleased him. "Hi. I don't suppose Wilma would be too happy with me if I kissed you right here."

She reached up and brushed his cheek quickly with her lips. "You bet she wouldn't. She'd probably chase us out. Do you know, mister, you'd be surprised at the number of things I ought to be doing right now."

He seated her and then himself and opened the menu in the hope of straightening out his mind. The more he looked at her, the more his need gnawed at his loins. "I've got a few things back there on my desk too, but they can wait."

She might turn him down, but he had to take the chance. Nothing had changed; he'd be the first to admit that, and yet, everything was different. He reached across the table and took her hand in his. "Veronica, I want to spend Saturday, Sunday, Monday and Tuesday at the lighthouse. And I want you to be there with me."

When she dropped her gaze, he knew she'd understood him. He stroked her long, satiny fingers and waited. And when he thought she was about to refuse him, she said, "Four days? What'll we do for a refrigerator?"

Relief flowed out of him in a grin that he knew covered his whole face. He squeezed her fingers and could have shouted with happiness when she turned her hand over and caressed his palm.

"Do you understand that I want us to be together?"

She didn't hesitate. "I understand that we'll be together and…and follow our hearts. Right?"

He nodded. "Yes. We won't have preconceived notions or plans, but we'll leave here with open minds and hearts. Okay?"

She smiled her agreement. "Now I won't get anything done for days. You could have waited and brought this up Friday night."

He glanced at his watch. "Would you believe it's three o'clock? I've got to get back to my office. What's the dress code for Friday?"

"Enid says she's still wowing Madison, and she's going to dress to the nines."

"Are we speaking tux?"

"I'll be wearing something red and something long."

He could imagine. "And something you poured yourself into, I suspect."

"You complaining?"

"Not as long as Madison keeps his eyes on Enid. If you can put the next hour to good use, I'll drive you home."

"Okay. Meet you out front of your office building in one hour."

He'd taken a chance in asking her to spend four days and three nights alone with him on Rock Island, but he hadn't a choice. They couldn't continue as they were, unable to stay away from each other, resolving nothing, and yet becoming more deeply attached with every passing hour. They stepped out of the Blue Moon and he brushed the pad of this thumb across her bottom lip and stood gazing down at her.

"See you in a hour."

Her smile was a beautiful thing, fuel for his engine. He waved at her as he turned and headed for his office. As he walked, he made mental notes to get a small refrigerator and adequate supplies and to rent a minivan for their trip. He had to cover a lot of territory in those four days, and he couldn't leave anything to chance.

"Would you please stop at the corner of Reisterstown Road?" Veronica asked Schyler as they neared Jenny's corner on the way to Owings Mills. "I want to see a friend. It'll only take five minutes."

She dashed across Bock Street to where Jenny sat beneath the shade of her precious umbrella.

"Ronnie. Ronnie. I ain't seen you in ages, and I sure did miss you. Don't you work this way no more?"

Veronica explained that she was using up some accumulated leave, but Jenny didn't seem convinced.

"Yeah? Well you sure did have a lot of it." She pointed to Schyler's Buick parked across the street. "That your car over there?"

"Why, no." Veronica beckoned for Schyler to join them. He got out of the car, and she thought he loped across that street with the litheness of a young panther.

"Now, I see where you been," Jenny said. "Is this your man? Come to think of it, I never seen you with a man."

Schyler joined them. "Hi."

"Jenny, this is Schyler."

"Hi you doin', Schyler? I'd shake, but—"

He held out his hand to her. "Glad to meet you, Jenny."

Veronica wondered, not for the first time, about Jenny's life before she became homeless. As she watched her, she concluded that she'd never seen anyone appraise another person more thoroughly than Jenny did as she sized up Schyler.

She wiped her right hand on her dress and accepted Schyler's handshake. "Is he your man, Ronnie?"

Now what was the answer to *that* question? She couldn't look at either of them, but managed to say, "He's my friend, Jenny."

Jenny pulled a few centimeters of air through her front teeth. "You kiddin'? Wouldn't just be *my* friend, if I was you. Not this one. What kinda work you do, Schyler?"

When he smiled at Jenny, Veronica wanted to hug him. "I'm an engineer."

She nodded and smiled, as if satisfied. "Don't you let Ronnie get away with that friend stuff. She a wonderful person, Schyler. You be good to her."

His face bore an expression of one deeply touched. Still, it surprised her when he stepped closer and rested a hand on Jenny's shoulder.

"Don't worry, Jenny. She's precious to me, too."

Jenny's smile revealed a full set of white teeth, and Veronica realized that she used what money she got to take care of herself.

"That's more like it," Jenny said.

Veronica stepped closer to Jenny and, unobtrusively, slipped her the folded bills that she hid in her palm. "We'd better be going, Jenny. See you next time."

But Jenny evidently saw no reason to keep Veronica's gift a secret. "Thanks, Ronnie," she said. "The money you gave me when you went off on vacation just gave out, and I was hopin' you'd come see me. I needed a coupla things. Bye now, Schyler, and thanks for my umbrella, Ronnie. You can see how handy it is."

Schyler drove down Reisterstown Road for three blocks, found a parking spot and stopped there. "Where'd you meet Jenny?"

"On that corner. That's where I get the train to go home. Why do you ask?"

"What's she doing out there? She's clean, intelligent and aware of what goes on around her. I can't see that woman living on the street."

She told him what she knew of Jenny's life and of her inability to get the woman to a social agency. "I gave her the forms, but she won't fill them out."

He put the car in Drive and pulled away from the curb. "Things like this make me want to run for mayor. If you get me a copy of those forms, I'll see that she gets off that corner."

"Oh, Schyler. If only you could. I'll give them to you Friday."

"You're a caring, nurturing person. You'll make a wonderful mother."

"If I ever get the chance."

He glanced quickly at her. "Just say the wor... No. I'd better not go there."

"Chicken?"

"You betcha. I'm not backing myself into that hole."

She wasn't sure she ought to pursue that, but the implications didn't sit well with her. How could saying he'd give her a baby back him into a hole?

The heck with it. She plowed in. "Are you saying you wouldn't care to be the father of my children? Is that what you just said?"

He slowed down to the speed limit and switched to the right lane. "Veronica, don't give me a heart attack. How in the name of kings did you come up with *that?*"

She let herself relax a little and told herself not to be annoyed with him, but that answer didn't satisfy her. "From what you just said."

He took his gaze from Reisterstown Road long enough to look at her and grin. "Honey, I was trying not to get out of line and give a flippant response to something that had to be important to you. And to me. But trust me, babe, I can't think of anything I'd rather do—given the right conditions, of course."

She couldn't help laughing. "You're a prize. You've even got stipulations for *that.*"

He pulled up in front of her house, parked and turned to her with a somber face that stunned her. "Yeah, I've got qualifications for *that,* as you put it, just as you have. I want my children conceived in the best possible circumstances and with a loving woman who wants them as much as I do."

Better get off that topic before it got out of hand, because she didn't trust herself not to ask him what he wanted out of their four-day tryst. Ordinarily, he'd probably consider that a reasonable question, but not in the present context. Besides, he'd already made it clear.

"Want to come in?" she asked, though she knew he wouldn't.

He put his right arm around her shoulder, brought her to him and nestled her close. "Don't think I wouldn't love to, but I've got to work on my case tonight, and I need a clear head. I have some leads, but they may take me no place. I've started this, and I can't let up now. I'm going all the way to the Supreme Court, if I have to."

She stroked his cheek with the pads of her fingers. "And don't forget. I'll do whatever I can to help you. You only have to ask."

Snug against his body as he locked her to his chest, she thought she never wanted to move. Her arm went around his shoulder, and she let her lips graze his square jaw.

Frissons of heat skittered throughout her body as his

fingers stroked her arms. "You believe in me, and that's all I need. I'll be here for you Friday evening at a quarter to seven."

He stared into her eyes, and she wondered if she could trust what she saw in his. But he bent to her mouth and claimed her, scattering her thoughts and filling her belly with dancing butterflies. When he'd sapped her will, he raised his head. "Woman, you do something to me."

At her door, she blew him a kiss. He'd given her a lot to think about, but she'd handle it.

He let out a soft whistle when she opened the door that Friday evening. "Hmmm. You're a knockout. You'll need some help getting out of that dress, won't you?"

Her delicate perfume teased his senses as he bent and kissed the side of her mouth. "You look good yourself, mister," she said, ignoring his suggestive remark. "Hmmm. And you smell good, too. Thanks for choosing red accessories."

A woman who noticed the little things you did to please her was a breath of fresh air. He shrugged as if it were inconsequential that he'd gone into three different stores before he found a red cummerbund, tie and handkerchief that he thought would complement the red sheath he'd seen her wear at the club.

"Is it surprising that I like to please you?"

She gazed up at him, her face an open cameo of her emotions. "Do you? None of this makes sense, but I'm glad."

He told himself to stop his automatic reaction to her frank sensuality, that he ought to be used to it. They walked across the street to his car, and he opened the front passenger door, shook his head and stared at her.

"How are you going to get in without ripping that dress?"

"Just hold the door," she said, then with her feet still on the pavement, sat in the car and swung her legs around until she'd properly seated herself. "Piece of cake."

He walked around to the other side, got in and put their seat belts in place. "Just do me a favor and don't move a muscle."

Her laughter seemed to enclose him in a kind of sweet madness, and he had a vision of himself taking her to a place unspoiled by humans and keeping her there forever.

He looked over at her and made himself grin. "What would you do if I abducted you?"

She turned to him, her face radiant. "I'd probably go nuts waiting to see what you had in store for me. If that's what you're planning for tomorrow morning, forget it. I'd be abducted willingly, and I'm looking forward to helping you inspect the lighthouse."

He banished the frown as quickly as it appeared. If he'd needed help inspecting the lighthouse, he'd have asked one of his colleagues. He pushed it to the back of his mind; he'd play it by ear.

Madison Wright lived in a style befitting a corporate lawyer. His penthouse apartment offered a tranquil view of a tree-lined park, and the interior furnishings bespoke good taste and the wealth to support it. Original paintings graced the walls, fine Oriental carpets lay underfoot and modern, Italian-design furniture completed the picture. Italians were known for their butter-soft leathers and excellent craftsmanship, but it pleased Schyler most that the chairs were big enough for his body. Few things could ruin his evening more completely than to find himself sitting in a chair with three-quarters of his thighs hanging out of it. He couldn't remember when being a guest in someone's home had been more delightful.

After a dinner that would rival the fare at New York's famed "21" Club, Madison got him alone. "Enid hates smoke, and I like a pipe after dinner. If you can tolerate it, we can go to my office and have a word together."

Now I'll get the real reason for this dinner invitation. "Won't bother me. What's on your mind?"

He took a seat in the big black leather chair, draped his left ankle over his right knee and waited, as Madison sat on the edge of his imposing mahogany desk.

"I'm considering taking a case for Robbins Electrical. One of my partners remembers a similar case a few years back that involved you, and I have a queasy feeling that I may have stumbled on something unsavory. Robbins is accused of fraud in building a machine, tying a three-hundred-dollar warranty to it and putting imperfect parts in the machines sold without that warranty. You know the rest. He swears that one of his employees is responsible."

Schyler lurched forward, his senses sharp, alert. "Have you spoken with the man Robbins is accusing?"

"Yeah, I think he's in shock. He said he did the original design but had nothing to do with overseeing the construction."

A numbness seemed to creep over Schyler's body as he re-membered the blank wall he'd faced eight years earlier. "Who is Robbins's witness, his accountant?"

Madison's eyebrows shot up. "Yeah. She says she has records that support Robbins's statement."

Schyler sat back in his chair. This time Robbins would pay. "The accountant is his daughter, my ex-wife. Because she vol-unteered to testify against me on her father's behalf, I spent three years in jail for something I didn't do. That man Robbins is accusing is in precisely the same position I was in. It's a scam, and he shouldn't be allowed to get away with it. Do you know who your opposing lawyer will be?"

"I'd better tell you that I got the court records of your case yesterday, and I saw the similarity. I wondered about collu-sion, but I couldn't be certain. I didn't know that the accoun-tant is his daughter or that she is your ex-wife."

"I'd like to have that man's name, but I can't ask you to do anything unethical."

"I've just decided I'm not taking that case. The man is Jonathan Seals. I'll call you and give you his number."

He had to get a few things straight. Was this dinner a social engagement or an opportunity for Madison Wright to pick his brain? "When did Robbins contact you, if you don't mind telling me?"

Madison relit his pipe, savored a few puffs and grinned. "He called me Wednesday morning, day before yesterday. You're a sharp one, brother. I believe it was Monday that Enid called Veronica about the dinner party. Enid and Veronica are friends, and I wanted to find out if we'd make a companionable foursome. I've enjoyed this evening, and I hope we can see each other often."

"I'd like that. Are you planning something permanent with Enid?"

"If she'll hold still for it, yeah. What about you and Veronica? From what I've observed, it looks as if you're both in for the long haul."

Ask a question, and you get a question. "Looks like it. We've got a few hurdles, but…I hope for the best."

Madison stood and seemed to mull over something, as he stroked his chin. "If you decide to reopen your case, I'll give you any help I can. I'm convinced you got railroaded, and I'm just as certain that you can get the evidence to clear your name."

Schyler extended his hand. "I've just begun to work on that, but I needed someone with inside information about that company."

"Now you don't need it. Robbins will sue to protect his name and you will file a brief in support of Seals. Then, you'll sue Robbins and the system. You have to win."

"How'd you and Madison get on?" Veronica asked Schyler as he sped along Reisterstown Road en route to Owings Mills. "Enid and I wondered about that *tête-à-tête* in Madison's office. It doesn't take forty-five minutes to smoke a pipe, does it?"

"I'm still digesting that conversation." He related the gist of it. "It's an unbelievable coincidence, but a fraud that big and that brazen has to come out. Who knows how long and how often Robbins has gotten away with that scheme? And to think that Ada is a knowing participant. I thought she supported him against me because she was so heavily influenced by him, because she idolized him. But eight years later, she still has her eyes closed? I don't believe it."

"You're going after him?"

"As sure as my name is Schyler Henderson. That brother's number is up." He patted the hand she'd rested on her thigh. "Enough of that. I want you to start thinking about tomorrow and the next few days. You all packed?"

"My bag is in the foyer beside the front door. You want to eat breakfast at my place?"

He switched into the left lane to exit at Lastgate Road. "I'd love to, but that'll take extra time. It's best we start for Kinnicock and eat along the way. Can you handle that?"

"Sure. I won't invite you in tonight, because it's late, and you won't get more than four hours of sleep."

He parked, cut the ignition, got out and walked around to her side of the car. "You sure you want to go with me tomorrow, honey?"

She nodded, looking him in the eye. "I'm sure. Positive."

It was right. She knew it was, as he took her hand and walked with her to her front door. His strength, the security he offered and his tenderness flowed to her from the fingers that caressed her hand. At the door, she waited for the kiss that would set her afire, but in his encircled arms, his gentle touch, featherlike kiss and whispered words, "You're so loving, sweet, so precious," suffused her with a feeling more pervasive, more binding than any he'd ever generated in her, shattering her last defense. She knew that in those seconds he'd locked her to him as solidly as a raw diamond is anchored in rock. She would love him forever.

Inside her house, alone and bereft of his nearness, she leaned against the dining room table and blinked her eyes in the darkness, for she hadn't bothered to turn on a light.

What had caused him to change? As recently as ten days earlier, he hadn't altered his position that she had to meet his father halfway, to extend herself or there could be nothing between the two of them. She switched on a light and went to the phone. He hadn't gotten home, so she dialed his cell phone.

"Henderson."

"Hi, Schyler. It's Veronica."

"What is it? You've changed your mind?"

She sat down on the edge of her bed. "No, I haven't. I had accepted that you weren't going to let us get closer until I made peace with my father. What caused you to change?" She jumped at the sound of screeching tires. "What's that?"

"Nothing serious. I said that, and I meant it. But you've taken a step, and you've told me that you will take the next one. At the lighthouse, something changed in me and for us. Irrevocably. I can't leave our relationship to chance, risking my well-being on what happens between you and Dad. If necessary, I'll teach you to love him, and I can, because I know who and what he is. But that isn't all. It's no longer chemistry that won't let us stay away from each other; it's deeper."

She swung her legs up on the bed and lay down. "You're right, and I've realized the difference. Thanks for telling me this."

"You go to sleep now. Be with you in a few hours."

She blew him a kiss. "Good night."

She got up and headed for the bathroom. So his conditions remained. The difference was that he intended to see that everything worked out to his liking. Well, she couldn't quarrel with that.

He parked the rented minivan in front of Veronica's house, jumped out and raced up the steps to her door. Anticipation of the days to come stoked him into a blaze, a roaring furnace. Energy boiled up in him, doubling itself and its strength by the minutes. The door opened as his finger touched the bell.

"I love a punctual woman," he said, leaning forward and kissing her quickly on her mouth. "Where's your stuff?"

She pointed to the corner. "Hi. I see you could use the coffee."

He looked at the two cups she held. "If I didn't have my hands full, you'd get thoroughly kissed."

Her wink, with those long black lashes, never failed to trigger his heat. He stood holding her luggage and tote bag, staring down at her. "I can drop this stuff, but if I do, we may not get to Kinnicock today."

She grinned, walked past him and held the door open. "Come on. You've already made me enough promises for the next four days."

He could only stare at her. "What promises did I make?"

"What were you doing last night, but promising me? And how about the night of my party? And at lunch the other day. Honey, you don't have to remember; I've got a mind like an elephant, and it will be my pleasure to remind you."

So she planned to tease, did she? Good. He liked that. "Just name the tune, sweetheart," he said, locking her door. "You've got more keys than a baby grand, and I aim to play every single one of them."

She eyed him with a look of skepticism and an air of disdain. "Really? Where'd you study music?"

He grinned, relishing the banter. "At the finest university nature has to offer, and I earned my Ph.D. with distinction. I'll be glad to show you my credentials."

She tossed her head. "I'll bet."

He settled them in the minivan, drank the precious coffee, put the vehicle in Drive and headed for Kinnicock, whistling as he drove. He didn't know when he'd been so alive.

Bright sun and a cloudless sky buoyed his spirits as he anchored at Rock Island. They'd have good weather, and he'd be able to treat her to an idyllic interlude. She insisted on helping him unload the supplies and carrying them into the lighthouse.

"I may be nothing more than a human female, Schyler," she said, her tone mocking, "but I can carry ten pounds. Even thirty, if I use both my hands."

"All right. All right. I didn't want you to think I expected you to lug this stuff in there, because I can do it."

He strapped a dolly on to the refrigerator, heaved it off the boat and pulled it into the lighthouse kitchen where Veronica busied herself organizing what they'd brought.

"You bought a refrigerator?"

He rubbed the back of his neck and scrutinized her. "You said we'd need a refrigerator, didn't you? So I bought one."

Her eyes seemed to increase in size. "For four days?"

"For one day, if it's what you want."

Her bottom lip dropped, and she stared at him for a full minute. Then she slid across the kitchen with her arms wide open. He pulled her to him. Hungry. Starved. Three and a half hours with her beside him and he hadn't touched her. Hours of waiting for her to reach out to him. She meant to say something. He didn't know what and couldn't wait to hear her words. At the touch of his lips, her sweet mouth opened to him, and his tongue could at last frolic in her warm mouth, receiving her promise of the loving she'd soon give him. Her arms tightened around him, and he felt her nipples harden against his chest. He had to get some space between them and do it in a hurry, but she undulated against him, sending the fire to his loins, and he rose against her.

He grabbed her hips and stilled their tantalizing motion. "Veronica, honey, slow down. I want more for you, for us than quick relief here in this kitchen. Okay?"

He nearly laughed when she blinked her eyes as though awakening from a deep sleep. "Oh, uh… Of course not. Besides, it's barely noon."

He let himself laugh aloud. Heartily. Releasing his frustration. "Sweetheart, let's not confuse this. Any time of day is a good time. But not on the kitchen floor the first time."

She shrugged and hid her face against his shoulder. "I'm not up on these things. We'd better figure out what you'll do each day, or you won't get anything at all done."

"You're right."

They installed the refrigerator, cleaned the electric stove and the utensils they thought they'd use. Together they prepared a lunch of hot dogs and the potato salad that Schyler had bought at a delicatessen, and by two o'clock, they'd begun inspecting the wires and electrical outlets on the first floor.

At five o'clock, he walked over to where she worked, on her knees with a scraper cleaning grit from a grate that allowed heat into the upstairs hall. "You don't have to do that. The owners can get someone to clean the place."

She looked up at him, her face decorated with soot and her hair stringing from the knot into which she'd pinned it. "But how will you know whether the heating system is working if we don't open these holes?"

He thought about it for a second. "You're right, and I'll do it."

She shook her head. "You look around for any others that I might have overlooked. I'll finish this one."

He reached down and lifted her to her feet. "Then you'll finish it tomorrow, my lovely. It's knock-off time. I want to go fishing."

She patted her hair, looked at him and made a face. "I'm a mess. I need about twenty minutes."

"You look good to me." He watched her run up the stairs, the motion of her rounded hips quickening his loins into an engine revved and ready to go. He told himself to think about something else. Anything. Just get his mind off her body.

He showered, changed into black jeans, a yellow shirt and a long-sleeved cotton knit cardigan, got the fishing gear together and headed outside prepared to wait for her, but he found her sitting on the front steps looking at the ocean.

"What are we fishing for?" she asked him, as they began casting their lines.

He let a smile crawl over his face as he gazed down at her, contentment springing to life inside him. "Honey, you do ask the most provocative questions. I'm going to take that one at face value, though. Whatever bites that's edible."

Half an hour later, they had three large bluefish, which he cleaned at the water's edge. "Wonder if we can make some cornbread?" he asked her. "I love cornbread with fried fish, but Dad usually makes it. I don't make bread."

"If you brought cornmeal and flour, I'll make the bread while you put the rest of this fish in the freezer."

He fried the fish and steamed a package of frozen green beans. "Let's eat outside."

She nodded and went upstairs where he hoped she'd get a sweater. He spread a blanket on the lawn, got a tablecloth, plates, glasses and utensils and set their table a few yards from the Atlantic Ocean. Then he brought out the wine and food, sat down and waited for her.

She returned wearing a jacket and carrying a lighted hurricane lamp and a radio. "I don't want us to have to rush because of the darkness," she explained. "And I thought it would be nice to have some music."

He didn't kiss her, but the restraint cost him some effort. She, too, was doing all she could to ensure them a memorable four days together. *I won't rush her,* he promised himself. *I'll make myself wait until she comes to me.*

She ate with her legs crossed lotus-fashion, listening to the ocean as it sloshed and the wind as it flirted with the trees. "It's so peaceful here. I felt it when we came before, as if I could stay forever."

He leaned toward her, and her nerves began crawling along the inside of her skin. "Would you find it so...so peaceful, so pleasant, if I were not here with you?"

If she answered truthfully, it would amount to a confession, and she wasn't ready to tell him how she felt about him. But if he was as smart as she thought he was, he ought to know. "I don't suppose so. You are a part of this scene." She spread her arms. "And when I recall it in the years to come, it will be you that I see first."

His fingers gripped her arm. "No hedging, Veronica. You're here with me because you want to be. Would you be as contented here if I were somewhere else right now?"

"I...I'd be a caged tiger, prowling from one end of this island to the other, impatient to leave here."

He crawled over to her, lay on his back and rested his head in her lap. She stroked the side of his face with gentle caresses until he turned his face to her belly, nestled there and locked his arms tight around her.

"Sing something. You've never sung for me. Just me alone, I mean."

She let her fingers skim over his back, arms, shoulders and his head, while she gave voice to one of her favorite ballads, "Tenderly." It wasn't sexy or seductive, blue or sad, but a lover's declaration of happiness found in the beloved. He turned over and gazed at her as she sang, but said nothing for a long time after she finished.

"Did you like it?"

"The song? More beautiful than anything you sang in Round Midnight." He spoke in a voice that was deeper than usual, that shimmered with what she recognized as a gut-level need.

"Thanks." She didn't know why, but her nerves had suddenly gotten out of hand, seeming to slide up and down her limbs, and her stomach clenched tight. She closed her eyes to get her bearings, to regain her equilibrium. This was no time for panic.

"Listen, sweetheart," she heard him say. "We are here to know each other, to get closer, to find out if what we feel for each other is solid. If we make love, you have to let me know you're ready. Tonight, let's enjoy each other's company. What will be, will be. So don't be nervous. You're not my captive."

He put his head back down in her lap. "I love to hear you sing 'Solitude.'"

She laughed a little harder than his remark warranted, but quickly contained herself and sang Ellington's famous torch song. At its end, he got up and reached for her hand. "I could listen to that all night, but I want to get up early tomorrow morning. Let's get all this in the kitchen and turn in."

They cleaned up the kitchen and walked up the stairs holding hands. At the landing, he asked her, "You scared to sleep in that room by yourself?" When she shook her head, he said, "If you get scared, come crawl in with me. I won't bother you."

She threw her arms around him and hugged him. She couldn't help it. "There can't be another man on earth like you."

He smiled ruefully and gave the floor a few light jabs with the toe of his left shoe. "That may be a good thing. If you need me, yell." He brushed a kiss on her cheek and left her standing there.

She went to her room and closed the door. He hadn't seemed disappointed, and she figured that was because he knew he had only to get her into his arms. Maybe that was what she'd waited for, but she sensed the time wasn't right, that their moment had yet to come. She looked out of the window at the moon and the swirling waves. No. It wasn't their night.

Schyler sat up in bed with the reflection of the bare, unshaded lamp against the whitewashed walls glaring in his eyes. He gave up trying to write what he remembered of Robbins's argument that had convinced the jurors to find an innocent man guilty. He hoped that the papers Madison had promised to send him would be waiting when he got home. He thought of Veronica sleeping across the hall from him and wondered why it hadn't distressed or disappointed him that she hadn't indicated a wish to share his bed or to have him join her. He'd sensed her fear and had tried to reassure her. He put his writing pad aside. Why would a thirty-two-year-old woman be nervous about making love with a man whom she wanted and for whom she cared? He turned out the light and put the pillow over his head to absorb the ocean's sound. He promised himself that within the next twenty-four hours he'd have all the answers.

By four o'clock the following evening they had finished the inspections, except for the stairs and tower, and sat on the light-house steps to make notes of the few problems they'd found.

"These little goofs can be fixed in an hour or so," Schyler said. "We could come back one Sunday and do it, but Dad won't let anybody finish a job for him."

Veronica recognized a familiar trait and wondered if such could be inherited. "I don't blame him. I wouldn't let anybody finish a job I started either."

He looked at her strangely, she thought, and wondered if he was also comparing her and her father. "Let's freshen up and have a cookout. I brought some steaks and frozen lobster tails. We can roast potatoes and vegetables. What do you say?"

"I'd love it."

They cooked the food outdoors on an open grill and ate as they'd done the previous evening. Then they worked together to clean away the evidence of their meal.

She didn't want to go in. "Let's sit out here on this blanket and watch the moon rise."

He eased down beside her and uncorked a bottle of char-donnay wine. "Let's find some music on your radio," he said, handing her a glass of the cold white liquid. "I don't believe I can ever forget these days here with you."

"Neither can I. I was just wondering if I've ever been happy before now. If so, it was certainly a different kind of happiness."

The strains of pan-flutist Georghe Zamfir's gypsy melody floated around them from the radio, wrapping them in a sensuous cocoon, and he positioned himself to lie with his head in her lap.

"What about the moon? Shouldn't it be rising by now?"

He sat up just as the silvery disk climbed slowly out of the Atlantic. "It's unbelievable, isn't it?"

She grasped his hand, needed to have something of him, as the moon slowly made its way upward. They watched in silence, and suddenly it disappeared behind a cloud. He shivered, and lay with his head in her lap as he'd done the previous evening. This time his lips pressed against her belly to her naked flesh where her shirt gaped open above her slacks, and frissons of heat shot through her.

He looked up at her. "Kiss me." He barely whispered it.

She bent her head for the kiss and tasted an urgency in him. Her breathing accelerated and excitement gripped her. She laced her fingers through his silky curls, stared into his eyes and parted her lips. In the near darkness, she could see the fire in his gray gaze and the breeze trapped his smell, teasing her olfactory senses. He sat up, braced himself on his right elbow and looked at her as if awaiting a signal. Wave after ocean wave struck the boulder beneath them, but he didn't shift his gaze. Excitement coiled in her.

"Veronica." His voice whispering her name sent the heat of desire arrow-straight to the center of her passion.

"Schyler. Schyler." She fell backward and raised her arms to him.

"Baby, is…is this what you want? Now? Tell me?"

"Honey, kiss me. Love me. Schyler, I need you."

She shifted her hips as she reached for him. He buried his face in the curve of her neck, and his lips hot on her neck and shoulder brought her cry of "Darling, please."

She had to feel his hands, his lips on her body, and her fingers went to her blouse, popping the buttons. She arched her chest and unhooked her bra, letting her breasts spring free. His lips closed over her nipple, and she cried out from the pleasure of it. His hand found the other one, and she could hardly stand the sweet torture of his fingers stroking, pinching and pulling on one aureole while he nourished himself on the other one. Her groans seemed to excite him, and he went at her, pulling and sucking until she spread her legs and reached for him.

"No, sweetheart, not yet."

But she had touched him, had felt the hard length of him, and her desire reached fever pitch. When her hands went to his belt buckle, he imprisoned them in his own and held them above her head, while he tormented her breast with his ravenous mouth.

"Schyler, I'm...I'm dying for you. I ache deep. Can't you—"

"Be patient, sweetheart. I want this to be the one experience we will remember forever."

When he released her hands to make use of his own, she unzipped her slacks and tugged them below her hips. She kicked them off, threw her left leg across his waist and grabbed his hips. She felt his hands move down over her belly, and stilled, waiting for his caress. At the touch of his fingers on her woman's folds, she let out a keening cry, but he stroked her, all the while suckling her breast until at last the evidence of her readiness flowed over his fingers.

He quickly disrobed, protected her and rose above her. "Look at me, sweetheart."

"Honey, please. I'm going insane."

Even in her heated passion, she could see his smile. "All right, sweetheart."

He wrapped her fingers around his steely length and let her guide him home. "Wait a minute. What's this? You aren't—"

"No, but it's been a long time."

"I'll be careful. Just try to relax."

She lifted her body to him and rejoiced in the feel of his difficult entry. He stilled himself and gazed into her face. "You are mine now, Veronica. You understand? *Mine!* And I am *yours!*"

She didn't speak, couldn't speak, for he moved, and fired her up again. He put an arm around her shoulder, a hand beneath her hips and drew her breast into his mouth. Tremors raced through her, and with each stroke she strained for the result that had eluded her. As though sensing her problem, he stopped.

"Relax, sweetheart and let me take you where you want to go. Just give yourself to me."

His powerful strokes quickened within her, and she wanted to explode. Tension gathered in her, and he drove faster and harder. Thunder roared in the distance, and the ocean growled at the shore's edge, its angry waves gnashing in jealousy at the lovers. Raindrops splashed on her arms and face, the wind shouted its loud fury, and still he drove mercilessly within her, bringing her to the brink of fulfillment and pulling her back. She raised her body to him, but he held her still.

"Do you feel what I'm doing to you? Do you? Do you want more, different, harder? Tell me."

"I want to burst. I can't stand it."

He eased up, and drove again. "Yes. Now. *Now!*"

He put one hand beneath her hip and the other between them intensifying the pressure, and she thought she'd lose her mind when the throbbing began.

"That's it, sweetheart. Let it go. Give yourself to me. I want all of you."

The voluptuous squeezing and pinching, the throbbing and finally... She wrapped her legs around his waist to keep from dying.

"Oh, Schyler. Schyler, what have you done to me?"

He looked down at her face as her body gripped him with its powerful spasms. He had to control his release until he'd given her all he could and all she needed. She quieted, and he moved within her, teasing, and at once her quivers began again. He stroked her, reaching for all the control he could muster until she sucked him into a cyclonic explosion as he gave her the essence of himself.

He collapsed. Spent. After a moment, he braced himself on his forearms and gazed into the face of the woman who'd etched a permanent place for herself in his heart.

"Are you all right?"

Shy? She couldn't look him in the eye. He kissed her nose. "It's bad manners not to answer that question."

"I figured you'd have to know the answer to that."

He kissed her eyelids. "A guy likes to be told."

"You may never get rid of me," she joked. "I never had that experience before."

"You may think you're kidding, but I don't, and I never had that experience before, either. Do you know it's actually raining on us?"

Her laughter was joy to his ears. "I felt something wet, but I thought you'd dragged us out into the ocean or something. My mind wasn't working."

"We'd better go inside. It's starting to rain harder. You grab our clothes."

She did, and he picked her up and sprinted to the lighthouse.

Chapter 9

Veronica leaned against the kitchen window and drained her coffee cup, trying to acquaint herself with the woman who'd flown to heaven in Schyler Henderson's arms time and again the night before. If the price she'd have to pay for it proved to be anywhere near equal to the pleasure, to the joy she'd found with him, she was in for a rough ride. She heard his footsteps, turned and basked in his blinding smile. If he was sorry, he hid it well.

He stood before her, so close that his shirt almost touched her blouse, but he didn't touch her, merely stood there, diffident, as though unsure of his right to touch her. "Hi. Have you been in here flailing yourself with regret?"

She resisted caressing him, though after all they'd shared, she felt she had the right to do with him as she pleased. "If I'm sorry, it isn't for what was, but for what may never be."

He reached for her then, letting his hands caress her shoulders. "I can imagine why you have misgivings, but remember that it won't be a problem unless we make it one."

She didn't want to discuss what would probably never be. With just two more days and one night alone with him, she'd rather invest the time in cementing their feelings for each other. "I'll keep my promises to you, but you'll have to accept that I can't stop being who I am."

"I don't want you to change, but dig deep, honey. That's what I'm doing, and I'll keep on doing it. My dad says I'm too stubborn, and I've begun trying to repair that. If I hadn't, we probably wouldn't be here."

"Why are you telling me?"

"I'm saying, you're not alone in this. The way we feel about each other, we can't lose."

"I see. You're willing to…to try for…for something permanent?"

Pure giddiness flushed through her as his arms encircled her, and she bloomed in awareness of his manliness. She knew him now and knew the woman she had become in his arms, and she tightened her arms around his body.

His lips brushed the tendrils of hair at her temples. "I want to reach for that. Yes. Otherwise, I wouldn't have asked you to come here with me."

The feel of his lips moving over hers, begging for the entrance of his tongue, sent jolts of electricity whistling through her veins, and she opened to him. She took his loving, welcomed him, her woman's heat rising around them and mocking them with temptation. Tremors betrayed her arousal, and she burrowed into him, demanding to know again the ecstasy of love in his arms.

He broke the kiss, folded her to his body and whispered, "Slow down, honey. After what you did to me last night, I'm not sure I can make it all the way up those 130 steps. If we start that this morning, I won't get past the first flight."

She stepped away and pretended displeasure. "Then don't stand so close to me. If you dump gasoline on a fire, what do you expect?"

His eyes widened, and he tilted his head slightly and pursed his lips. "Hmmm. Try that one on me another time. Right now, I think I'd better not go there. I've got some great country sausage. Want me to cook you some for breakfast? Scrambled eggs? Toast?"

She stared at him. If he knew how much she loved him... "Sounds good to me," she said, reining in her thoughts.

For the remainder of the day, they worked together as smoothly as a well-rehearsed symphony orchestra. At dusk, they stood at water's edge, arm in arm, not sharing their thoughts, but she'd never felt closer to him. She finally understood that to need a man exceeded physical hunger for him, that it meant desiring his companionship, wanting him to need her, longing to bear his children and knowing that without him you were incomplete. In his arms, she'd been a whole woman, a woman she hadn't known existed. She had found herself. In the evening cool, moisture accumulated in her mouth, on her limbs and beneath her breast as she anticipated the hours to come, hours when she would again come alive in his arms. He held her closer, but he continued to look into the distance, and she wondered at his thoughts, whether he still held to his terms for total acceptance of her in his life.

Nothing in his demeanor supplied the answer to that question, nor did the gray eyes that she could barely see in the growing dusk and the light of the rising moon. "Will you spend the night with me?"

She didn't know what to say, and she wished he hadn't asked. Perplexed at his strange behavior, she didn't speak, but took his hand and began the short walk with him to the lighthouse. He stopped in the kitchen, got two glasses and a bottle of wine from the refrigerator.

With their arms around each other, they climbed the stairs. "I hate for these days to end," he said, more to himself than to her, she thought. "I've always known exactly how I felt about everything, but I can't quite get a handle on..." He ran his hand over his hair. "Heck, I just don't want to leave here, and that doesn't make sense. I've got obligations, a life elsewhere. I *have* to leave this place."

"What is it? Schyler? What's wrong?"

"I don't know. I don't remember having…well, I've never been at sea like this." His shoulder lifted in a slow admission of perplexity. So uncharacteristic of him, she thought. "Let's have a glass of wine and enjoy what's left of our time together."

She nodded, accepted the glass he handed her and gazed up at him as he locked arms with her and sipped the wine. Free of self-doubt, knowing who she was and what she wanted, she let him have his thoughts.

"Woman, you do something to me. I'm not myself here."

She searched his beloved face for the man who'd loved her so fiercely and so tenderly the night before. "Does what you feel for me make you sad?" she asked, though she wasn't sure she wanted the answer.

He shook his head. "It confounds me. It damn near stupefies me, but I'm nowhere near sad. You said you could stay here forever, but you're willing to leave."

She rested her glass on a nearby table and laid a hand lightly on his arm. "You're thinking of what you'll come up against trying to clear your name?"

His face clouded in a slight frown. "I'm not afraid of anything I have to do, and clearing my name will be tantamount to finding a bag of pure gold." He kissed her nose. "Stop worrying. I've always fought my battles alone; not even my dad knew when I was troubled. But you…you've gotten so close to me, so much a part of me that I…well, I didn't… I let you see me exactly as I am. But… It's all right."

"Does what we've had these past few days have any meaning?" she asked him. "Do you think the battles we fought with ourselves before we could come this far were over trite, worthless issues? Honey, we're standing here right now because we care for each other. We can't change what we feel as if it were a gadget that didn't work properly, and we can't send it out to be pressed when it gets wrinkled. It's with us, as much a part of us as our skin, and we won't always be happy about it. Whatever's bothering you isn't all right, but I'm not entitled to your mind."

His fingers gripped hers, and she sucked in her breath when his eyes lit up and sparkled with something that she could only describe as a kind of *knowing*. He gazed at her until the sparkles flared into flames, intense, electrifying, like the last blush of the sunset they'd just witnessed.

"I know you're inside of me," he said, and the dark, huskiness of his voice, so like his lovemaking sounds, triggered her need of him.

"It seems as if you've taken up permanent residence in here," he went on, pointing to himself. "My head has ruled my emotions ever since I knew myself. But this…this release is…terrifying, almost unbearable, because there's so much more inside of me."

"Darling, please. We both have dragons to slay. Let's leave them for another time and enjoy these last few hours together."

Before he spoke, she knew from his stare that he would challenge her. "Am I your darling? Am I?" he repeated, when she hesitated to answer.

She looked him in the eye. "I think of you that way. Yes. Don't you want to be?" From the heavy breath he released, he didn't have to tell her the joy her answer gave him.

"Don't you?" she persisted.

His countenance bloomed, and his smile seemed to radiate love, but she didn't dare trust that possibility, though his words came in guttural tones, as though torn from him. "That and more. So much, much more."

Even before he stepped closer to her, tension began crackling and dancing between them like an unharnessed current, wild and dangerous. She moved into his arms, her body already abloom from its memories of his touch. She wrapped her arms around him and parted her lips for his kiss, and tingling sensations zipped through her as she knew once more the sweet torture of his tongue plunging in and out of her mouth. His groan was a raw, tortured sound that seared her, constricting her body's life vessels. She didn't care that his arms tightened almost to the point of pain as his passion exploded in a hard, hot and demanding kiss. With its uncontrolled undulations, her body signalled to him its impatience, and he lifted her and carried her to his bed.

Schyler lay on his back holding Veronica above him, tight in his arms. He had needed her so badly, needed confirmation that he meant to her what she meant to him, and she hadn't disappointed him. He marveled that she could share herself with him in such total abandon. She'd pulled out the stops, had given him everything, winding him up like a top and spinning him around. He'd been more vulnerable to her than he'd ever been to any human being, and she'd sensed that he was exposed, bare to her, and had loved him with exquisite sensitivity.

"Are you happy now?" she murmured.

He let his fingers stroke the satiny skin of her back. "How could I not be happy with you lying in my arms?"

Her body tensed a little, and he knew she'd responded to his evasiveness, his failure to declare himself. But he couldn't, not right then when he would say just about anything, or do anything that would make her happy. He didn't trust himself.

She pinched his shoulder. "If I could answer that question, I doubt I would have asked it." She stroked his body, teasing him.

"Careful now, a loving woman does not get smart-alecky with her darling."

She rolled off and lay beside him, supporting herself with her right elbow. "I'll have to remember that. When we get back to Baltimore, how am I supposed to act?"

He bolted upright. "What kind of question is that? I didn't ask you to come down here with me because I wanted to hide our relationship." He softened his posture, realizing that she, too, was vulnerable. "I wanted us to be together, to learn each other and have a chance to be ourselves without the distraction of the media and the intrusion of family, friends or…or anything else. How do you want to act with me when we get back? You want to move in with me?" He'd meant to shock her with that last question, though he'd consider himself lucky if she said yes.

"Wh…what? Move… You're…" He could see understanding light up her face. Then she lowered her gaze. "All right. I apologize."

"That's better." Gently, he eased her on to her back. "In case you'd like my address better than yours—"

Both her eyebrows shot up. "That's not my style."

"I didn't think so, and I want more than that for myself. Still, I'd welcome you if you got lonely out there in Owings Mills."

Her expression had become guarded; the open, confident lover she'd been half an hour earlier had vanished. He wrapped her in his arms, brought her close to his body and gazed deeply into her eyes. "You're special to me. I… You're important to me." He couldn't say what he felt; the words wouldn't come. If only he could believe that what he saw in her eyes was strong enough to make her pull down the walls that separated them. If she'd move in that direction, he'd move with her. He let his gaze roam over her face, adoring her until she grasped the back of his head and parted her lips. Then she opened to him, and the world spun off its axis.

Several days later, Schyler scanned his mail, found a letter from Veronica and opened it at once, curious as to its contents. To his disappointment, he found only the forms for her friend, Jenny. Three pages of questions. No wonder the woman hadn't wanted to tackle it. He left his office shortly before five o'clock, went home and changed into jeans, a T-shirt and sneakers. He drove to Reisterstown Road and Bock Street, parked and crossed the street to where Jenny sat beneath her umbrella, though it was neither raining nor sunny.

"Hello, Jenny. Remember me? I'm Veronica's friend Schyler."

She grinned up at him. "I may be broken down, but I ain't gone blind and I got my senses. If a woman don't remember you, she blind and crazy, too." Her smile was broad and frank. "Hi you doin'? And where's Ronnie?"

He leaned against the building. "She's home, I guess. Mind if I sit down?"

She looked around. "Where?"

He couldn't help grinning when she took a rag from her shopping cart, dusted the pavement beside her and patted it.

"Ain't no place else, if you got to sit."

He sat down, braced his back against the wall and raised his knees. "I've got a copy of those forms Veronica wanted you to fill out. I'll read the questions and fill in your answers. Okay?"

It pleased him that she'd seemed affronted when she sat up straight and stared at him. "I can read, Schyler, and write, too. I'm down on my luck, but I ain't ignorant."

"I never thought that, and that's why I'm here. Veronica said she couldn't get you to fill out the forms, so I'm filling them out. I intend to see that you get off this street."

"Just 'cause I'm out here don't mean I ain't got no pride. My hands ain't hardly ever clean, and I ain't sendin' nobody no dirty forms."

During the next half hour, he learned that Jenny Sowell had been a seamstress, able to design and to copy from pictures or a garment, and to duplicate the work of any designer. However, her employers had exploited her, paying a minimum wage, and she couldn't save money. A fire had destroyed the tenement building in which she lived, leaving her with only what she wore and no means of traveling to her job. She became a homeless person, and had lived on the street for over a year and a half.

He completed the forms. "I'll be right back."

"Don't you want me to sign it?"

"When I get back," he called over his shoulder.

He found a convenience store and bought two boxes each containing twelve Wash 'n Dri disposable towelettes. When he got back to her, he opened one box and gave her a packet.

"Now you'll have clean hands all the time." He pointed to the line for her signature. "Sign right there."

He watched her make a ceremony of cleaning her hands, her face expressing her pleasure. She put the used ball of paper in her shopping cart and grinned at him.

"You made my day. I can clean my hands before I eat. Let me see what you put down there." He nodded his approval and handed it to her. She read it, signed her name and gave it back to him. "For a man, you sure do write good. Now what you gon' do with it?"

He wouldn't comment on her jab of female chauvinism. "I'll walk it through that minefield of Baltimore bureaucracy. Be patient. We've made the first step, and soon as I know something, I'll get back to you." He took some bills out of his pocket and handed them to her.

She counted them and looked up at him. "Schyler, Ronnie don't give me this much. Twenty is enough. That way you and her will come back to see me soon."

His heart went out to her; she needed friends. "I'll be back, and so will Veronica. Don't worry."

"All right, now. And you hurry up and marry Ronnie. She ain't got no business bein' by herself."

He grinned, mostly to let her know she hadn't displeased him. "I'm working on it. See you next time."

"You better be serious 'bout Ronnie. She a wonderful person," he heard her yell after him. She had chutzpah, no doubt about that.

He hurried home and began reading the thick package of trial documents he'd received from Madison Wright. A look at his watch told him that if he settled for a sandwich supper, he could get in three good hours of work before calling Veronica around ten o'clock.

Meanwhile, Veronica sat in her kitchen with a salad, a pen and stationery, pondering her answer to her father's letter. Instead of annoyance at having to answer the phone, she welcomed the opportunity to procrastinate.

"Hello."

"So you're home finally. I was beginning to think you'd left town for good."

A sinking feeling pervaded her. "Hello, Jack."

"I've probably been greeted with less enthusiasm, but I don't remember it. At least you recognized my voice."

Who wouldn't spot that nasal twang? "I'm busy right now, Jack. What can I do for you?"

"You're always busy." She didn't miss the impatience and irritation in his voice. The man was used to getting his way and had a habit of behaving childishly when he didn't. "I want you back at the club, and I'd like to…to take you out."

Jack wasn't a man she'd choose for a personal friend, and she didn't intend to let him browbeat her into going anywhere with him.

"Jack, I told you—"

He cut her off. "I'm not giving up, honey, and I get what I go after."

Becoming more and more peeved, she got up from her chair, faced the window and gritted her teeth. "Jack, there's a man in my life, and he suits me perfectly in every way. So I neither need nor want another one. I'd appreciate if you'd accept this gracefully."

"You coming back to the club?" He practically growled it, but she didn't care. She wasn't moved.

"That's not in my plans."

"Your fans are begging for you."

"Thanks, but that was a pleasant interlude in my life, and

it's over. I'm going back to my profession, because I'm not happy doing anything else."

"Don't tell me you weren't happy at Round Midnight with all those guys whistling, yelling and screaming for you after every song. You think I didn't have ears?"

His persistence had begun to wear on her. She'd rather not treat him rudely, but she'd had it. "Jack, I'm very busy. Please excuse me."

But he hung on. "Is that fellow Henderson over there?"

"Goodbye, Jack." She hung up. He was going to be a problem, but she'd handle him.

As though suddenly inspired, she began to write:

Dear Father,

Thank you for writing. I didn't invite anyone to my performances at Round Midnight because I didn't want my friends present if I flopped. You gave us a terrible scare while we waited to learn if your plane had landed safely. The unsettling event carried some lessons, at least for me.

I hope the day comes when I shall be able to answer your questions about my mother. I don't think I can do that right now. Please be patient while I try to find my way through this maze of seeming contradictions.
Yours, Veronica

She reread the letter several times, put it in an envelope and quickly sealed it. She hoped she hadn't promised more than she could deliver, but she admitted that thinking him lost in a plane crash, and his help as she drove home from Crystal Caverns, had caused a change in her feelings about him. And she found it difficult to remain unyielding after repeatedly hearing Schyler's stories of her father's warmth and goodness. But she wasn't going to second-guess herself. What would be, would be.

Schyler. Three days had passed since their return from the

lighthouse, and every minute she spent away from him was like wasted time. She took pride in her progress on the review of foster-care homes, but her joy came when she lifted the receiver and heard Schyler's voice, opened her door and saw him standing there, or felt the touch of his hand. She tried to imagine what their relationship would be like if nothing stood between them, if neither of them had reservations about the other. Though she loved him, she hadn't opened herself fully to him; she couldn't, knowing his unwillingness to bind their lives together as long as she withheld herself from her father.

She had to take the next step, and she didn't look forward to it. Uncertainty and misgivings crowded her thoughts as she lifted the receiver and dialed her stepfather's number in Pickett.

She looked at her watch and began to pace from the kitchen window to the stove as she waited for him to answer. "What took you so long, Papa?"

"Now this is a nice surprise. My back hasn't been too good recently, and getting up and down takes a little time."

Surprised, since she hadn't known he had back problems, she jerked the telephone cord. "Since when have you... Oh. Oh. You've been working on that church. Did you fall?"

His reply was tinged with reluctance to discuss it. "I might've strained it a bit. It'll be all right pretty soon."

She didn't like the sound of it. If he'd ever gone of his own accord to a doctor, she didn't recall it. He'd go only after her mother's prayerful pleading. She'd better go to Pickett. Besides, she'd learn more about what she had to ask him if she was looking at him.

"Papa, I was calling to tell you I thought I'd get down there this weekend and stay for a couple of days. How's the weather?"

"I sure will be glad to see you. You know it's warm, eighty-five to ninety-five degrees, but it's nice in the house here, so you don't have to feel it. What time should I meet the bus?"

She was grown and able to take care of herself and him too, but he still put her interests before his own. He shouldn't attempt to drive if he had a back ailment, but she knew he loved sitting behind the wheel of that Chevrolet she'd given her parents a few Christmases back.

"I thought I'd fly to Durham, pick up a rental car at the airport and drive to Pickett. I'll call you before I leave here."

"All right, if you'd rather do that. I'm just glad you're coming."

She told him goodbye, straightened up the kitchen and glanced at the wall clock. She didn't think she'd get used to waiting on a man's call, not even Schyler's. The phone rang just as exasperation had begun to threaten her good mood. She had to laugh at herself. It was exactly ten o'clock; he wasn't even a second late. *Put on the brakes, girl,* she admonished herself.

"Hello." To her embarrassment, it came out like a purr.

"With that kind of greeting, I certainly hope you had me on your mind."

"You couldn't be serious," she teased, curling up on her bed to get comfortable. She stretched out one long leg. "How are you?"

He told her he'd filled out the forms for Jenny. "She's intriguing. You'd be surprised at what I found out about her." He related the information Jenny had given him. "Now what do you think of that?"

"I always thought she only needed a chance. Schyler, you do so many things that endear you to me. I'm happy for her."

"What surprised me was that deep-seated dignity of hers. She hadn't filled out the forms you gave her, because she didn't want to send in a soiled application, and her hands were rarely clean. If that didn't beat all! An interesting visit with her. Very interesting."

She didn't want to raise his hopes, but she had to tell him. "I'm going to visit my stepfather this weekend."

"Really? I'm glad you're taking this step, and I'm praying it goes smoothly."

"Me, too. I'm leaving Friday afternoon."

"Hey! That's day after tomorrow. Can we see each other tomorrow evening?"

She would have been disappointed if he hadn't suggested it. "I'd love it. Did you get any more leads that'll help get that case reopened?"

"Did I ever!" His excitement floated to her through the wires. "Madison sent me precisely what I needed and made notations on the papers. He's a sharp lawyer."

She rolled over on her stomach and propped herself up on her elbows. "I think I'll shout for joy. Your ship's headed for shore. You're going to beat this thing. Oh, Schyler, I could fly!"

She loved his laughter, and it poured from him. The lush sexiness in his voice sent excitement scooting through her. "When you get ready to fly, baby, be sure I'm there to go along for the ride."

He had to know he was being suggestive. "I wouldn't dare take off without you," she shot back.

Every molecule of her body responded to his low, sexy laugh. "I'm glad to hear it. If anybody else applies for the job of pilot, you tell 'em the position has been filled."

"Shouldn't I...uh...just take their name and phone number in case the...er...fellow who has the job makes a few choppy landings?"

She imagined that a wide grin split his face, because he laced his words with humor, seemingly happy to do what he did so well—bantering and giving every sentence a double meaning.

"Landings? What you got to watch, baby, is that takeoff. If it doesn't start right, there won't be any landing, with or without radar. You still with me?"

She warmed up to his game, squelching a giggle. "I'd like to see this pilot in action."

"I may be able to manage that. What time will I see you tomorrow?"

"Is six-thirty too early?"

"Right now isn't too early. Six-thirty it is. When you get

into bed tonight, think about the last time you flew. See you tomorrow."

"Okay. And you give some thought to the last time you cranked up that engine. Here's a kiss."

She made the sound of a kiss, hung up and wished she could turn out the light and dream. Sometime during their weekend together, she'd developed a sensitivity to him. He'd teased, but his jests had lacked the robustness of his usual verbal pranks. He still had that rawness inside, though she knew his laughter had released some of it. But the pain of uncertainty remained in him as strong as when they'd stood arm in arm on Rock Island watching the setting sun.

Schyler hung up, rubbed his chin and pursed his lips. She was a challenge for any man and, Lord, how he loved her! If she could have a good talk with her stepfather, she might learn all she needed to know. He found himself smiling at her wickedness, something he wouldn't have associated with her when he'd met her all those months ago. He remembered that she'd loved La Tavola and decided on that restaurant for their dinner.

A sharp whistle slipped through his lips when she opened her door to him that Thursday evening. In that mauve-pink silk dress and matching coat and with her hair up in a high twist, she was Venus incarnate. He stared at her until she grinned and opened her arms. But he could only hug her; if she got him into a clench, they'd never leave her house. She took his hand and pulled him inside the door.

"Thanks for the orchid. I know it's old-fashioned, but I'm going to put some ribbon on it, make a bracelet and wear it on my wrist. Sit down a minute; it won't take long."

"How'd you do that?" he asked when she returned wearing the orchid on her right wrist.

"I dampened the stem, wrapped first a bit of damp paper towel and then some plastic wrap around it, covered that with ribbon and tied the whole thing to this bracelet. You like it?"

"It's ingenious. I've noticed that you're pretty inventive."

"I've had to be. My stepfather preached self-reliance. He wanted me to learn how to do things for myself so I would never have to depend on other people. And he said if a girl could take care of herself, she wouldn't have to tolerate abuse."

He nodded. "She shouldn't put up with that even if she is dependent on a man. Better to leave him and take life as it comes. What else do you do that you haven't told me about?" He couldn't resist kissing her cheek as they walked to the front door.

"I can make my clothes, cook and...let's see. That's enough."

"Do you play that piano?"

"Of course. Not as often as I should, but I play. Sometime when you're here, I'll play something for you."

He wished he hadn't planned an evening that began with dinner in Baltimore. He didn't want to share her with a bunch of strangers. "Maybe when you get back."

The time sped by too rapidly to suit him. He'd been careful not to raise any issue likely to cloud their time together, but his unasked and, hence, unanswered questions left him dissatisfied. As he parked in front of her house, he told himself not to think about anything negative, to concentrate on the pleasure he got from just being with her.

"Dinner was great, and your company beats anybody else's," she told him. A lame compliment, from where he stood.

"I'm not sure I know how to take that last part. Maybe you've been in lousy company recently."

She handed him her key and stood aside while he opened the door. "I don't allow myself to suffer lousy company, as you put it."

But he wanted more. "If you like being with me, can't you just say so?"

She leaned against the wall inside the foyer and raised her arms to him. "You make me happy. When I'm not with you, I wish I was."

She raised her lips for his kiss, but laughter bubbled up in him, and he couldn't follow through. When he could control it, he said, "You are one contrary woman, but you suit me to a tee."

"What do you mean, I'm contrary?"

Then, he did laugh. It rolled out of him until, as though exasperated, she pulled his left ear. "What's so funny?"

"I asked if you like being with me, and I loved hearing that I make you happy and you don't like being away from me. But, Veronica Overton; woman, what I want to know is whether you like just being with me. Not going somewhere or doing anything. *Just being with me.*" He couldn't help grinning at her raised eyebrows and the frown that marred her beloved face. "Like now. Just standing here close to each other."

Her laughter thrilled him. "Oh, yes. I wasn't thinking right. You were asking me how many threes equal nine. Poor me, I said three times three, and you wanted me to say three plus three plus three. Right? Not to worry. I *love* being with you."

He gazed down into her face, wide-eyed with a look of pretended innocence, wicked and daring at the same time. He'd never get enough of her. And as if she knew it, her tongue started its slow sweep around her tempting lips, dampening them for his kiss, and he grabbed her to him, squeezed her and tasted her. A harsh groan escaped him, and he had to back away from her. For the first time in his life, he teetered toward a complete loss of control. If he touched her, he'd incinerate.

"What's the matter?" He didn't miss the disappointment in her voice. "Where's that pilot you were telling me about?"

He shook his head, amazed at himself. "He's here, but he's so hungry, so ravenous that he's out of control." He stopped the game. "I'm burning up for you, but I'm not sure I can rein it in. I've never had this feeling before."

She flicked off the foyer light. "I could use a glass of wine, and I'll bet you could, too. Come on." With his hand in hers, he followed her to the kitchen and stood there, marveling at her self-possession as she poured two glasses of chardonnay.

"Thanks," he said as they stood in the kitchen drinking high-priced wine out of juice glasses. "I think I'd better go home."

He wasn't sure he liked what he saw on her. She was priming herself for a good tussle, and from what he'd seen of her when she became adamant, she didn't intend for him to leave the way he'd come in that door. He didn't let women get the better of him, nor men, come to think of it. But this time, he didn't have the advantage. She bit her bottom lip and transformed her face into the embodiment of innocence.

"You think you'd better go *where?*"

Since he'd left her on Sunday afternoon, he'd thought of little else but the pulsing of her body tight around him. He put his glass on the kitchen counter and looked her in the eye. "That depends on what you're willing to risk."

She put her glass on the counter, leaned against it and crossed her ankles. "With you, there is no risk. I want whatever you're offering."

He straightened up, jammed his hands in his pants pockets, walked over to the window and took a stance similar to hers. "You think you know me better than I know myself; is that what you're telling me?"

The woman let a grin crawl over her face as she started toward him. "I never said that. But I can't believe you'd walk out of here right now, if you knew I wanted you to stay here with me."

He cocked an eyebrow. He'd walked out on women, a number of them. But he hadn't had in his heart for them what he felt for Veronica. "You want to test me, is that it?"

He knew the second she decided to change tactics, and it didn't surprise him when her fingers rested on his chest briefly and started their slow climb toward his shoulders.

"This isn't a game with me, Schyler. I've thought of nothing this week except the way you made me feel." Her fingers stroked his left cheek and her eyes softened, not with passion, but with something deeper that sent his heart into a drumroll.

"Baby, if you knew how badly I need you, you'd be scared to death."

Her fingers continued to soothe his skin. "I wouldn't be afraid of you if you had a gun in your hand." She eased her arms around his neck and kissed his cheek. "I need you, too."

She wasn't offering her body, he knew that, but her whole self, the inner part of her that she'd let him glimpse on Rock Island, her understanding and acceptance of all that he was, had ever been and would ever be. His body quickened with the blaze that started in his heart and spread all over him. He inhaled the sweet scent of her, the delicate woman's perfume that always fired his furnace. He put his arms around her then, knowing what it meant and realizing that no matter what he'd told her, he'd get the control he needed or die trying. She relaxed in his arms, and he sensed the softening of her body and the easing of the pressure of her fingers on his face. Without a word, she'd told him she was his and that she trusted him to love her however he needed to.

His pulse took off in a rapid beat as he anticipated what was to come, and he lifted her and took her to her bedroom. To his amazement, she carefully removed the orchid from her wrist and placed it on her night table. He eased the silk coat off her, but his fingers shook when she turned her back to him so that he could unzip the sheath she wore. He slipped the dress off her, lay her on the bed and removed her sandals. It pleased him that she didn't wear pantyhose, because he hated them. He looked down at her, the treasures she offered shielded from his eyes only by the tiny scraps of mauve silk covering her nipples and love nest, and he hardened to a full arousal. She reached up to him, and he'd never know how he got out of his clothes so quickly.

The minute he joined her, her hips shifted, and he thought he'd burst with need. "Honey, try to slow down. If you don't, I won't be able to find much for us."

"Stop worrying, and just…just love me."

"I am, honey, I am." When she parted her lips for his kiss,

his body revolted against the prison of denial that he'd fenced around it since he'd last been in her arms, and he had to restrain himself when she took his tongue into her mouth. He stilled her dancing hips, gathered her to him and let her feel the force of his passion. Then, her fingers went to the back of his head, and he knew she wanted his mouth on her breast, but he teased her, prolonging the act and intensifying the pleasure.

"Please. Please. I need you to…" She grabbed his hand and attempted to press it to her flesh. He took the sweet bud into his mouth, and she rewarded him with a keening cry for more. He didn't want to rush her, but her cries excited him, and his body pained him with its need to find its place within her. He stroked her other aureole, as his lips loved her face, neck, ears, and shoulders. His mouth skimmed her inner arms and teased her belly. He told himself to think about the size of his income taxes, the case he wanted reopened, Jack McCrae, what the founding fathers didn't put in the Constitution, anything but the way the perfume of her loving teased his olfactory glands and made him want to chuck common sense and get into her. Her undulations set him afire and he tried to still her, but she grasped his buttocks and spread her legs, inviting his entry. He had to skip the next step he'd planned for her, and let his fingers part her woman's folds to stroke her into readiness. Finding the evidence that he wanted, he rose above her and looked into her face at the love light in her eyes and the loving smile that welcomed him. He knew he'd find that control and anything else she needed, no matter what. Her hand found him, guided him to her and at last he plunged into her.

He meant to drag it out, to love her so thoroughly that she'd never want anyone else, not Jack McCrae, that marriage hunter in Switzerland or any man but him. He stroked her with all the power he could muster, bringing her to the brink, dragging her back and heating her up again.

"Honey, please stop teasing me, I'll go crazy if I don't… don't burst."

He drove harder. "I want you crazy. Crazy for me. Do you hear me? I don't want anybody else near you."

"Oh, honey, there's only you."

Her body jerked, and he felt her tremors. He tightened his grip on her and whispered, "Go ahead. Explode all around me." Her powerful pulsations began, and he wanted to rock her forever, but he couldn't stand the pleasure. She wrapped her legs around him, clutching him, until at last she screamed his name.

"Schyler. Schyler. My love."

Shaken to the core, he burst within her, giving her all of him. As though she sensed his vulnerableness, she squeezed him to her as he lay wrapped in her arms and legs, exhausted from the loving and what it had taken out of him. He couldn't speak.

After more than half an hour, she spoke. "It was wonderful. I didn't notice you having a problem with control. You know, I didn't think it could get any better than that last time, but it did."

He raised his head from her shoulder and kissed one brown aureole. "If things stay good between us, it'll get better and better. The more we learn about each other, the better we'll be able to please each other. As it was, I had to skip some steps, some of the things I've learned that you enjoy, but I was fighting myself all the way."

"Oh."

He needed to let her know he adored her, and he let his lips brush her long lashes, cheek and neck. Gathering her to him, he gazed into her eyes. "You...you get to me."

Her soft, sweet smile seemed to light up her face, a loving smile that told him what he'd never heard from her lips, making him want to lose himself in her.

"Happy as I am locked up in you like this, I have to leave."

"I'll call you before I go tomorrow."

He sat up and looked down at her. "What time are you leaving?"

"My plane takes off at ten after one, so I'll—"

"I'll be here at eleven thirty and take you to the airport."

"Oh, but you don't have to—"

"I know I don't have to. When are you coming back?"

"Sometime Sunday. I don't have a reservation, yet."

"Call me and let me know what time to meet you. I'll be in Tilghman until Saturday, and I should get back to Baltimore no later than nine o'clock Sunday morning. You'll call me?"

Her reticence was one more indication that she didn't like giving up her independence, not even for a minute. He figured she was pampering him when she said, "All right. Thanks."

He got up. "You stay right there," he said caressing her forehead. "I want to leave you lying in bed. I'll let myself out." He had to hold her again, if only for a second, and when he leaned over to kiss her, she clung to him. He gazed at her in-quiringly. "What is it, sweetheart?"

"Nothing. I…I guess I won't ever be ready for you to leave me."

"That's the way it should be. You don't see me dancing for joy right now, do you?"

He turned out the light beside her bed, dressed as fast as he could and let himself out. More than anything, he wanted to awaken in her arms the next morning, but he wasn't ready for what that implied. Not yet.

Schyler watched the departures board as Veronica stood and hooked the strap of her carry-on bag over her shoulder. "US Air flight 1126 now boarding," reached his ears as though from a distance. She was going to get on that plane without telling him where she was going or how he could reach him. He faced her, his hands on her shoulders.

"Call me on my cell phone as soon as you get there."

"I will, and thanks for bringing me to the airport."

He was about to squeeze her shoulders when he realized it would have been a reprimand, not a gesture of affection. "Don't thank me. I'm here with you because I'm supposed to be and because I…I have to be."

He hated public displays of affection, but as he gazed into her face, her eyes adored him, and he pulled her close. When he touched her mouth for a brief kiss, her lips clung to his, and he let her have her way.

"Last call for US Air flight 1126."

He released her and watched her walk away from him, but he stood there long after she was out of sight, until the gate closed, pondering what had not transpired between them. He'd taken her to the airport, but she hadn't so much as mentioned her destination. He could see from the departure listings that the flight terminated in Durham, North Carolina, but did it make intermediate stops? And would she transfer to another plane when she got to Durham? He made slow steps out of the airport to his car. As he opened the door of the driver's seat, he let out a long breath. She'd never told him her stepfather's name, nor the place where he lived, either.

He got in, put the car in Drive and stepped on the accelerator. She was intentionally hiding something. And for the first time, it occurred to him that his dad hadn't voiced either question, which meant he might know more than he was telling. He made up his mind not to torture himself with it; if and when they straightened out their relationship, it wouldn't matter. If they didn't get together, it still wouldn't matter. One more reason why he'd better roll up his sails and mark time.

Chapter 10

Veronica turned the rented Chevrolet into Cooks Row and parked in front of her stepfather's house. With its yellow brick facing, white molding and awnings, it stood as a palace among the neighborhood's comparatively shabby dwellings. Her parents hadn't wanted to move away from the people who had befriended them when they'd been jobless with a small child to support. So she had remodeled the house instead of buying them a new one. She didn't marvel that the neighbors showed no envy when she'd refurbished her parents' home but had rejoiced that at least one of the neighborhood children had done well, for they had always supported one another.

As she got out of the car and started up the short walk along which her mother had planted the red and yellow roses that perfumed the air, the front door opened and her stepfather struggled through it. A wide smile softened his beloved face, now lined not from age but his life's hardships.

"Veronica! It's so good you're home."

She stifled a gasp and did her best to hide her shock at his appearance and to keep the concern out of her voice. "Papa. I'm so glad to see you. But you said you didn't fall, so why are you limping?"

"I didn't fall. I kind of wrenched some muscles in my side when I was reaching for a pillar instead of moving the ladder closer to it. I've been getting some spasms, but it's better today."

She didn't like it. "Are you sure?"

"Yeah. Don't worry now. I got it a few times years ago, maybe before you were born, and it always went away on its own."

When she hugged him, he stepped back, looked at her and laughed. "You been getting your vitamins? That weak little hug wouldn't crack an egg."

She hugged him harder. "In spite of that limp, you look good."

It wasn't the one hundred percent truth, but at least he'd gotten back the sense of humor that had deserted him after her mother's death. She locked arms with him and walked into the house, noticing the changes he'd made. In the foyer, soft beige paint had replaced the striped wallpaper, and brown-and-beige-marbled tiles covered the once-carpeted floors. Thank goodness, he'd thrown out the artificial pussy willows that had filled an old urn in the foyer for as long as she could remember.

"I hope you didn't eat on the plane, because I've cooked all your favorites."

"And I'm ready to eat them, too. These airlines don't give you a doughnut unless the flight's over two hours. I'm starved."

He limped toward her old room. "Put your things in there and get comfortable. It'll be ready in a few minutes."

"Give me five extra, Papa. I have to make a phone call."

"Sure. You can use that phone in the hall right by your room."

She started to dial, hung up and took out her cell phone. No point in putting a long-distance call on her stepfather's bill.

She dialed Schyler's number and waited for the thrill of suddenly hearing his voice.

"Schyler Henderson speaking."

"Hi. It's me. Veronica."

The vibrant tones of his deep, throaty laugh filled her with warmth and contentment. "You think I don't know your voice? You only had to say hi. How was the flight?"

"Exciting beyond words. They gave me a seat, a safe trip, about twenty peanuts and a choice of coffee, tea, milk, juice or soft drinks. My stepfather is getting me some lunch. He didn't tell me, but I know it's going to be Cajun-style fried catfish, hush puppies, stewed collards and iced tea. I'm drooling."

"If he didn't tell you, how do you know?"

"What will your dad give you for dessert this evening?"

She imagined that a grin started around his lips and eased its way to his wonderful eyes, for she could hear the merriment in his voice. "I get it. Your stepfather does the cooking?"

"I'll say. Mama couldn't have cooked her way out of jail if that had been the only stipulation for her release."

"Do you see a similarity here?"

"I hadn't thought of it, but there sure is one. I'd better change and go eat. I smell the fish. I'll call you tomorrow."

"See that you do. And stay sweet."

"You too. Oh, and give my regards to my father." She glanced around to make sure Sam Overton hadn't heard that last remark.

"Thanks. I...I will, and he'll be happy to know you thought of him. I'm waiting for my kiss."

She made the sound of a kiss. "Bye now."

At times, she forgot how much her stepfather enjoyed doing things that made her happy. From childhood, he'd whittled little animals, made straw dolls and numerous other little things for her, compensating for his inability to buy what other children took for granted. He couldn't afford books, so he took her to the library and let her read there, told her wonderful stories that she still remembered. She swallowed the last hush puppy, dabbed her napkin around her lips and drank the remainder of her iced tea.

"Papa, it's sinful the way I eat when I come home. You shouldn't spoil me like this."

He sipped his own tea, set the glass down, leaned back in his chair and smiled. "You always did spoil easy, and I just got a kick out of doing it. Your mother said you wouldn't be worth a cent if I didn't stop catering to you, but she saw how wrong she'd been. Did you make your call?"

She nodded and primed herself for the conversation she had to open, but he, too, had some questions.

"Was that a man, somebody special you called?"

"He's special, Papa, but so much separates us right now that I'd better not talk about him. If things work out, I'll be proud to let you meet him."

Sam Overton cocked an eyebrow, and his reproachful stare was one to which she was unaccustomed. "He isn't married, is he?"

"He's been divorced for four years. I don't get involved with married men, Papa. That's a no-no."

He let out a deep breath that signified his enormous relief. "I'm glad to hear it. That's something I don't approve of."

"Excuse me, will you? I just remembered I have to make another call."

She went into her room, and called a friend, an administrator at Duke University Hospital in Durham. "Gladys, this is Veronica." She told her about her stepfather's injury and got an appointment for an examination the following Monday morning. That meant she wouldn't see Schyler on Sunday, but she couldn't help it. She'd call and explain, and she knew he'd understand.

She found her stepfather sitting on the back porch, which she'd had fitted with removable glass so that it could be air-conditioned in the summer and heated in the winter. "Papa, there's something I probably should have told you right after Mama died, but I couldn't make myself do it. Now I have to, and I don't know how."

He stopped rocking in the Shaker chair he'd had for as long as she could remember. "What is it? There isn't anything that you can't tell me."

She leaned toward him. "Don't take this the wrong way. Please don't, because I'm convinced it isn't what it seems."

He placed both hands on his knees as though prepared to spring forward, and it occurred to her that there was much she didn't know about him. "Just say it, Veronica."

"When I came back here from Switzerland, Mama was... she was—"

"I know. She was leaving us. What else?"

"She...she told me to find my father. She said, 'Find your father...please...find him...sorry.' Those were the last words she said."

"I was expecting anything but that."

"It was for me, not for herself. She didn't say so, but she seemed to be apologizing to me. Anyway, I got a private detective, gave him what information I could gather and he found him." She looked at her stepfather, at his stricken expression, and wished she didn't have more to tell.

He rubbed his fingers across his forehead as though erasing an error. "And...and have you seen him?"

She'd never seen him so agitated, and she was fearful of continuing, but she had promised Schyler that she'd seek answers from her stepfather. "I visited him once, Papa. He was overjoyed at meeting me, and everything about him was different, almost the opposite of what Mama taught me. If I hadn't disliked him so intensely all my life, I could have enjoyed being with him. Papa, I know Mama loved the ground you walked on, so she didn't regret marrying you. In fact, she told me many times how sweet you made her life and cautioned me to marry for love; that money and material things couldn't compensate for having to lie in bed with a man you didn't love. So what was she saying to me?"

He got up, limped to the door and gazed out on the garden,

though she doubted he saw what his eyes beheld. "She's gone, and she can't tell her side of it now. Let it lie, Daughter. Don't dig up that old stuff that won't make anybody happy. Let the sleeping dogs stay asleep. I never was pleased with the way it was handled, but it wasn't my story to tell. Just…just let it lie."

Hearing the sadness in his voice, she rushed to him and put her arms around him. "I didn't mean to upset you. I didn't ask you earlier, because I was afraid I would. But it's all right. Maybe one day you'll feel up to talking about it. If not, I'll understand. I want you to know that nothing and no one will ever take your place with me."

He patted her hand, absentmindedly, it seemed. "I know. I always knew that. Don't worry now. Just remember that when you open Pandora's box, you don't know what you'll find."

"All right. That's that. I made an appointment for you to see a specialist at Duke University ten o'clock Monday."

"Thanks, but I can't make it over there at least for a couple of weeks."

She didn't imagine the satisfaction his voice conveyed at the thought that he could avoid going. "Sorry, Papa. That old trick won't work, because I'm staying right here till we get the results of whatever tests they give you and treat you for the problem. I may be here for days, so you might as well not even try to get out of it. We're going Monday morning."

His sheepish grin meant that he'd capitulated. "You always did have a broad streak of Esther in you. I'll go, but don't remind me again until Monday morning. Want to drive by the church and see what I've been doing over there?"

She agreed, and for the next few hours, she marveled at the talent she hadn't known he possessed. "You're practically re-building the apse of this church. In all these years, I never knew you could do anything like this."

His chest seemed to expand, and in spite of his obvious pain, he stood straighter. Pride radiated from his face. "I can do a lot of things, or I could once. That wasn't simple, and it's not perfect, but at least Reverend Cox won't get rained on when he stands before the altar, where he likes to preach."

She wanted to question him, but years of trailing around behind him eagerly absorbing all that he did and said had taught her the futility of asking him personal questions. If he wanted you to know, you didn't have to ask. He told her his other plans for renovating the church, and she noticed that, as he spoke, he'd begun using technical terms. Talking about Pandora's box. She had a thousand questions that she didn't dare ask.

Their visit to the specialist, a leading orthopedist, netted the information that Sam should refrain from energetic movements for the next several weeks. He left the doctor with his side tightly bandaged and a prescription for pain. A grimace was the thanks he gave her when she returned from the market with a dozen packages of frozen dinners, several pizzas that she prepared for freezing and a ready-to-eat smoked ham.

She brushed aside his complaint. "You took care of me when I wasn't well, I'm just returning the favor. This would be a good time for you to learn the guitar, and I'll send you one soon as I get back to Baltimore."

He raised an eyebrow. "I hope that fellow up in Baltimore likes to be bossed around. I'll eat that stuff, and I thank you." He waved a hand as though dismissing the food. "But I'm not about to learn the guitar. I got lots of things I want to read."

"Fine with me, long as you do as that doctor told you."

She went into her room, called the airline for a reservation and then telephoned Schyler.

"What's the news?" he asked, a note of urgency in his voice.

"It's just strained muscles. He'll be all right in a couple of weeks, if he follows orders—the doctor's and mine."

"I'm glad it isn't serious. I'll be waiting for you."

She quickened her steps as she left the plane and made her way through the airport, and her heart threatened to run amok when she saw him standing just outside the security area. He removed her carry-on bag from her shoulder, dropped it at his feet and opened his arms, and his fierce hug was all the proof she needed that he'd missed her.

"You're a sight for sore eyes," she told him, because all the things she'd planned to say to him had gone out of her mind.

"You're the one."

From his eager expression, she knew he had to use a lot of restraint to prevent himself from asking her about her talk with her stepfather. And she was glad he didn't ask; she wanted to postpone his disappointment for as long as possible.

"Any progress toward getting your case reopened?"

His swift glance and the sparkles in his gray eyes told the story. "I have, indeed. I've had several meetings with Madison, and he's laid the case out for me. I'd like him to take it, but the judge would probably disqualify him, since my former father-in-law had attempted to retain him for a similar case. One of his partners will represent me. It's an unbelievable stroke of luck."

"Does your dad know?"

"Yeah. He's agreed now that I have no choice but to do this, and he's stopped worrying. How about spending next weekend with us?"

"I don't—"

"Wait. Hear me out. A bell won't ring by itself. It has to have help. If you and Dad don't see each other, how can you get to know and understand each other?" He pulled up in front of her house and stopped. "How could I have forgotten? Your letter made him very happy. Thank you for writing him. Do you know he hasn't showed me either one of your letters? You didn't by chance, tell him you think I'm a great guy and that you can't live without me, did you?"

She flexed her eyebrows. "Of course I did. You don't think I'd keep a thing like that from him, do you? I told him you played the music that made me dance."

His eyelids lowered into a half-squint, and she couldn't help grinning at him, because he didn't know whether to believe her.

"Are you pulling my leg?"

She laughed outright. "Would I do a mean old thing like that?"

The words had hardly cleared her throat before he had his hands on her, squeezed her to him and torched her lips with his mouth. "I have an appointment exactly thirty-four minutes from now, and that's all that saved you. But I'll call you as soon as that guy walks out of my office."

He got out and opened the front passenger door for her. She didn't know what got into her when she let her skirt ride halfway up her thigh, glanced at him from beneath her lashes and let him feel the breeze from her body as she stepped past him. Then, for good effect, she tossed her head. "Whatever made you think I wanted to be saved?"

His sharp whistle matched the surprise that blazed in his eyes. "Whew! I'll bet you've got layers that haven't been uncovered."

She kissed his cheek. "I'm sure you're equal to the task."

"Uh…yes, ma'am," she heard him say as she opened her door.

She turned and waved at him. "Call my cell number. I may be lounging on my deck."

She went on into the house, certain that she'd given him enough to chew on for a while. She had a hunch that her sauciness affirmed something for him, though she didn't know what it was. She'd begun to like that side of herself; it made her feel strong in her relationship with Schyler, and she needed the assurance that she could hold her own with him.

Veronica's behavior did not perplex Schyler. Their idyll on Rock Island had given him a better understanding of her, and as far as he was concerned, her flirting was right in character. The brainy, circumspect woman he'd first seen in Family

Court had set herself free and allowed the female who'd always been there—submerged beneath walls of proper behavior and public persona—to emerge, a butterfly fresh out of its cocoon, eager to relish nature's bountiful nectar. She'd challenged him in the courtroom, and she hadn't spared him in the bedroom. The woman went after what she wanted and for that alone his admiration for her was boundless. He just wished she wouldn't pull those audacious stunts when he didn't have time to deal with them. He looked at his watch as he parked in front of the Drake building where he worked and saw that he still had eleven minutes. Good thing a patrolman hadn't spotted him.

He pushed aside his mild annoyance at seeing his four o'clock appointment waiting for him and checked his watch to see how long the man had been there. "Good afternoon, Mr. Reid," he said, pausing on his way into his office. "Be right with you."

He read over the notes he'd made in preparation for the meeting with his client and buzzed his secretary. "Daphne, would you please ask Mr. Reid to come in."

"The design's perfect," Reid said, "but we're putting up a modest building for tenants with limited means. Won't it be pricey?"

He'd expected that argument. "I can make a cheaper model, but the money you'll spend in maintenance will cut your profit in half. And another thing; if you put in the cheaper one, you can't advertise this company as the designer. A heating unit that needs constant repair is a headache for any builder owner."

Reid finally agreed to purchase the costlier and more efficient heating systems for his new building complex. After he left, apparently satisfied, Schyler telephoned Veronica.

"This is Schyler. Still feeling your oats?"

Her laughter soothed him like a dip in the bay on a scorching-hot afternoon. "I was just about to call you. A dear friend, one of my teachers, is in town, and I'd like her to come over this evening. She'll only be here two days, and I have to entertain her. She was my psychology teacher, and she wants me to tell her about my work."

"This afternoon?"

"This evening. I thought I'd take her to one of our local restaurants."

"Am I getting the message that you can't cook?"

"Of course I can cook. It just isn't something I get a charge out of. Did your appointment go as you wanted it?"

"Just about. If I'm not seeing you tonight, that may be a good thing. Madison's firm got a court date for my retrial hearing, and that means I have a lot of work to do. Give some thought to going out to Tilghman with me Friday. All right? Call you tomorrow."

He hung up and called his father. They discussed the lighthouse and the additional work Schyler had recommended.

"You did a great job. I didn't even see those heat grates. I'd like you to go down there in a few weeks and check on the builder one last time."

"I didn't see those grates either, because they were sealed over with rust and grime. Veronica discovered one, cleaned it and found the others. She's one hard worker, and she didn't mind getting dirty and unkempt. She amazed me."

"I like everything you tell me about her. What's going on with the two of you?"

He propped both elbows on his desk and closed his eyes. "I'm not ducking the question, but I don't know. We're... we're good together, because we like so many of the same things and she's witty as well as smart. But...well, we'll see. That's all I can say."

"I see. All that tells me is that you're still putting up roadblocks."

He had been, perhaps, but nowadays he was looking for every reason to knock them down. "Give me credit for not wanting to shoot myself in the foot, Dad. If I can be patient, so can you."

He imagined that his father's face glowed as it always did when he found pleasure in a thing, and a union between his adopted son and his daughter would appear to Richard Henderson as manna from heaven.

Schyler had learned to value his father's judgment, but he dared now to question his opinion. "Why are you so certain that a relationship between Veronica and me would be a good thing?"

"Because you love her, and you hurt deep inside because you don't have her and you're scared you won't. Oh, you've made headway with her, but you're not there yet. You've got a test for her and she's got one for you. I hope I live long enough to see you two raising my grandchildren."

"I have a feeling she's not much of a cook." He didn't know why he said it, but hearing the words as they slipped out of his mouth gave him a great feeling. In that respect, at least, she wasn't perfect.

To his surprise, his father's laugh greeted him strong and hearty. "Neither was Esther, but considering her other attributes, that didn't make one bit of difference to me. Learn to cook."

He decided to have the last word. "I used to wonder how you happened to be such a good cook. Enough said."

But Richard had other ideas. "Happiness doesn't come ready-made and perfect, Son, and a smart man supplies whatever's missing. See you this weekend, I hope."

"I'll be there."

And with luck, he'd have Veronica with him. He got up from his desk, walked over to the window and gazed down at the strangers rushing along Calvert Street. Veronica had promised to ask her stepfather if he knew why her mother wanted her to find Richard Henderson, but if she'd spoken to the man about it, she obviously hadn't wanted to share his answer. Her stepfather had to know. How could you live with a person for thirty years and not know the things that were important to them? Unless, of course, Esther Overton had lived with a heavy secret. No point in thinking the worst; he'd have to wait, but the thing had to come to a head. He only hoped it wouldn't be painful for Veronica.

He awakened the next morning restless and agitated after a night of fitful sleep during which he'd watched Veronica beg a faceless man for the keys to her house. He knew what it symbolized and scolded himself for letting his doubts frustrate him to the point where he couldn't sleep. When he got to his office, he tossed his briefcase onto the chair beside his desk, sat down and telephoned Veronica.

He'd meant to ask her outright what she'd learned from her father, but when she answered, he thought better of it. "The National Symphony's playing in Druid Hill Park this evening, if you'd like to go, I'll order us a picnic supper and a couple of folding chairs and pick you up at five-thirty. What do you say?"

"Great, and I'll bring along a couple of umbrellas."

He didn't feel like bantering, but he tried to keep his tone light. "That means you'll go?"

"Why, yes, I'd love to go."

"See you at five-thirty."

He hung up and stared at the phone. She hadn't seemed a bit more sociable than he felt. He ought to call her back, but he wanted to be with her when they talked. He fidgeted with the papers on his desk, gave in to his hunch and called her.

"You didn't seem quite yourself a minute ago. Are you all right?"

"I don't feel like jumping for joy, and I gather you don't either, so maybe we'd better not go to that concert. I'd enjoy being with you, but tonight I doubt I'd hear the music."

"Just as I thought, and I probably wouldn't either. You haven't told me whether you'll go home with me this weekend. It's important to me, Veronica."

He heard her sigh and knew that she, too, wrestled with her feelings and her demons. "I haven't forgotten. Couldn't we just…just be together somewhere where we can talk. If we go to your place or mine—"

"I know. That's why I suggested the concert. Tell you what. Let's drive out to Brackton Park and picnic beside that little lake. Darkness won't fall before eight o'clock, so we'll have plenty of time."

His heartbeat returned to normal and he relaxed, relieved that she agreed. "I'm anxious to see you," he told her, aware that his words lacked passion. But she had him worried, and he didn't believe in faking his feelings.

"Me, too. See you this evening."

Veronica leaned back against the trunk of an old oak that stood in the midst of a grassy knoll not far from the lake's edge. The moon's brightness gave shadows to the well-manicured foliage and to the big oak under which they lounged. She longed to enjoy the night's beauty with Schyler but couldn't because his almost solemn mood gave her a feeling of unease. She wondered if that night would be the time when he handed her his knockout blow, his now-or-never proposition. In her state of uncertainty, her nerves seemed to scatter when he pushed the picnic basket aside and took her hand.

"Have you spoken with your stepfather since you got back?"

She told him that she had and that his condition had improved, thanks to the doctor's care, but she dreaded the topic she knew he intended to open and she didn't offer more.

"Did you ask him why your mother would want you to find your birth father?" From his voice, one might have thought he faced despair, for he spoke with a reticence that belied his normal self-assurance.

She had to work hard at controlling her emotions and her voice. "Yes, I asked him. I said I would, and I did."

"And you aren't planning to tell me what he said?"

She removed her hand from his and rubbed her elbows, well aware that she did that only when her nerves got out of hand. "I'd as soon I hadn't mentioned it to him, because I've got more questions now." She summarized her stepfather's reply. "And that's not all of it. All these years, he worked at odd jobs as a laborer, doing anything he could to eke out a meager living, and I mean *anything*. Would you believe he hurt his back rebuilding the inside of the church apse—and as a volunteer? You should see what he did; a professional couldn't have done it better. I still can hardly believe it."

He remained silent for a while, obviously musing over what she'd told him. "So we won't find out from him."

"Depends. Maybe he'll talk about it when he's more comfortable with the fact that she asked me to do it, but he won't talk until he's ready, and when he's ready I won't have to ask."

"Then it's up to us to straighten out our lives, because nobody's going to do it for us. Will you come with me this weekend? I'm not asking you to make any promises; I just want you to give a relationship between you and Dad a chance."

Might as well be honest. "Can you accept the fact that I'm petrified of the idea. He and I have begun a…a friendship, I guess you'd call it, through the mail. Suppose it's superficial and when I see him I find my feelings haven't changed? I don't want to risk hurting either of you."

"But what you feel for him *has* changed. Maybe I'm not being realistic, but I want the two of you to care for each other."

She wanted to go with him, but she got cold feet whenever she thought of her stepfather's ominous advice. "All right. I want a healing too; I just don't know how much I'm willing to invest to achieve it."

"I told you I'd always be there for you, and I mean that. I'll be by for you about noon Friday. Can you make that?"

"Sure." Three hours had elapsed, and she hadn't felt his arms around her. She leaned against his shoulder, closed her eyes and breathed deeply.

His arms immediately enclosed her. "What's the matter? Has this whole business wrung you out? It's heavy, no doubt about that, but we can't let it beat us down."

She kissed his cheek and stroked his chest, seeking evidence that he cared as deeply as she did, and his arms tightened about her. He tipped up her chin, and when she gazed into his face, what she saw in his eyes sent shivers coursing through her. She'd barely parted her lips when she felt the electric shock of his tongue probing and demanding. She gave herself over to his loving, relaxing as his kisses on her eyelids, ears, cheeks, nose and throat told her that he adored her, and she held him as tightly as her strength would allow.

"We'd better not go there, honey."

"I know, but you didn't even kiss me when I opened the door for you this evening."

His sheepish grin sent her pulse into a roll. "I wanted us to get away from that house, and anytime we get into a clinch…well, you know the rest."

Feeling reassured, she let her head loll on his shoulder. "But that's a good thing, isn't it? A good relationship needs a lot of chemistry."

He shook his head as though bemused. "You bet, and we've got enough of that for a dozen other couples. I'd better take you home. It's late, and those clouds covering the moon are getting pretty dark." He pinched her cheek playfully. "Up with you, brown-skinned beauty."

She reached for the back of his head, held it and kissed him on the mouth. "Sweet man. You've got a hold on me, you know that?"

A grin played around his lips, and his wink suggested something she knew wouldn't happen on that knoll that night. "I should hope so. I wouldn't like to be suffering from this devilish little bug all alone. Come on."

Veronica glanced at the clock on her kitchen wall and made up her mind. If her stepfather wouldn't give her the answers she sought, she had to look elsewhere. She dialed the airline, made reservations for a seven-thirty flight to Durham, reserved a rental car there and phoned for a taxi to pick her up at six the next morning. She left a message on Schyler's office phone, deliberately thwarting attempts he might make to question her about her mission. Time enough to face that when she got back. By the time he got to his office, she'd be within a few miles of Pickett.

She called her stepfather from Durham airport so as not to alarm him by walking into his house unannounced.

"You're welcome to look," he said, though she could see that he'd rather she didn't. "All your mother's personal belongings are still in those two drawers and that back closet. Keep an open mind, now, because things don't have to be what they seem. I'll fix you some breakfast."

"I don't think you should move around so much, I'll do it."

After they finished the meal, she straightened up the kitchen, went into what had once been her parents' bedroom and began her search. She discovered old photos of her maternal grandparents, and found scraps and memorabilia from every stage of her mother's life, but only a single snapshot of her life with Richard Henderson. She found old payroll and bank deposit slips dating back to her mother's single days as a high school science teacher. Totally discombobulated, she sat on the edge of the bed, breathing heavily. *A science teacher?* Then why was she living in the backwoods of Pickett, North Carolina, house cleaning and taking in laundry? And why hadn't she taught in the local high school? Another hour's search produced nothing helpful.

"Did you find anything?"

She stopped herself as she was about to tell him about the payroll and bank deposit slips, certain that he wouldn't want to answer her questions. "I went through all that before; I just wanted to satisfy myself that I hadn't missed anything."

His obvious relief was so immense that he didn't detect her evasiveness. "Do you have to go back today?"

"I'd better. I'm developing a strategy for reorganizing

the city's foster care systems, and I need to finish it as soon as possible."

"I'm glad to know you're sticking with your profession. You've put so much into it. Come see me again soon as you get a chance."

She hugged him to her, wanting him to know that despite her questions about her mother and birth father, she loved him and always would. "And next time, I'll give you enough notice so you can fix my special."

She said goodbye and left him, a lonely figure standing at the front door watching her leave. Once more, she'd come away empty-handed, this time with questions about her mother.

She walked into her house at seven-fifty that evening and put the documents she'd taken from her mother's things in her desk drawer. She had a feeling she'd need them.

Schyler listened to Veronica's voice tell him she'd decided to go back to her stepfather's home to look through her mother's belongings and that she'd be ready to go with him to Tilghman at noon on Friday. She could have called him on his cell phone or phoned him the night before, so he had to conclude that she hadn't wanted to discuss her plan with him. He didn't mind though, because she'd said she wanted a healing, and he believed she meant it. He phoned his father. No point in shocking him.

"Hi, Dad. Veronica agreed to spend the weekend with us, and we'll be down there early tomorrow afternoon. She told me she hesitated because she didn't want to hurt either of us, but that she wants a healing and that's why she's coming with me."

His father's uncustomary failure to respond where the issue of Veronica was concerned didn't sit well with him. "What's the matter? Don't you want her to come?"

"Of course I do, but I don't want either one of you to get the impression that Veronica or anyone else has the right or the power to bestow beneficence on *me*. We'll have a proper relationship when she meets me as daughter to father, not as some baroness bestowing favors."

"Wait a second. I didn't intend to imply anything of the sort."

"I know you didn't. I want a normal loving relationship with my daughter, you know that. But I pray only to God, and I don't want you to interfere. Veronica and I will come to terms. Good terms. And when we do, it will be in an atmosphere of mutual love and respect."

He defended her. "I didn't detect any arrogance in what she said. She confessed to being petrified at the possibility that she might offend us. Where's the conceit in that? I had both my arms around her when she said it, and her voice as well as her demeanor conveyed nothing but softness. Go easy, will you, Dad?"

He hadn't expected his father to laugh so soon after his testiness of minutes earlier, but laugh he did. "I'm not sure I see the humor in this," he told Richard.

"I'm not surprised. You defended her, and staunchly, too. I laughed because it pleased me. You care deeply for her. Get it into her head, Son, that her relationship with you is independent of what goes on between her and me."

"Dad, you don't—"

"I know I'm talking to the clouds. Tell her I'm looking forward to seeing her again, and that I hope she's planning to stay here this time."

Schyler allowed himself a laugh. "I didn't ask her where she's staying, because she's our guest. That means she stays here."

Richard's words were tinged with merriment. "In the fifty-eight years of my eventful life, I've never once been that certain of any woman. Right on, is all I've got to say to that."

Veronica had a premonition that she would be tested, and though she tried to imagine ways in which that could happen, she hadn't thought she'd face it as soon as she entered Richard Henderson's home. Her father opened the door for them and stood speechless while they gazed at each other. She was conscious of Schyler standing behind her not making a sound. But as she looked at her father, all she saw was her resemblance to him, and the smile that spread over her face was in recognition of that likeness. However, he accepted it as a gesture of warmth and friendliness and once again opened his arms to her. She could feel Schyler's tension radiating all around her, but in her father's eyes she saw not a challenge but an invitation. She didn't know how she did it but, with her own arms open, she stepped into his embrace.

Her father didn't prolong the embrace, but hugged her tightly, stepped back and said, "Welcome home, Daughter." She wanted to move but couldn't and stood looking up at him. There hadn't been anything phony about the way he'd held her; she felt his sincerity in every atom of her being.

"Thanks," she finally managed. "Thank you."

Schyler's hand gripped her waist as he moved to stand beside her, and in spite of her promise to herself that she'd stay cool and laid-back, she turned to him, rested her head on his shoulder and held on to him.

"All this is a bit much for her," she heard Schyler say.

"I can see that. I also see that she knows how to handle herself. Come, Veronica, and I'll show you your room."

She moved out of Schyler's arms, thankful that she hadn't cried, and followed her father. He placed her bag on a luggage rack and turned to her. "I want you to consider this as your room and you're welcome to use it anytime you like. You don't have to wait for my son to bring you."

"Thanks. It's a lovely room, and the colors are some of my favorites."

For a minute, she thought him lost in the past. "These were your mother's favorite colors, at least when I knew her."

Before she could recover from that, he spun around and left the room. Lavender, rose and pale green. Those colors remained in the bedroom that her mother had shared with her stepfather. If she didn't get to the bottom of that increasingly befuddling request, she'd lose it. She unpacked and changed into white cotton slacks, a pale green cotton T-shirt and white espadrilles. Remembering that her father relaxed in his solarium, she started toward the back of the house.

"You okay?" Schyler asked her.

"I'm fine."

"You weren't prepared for that, but you handled it well."

She didn't want him to misunderstand. "I didn't handle it. I obeyed my feelings. I turned to you because it…he'd shaken me up. I'm not going to play games; that wouldn't be fair."

"No, it wouldn't. Where were you headed?"

"Back there to his office."

"I think he's got a meal ready. It's a little late for lunch, but our supper this evening will be light."

They sat down to the table, and Veronica could hardly believe her eyes. After Richard said grace, she asked him, "How did you know I love fried catfish, hush puppies and collards?"

He nodded toward Schyler. "He told me. I also like it."

She wouldn't tell her stepfather, but she was eating the best hush puppies she'd ever tasted. "These are wonderful," she told him. "I'd love to have the recipe."

After the luncheon, which ended with chocolate cheesecake, Schyler went out back, returned with Caesar, and introduced Veronica to his dog, adding, "This woman is important to me, boy, so you take care of her." To her amazement, Caesar walked over to her, stood beside her and received a pat on the head from Schyler.

"Want to go for a walk on the beach? Caesar needs a good run."

She looked toward her father. "You don't mind staying alone?"

His smile told her she'd made him happy. "I doubt Schyler wants me to tag along with the two of you. Go ahead and enjoy yourselves."

As they walked along the narrow strip of beach, she prayed that they'd be spared a repetition of their previous parting after their first walk along the bay. He seemed content to stroll along silently, holding her hand. But she wanted to know his feelings about the way she and her father had greeted each other and the camaraderie they'd enjoyed throughout the meal. Yet, if she asked him, she might get more than she wanted to hear. After all, what was so extraordinary about a father and daughter expressing affection?

"Do you have a boat?" she asked him.

"We have one, but it's docked some miles from here. This water's too shallow for a boat. If you're here on a good day, we'll take you out. Dad sails much more often than I do, and he's a better sailor than I am. Let's start back."

When they got back to the house, Richard joined them in the living room. "Would you like to know where you got your vocal talent?" Schyler asked her.

She raised both eyebrows. "Do you sing, Father?"

He nodded, left the room and returned with a guitar. "I don't play this thing very well, but I like to strum it. Learned what little I know from my college roommate." She stared at him openmouthed when the first words of Gershwin's "I Got Plenty of Nothin'" pealed from his throat. His rich baritone flowed around them until they were caught up in the music. When at last he ended it, their silence told him how he'd awed them.

"I never dreamed... Didn't you ever consider a career as a singer?" she asked him.

He lifted his shoulder in a quick shrug, much as she'd often seen Schyler do. "It didn't once occur to me."

"I'd like to hear you," Richard told her. "Schyler and half of Baltimore were enchanted with your singing."

She didn't know why she chose it, she just opened her mouth and out flowed the first words of "If You Are But a Dream." To her embarrassment, when she glanced at Schyler, his eyes reflected every sweet thing that had ever happened between them. At the song's end, the men applauded her.

"This must be tiring for you," Richard said. "If you want to rest, we'll excuse you." She thanked him and grasped the opportunity to be alone, to think and to settle her nerves. Saturday morning and early afternoon went smoothly and without incident. She admitted to herself that she could like her father if only she could come to terms with his having deserted her mother and her when she was only two years old. It seemed out of character, but many men had reformed as they aged and matured. She'd do as she promised herself before leaving home; she would not voluntarily say or do anything that would cause Schyler pain.

However, she would learn that it was not she alone who could guide the course of their weekend. "How about getting a lesson in crabbing," Richard said to her when they'd finished lunch Saturday afternoon. "I'll get what we need, you just bring yourself."

Her instincts told her to invite Schyler to join them, and she did. However, Richard spoke before Schyler had a chance to answer. "I thought we'd give him some time to work on his project while you and I enjoy getting acquainted."

She hid her disappointment when she realized he didn't want Schyler to go with them. Richard baited the line with some uncooked chicken and dropped it behind a boulder at the edge of the water.

"That's all there is to it."

"You mean catching crabs is that simple? I had no idea."

He smiled, and she liked the way his eyes sparkled. "If you just want a mess or two, yes. But commercial fishermen bait with herring or some other oily fish and use wire crab pots that are constructed in such a way as to trap the poor crabs when they smell the fish and go after it. Just say they can get in, but they can't get out. The pots sit on the sand below the water with a long string and the crabbers' marked buoy attached to them. Frankly, it's a hazard. The men have to wear special gloves, and—"

"What's dangerous about it?"

"Those crab claws are like scissors. Anyway, that's enough of that. I've been worried about a number of things that just plain mystify me, Veronica, and I believe in cutting to the chase. There's no point in my trying to guess at the answers. I'm aware that you must have been taught some things about me that have sullied my image with you. But first, why is your name Overton? When you were conceived and when you were born, Esther was my wife, sharing my bed."

How dare he question her mother's virtue? "Are you saying you doubt you're my father?"

He bristled at that, and she could see that he had a temper. Well tough, she had one, too.

"How could you think such a thing?" he asked. "Of course not. I want to know why your last name isn't Henderson when I did not give permission for your name to be changed."

"You ought to know the answer to that," she returned hotly. "I bear the name of the man who cared for me and my mother after you walked out on us and deserted us."

He stood looming over her, his eyes wide and the veins in his face and neck protruding to twice their normal size. "What the devil do you mean by that? How dare you or anybody tell me I deserted my family! If a man said those words to me, I would flatten him and stand on him. Young lady, you apologize this minute."

"You're asking me to believe my mother lied to me. I'm sorry. She isn't here to defend herself, and I won't listen to a word against her."

Shaking uncontrollably, she gazed at him standing three feet from her as out of control as she. Shocked at the way their budding rapprochement had deteriorated, she turned and ran back to the house.

"What happened?" Schyler asked as she plowed into him, unseeing.

"It's no use. I tried. For both our sakes, I promised myself this would be a loving weekend. But he wouldn't have it that way. If you want to know what happened, ask him. I'm going home."

"But you can't."

"Don't tell me what I can't do. I'm not staying here in this house."

"All right. I'll take you home."

She'd never heard desperation shout so loudly, nor seen a man's hopes wither as he stood before her, but she heard it and saw it in Schyler. She hurt for him, but the pain that throbbed in her heart was for herself. She'd never been so at sea. She had to find out why her mother had wanted her to meet Richard Henderson, but he was no longer a source of information because they had just aborted their relationship.

Chapter 11

Schyler parked in front of the little brown town house at 31 Comfort Road and turned to the somber-faced woman beside him. "I'm sorry it didn't work out the way I'd hoped. When you put your arms around him as we entered the front door, I could barely contain what I felt."

"I'm sorry, too. Will you...come in for a few minutes?"

He knew she was reaching for some way to bridge the chasm that gaped between them, and he'd make the effort, but not right then. He was still dealing with the shock of having his hopes scattered around him like so much discarded rubble.

"Not this evening. I told Dad I'd be back as soon as I took you home."

"You're going back to Tilghman now?"

"I've to talk with him. I'll call you later tonight."

She turned to face him. "I thought this was it, that after what happened, you'd break things off."

He leaned back in the seat and closed his eyes. "If you didn't mean anything to me, I'm sure I would."

He got out, got her bag out of the trunk, opened the passenger's door and walked with her to her front door. He didn't feel affectionate, but he didn't want to widen the breach or to hurt her, so he kissed her briefly on the mouth, looked down at her and at his dreams.

"I imagine you feel as rotten as I do. Remember, nothing stays the same. Call you later."

Driving across the Chesapeake Bay Bridge on his way back to Tilghman, he wondered not for the first time what his father might have said or asked that set off Veronica. He was certain that Richard had planned that crabbing trip to the beach in order to have time alone with her, and he knew his father didn't bite his tongue when he had something to say.

"I expect you broke all the speed limits again," Richard said when Schyler walked into the house at eight o'clock that evening.

"You could say I didn't waste any time. What do I smell?"

"Stuffed crabs with shrimp sauce."

"Any garlic left in the state of Maryland?" Small talk. When had he and his father ever been self-conscious around each other? After one of the best meals he'd had recently, he cleaned up the kitchen and went to his room to get his thoughts together. But Richard didn't give him time to simmer.

He answered the soft knock. "Come on in. I'd planned to go have a chat with you, but as long as you're here, have a seat."

Richard sat on the bench at the foot of Schyler's king-size bed. "I don't remember things having been strained between us, and I don't want that to happen now."

"There's no need for that now, either. Tell me what happened out there."

Richard related to Schyler his exchange with Veronica. "It's been galling me that her name is Overton, and that Esther allowed another man to adopt my daughter. Every time I think about it, my gut ties in a knot."

"And that caused the argument, I suppose."

Richard got up and began to walk from one end of the room to the other. "No. I told her that if a man had said to my face that I deserted my family, I'd knock him down and stomp him. Yes, I was furious and demanded that she apologize, but she's been so thoroughly brainwashed for so long that she refused to believe Esther could have lied to her. She walked off, and it was a good thing, because I was almost insane with anger. Damn it, I loved my family, I…never mind. That's water under the bridge. It's enough that I have to live with the pain."

"She told me you'd deserted her and her mother, but I didn't believe it, and I told her it was impossible. I've known since she met you that she believed that story and that her coolness toward you was because of it."

"Not one word of it is true."

He stood, jammed his hands in his pants pockets and leaned against the doorjamb. Just as Schyler had feared, he stood between them.

"I knew that without your telling me. I…I've got some thinking to do."

Richard stopped pacing and pointed a finger at him. "Now you just wait a minute. This has nothing to do with you and Veronica. I've told you before that it's between her and me."

"It's not that simple. I'm split in half right now. I left her to come back here and comfort you, but my mind and my spirit are in Owings Mills with her. If I dropped it, I'd at least have my sanity."

"You can't drop it, Son, because it won't leave you. Loving a person doesn't mean things are perfect, and you'll learn that whatever and whoever gets in its way has to move, because love doesn't give quarter. So when you decide you can quit loving her, remember the story of my life."

Schyler ran his fingers through his hair as a restlessness suffused him. "Dad, if she grew up with lies about you, what about me? The social workers led me to believe that my mother was probably little more than a streetwalker. Suppose that isn't true either."

He had to wait a while for his father's response. "You're up against a hard rock right now with a lot of things piled on you, so don't go adding another one."

"But wouldn't I feel a lot better if I discovered that what I believe isn't true?"

"And how would you feel if you discovered that it is true?"

He shrugged. "I can take it. Having you for a father has been the best buffer a kid could have. None of that can hurt me." He looked at his watch. "I told Veronica I'd call her, and I don't know what kind of shape she's in, so—"

"I'll be in the solarium if you still want to talk."

"Thanks, I...thanks."

He took a moment to meditate, then dialed her number.

She lifted the receiver hesitantly, anxious as to what the call would bring. She'd had five hours during which to relive the encounter with her father and the silence that had hung so ominously between Schyler and her as he drove her home. In her heart, she knew she didn't want a break with her father, and the thought of a permanent breach with Schyler had robbed her of her appetite.

"Hello."

"This is Schyler. How are you right now?"

Her heartbeat fluttered madly. "I'm so glad you called. I've gone over and over that incident with my father. I... Oh, Schyler, I'm drained."

"We all are, but this isn't the end of the world, Veronica. We'll salvage what we can; if we can't mend this, we'll be adults, say we tried and get on with our lives."

She bristled. "I forgot how mad you can make me when

you put yourself to it. If you're telling me you can snap your fingers and I'll be out of your life, hang up, or I will."

"Honey, what's wrong with you? Your misunderstanding is with your father, not me, and I'm talking about the two of you. Get off your high horse. Oh, for Pete's sake. I didn't call to aggravate you."

She shook her head in dismay. If she weren't so vulnerable to him, she wouldn't say things to him that caused misunderstandings. "I know you didn't call to upset me; it's just that I'm…I'm—"

"You're miserable, and that's understandable."

She rubbed her forehead with the tips of the fingers on her left hand, symbolically erasing her pain. "The more I mull over this, the more I realize I don't want a break with my father, but, Schyler, he implied something awful about my mother. Somebody has to straighten out this mess. I can't figure out whether she was telling me she wronged him or me, both or neither of us. And Father reacted so harshly. He erupted in fury."

"He's got a temper all right, and if he's wrongfully accused, anger hardly covers it."

She couldn't help laughing. "I suppose you noticed that my own temper takes a lot of managing. Since Mama never got angry at anybody, I can see where I got it," she said when he questioned the humor in the situation.

"I suppose he told you I defended my mother. That finished it. I walked off because I figured he couldn't stand the sight of me after that…that awful business out there on the beach. I wish I hadn't gone home with you."

"You're wrong. Did you think you two would never have a confrontation, that you'd tiptoe around each other pretending things were getting better? Now that you know where you stand with each other because you've aired your grievances, maybe you can make some progress."

"You haven't given up?"

"It takes more than a little wind to knock me over. I won't say I'm unaffected; what wounds you or my dad also hurts me, so I don't feel any better than you do. But I know both of you deep down, and I still have hope. Could we see each other tomorrow? I need a professional consultation with you."

She couldn't imagine what for. "Sure. Where? How about lunch or dinner?"

"Dinner. I'll cook," he said.

"It's a date."

"I'll send a car for you at six-thirty. Till then—"

"Wait. May I speak with my father?"

She knew she'd surprised him, but if she didn't reach out to her father now, it would be that much harder in the days to come.

"You want… Sure. Good night, sweetheart."

She made the sound of a kiss. "Good night, honey."

"Hello, Veronica. I'm glad you want to talk," Richard said, "because we have to settle a few things. But meantime, I want you to remember that a father's love isn't easily lost. It is without end."

"Thanks. I wanted you to know that I'm sorry for upsetting you, but I've been on edge ever since Mama told me to find you. I hope we…that we can get past this explosive topic."

"We'll get past it, now that I know what I'm up against. Try not to worry, and come to see me often. Your room is here for you."

She thanked him and meant it, though she wouldn't have thought his anger had dissipated so thoroughly. Just like me, she thought. She hung up, warmed up the soup she hadn't been able to eat, made a sandwich and ate her supper.

She answered her doorbell at exactly six-thirty the following evening and could hardly suppress a laugh when she looked at the man standing there in his chauffeur's uniform. She followed him to the silver gray Lincoln Town Car and settled in for the twenty-minute ride, wondering what Schyler was up to. She hadn't gone for broke but had worn a royal blue Fuji silk tunic over matching pants and a single strand of long pearls.

When he pursed his lips in a mock whistle, she knew she'd chosen the right thing. He stopped her just inside the door and opened his arms to her. She hadn't known what to expect, and as her blood zinged through her throbbing veins, she reached out to him.

"Baby, come here and let me hold you." Tension gathered in her and she flung her arms open wide, eager for his touch, his taste, his scent, all of him. He lifted her up and twirled her around, but she wanted, needed more. She grasped his shoulders and shimmied down his body until she could reach his lips.

"Kiss me. Love me. Tell me it's all right with us," she whispered.

He held her away from him and looked down into her face, and what she saw in his eyes nearly unglued her. His mouth was on her then, and her parted lips soon knew the wonder of his tongue claiming, branding and loving her. She could hardly bear the tenderness with which he held her close, stroking her back and telling her that he needed her as much as she needed him.

He tipped up her chin with his right index finger. "Honey, you know it isn't perfect. It's never been, but you also know that it will take more than an argument or a misunderstanding to keep us apart. We'll work through this. You took a big step telling my dad you hadn't wanted to upset him and in letting me know that, cool as things were between us, you'd still help me if I needed you."

She let her head rest on his shoulder. "Is there really some way I can help you?"

He led her to the living room. "I meant that. I'll tell you after dinner."

"Thanks for that classy trip over here."

He raised an eyebrow. "You didn't think I'd send a taxi for you. Since I was stuck here in the kitchen, I sent the next best thing."

She trailed him into the kitchen, sat on a stool and crossed her knees. "Want me to help?"

"What? And ruin my reputation? Definitely not." He tossed the salad with what seemed like homemade dressing. "You're my guest."

After their meal of roast chicken, potato fritters, steamed asparagus, arugula salad and double-chocolate ice cream, he closed the kitchen door and headed for his den.

"I'll clean the kitchen tomorrow. Want to hear some Buddy Guy?"

She couldn't believe it. "You like him, too? I love the man, but I've had enough of the blues for one day."

His grin began around the edge of his lips and fought its way to his remarkable eyes. "Me, too, for that matter. Veronica, hearing my dad swear that he'd been misrepresented to you brought back a question that has plagued me since my childhood. The agency records indicated the possibility that my mother may have been a street woman, and one of my foster mothers as much as told me that. I want to know if it's true."

"But...Schyler, do you want to dig into something that may make you unhappy?"

"The answer won't upset me. What happened before Dad adopted me can't ever hurt me again. Except for my marriage and the trouble it brought me, my life since I met my dad has made up for everything I suffered before. He's given me a wonderful life, but I want to know the truth about my parentage."

"But suppose she doesn't want to be found. I mean—"

"I don't want to find her. I don't even want to know who she is, only the truth about her. Can you help me?"

"If you're sure."

"I am."

He might be sure, but she wasn't. "All right, and while we're straightening things out, what about your case?"

"I have a court date three weeks from now, and all of my papers are in order."

She folded and unfolded her hands, hoping he hadn't noticed, because she didn't want to put a damper on his optimism. "That's great. Let's hope your ex-father-in-law doesn't settle out of court."

"He can't, because the employee he's accusing has entered a countersuit against him." She made a show of looking at her watch, because she believed the first bed she got into should be her own and that, when she did, she should be alone.

"Thanks for a wonderful dinner. It's time I headed home."

His fiery gaze held an unmistakable question. *Are you sure?* he silently asked.

She stood and reached for his hand. "You're a wonderful host, and your cooking skills will beat etchings as a lure for us females any day."

His laughter surprised her. "Didn't you do the cooking?" she asked him.

He laughed harder. When he could, he said, "If I cook dinner for you fifty times, you'll get the same thing, except sometimes I change the vegetable."

She nodded. "Maybe I'd better do something like that, perfect two or three menus, I mean."

That grin again. "Works for me. Say, how're you coming along with that plan for reorganizing the foster care system?"

"I sent it in last Friday. I called someone I knew and was told that if I made even a crumb of sense, it would probably be accepted, because everyone's unhappy with the current directives."

"I wish you luck. The thing's archaic, practically the same as it was when I was a child." He walked with her to the door. "I'm driving you home. Why should that chauffeur have the pleasure?"

An hour later, she tuned her television to a late-night talk show and listened to a condemnation of the foster care system. She went to bed confident that her plan would make a difference, that Schyler cared for her, and that her father wouldn't rush her into a superficial resolution of their relationship.

For hours after he'd returned home, Schyler sat on his balcony listening to the night's sounds. He conceded that he was at a crossroads in his life. Veronica and his dad would mend their relationship, because they had planted the seed and begun cultivating it. Furthermore, she'd said she didn't want to break with her father. What remained was for the two of them to work out their problems. He hadn't wanted her to leave him, though he knew she'd done the right thing, because sex was no substitute for understanding; it only camouflaged the problem. They were at a standstill in their relationship, and that wasn't a good thing. He didn't believe in treading water. You either swam or got out of the pool. He needed her with him all the time. Permanently. But she hadn't given him one clue as to whether she had similar thoughts about him.

And another thing. It didn't make sense for a woman of her competence to while away the time, but whose fault was it? If he'd investigated Natasha Wynn's case more thoroughly, he wouldn't have sought an indictment against Veronica and CPAA. Oh, hell. He *had* investigated it properly, but his own experience with foster homes had made him so emotionally involved in the case that he'd misjudged it. He got up and began pacing the balcony. In spite of all she'd suffered because of that indictment, she didn't hold it against him. And even though their relationship wasn't what either of them wanted and needed it to be, she was ready to help him with his own personal problem. He'd find a way to make it up to her, because she deserved better than she'd gotten.

The next morning he telephoned her as soon as he reached his office. "Hi. Could you sleep well last night?"

"I dozed off thinking about you. That usually works."

"When are you going to end your long vacation? Things

are going well for me here at Branch Signal, and I'd feel more like rejoicing if you could say the same."

"Don't punish yourself about that case, Schyler. You—"

He interrupted her. "Could you call me honey, dear, friend…something other than Schyler? I love my name, but I want to hear something more intimate from your lips."

Her silence told him he'd surprised her, because Veronica was never speechless. "If that's the way you're feeling," she said at last, "maybe insisting on going home last night was a mistake."

Energy began gathering in his belly. "I wanted you to stay. Make no mistake about that, but I knew you read it right. We've hit the heights, and we did that because we were open to each other. Last night, we were trying to heal. Our day will come again, babe. Look, I know you don't hold that Natasha Wynn fiasco against me, but it sticks in my craw like wet cement. Have you looked around?"

"I'm on a three-month leave of absence that expired last week, and I got paid for every day. The board of directors extended my leave for six weeks without my having asked. So I'm employed. The question is when or whether I want to go back there and resume that thankless grind. And another thing: I refuse to work with that obsolete foster care system."

"You've done what you can to change the system. If the plan goes through, will you go back soon?"

"I don't know. I'm not the same person, and I like myself better. Why should I—"

"You are even more admirable now. I know you miss that status, but you can get it back."

"I don't miss it, Schy…, but I'm not sure I want to work twelve hours a day for people who cast me aside even after I'd been exonerated."

"I understand that, because I went through it, and I'm still feeling it. I won't press you more right now, but please think hard about this. Promise?"

"Promise. Here's a kiss."

"Back at you. Bye for now, sweetheart."

What was he thinking about? "Wait. Fax me a copy of that plan."

He read it as it came through his machine. Brilliant. Simple and brilliant. He dashed over to his office at Advocates for the Child, called a meeting of the paid staff and gave them copies of Veronica's plan for overhauling the foster care system.

"Call everybody you know who has any influence and push for its adoption. If you have any problems, call me over at Branch Signal."

He strode back to Branch Signal on wings, whistling as he went. Veronica had laid out a wonderful system, so simple he couldn't imagine that no one else had thought of it. His chest swelled with pride. He intended to fight for it as hard as he'd ever worked for anything.

This was his day, he decided, when he walked into his Branch Signal office and looked at the papers his secretary had spread out on his desk. *An apartment for Jenny.* He had plenty of work facing him, but he rushed out of the Drake building, got in his car and headed for West Baltimore and the social agency that had taken responsibility for Jenny. He got the keys and went to the apartment. A comfortably furnished bedroom, living room, dinette, kitchen and bath. He sat down in the nearest chair and said a prayer of thanks. More excited than he remembered having been in years, he'd driven halfway to Owings Mills before questioning the wisdom of going unannounced to Veronica.

He called her on his cell phone. "I've got such wonderful news that I'd driven almost to your place before thinking about where I'd headed."

"Come on. I can't wait to know what happened."

He walked in the door, picked her up and whirled around with her before putting the keys in her hand.

She looked from him to the keys she held. "What's this for?"

"Jenny's apartment. Can you believe it? She'll be off the street."

A look of disbelief spread over her face. "You wouldn't joke about this, would you?"

He shook his head. "Come on. Let's go get her. She has to go to the agency tomorrow morning."

She hugged him fiercely, and he basked in it. "You're a wonderful man. I'd better find something for her to wear. I've got a couple of shift dresses that might fit her. Oh, what the heck. I'll take her shopping."

At five o'clock that afternoon, they sat in the living room of Jenny's new apartment waiting for her to take her shower, something she'd insisted on doing as soon as she'd looked around her new home.

"Did you ever see such happiness on anybody's face?" Veronica asked him.

He shook his head. "This is one of the best things that's ever happened to me." He turned to face her fully. "Honey, this is almost the way I felt when my dad showed me the papers that said he was officially my father. Do you still resent his having adopted me? Do you?"

Her eyes, soft but devoid of passion, sent him a new and very different message. "I don't begrudge you that or any other good thing that has ever happened to you. Schyler, I love you."

His heart skidded down into his belly, thundering wildly. "Wh…What did you say?"

Her fingers stroked his cheek. "How could you not know it? Did you think I would have gone to that lighthouse with you, even the first time, if I hadn't loved you?"

The words he would have spoken were held captive, trapped in the air that lodged in his throat. He wanted to believe her; he *had* to believe her. Practically springing from his chair, he lifted her and held her tight to his body, praying for the words that would tell her what he felt. "I love you, baby. *I love you!* I…"

He found her parted lips and settled his mouth on her, letting his pent-up, fermented passion flow into her. "I've loved you since the first time I saw you. Oh, I fought it, and I may wrestle with it again, but it's always been there. I knew you cared, but to love me—"

"If you'd hurry up and marry Ronnie like I told you, Schyler, y'all could make out in y'all's own house. Not that I mind. Ronnie, I'm gon' make your wedding dress, and Mr. Dior gon' turn black when he sees it. I'm gon' plain outdo myself."

At Veronica's stunned expression, she assured her. "Child, they sold my clothes in the big Madison Avenue stores in New York. I know what to do when it comes to sewin'. Give me six months, and I'm gon' kiss welfare goodbye. And I ain't chargin' you nothin' for that dress neither. Y'all got me this place, took me shoppin', filled up my refrigerator and give me money to start me off. Child, I plans to make all your children's clothes."

She threw out her arms. "Schyler, I can't count the money Ronnie done give me. 'Course, I'm gon' make her bridal clothes."

"You don't have to go that far, Jenny," Veronica said. "I just want us to remain friends. Good friends."

Jenny sat down, barely recognizable in her powder blue pique shift and white sandals. "I know I ain't in your class, Ronnie, and I don't expect to be buddy-buddy with you, but I appreciates your friendship."

Happiness radiated from Veronica, happiness not for herself but for Jenny. He thought his heart would burst. At last he had the love of a compassionate woman, a caring woman. A sweet woman who knew how to give of herself and enjoyed doing it. He squeezed her hand, but he knew that nothing he did or said could communicate to her the depth of his feelings.

Chapter 12

Veronica knew she could find out about Schyler's mother on her own, but decided against it, lest she arouse media attention. She called Enid.

"He wants to know his mother's background," Veronica explained when Enid questioned her. "He doesn't want to meet her or to know who she is. And don't send what you find to me. Mail it to him at his home address. Here's the information."

"Okay. Call you back this afternoon," Enid said. "Oh, by the way, I'd like you to be my maid of honor."

Could that shriek have come from her mouth? "Enid! Oh, honey, I'm so happy for you. Of course I'll be your maid of honor. Have you picked out your dress?"

"Not yet. He just asked me last night."

"How about going with me to talk with someone about your dress? You're not obligated. Just see what she has to offer."

"Sure. How's tomorrow after I get off?"

They agreed on a time and place to meet. "What's happen-

ing with you and Schyler?" Enid asked. "Isn't it time something started cooking with you two?"

"Something *is* happening. A lot, in fact. I—"

"You love him?"

"Enid, I loved that man ages ago, and he…loves me."

"Then what's his problem? Isn't he ready to take the next
step?"

"You got engaged last night, and we confessed to each
other yesterday afternoon, so we're a little behind you. Our
relationship has been staggering under some heavy weights,
but I think we may get there."

"I sure hope so. You can't stop love, kiddo, so quit fooling around. A woman is supposed to tie a guy like Schyler
into knots and, if necessary, hit him over the head and drag
him to the altar. He's a peach of a man. If he loves you and
it swings good in the sack, what on earth are you waiting for?"

"Is that how things worked with you and Madison?" she
asked with tongue in cheek.

Veronica crossed her leg and swung it back and forth, delighted that she'd made Enid back down. But her friend surprised her.

"I didn't have to hit him over the head and threaten to drag
him to the church, but you can bet on the rest of it. By the way,
I've crocheted six more caps and mittens, and I'm out of thread."

"My. My. We did get out of that one in a hurry, didn't we?
I've got a couple more sets to knit, and I'll have my quota.
Crochet as many as you can."

"Say, you didn't tell me whether you went to see your
birth father."

"I did, but I still don't know why Mama wanted me to.
We're working on our relationship. He's likable, handsome,
a striking figure of a man. And would you believe I look just
like him? We can talk tomorrow when we meet."

Veronica hung up and went to her front door to get *The*

Maryland Journal. She drained her second cup of coffee and turned to the features page.

Her eyes widened in stunned disbelief. For the last five years, she had presided over the city's annual social welfare conference, but this year, she hadn't even received an announcement. Her stomach burned and wobbled until it could hold nothing. She washed her face in cold water and shrugged her shoulders. Just one more indicator of human fickleness. In years past, the organizers had said they couldn't manage without her. At least she hadn't believed them.

Thoroughly shaken but determined not to let it beat her down, she put on a pair of white jeans, a green T-shirt and sneakers and walked six blocks to the bowling alley. She hadn't been there in nearly a year and didn't expect to see anyone she knew. Her friends would be working that time of day.

"What a surprise! Haven't seen you around. Did you come for a game or an early lunch?"

Her mind told her lunch took less time than bowling, because she could leave when she finished eating. If she bowled, Heddie Morton would insist on "one more game" until nightfall.

"I'm headed for the dining room," she told her.

"Good, so am I," was Heddie's expected response. "I heard your Mom passed, and I wanted to tell you how sorry I am. She taught me in the sixth grade, you know, and she was such a nice teacher. Never got upset about anything. Must have been wonderful having a calm person for a mother. Mine screamed and shouted at us children from morning until night. I thought every adult was like that until I went to school."

Fortunately, Veronica didn't splatter the soup all over herself when she dropped the spoon. "You sure it was my mother who taught you?"

"It was the same name, and the notice said she taught sixth grade science at McKinley, and that was my school."

The sudden dryness of her mouth made it difficult to speak,

so she took a few sips of water. She didn't need this reminder that she had no idea who her own mother really was. No one had ever told her that Esther Overton had taught at McKinley. "You never mentioned to me that you knew her."

"I didn't know until lately that she was your mother. You know, this good-looking man used to meet her after school, and us kids always watched to see if he'd kiss her. Some of us girls had an awful crush on him."

Her antenna shot up, but that bit of information didn't help, because both her father and her stepfather were strikingly good-looking. She'd better not encourage Heddie, because the woman always embellished things, and you had to piece the facts together.

"Thank you for telling me that, Heddie."

"She left right in the middle of the term. For such a nice lady, you would have thought she'd have given notice, or at least told us kids she was leaving, but one day she just didn't come to school."

Veronica frowned. Something didn't add up. "How did you know she was my mother?"

Heddie lowered her gaze, as though in deference to the dead. "I always read the obituaries. Every single day, I read them, and I saw this notice about Esther Overton nee Hunt who was survived by Sam Overton and their daughter, Veronica. I sure was sorry."

She got away from the woman as soon as she could and left the sports club. Her steps lacked their usual spring as she walked home, nearly unraveled by Heddie's words. Her stepfather had just demonstrated that he could rebuild a church apse, giving it an elegance superior to its original state. Yet, for thirty years he'd eked out a living cutting and hauling wood, cleaning anything anyone would hire him to clean, scraping floors, unclogging drains and trenches and doing assorted other kinds of laborious work. And her mother! If she could teach science in a Baltimore middle school, why had she worked all those years as a domestic and laundress? What else didn't she know?

She let herself in her house and sat down. She had to think. After a while, vacillating between anger and sadness, she pulled herself together and called her stepfather.

"Papa, did you put an obituary for Mama in the paper?"

"Yes, I did. In the *Afro*. Why, did you see it? I saved a copy, but I keep forgetting to give it to you."

"I'll look at it next time I go home. Have you thought any more about why Mama would want me to find my birth father?"

"You could say I've hardly been thinking about anything else. I hope you'll take my advice and drop it. She might not have known what she was saying."

Veronica knew better, but she kept that to herself. After the shock she'd just had, she didn't have the strength to confront him, but she was beginning to realize she'd have to do exactly that. "You feeling all right now?" she asked him.

"I'm fine. I've almost finished figuring out what to do with that church. When you get back here and see what I've done, you will be surprised."

She was already surprised. She laid the phone in its cradle and for the first time, considered that her parents might not have squared with her. Mother said yes, and Father said no. Whom was she supposed to believe? What a cloud of confusion to lay on a child!

As soon as she hung up, Enid called. "I just mailed Schyler the information he's after, and I'm sure he'll be pleased with what he sees. I gotta get back to work. See you tomorrow."

Veronica wrapped her arms around her middle and stretched out her feet. She wanted to call him, but she couldn't because she wasn't supposed to know what was in that letter.

"If we have any children, at least we won't have to tell them their grandmother was a streetwalker," she said aloud. She got

up and walked out on her porch and stood there looking at
nothing in particular, killing time until he called.

At that very moment, Veronica filled Schyler's thoughts.
He looked at his engraved invitation to the banquet of the
annual social welfare conference and the program listing the
names of the notables expected to attend, and the wind gushed
out of him. They'd ignored her. In seven months, she'd slipped
from star attraction to *unperson.* He had two invitations, and
he'd invite her to go as his guest. If she refused to accompany
him, he wouldn't attend. He called her.

"Hello, sweetheart. This is the most important man in your
life. Scratch that. This is *the* man in your life. How are you?"

"Hi, honey. I'll second that as long as you understand that
you're speaking to the one woman who lights up *your* life."

He settled back in his high-back, tufted leather chair and
strummed the desktop with the fingers of his left hand. "Well
now, it wouldn't make sense to waste my time arguing against
that. This...er...woman you're talking about...does she have
a tall, shapely brown frame and big brown eyes with long
sweeping lashes? Fine. This dame who lights up my life is
something fine. You talking about her?"

"Could be. She has her moments. But she's got this
guy...this fellow who strokes her whole being, just gets her so
mellow she hears the angels sing. This brother... Lord, sometimes when I think about him, I see gray stars. You know, like
the ones always sparkling in those eyes of his. Talking about
fine! He's out of sight! That the one you're talking about?"

She'd lifted his mood, and he let himself enjoy a good
laugh. "Baby, I'll take all the flowers you send me. Sure, I'm
talking about that guy. Makes the angels sing, huh? Not bad
for a fellow who started life as an orphan. Reminds me I've
got to make a final check of the Rock Island lighthouse a few
weeks from now. Dad hasn't had time to draw plans for all
the changes we suggested, but he ought to finish them soon

and send them to the architect. I think of it as our lighthouse,
and I'd like you to go with me."

"Just say when, and I'll start packing."

No point in putting it off. "I got an invitation today to the
conference banquet, and I noticed that you aren't among the
expected guests. I'd like you to come with me."

He should have waited until he was with her. "What is it?
Veronica, please say something."

He supposed she was struggling for control, because being
excluded from an event that she'd championed and over which
she had presided had to hurt. "Listen, baby, I know this is a
nasty pill, but you're not alone in this. I'm here for you. Come
with me and show them they can't beat you down. I'd give
anything if I cold relive the month of March."

"You mean February, since that's when you made that fatal
decision. Schyler, I want you to get rid of this guilt. You did
what you thought was right, and you are not responsible for
the fickleness of humankind."

A feminist to the core. "All right, but will you go with me?
Let the bastards know you're unbowed."

Her laughter wrapped around him, a spirit that renewed and
uplifted him. "Why are you laughing?"

"Such strong language coming from you. If you're that exasperated about it, I'll go. I confess to being hurt and angry when
I realized they'd ignored me, but after an hour or so, I said the
heck with it and let it roll off me like water off a bird's back."

"You'll go to that banquet with me?"

"Yes, and the more I think about it, the more I love the idea.
Pull out your best tux and your red accessories, because—"

He howled with laughter, with relief and joy that she'd
come through it and could laugh in their faces. "I know. I get
the message. You're going for broke, and with all those old
fuddyduds there, you'll be the only one in the place wearing
a daring red dress."

The peals of laughter that reached him through the wire

brought him to his feet; he wanted to embrace her and the whole world.

"Sir, you know me too well. I'll have to call Enid and ask her not to wear red. Say, did you know she and Madison are getting married?"

"No I didn't, but he once indicated to me that that was his aim. I'll have to call and congratulate him. Stay sweet."

"You, too. Here's a kiss."

She'd show the whole bunch of them, bless Schyler. And wouldn't they be shocked to see her stroll in with the CEO of Advocates for the Child, the same man who'd prosecuted her and her agency and lost the case against them. She got her knitting bag and worked on the last three caps and mittens until eight o'clock that evening, when she finished them. She let out a long breath, satisfied with what she'd accomplished, and put them away. Eventually, she'd wrap them in twenty-five separate gift packages and store them until the homeless shelter had its annual Christmas party.

What a day! She'd been down, and she'd been up. She went to sleep wrestling with the mystery of her parents and step-father, as their images frolicked along the unpaved road called Cooks Row in Pickett, North Carolina. She woke up shortly after midnight exhausted, imagined herself in Schyler's arms and was soon asleep again.

As agreed the previous morning, Veronica met Enid at Wilma's, where they each had a glass of wine. She told her friend what she knew about Jenny and suggested they visit her and see what she could do.

Enid rolled her eyes and tapped her fingers on the table. "Veronica, are you suggesting I let this woman make my wedding dress, when she hadn't even been inside a house in nearly two years until a couple of days ago?"

"I said let's go talk with her and see what she can do. If her things sold in New York's Madison Avenue shops, I'll know it as soon as we get to talking. And if they didn't, I'll know that, too."

Enid took a small mirror from her purse and checked her lipstick. "That's right. I forgot you always wear designer clothes. Let's go."

They found Jenny hard at work making sample dresses. "This shore is a fine sewin' machine Schyler bought me, Ronnie. I went out and got me three fashion magazines and things I needed. Let me show you what I made."

Enid's bottom lip dropped when Jenny showed them an ice-blue silk sheath and matching redingote, both lined with a lighter weight, printed silk of blending colors.

"I copied it from this *Vogue,*" Jenny said, showing them the picture. "What you think, Ronnie? You like my work?"

Veronica shook her head in wonder. How a person with such talent could have floundered on the street for nearly two years was beyond her comprehension. "Jenny, honey, I've been wearing designer clothes for years, but I haven't had anything of this quality. Where'd you learn to sew?"

The woman's pride shone like bright sunlight. "Right at my mama's feet. Her and her three sisters all sewed, and I learned just watchin' them from the time I knowed myself. I sure am glad you like it, but I knowed you would."

Veronica noticed that Enid had dropped out of the conversation and was concentrating on the fashion magazines. She handed Jenny the *Elle* magazine and pointed to a wedding dress.

"Can you make this one for me?"

Jenny glanced at it. "I sure can, but here, look in this bride's book before you makes up your mind. They's higher-class styles in there."

"Look at this, Veronica. Just look at this. It's the one. Can you make it, Jenny?"

Jenny didn't look at the picture Enid showed her. "Honey, I can make anything in there just like you sees it. Just give me what material I ax you for, and I'll make it."

"What do you charge?"

Jenny looked at Veronica, obviously distressed. "I don't know. You my first customer. I just needs enough so I can get off welfare."

Veronica didn't intend for Jenny to work for donkey wages. "Charge by the amount of time you have to spend on it, Jenny. How long will that take you?"

She could see that the woman was uncomfortable. "With that beadin' on it, it'll take a while."

"Start with twenty-five dollars an hour. If you know the person is rich, charge more."

"But Ronnie, I ain't never made that much money in my life."

"That's why you were on the street," Enid chimed in. "You make that dress for me, and I'll pay what you charge. I'll bring the material one day next week. Do you have a card?"

Jenny laughed. "A card? You makin' fun of me?"

"No, I'm not," Enid said. "And when I come back, I'll bring you a box full."

Veronica handed Jenny the *Vogue* opened to a page that showed a striking white evening gown. "I want that in red," Veronica told her.

Jenny looked at it for a few minutes. "If you want somethin' great, bring me seven yards of silk taffeta and seven yards of silk crepe de chine same color."

Just before they separated after having left Jenny, Enid said to Veronica, "Give me her phone number and I'll put ads for her in *The Maryland Journal* and the *Afro*. That ought to get her started."

Veronica hugged her friend. "That's great. Let me know what you want me to wear in your wedding, because she'll have to make that too." All she could think of as she passed Jenny's now-forsaken corner on the way to her train was Schyler. He'd gotten Jenny off that corner, and for that alone she'd do anything for him.

* * *

He bolted upright, banging his kneecap against the edge of his desk as he did so. But not even the pain engaged his attention.

"Well, I'll be." There it was, spread out before him. He rang Veronica's phone and got no answer. When his father didn't answer, he dialed his cell phone.

"Richard Henderson speaking."

"Dad. I've got it. It's right here in front of me, and—"

"Slow down, Son. What is it?"

He stared down at the notarized form. "It's about my mother. She wasn't what they said. All these years, I thought she was a prostitute or pretty close to it. Dad, she belonged to a prominent family that turned her out when she got pregnant. She was seventeen. The social agency placed me with a foster care family until they could arrange an adoption. I lived with five foster mothers before you adopted me."

"I'm glad for you, Son, but I want you to know it never mattered to me. Are you going to look for her?"

"No. The funny thing is I don't care who she is. I don't want to foul up her life, and I don't want mine turned around. And I don't resent her, though at seventeen, she could have made other arrangements. I have all the information about her that I need."

"How'd you find out?"

He rubbed the left side of his jaw, still unable to believe what he saw. "Two or three days ago, I told Veronica what I wanted, and I just got this report from her agency. This is great, I tell you."

"Have you told her?"

"She's not home."

"Well, you keep that document. Your children may someday want to know."

He hadn't considered that. "Yeah. You've got a point. Have you finished that plan?"

"I sent it off yesterday, and I've told that architect I don't want any fuzzy work this time—he either does what I want or he doesn't get paid."

"He did a good job, Dad. Veronica and I didn't find too many problems."

He heard his father clear his throat, which meant don't press it. "One of those boo-boos was one error too many."

"Well, let me know when he finishes it."

"Are you taking Veronica with you when you go back?"

He frowned, not sure what the question meant. "Uh… Yes, I am. She's anxious to go. And she made an excellent inspector, because she questioned everything. Besides, she enjoyed being there so much that I…I wouldn't go without asking her if she'd like to join me."

"Hmmm. I see. Give her my love."

"Thanks. I will."

At least his father had the grace not to say what he thought. He knew his dad wanted them to get together, but it would work itself out. He wasn't stupid; he knew what she meant to him. He wondered if he could wear the same red accessories he'd worn when they visited Madison. Better be sure. He rummaged in his pockets until he found Jenny's phone number.

"Jenny, this is Schyler. How's it going?"

"Schyler?" She sounded mystified.

"Right."

"Schyler! I got work, Schyler. Ronnie brought her friend over, and I'm makin' her wedding dress."

"Did Veronica ask you to make anything for her?"

"Did she! She shore did, but I ain't sure I'm supposed to tell you."

"Is it a red evening dress?"

"How'd you know? I…mean. You caught me."

He'd give it a shot. "Can you make me a cummerbund?"

"Sure. The tie and hankie, too. You tie your own, don't you?"

He assured her he did. "Well just send me your shirt size

and your belt size, and I'll make them out of the cloth I use for Ronnie's dress. But you let that surprise her now. You hear?"

"You sound elated, Jenny, and I'm happy for you."

"The Lord's gon' bless you, Schyler. What you done for me ain't no words to thank you. Ronnie said I has to charge twenty-five dollars an hour for the kind of sewing I do. You don't think that's too much? I hates to take advantage over people."

He'd been right about her; she had integrity. "If Veronica suggested it, she would know what it's worth, because she wears top-quality clothes."

"The one I make her gon' be top of the top quality. You wait'll you see it."

He gave her his phone number. "Call me when my things are ready, and I'll pick them up."

"Oh, I'll be glad to bring them to you."

"I'll pick them up. If you need anything, give me a call."

Schyler couldn't give his news to Veronica until after nine that night. A storm had knocked out power lines in Owings Mills and he could neither call her nor, with Reisterstown Road blocked at the Owings Mills Boulevard crossing, could he drive to her home.

Alternately, he paced the floor and dialed her number until at last he got a ring.

"Are you all right? I've been out of my mind. Where'd that storm come from anyway?"

"Hi. You haven't been listening to your radio. My place is fine, but I understand there're trees down all around here, so don't try to come out."

"Trust me, lady, if I could have gotten there, I'd be at your place this minute. I wanted to thank you and share my good news with you." He told her about the report Enid sent him. "You'll never know how relieved I am."

"I'm happy for you, because it could have been different, though surely you had to know you've got fine genes."

"I didn't know any such thing. I was a pure hellion until

I met my dad, but he made me understand that I wasn't bad, just unhappy and that I was only hurting myself. He sent love to you."

"I'm sure you'll soon be tired of transmitting these messages between us, but thanks, and please give him my love when you speak with him."

His pulse beat accelerated. She hadn't sent regards, but love. "Did you say precisely what you meant?"

"I always do."

"I see. I'll tell him. I love you, Veronica. Good night." For a short while, she didn't say anything. "I love you."

She hung up, and he stared at the phone, recalling the emotion he'd heard in her voice. He needed to spend more time with her. A lot more time.

Veronica had a premonition when she answered the phone that she wouldn't like what reached her ears, and hearing Jack McCrae's voice didn't please her.

"You don't think I give up so easily, do you?" he asked when she told him she hadn't expected to get a call from him.

"Why are you calling, Jack?"

"Still cut and dried, I see. You know how to slice into a guy, don't you?"

"I'm honest with men, yes." She wasn't going to get into matching wits with the man, so she let her silence fill the air.

"I want you to come back to Round Midnight. Every night, my patrons are asking me when you'll be back and where you're singing now. Doll, you made the biggest splash I ever had in my club. I could make you rich. You want a recording contract? I can get it for you."

"Jack, I told you I am not interested in a career as a singer. I meant that."

"You're not listening to me, doll. You and me, baby, we can make great music together. I'll set up a round-the-world tour for you. You'll be even bigger than Lady Day. I'm talking big-time here."

"Jack, you're wasting your breath."

"I can't believe you'd blow an opportunity most other singers dream about. Have dinner with me tomorrow night, and let's discuss it."

"We're discussing it now, and please don't ask me for any dates. I have someone who's very important to me, and I don't go out with other men."

"Still Henderson? I can give you more than he'll ever have. I only want a chance, doll."

"I'm sorry, Jack, but that's not my way home. I wish you well."

"That's it, huh?"

"'Fraid so. Goodbye."

Veronica slipped into the red silk-taffeta strapless ball gown, the fitted hip of which was emphasized by the huge bow tucked beneath it and the short train that trailed behind the wearer. The tucking at the bosom allowed a modest dé-colletage, and Jenny had made above-the-elbow evening gloves that hooked to the thumbs and left the other fingers free. The tailoring and fit far exceeded her hopes, for the work was of true couturier quality. She brushed her hair down, decided that jewelry would only detract from the dress's stunning effect, dabbed some Opium perfume in the right places and put on the gloves just as the doorbell rang. Her pulse kicked into a rapid trot as she headed for the door.

They gaped at each other until Schyler laughed. "You're beautiful, and that dress is a...a knockout. You must have looked for it all over town."

She stared at him until she could no longer contain the mirth fighting for release. "Wait'll I see her. She's supposed to be *my* friend, but she's just like the other women who can't resist a good-looking guy."

His grin went to work for him, accentuating his striking good looks and elegance in his navy tux and accessories cut from the same cloth as her dress. "You talking about me?"

"I won't ask how you did it, because I've learned that you can be very resourceful, but I do appreciate the effort you made to match what I'm wearing. Jenny is a wonderful designer and seamstress."

"She sure is. She wouldn't let me see your dress, but she gave me a peek at what she's making for Enid. I'll have to put some notices for her on the bulletin boards at Branch Signal and AFTC. She'll do well."

He draped his arms around her, loosely, as though not wanting to spoil what he saw, and kissed her cheek. "You look to me the way a seven-course gourmet meal must appear to a starving man. Let's get out of here."

She smiled her pleasure at the comparison he'd drawn and restrained the impulse to rim her lips with her tongue. "You're an eyeful yourself."

His perfect white teeth sparkled against his tan skin, captivating her, as if his charm had been set on automatic pilot. "Ready to go?"

Indeed she was. She couldn't wait to show him off and to let her detractors know what this man whom they held in such high esteem thought of her.

Schyler held Veronica's hand as he led her to their table. He'd been able to get one directly facing the center of the dais, and he'd chosen it because he wanted them to see her, to know that their pettiness hadn't been worth the time they spent on it.

"We'll be sharing a table with the Roundtrees. I thought you might like that."

"Good. I've been hoping I'd get to see more of Banks."

Wayne stood when they reached the table, and Schyler had a sense of relief when Veronica greeted Wayne and Banks and sat down without seeming to attach any significance to the position of their table.

"You pulled out the stops tonight, Veronica, and do you ever look great," said Banks, whose white silk gown befitted the famed Roundtree wealth and status.

Schyler relaxed in his seat beside the woman of his heart and let himself bask in her elegant good looks. She returned Banks's compliment, and he couldn't help thinking that he was sitting with the two best-looking, most elegant women in that room filled with at least two hundred wannabe socialites. He surveyed the dais and enjoyed the discomfort he could see in the expressions of half the people sitting there. He knew that none of them had expected to have to look Veronica Overton in the face. Veronica seemed oblivious to them. What a champion!

"If anybody puts one of those silly little pastry cups full of chicken à la king in front of me tonight, I may scream," Banks said.

"Thank goodness you didn't say you'd murder somebody," Wayne interjected, "because ten to one, that's what we'll get."

Schyler listened with half an ear. He'd set his attention on the dais, and the whispers and glances satisfied him that he'd achieved his purpose. Their gazes and their attention focused on Veronica. The chicken à la king arrived in the expected pastry cups along with the de rigueur green peas and carrots, and he looked at Banks for a reaction.

She nibbled at the chicken as though tasting it for poison, looked into the distance and took a bigger bite. "Darned if they didn't learn how to cook it."

"No screams, I take it," Wayne said.

"No," she replied, "but they forgot to cook the peas. No problem though; their color looks great with my dress."

The conversation ceased when the president rose and introduced the guests and the gala's presiding officer. Schyler scrutinized Veronica's face and bearing for a reaction, but she seemed impervious, unmoved by the proceedings. He moved his chair closer to hers and draped an arm around her shoulder, and when she leaned toward him, he knew she'd found comfort in his touch. After half an hour of the necessary speeches and toasts, the orchestra signaled that dancing could begin.

"Dance with me?" he asked Veronica, and she was already moving her chair.

"How'd you get that table? It's usually the lieutenant governor or the chief of police who sits there."

"No sweat. I asked for it. Enjoying yourself?"

"Thank you. I am indeed! I've bamboozled the bunch of them, and they don't know what to think. I'm having a ball."

He held her closer, enjoying the spicy scent that wafted up to him and the carefree way in which she moved in his arms. "Me, too. I wouldn't have missed it for anything. You've slain them. Royalty couldn't have ignored them with greater finesse. And they'll eat crow, yet. Trust me."

He looked down into eyes that smoldered like hot bituminous coals at their peak. "I want to spend more time with you. Seeing you two or three times a week doesn't suit me. You told me you weren't seeing anybody else. Does that still hold?"

She missed a step, and he wondered whether it was his question or her answer that bothered her. She didn't keep him guessing. "Mister, you know exactly how to ring my bell. What kind of question is that? Would I have an affair with—"

He interrupted her. "Hey! Hold it. I never said anything about an affair."

"Oh, all right. No, I'm not, although McCrae asked me out."

"Tell that man to get a woman of his own and stop hitting on mine. Doesn't he understand the word *no?*"

For reasons that escaped him, she grinned. "Did I tell him no?"

"You bet you did, babe."

The music ended and they wound their way through a maze of tuxedos and ball gowns back to their table.

"Wayne wants you two to come out to our lodge one weekend so he can drag Schyler away from you while they fish," Banks said to Veronica.

Veronica leaned back in her chair and fixed her gaze on Wayne. "The last time I fished in the ocean, I caught over a dozen bluefish and I forget how many of something called mackerel. The boat was only out from midnight until five in the morning. I'd never had so much fun."

Banks's eyes glittered with mischief. "You heard that, husband dear. You'll have to take us with you."

They parted with the understanding that Wayne would propose a fishing date, and Schyler meant to hold him to it. It pleased him that Veronica and Banks liked each other, because he enjoyed Wayne's company.

"My place or yours," he asked after they seated themselves in the chauffeured limousine he'd rented for the evening.

"Mine," she said. "You really took me out in style tonight."

He let his eyes feast on her profile. "You wouldn't expect me to put you in the front seat of a car when you're wearing a ball gown, would you?"

She rewarded him with a squeeze of his arm. "I'm enjoying this pampering. How're you going to get home?"

An unearthly sensation shot through him, heating his blood. If she dared, so did he. He stroked the back of her hand, finding pleasure in just touching her. "You can drive me home tomorrow morning, or I can take the train."

"You'd get on the train in the morning in your tux? I wouldn't have thought so. Maybe you'll have to stay until tomorrow night."

He didn't want to play with that topic. She had to know that there were such things as taxicabs. But if she wanted him to stay with her all day tomorrow, he'd stay. He'd come a long way in the last couple of weeks, but she loved him. He hadn't known how much he needed to hear her say it, and the words had come from her with no prompting from him. She loved him, and she'd let him know she needed him. They weren't out of the water, but he could see the shore.

Chapter 13

Veronica stood on her porch that Monday morning reflecting on her weekend with Schyler and the many ways in which he'd showed her that he loved her, and asked herself what she was willing to give in order to make a life with him. He hadn't asked for a commitment nor had he pressured her; he'd simply found ways of letting her know what she meant to him. She had tired of her unstructured life, or moving its pieces around like so many pawns in a chess game, but never fitting them together. She had existed in a narrow world of success or failure that didn't tolerate individuality, and she had needed to break out of the mold. But that was a thousand years ago—before she liberated herself, before she loved Schyler Henderson, and before he showed her what a man's love could mean to a woman.

She thought of Kurt in the lonely Swiss Alps, tall, handsome and discombobulated, his life barren in the midst of beauty. An individual caught between the known—his family's history and traditions—and the uncertain, unattractive demands of modern life. Her mind dwelled briefly on the blustering with which Jack McCrae covered up his loneliness. And she thought of Schyler. Warm. Loving. A man who reached out to her openly and frankly because he needed her. It was time she got her life in order.

She went to her desk, sat down and dialed the board chairwoman of CPAA. "Mrs. Rothenhaus, this is Veronica Overton."

"My dear, I hope you're not calling to tell me you're not coming back. We're anxious for you to return, and especially now that Ms. Dupree wants time for her honeymoon."

Veronica closed her eyes and said the words that she had thought would pain her, but which gushed out with ease. "I'll be in my office next Monday morning."

She'd never heard the staid woman exclaim so loudly. "Wonderful. Wonderful. I'll be there to greet you."

That settled, she telephoned Enid. "See you Monday morning at eight-thirty."

"Get outta here! Just wait'll I tell everybody." Calmer now, she added, "You don't know how happy I am. By the way, how's that dress coming? When you see what she did with mine, you'll be ready to give her some financial backing. That's what Madison wanted to do when he saw our ball gowns. I have to attend a meeting. Be in touch. Way to go, girlfriend."

She telephoned her stepfather. "I'll be back on the job Monday morning, Papa."

A few seconds of silence passed before he asked, "Back to your old job?"

"Right. And now that I've announced my decision, I can hardly wait for Monday morning. A lot has transpired in these past months, and that means racing to catch up, but I'll—"

"Now, just a second, Veronica. Seems to me you're going right back into that trap you made for yourself before you got fed up and took a six-month vacation. One of these days, I'll tell you about traps. You be careful."

Did she have a choked mind? Hadn't she learned *anything?*
"I hear you, Papa. Real loud. Thanks for reminding me."

"You came to a crossroads back there in March, and you
reviewed your life. Just don't forget what you found,
because if you do, it'll be a wasted six months. You hear?
Come see me soon."

Her stepfather had always given her a sense of peace, had
always made her feel brighter and more clever than she was,
because he believed in her.

"Thanks, Papa. You always made the sun shine brighter.
Love you. See you soon."

She wanted to tell Schyler, but he'd said he'd call her
around noon. She'd wait. She thought of calling her birth
father, but what could she tell him? If he didn't know she'd
walked away from CPAA and why, her news would hold little
interest for him. While she wrestled with the idea, Enid called.

"You sitting down?"

"Yeah. What's going on?"

"I just got a directive from Social Welfare. From this day,
we're to restructure foster care according to your plan. Every
agency involved with placement received this. Your ship's on its
way back to shore, girl, and it can't get here fast enough for me."

"Well, I'll be! First thing I'm going to do when I get back
there is to start a systematic review of every foster care home
in this city."

She imagined that Enid's eyes sparkled with anticipation.
"That can't come soon enough for me. These politicians are
in for a surprise. From now on, they have to support scien-
tific guidelines. And just think, *they'll live in spite of it.*"

Schyler sifted through his morning mail, tossing out advertisements from child care centers, managed health care insti-
tutions, clinics, nursery schools and assorted other providers
of services for children. Thinking it was one of the endless,
time-consuming questionnaires aimed ostensibly at stream-

lining service, he tossed out the letter from the Department
of Social Welfare. Then he noticed that unlike most such
letters, this one bore a stamp rather than a frank, so he retrieved it. As he ripped it open, his mind wandered to his plans
for the coming weekend that he would spend with Veronica.

"What on earth?" He examined the letter more closely,
letting a grin split his face as he did so. She'd done it. She'd
forced a change in the archaic system. Exuberant, he dialed
her number.

"Sweetheart, you've done the impossible," he began, as
soon as she answered. "I'd begun to think I wouldn't live to
see it. From now on these agencies can't dictate where foster
children will live, but must first determine whether those four
years old and over *like* their prospective foster parents. This
alone will ensure that the children aren't dumped in the first
vacant spot and left there."

"I know you're sensitive about foster care and not just because of professional interests, and I confess I dreaded hearing
your views on my plan, but—"

She couldn't be serious. "Come on, love, you know this
thing is pure genius. I'm proud of you, Veronica. Wait'll I
show this to Dad."

"You're going to show it to *him?* Gosh, I…maybe I
should've sent him a copy."

"He wouldn't expect that, but he'll be pleased, because he
knows my concerns about the system." He let his eyes skim
the last provision. "And now the foster parents will have to
report what they spend on the children and provide receipts
for everything but food. Baby, you have pulled the plug on
one of the worst offenses. Right on."

"Does that mean I get a kiss?"

There had to be a reason why she could say a couple of
innocent words and set his blood racing, and he wished he
knew how she did it. "A kiss? Sure. Anything else you want,
just lay your head to the side and lower those come-hither

lashes the way you do when you're feeling…uh…warm. You won't have to say a word."

"Oh, Schyler, am I that obvious?"

He'd bet her face was one big scowl. "In my experience, sweetheart, you definitely are not, but I know you." He glanced at his watch. "I'd better sign off. I have to get back over to Branch Signal."

"Wait a minute. I've given notice that I'm returning to work Monday."

He sat down, certain that he hadn't heard her correctly. "What? What did you say?"

"I phoned Mrs. Rothenhaus and Enid and told them I'll be back to work Monday."

"Thank God. I… You can't imagine how happy that makes me."

"It was so important to you?"

"In a way, yes. To me, it means you're getting your life in order, and the fact that you came to that decision after our weekend together gives me hope."

"Are you getting ahead of me again?"

They needed to talk about what she wasn't saying, but he had to get to his office. Oh, the hell with it. He sat down. "Think of all we shared this past weekend—our dreams, goals, fears, ourselves and more. Think about that and tell me those two days shouldn't influence our whole lives, everything we think and do for as long as we live."

"I'm with you so far, but—"

"Listen to me, Veronica. What we had this past weekend was a soft, running brook. But when we come to each other with nothing left between us but our own identities, you'll know what it is to be caught up in a wild pounding ocean of feeling and passion. That will be the day when we give ourselves, and when we can finally receive each other without reservations of any kind. I promise you, it's only just begun. I'm cleaning my slate. Hurry up and do the same."

"Back there, I was wondering whether we're hoping for the same thing. That was my question."

"Of course we want the same thing. The problem is we still see it wrapped in different packages. Gotta go."

At six o'clock sharp the following Saturday afternoon, gowned in a dusty-rose satin dress that was identical to the bride's white one, Veronica began the long walk toward the altar of the Bethel AME Church where Madison Wright stood with Schyler waiting for Enid. A lump settled in her throat and threatened to cut off her breathing. Dampness cooled her bare arms, but at least there were no tears in her eyes. Schyler had said about everything to her that a woman could want to hear a man say. Everything but "Will you marry me?" To her way of thinking, the worst of it was that he wanted that. He hadn't said it, but she knew it, because his moves, his protectiveness, his loving and his growing possessiveness shouted the words. She reached the altar and stood opposite the man she loved as the music heralded the arrival of the bride. Finally, with her heart dancing wildly in her chest, she forced herself to look at him. His gaze captured her, and she had to steady herself against the sensation of being pulled to him like a nail to a magnet. Though she struggled to do so, she couldn't wrench her gaze from his, from the blaze of passion that burned in his eyes.

"I now pronounce you husband and wife."

The words pierced through her consciousness, slowly, like an old boat breaking through the fog, and she realized she'd missed the ceremony. Seconds later, Schyler touched her elbow, and her feet took her along with him, out of the church, into the limousine and to the reception.

"I'm beat," she told him later, as he walked with her to her front door.

He opened her door before he said anything, and she

wondered at his quiet manner. "I realize that, and I know it's mental. You missed the whole thing."

She didn't want him to leave her; she just needed to be alone. "Yeah. I wasn't sure I was in the right place. I... Schyler, would you excuse me, please?"

He stepped into the foyer with her and handed her the bunch of keys. "Of course. Will you call me?"

She nodded. What was wrong with her? She sucked in her lips to hide their quivering and squeezed her eyes tight to protect them from his knowing appraisal, but as she turned from him, he grabbed her. One of his hands went to the back of her head and the other wrapped tightly around her shoulders as he whispered to her words that could have been Greek or Finnish for all she knew. What mattered was his sweetness and his tenderness, that way he had of removing any doubt that he was there for her. She relaxed in his arms, that precious place she knew as home, and absorbed his gentle loving.

"It's going to be all right. You understand? Now be happy for Enid and Madison, and stop worrying about us. Our day will come."

She stared up at him, waiting for more, but she had to settle for the words of love and commitment mirrored in his eyes. She made herself smile, kissed him on the cheek and watched him leave her.

Self-pity wasn't a thing in which she indulged. She hung up the maid-of-honor's dress that had been a gift from Enid and stared at it. A month earlier, Jenny had been living on the street in beggar's rags. That day, she'd sat in the second row on the bride's side of the church, resplendent in a blue silk suit of her own making, and enjoyed looking at the elegance she'd created.

"I'm crazy," she mocked herself. *Nothing to be miserable about; the next move is up to me.* Her mood lighter now, she dialed Jenny's number.

"Lord, Ronnie," Jenny greeted her, "wasn't Enid the most

beautiful bride you ever seen? And that man of hers is...
Lord, just think of wakin' up and finding him right there
beside you. Ain't no flies on Schyler, though. Now, there's a
man. When you want me to start on your wedding dress? I
got the picture right here."

"Back up, will you, Jenny? I called to tell you what a great
job you did on our dresses. Enid looked like a young princess."

"Well, she still got a good shape. You can't sew nothing
nice for butt and bulges, as we used to say at the factory.
How'd you like how I dressed my men? I done everything but
they suits."

"I guessed that because they matched the dresses you made
for Enid and me. Congratulations, honey. You're on your way."

"I makes real pretty baby clothes, too."

She had to laugh; Jenny couldn't help behaving like a
mother hen, and that prompted a question.

"Jenny, do you have any children?"

The long silence told her she was too close to home. "I
guess so, Ronnie. I had a daughter, but when I lost everything
and had to go on the street, she didn't have no room in her
three-bedroom apartment. I 'spect now that I'm making a
little change again, I'll hear from her. But you and Schyler is
more like my children. So you hurry up and—"

"All right. All right. I'm working on it."

"That's exactly the same old line what Schyler give me. I
ain't gonna stop reminding you though."

Schyler stood on his balcony looking at the changing
season, wondering what his life would be a year from then.
If she had cried as she walked up that aisle, he'd have broken
tradition and gone to meet her. And she'd come close to it later
as they stood in her foyer, but the woman was put together
with stern stuff; his admiration for her had never been higher.
She wanted marriage for them. He wanted it, too, and he
knew it was right for them. But what if they had a formal

wedding—and he didn't doubt that she'd want one—which man was entitled to walk with her to the altar, her father or her stepfather? And how could she justify choosing one over the other, when she knew that either one of them would suffer mortification? And what of her future relationship with the father she didn't choose?

She'd been so beautiful standing there beside Enid, gazing at him as though transfixed. And in his heart, he'd said every word to Veronica that Madison had spoken to Enid. They had been lost in each other, and neither he nor Veronica had followed the ceremony as witnesses were supposed to do. He changed out of his tuxedo, put some underwear, socks and a T-shirt in a duffel bag, got in his car and headed for Tilghman. He'd give it another three weeks, and then he'd force the issue.

Veronica stared at herself in the mirror, stunned. "I thought I'd changed," she said aloud in disgust. She took off her Anne Klein suit and kicked off the spike-heel shoes that she'd always hated but felt compelled to wear for the sake of fashion. Her gaze lighted on the penny loafers she'd worn in Europe and a moss green, button-front dress that she loved. *Let them think what they like; from now on, I'm pleasing myself.*

She spent her first day back at the office doing precisely that. She rejected the two-hour lunch at Wilma's Blue Moon, skipped the morning and afternoon coffee hours that each usually consumed three-quarters of an hour and left promptly at five o'clock.

"Run that past me again," Schyler said in a tone of incredulousness when she told him about her day.

"What exactly does this mean?" he added, his voice confirming his bewilderment.

"I'm going to lead a normal life, and work will be a part of it, not all of it. See anything wrong with that?"

"No, ma'am." She thought she heard laughter in his voice.

"What are you planning to do with the other sixteen hours, assuming travel takes up two of them?"

She didn't know why but she had a need all at once to test his mettle. "Oh, there's plenty to keep me busy. I can work at Round Midnight. Jack's after me to—"

"The hell, you say. For the last time—if that brother doesn't quit hitting on you, I'm going to show him what darkness looks like."

"Show me, too. Just when you think it's dark, some light always filters in through—"

"Do you want McCrae?"

"Of course not. You know I don't."

"Then tell him to stay out of your way, and if he's got any sense at all, he'll avoid me as he would the plague. And don't play games, Veronica. I may appear mild, and I am most of the time, but if he gets on my turf, he'll discover that I'm like any other threatened animal. You can help him avoid the consequences of stupidity."

He wouldn't appreciate her laughing right then, so she did her best to control it. "I suppose that's as close to a commitment as I'm likely to get anytime soon. Just checking."

"Is that what you want?"

She buffed the nails of her left hand against her thigh and considered her answer. "Hmmm. Tactical error. I showed my hand." Her eyes rounded when she realized a giggle had escaped.

If he heard it, he ignored it. "Sometimes, that's not a bad thing. What do you think of this? You committed to getting some information from your stepfather, and so far you haven't done it. If you're still sitting on the fence, I can ask him for you."

How had that jocular exchange become a tug of war? So his terms hadn't changed. "I don't advise that. You said if I made a step, you'd take one, too. I'm going to make one. If the planes aren't flying, you can still get there by train."

"That's the way I like to hear you talk, sweetheart."

* * *

Several days later, the mayor gave her her first opportunity for revenge, but she declined the chance at pettiness. "Ms. Overton, we're so delighted to have you back with us. I want you to know how excited our social workers are about your foster care plan. We want to hold a meeting and invite our sister agencies throughout the state to attend. We hope to discuss the plan's advantages and means of assuring full compliance with it, and I'd like you to be the chairperson."

How sweet it was! "I'd be delighted to help in any way that I can, sir. Incidentally, I've been planning to ask if you would support a review of all the foster care homes under your jurisdiction?"

"Of course, Ms. Overton, and if you need some funds, not over fifty thousand, mind you, I'll be glad to help."

She'd done it. She'd get what she'd been after for years, and she'd have the mayor's support. Hallelujah!

Schyler disliked spending his time woolgathering, but his last exchange with Veronica had left him in a mental tailspin. He ran along the beach with Caesar just ahead of him, feeling the early fall chill. She had to know what she meant to him, but knowing that wasn't enough for her, and it hadn't been for some time. He wanted her for his wife, but he also wanted his life in order. *Stop second-guessing her, man,* he told himself. He had to await her next move, because he didn't doubt that she planned one. And a serious one, too. The hearing for his appeal had been postponed pending events in Robbins's case, adding to the disorder in his life. He wanted the freedom to ask Veronica to marry him, provided conditions became propitious, and he didn't want her to marry an ex-con, even if he had been railroaded.

He hadn't asked Veronica why she was too busy to see him during the weekend, because he believed in giving her as much space as she needed. He'd just put on his favorite Buddy

Guy CD, kicked off his shoes and stretched out on the floor with Caesar beside him, prepared to relax, when the doorbell rang. He sniffed the odor of andouille sausage, Cajun spices and buttermilk biscuits that wafted from the kitchen, pulled himself up and headed for the door where Caesar stood wagging his tail. He furrowed his brow. Caesar didn't greet strangers with a wagging tail but with a fierce growl.

He opened the door and gasped. There she stood in a red pantsuit with her hair flying everywhere, caught up in the swirling wind. As though she'd done nothing unusual, she handed him her small overnight bag, reached up and kissed him on the mouth and strolled past him.

He recovered and grabbed her hand. "Honey, what are you doing here? You said you'd be busy this weekend. I would have brought you down with me." He stepped closer, dropped her bag on the floor, and brought her to him with both hands. "Baby, what's this all about?" The mingling of the perfume she always wore and her own woman's scent teased his nostrils while he gazed down at her. "Suppose I hadn't been here?"

"Father knew I was coming. I called him last night."

His eyebrows nearly reached his hairline. He gazed at her for a long time, trying to add it up. "He's cooking, as you can probably tell from the odor of things. I'll put your bag in your room." He rubbed the back of his neck and let out a long whistle. She wasn't boring, that was for sure.

"Did you tell him not to tell me?" he called after her.

She walked back a few steps. "I didn't mention you. Honest. I just asked him if I could come out today and maybe spend the night, and he said I could come here as often as I wanted to and stay as long as I like. I hope you don't mind."

"Of course I don't mind; I'm glad to see you here. I'm just having a problem understanding why you couldn't tell me."

She had an interesting and unusual way of shrugging; when one shoulder went up, the other went down. "I was working on cleaning my slate as you suggested, and suddenly I just made up my mind about this and called him. You always said it was between him and me, and I agree with you. I was hoping you'd be here, though."

He had thought he understood her, but right then, he wasn't so sure. He remembered that he wasn't wearing shoes when Caesar's tail thumped his toes. "You're glad I'm here, huh? Well, that's something." She was looking down at his feet, and the grin she wore spread until it enveloped her whole face. She laughed.

"You laughing at my feet? What's wrong with them?"

"You don't know that I kick off my shoes as soon as I get in my house. If we lived together, I imagine we'd spend a lot of time looking for our shoes."

There it was again. A couple of simple words, and he wanted her so badly that his stomach cramped. The heat in him must have shone in his eyes, for she started toward him, slowly, almost zombielike until, within inches of him, she sprang into his arms. Arms that he didn't realize had left his side. With her body pressed to him and the feel of her breasts warm and tight against him, he hungered and ached to lose himself in her. Her parted lips invited the thrust of his tongue, and he yielded, finding every crevice, every sweet centimeter of her mouth until tremors ripped through him. Her accelerated breathing— always his sign that she wanted him—intensified, and when she climbed his body, the hot lava of desire snaked through his frame, gathering fire as it reached his loins. And though he fought it with all the energy he still possessed, he rose against her. Instead of backing away, she took it as a go signal for her greedy passion, pulled his tongue into her mouth and feasted on it. Pots and dishes banged and clanged in the kitchen but, for all she seemed to care, the noise could have been in China.

"Uh-huh." The sound of a throat being cleared rocked him back to full consciousness, and he set her away from him. He stared at her, lips half parted, as open as he'd ever seen a woman, and the expression in her eyes nearly unglued him. With more effort than he was normally required to exert, he shifted his gaze from her to where he expected to see his father standing, but his dad had mercifully left them alone. He drew her to him, took her into his arms and stroked her back.

"Encounters like that one keep me going, baby. They make me know that only you and I can spoil this fantastic feeling we have for each other. I don't want to lose it, and I don't believe you do. Get yourself together and go find Dad."

She rubbed her arms as she did when vulnerable. "I'll need a minute or two. I'm…I can't right now."

"Tell me about it." He wasn't in the best of shape himself. "You've got all night." She still gazed up at him, so he brushed her lips with his own and walked her to her room. "I'm always here if you need me."

Veronica combed her hair, headed for the kitchen and stopped short as she neared the open door. Richard leaned against the doorjamb, facing her and twirling a spatula. She didn't know what to think, since a smile lit his face and his mood appeared light and friendly, but it was clear that he knew she hadn't just walked into the house. This time, he didn't make the first move, and she knew he was telling her something important, reminding her of their respective roles. She told herself not to blow it. Returning his smile was easy, because he invited warmth, and besides, she found that she enjoyed looking at him and marveling at how much like him she was. She walked to him and kissed his left cheek.

"You knew I was here, didn't you?" she asked, hoping he'd let slip whether he'd seen her in that clinch with Schyler.

He opened his arms then, and she hugged him. His wink surprised her. "You have to get up early to hide anything around Caesar. I knew it was you when I heard his tail thumping against the floor. I've just about got lunch ready."

"Want me to help with anything?"

He told her she could set the table and make iced tea, and

she was glad for the opportunity to concentrate on something other than her feelings about Schyler and her father, and to get her emotions under control. She wondered why Schyler didn't help her set the table, and sought him in the living room, but he wasn't here.

"Where's Schyler?" she asked her father.

"Probably out back in the garden. You surprised him, didn't you?"

She nodded. "I didn't think of it as a surprise. Why didn't you tell him?"

"I wasn't sure how things were between you, so I figured if he didn't know, he'd at least be here when you came. I see I needn't have worried."

She'd walked right into that one. If she could have disappeared through the wall, she would have. "I…uh—"

He stopped clipping strings off the beef roll-ups. "Veronica, loving a man who loves you is just about the most priceless experience a woman can have. Not one thing to be shy about. I can tell you that for a man nothing beats it either. I must say Caesar had a very surprised expression on his face."

She fled to the dining room. It seemed as though her father liked to tease. She tried to imagine him and her mother together but couldn't, because Esther Hunt belonged with Sam Overton. They had fitted like hand and glove. She listened to her father singing and whistling in the kitchen and tried to catalog the traits she'd inherited from him.

I'm getting used to him in this role, she admitted to herself, and prayed that they'd still be on good terms when she left him on Sunday.

Richard's Cajun-style lunch proved to be one of the best meals she'd ever eaten and set the tone for their camaraderie during the meal.

She bit into one of the beef roll-ups and savored it as she chewed slowly, enjoying the fragrant smells and spicy flavors.

"Women ought to have it written into their marriage contracts that their husbands do all the cooking. Men make great cooks."

"Pshaw!" Richard said in mild disgust. "Love him right, and you don't need a contract. The poor fool will do any dumb thing you want him to do."

A glance at Schyler revealed a raised eyebrow. "I wouldn't go that far, Dad. I'd say, *most* any dumb thing." He gazed at her in what she took for a challenge. A strong one.

"Don't look at me. I'm not in this."

"You mean you're not showing your hand," Richard countered.

"Oh, she shows it all right," Schyler said, still gazing steadily at her. "She doesn't let you make mistakes with her."

"I don't say everything I think," she corrected, beginning to feel uncomfortable.

"Sweetheart, you don't have to say a word." He always told her that no matter what her mouth *said,* her body did the talking, and she suspected that her father understood what Schyler meant.

His words confirmed as much. "Oh. Oh. We mustn't get personal. And using what you know of her vulnerableness against her is hitting below the belt, Son. Let's stick to generalizations, which is where we started. Schyler says you're not a great cook, but that shouldn't bother you. He's a quick study."

"Thanks. I was hoping to keep my genius a secret."

That two grown, self-possessed men could be so completely compatible would have amazed her had she not known how deeply they loved each other. If only she could be a part of them. Both men had set their gaze on her, watching her, and she quickly brought herself out of her pensiveness.

"Is that usually a problem, hiding your superior mentality, I mean?" she asked Schyler.

Their laughter told her that she was theirs and they could be hers.

"Now that Schyler's had his chocolate fix, why don't you

rest a little," Richard said to Veronica. "I'm going out on the beach in about an hour, and I'd like you to go with me. The weather's perfect. Okay?"

"That would be perfect timing. I could use a nap." She ducked her head to avoid looking at Schyler and went to her room.

"The two of you are not going out there alone this time, I don't care what he says," Schyler declared. "I'm tired of these crash landings."

She walked between them with each man holding one of her hands. Richard whistled the hymn "Amazing Grace," as they went, but she could almost feel the tension radiating from Schyler. *I must be careful*, she thought; *I can't let it get out of hand this time.*

Richard put down the bait for crabs and turned to Schyler. "Why don't you and Caesar take a stroll?"

Schyler shook his head. "Not this time, Dad. I'm staying right here." He'd see that they talked civilly without blowing up and hurting each other. Making certain of it, he sat on a boulder, patted the space beside him and grasped her hand as soon as she sat down.

Schyler gave the appearance of not having a care, though he knew that belied the facts. But he realized that his father viewed this as just another visit with his daughter, albeit an important one.

"Is there anything you wanted to tell me, Daughter?"

"I… No, sir. I promised Schyler I'd get to the bottom of my mother's request. I asked my stepfather why she wanted me to find you, but my question upset him so visibly that I couldn't persist. It occurred to me a couple of days ago that you also know the answer."

Schyler squeezed her fingers, half in support and half as a caution, because he, too, had come to suspect that his father understood Esther Hunt Overton's request.

"If you seriously want to know and you're prepared to

listen without rancor, I'll talk. First, tell me once more what she said."

He felt her tremble, looked into his father's troubled eyes and wanted to shield them from what he now knew would pain both of them.

"She said '…find him. Find your father…please find him. Sorry.' And that was her very last word."

Richard looked into the distance, at the gray water speckled with sea gulls and ospreys, his gaze reflecting the great distance his mind traveled. "Howard Overton and I were good friends, had been since college days. He was the architect, and I the architectural engineer. We worked together, socialized together and we were together when we met Esther Hunt. Both of us fell in love with her. After months of uncertainty, we told her she had to choose, and she chose me.

"For three years, I was in heaven; my feet barely touched the earth. I loved her. She was my whole world. After that first year, our daughter came. I named her Veronica, because she was conceived in Verona, Italy, while Esther and I were there on vacation. Something had always been lacking in our marriage but I told myself that I loved Esther so much, she couldn't help but love me back. My work took me away from home occasionally, but after you were born, I shortened the trips, because I hated to be away from you even for an hour. And when I came home, you would laugh and dance for joy. I'd hold the two of you and wonder how I'd gotten so fortunate.

"One day I returned from an engineers' convention and walked into a quiet place. I thought of illness, an accident, robbery, even death. And then I found the letter on my pillow. She had made a mistake, and had discovered it soon after we married. She loved Howard, and she'd gone to him, taking you with her. I couldn't find her. Finally, knowing what had been in my heart all the time, that she really loved Howard, I divorced her and put a notice in the papers to that effect, but I also sued for child custody and put that notice alongside it.

I won custody, but I couldn't find you and Esther. I have the papers, and I'll be glad to show them to you.

"Until your detective came here, I had heard nothing from that day on, although I've spent a small fortune looking. When Schyler came into my life, I was a washout. I worked, ate, slept whenever my demons let me and tried to keep my faith in God, though I tell you it was hard. I have never loved another woman, and I know I never will. When you told me she was dead, you killed my dream that someday she'd come back to me, that someday I'd have the two of you again. I don't know where you got the idea that I deserted you. It was the other way around, and I have suffered for that every minute of the last thirty years."

Schyler hardly breathed. He had never known a living being to remain so still. Fearing that Veronica might have slipped into a catatonic state, he wrapped his arms around her and rocked her as water spilled from his eyes. A chill sank into his pores, and he had to struggle with the feeling of strangulation that stole over him. Nearly dumbfounded by the story of his father's lost love, he lifted Veronica into his arms, carried her over and sat beside his father. With one arm around his father's shoulder and the other embracing Veronica, he tried to comfort them both.

"At least you have each other now," he said, as more dampness settled on his cheek. "Don't hurt each other any more. Please. It's too much for all of us."

"B...But I'm asked to believe Mama lied to me. From the time I remember myself, she said *you* left *us*."

"I can't make you believe the truth. Do you want me to swear on a Bible in the presence of my minister?"

"Please. I didn't mean that. Can't you understand how confused I must be?"

"I certainly can, and I sympathize with you, Daughter, but you asked me. Hasn't it occurred to you that Esther wanted forgiveness when she said she was sorry? I thought so the first time you told me, but until you asked me the way you did just now, I didn't have the spirit to go over all that."

He pulled up the crab bucket and grinned. "Seven of 'em. Another haul like this one and Schyler can make stuffed crabs for supper."

Deeply troubled by the story of her parents' lamentable marriage, Veronica burrowed into Schyler as though denying all else. His father didn't fool him either. Rehashing the wrenching tale of his life had shaken Richard Henderson as much as it had Veronica and himself.

He stood. "Leave the pot there, Dad. I'll come back in a couple of hours and see what you caught. I want us to go in now. Veronica needs to rest, and I have a feeling you do too."

Richard didn't object, and he knew he'd guessed correctly. Reviewing a part of his life that had pained him so greatly seemed to have left his father totally enervated, though he offered them his usual serene facade. At last, Schyler understood Veronica's wanting to care for her father, but unable to stop believing her mother whom she had loved and trusted all her life. And his heart went out to his father. How could a man suffer so much and so unfairly and yet open his heart to a street urchin, still pray, still greet every morning with a smile?

He held Veronica and kissed her. "See you after a while," he said before grasping his father's hand and walking with him to the solarium.

"I don't know what I'll do if she doesn't believe you."

Richard lifted his left shoulder in a quick, dismissive shrug. "She believes me. It's what she does about that belief that matters. She's honorable, and I'm betting on that."

Veronica sat lotus-fashion in the middle of her bed, trying to digest all that her father had told them. He and her stepfather had been close friends… She jumped from the bed. Her stepfather's name wasn't Howard; it was Sam and always had been. She sat down, subdued once more. How did she know what it was or why? She threw on her robe and knocked on her father's door. Getting no answer, she went to the solarium where she found Schyler holding her father's hand and speaking to him in low tones.

"Excuse me. I think I have to go home. I have to talk to my stepfather. A lot of things are coming to me now. I've just realized that he's never mentioned your name to me, Father, nor spoken of you in my presence. He's never told me anything about how or where or when he and Mama got married. Please don't think I'm insulting you, I'm not. But Mama's gone, so he's the only one who can tell me her side of this. I think he'll be fair, because I realize now that he has always avoided getting between you and me."

Schyler rose, as she'd known he would, obviously preparing to leave with her. "No, love. You stay here. Please stay here with Father. I'm fine. I don't want to call my stepfather from here, because he'll ask me where I am. I'll phone you when I get home."

"I can't let you drive back when I know you're upset."

"Please, Schyler. I know myself, and I'm fine." She walked over to her father. "Why did you call him Howard Overton? I've never known him by that name, yet I know we're speaking of the same person."

She had the comfort of her father's arm around her shoulder and knew it belonged there. He looked her in the eye. "Ask him. I'm sure that will be a part of his explanation. Call me as soon as…as you can."

She kissed his cheek, stuffed her things into the duffel bag and headed for her rental Mercury Sable. Schyler walked with her to the car. "Try not to upset your stepfather. Somehow, I'm sure he has a harrowing story to tell. You have my cell phone number—here's Dad's. Drive carefully and call me the minute you get home. Okay?"

When she got home, she kicked off her shoes at the door, phoned Schyler and made a cup of coffee. She didn't need it

or especially want it and recognized the process as one of procrastination. She sat down at her desk and dialed her stepfather's number.

"It's a long painful story, Daughter. It's out now, and I'll
finish it, but I want you here when I do."

"All right, I'll be there tomorrow shortly after noon. Don't
worry, I'll get a rental car in Durham."

"I'll see you tomorrow. Drive carefully."

She hung up, made a plane reservation and called for a taxi
to take her to the Baltimore airport.

Sam Overton opened the front door as she came up the
brick walk. She held out her arms to him, for he needed to
know that no matter what she'd heard or what he told her, she
loved him and always would.

After relating to him as gently as she could all that her
father had said, she added, "I needed to hear your side of it."

She heard the deep breath that he expelled, a long, tired
breath that told of having been pent up for a very long time.
"What he says is true, Daughter. I didn't approve of the explanation Esther gave you, but she didn't want you to grow
up thinking she'd deprived you of your father. I didn't interfere because it wasn't my story to tell, but I knew it wasn't
right, and I told her so."

"Then you are an architect as he said?"

"Yes. I've designed many a building. I gave it up and
allowed myself to disappear into oblivion because I loved
Esther more than myself. I loved her almost to distraction, and
when she married Richard, I nearly died. I knew she loved me,
but I couldn't convince her, because he and I had said she
should choose. She knew right off that she'd made a mistake,
but she didn't contact me until the day she left him. She told
me she'd die before she'd give you up. Richard divorced her
at once, because he also knew she loved me, but when he sued
for custody and won it, she went into hysterics. So I brought

her down here where nobody knew us. I changed my first name and worked as a laborer to avoid detection. I did menial jobs, took my pay in cash and couldn't own a car even if I could have afforded one, because if I paid taxes, had a bank account or a decent position, I'd have to give my social security number and could have easily been traced through it."

She stared at him openmouthed. "You loved my mother so much that you gave up your profession, status, friends and comforts for her."

His smile seemed to mask a pleasant memory; then he shook his head as though to snap out of it. "It wasn't much of a sacrifice; I didn't design or build a single house during the three years she was with Richard. I didn't take to drink, but looking back, that's a wonder."

"But Papa, you did everything to keep us alive but dig ditches with your bare hands. Lord, I hope she knew what she had."

"She knew, and she loved me as much as I loved her. I don't regret a day."

"Will you go back to architecture?"

"Well, I've still got my credentials, and I've been doing some things over in Durham recently. I won't get back where I was, because I'm too old, but I'll be able to enjoy myself. Esther would want me to do that."

She had one more question to settle. "My father got hot under the collar when I accused him of deserting Mama and me, and I thought he'd blow a gasket when he asked me why my last name wasn't Henderson."

"I'll bet he did. He has a very short fuse. We had to change your name, Veronica. If it had remained Henderson, he would have been able to find you, and I couldn't stand to see that happen to your mother. I adopted you because I loved you, and not for any other reason."

"I believe that, Papa."

"I said I'd one day tell you what it meant to be trapped. Now you know."

"How about it! I've had bigger shocks yesterday and today than in all my previous thirty-two years. Thanks for straightening it out, Papa. My father adopted a boy who is now a man named Schyler Henderson. He's the man who prosecuted CPAA and me." His gasp echoed through the room, and he sat as though spellbound while she told him the remainder of the story.

"If we do get married, Papa, could I expect to walk up the aisle between you and Richard Henderson? It would be both or neither."

His laugh made her feel better than she'd felt in the last two days. "Well I'll be! We started with the same love and end up with the same daughter. And our daughter won't choose between us. If he's forgiving, I'll be happy to shake his hand."

She got up, twirled around and skipped to the kitchen. She knew false gaiety when she witnessed it, but she didn't want to look hard at her feelings. "Where's my catfish, collards and hush puppies?"

A smile burst out on his face. "I had to rise pretty early to get that fish before old man Moody closed up to go to church, but it's all cooked."

She finished her favorite meal and prepared to leave. "Next time I come down, meet me in Durham and show me what you've been doing over there."

"I can't think of anything that would give me more pleasure. That house I rebuilt is a real beaut. You'll see." He touched her arm. "Don't think harshly of your mother. She did wrong, but she did it out of love for you. You hear me?"

She looked into his eyes that pleaded with her. "I don't hold it against her, Papa. She also suffered and gave up a lot. I know the story now. We were all losers."

She got back home late that Sunday night, wrung out. Exhausted. She started to call Schyler, but her fingers wouldn't do it. Now that she knew everything, understood the suffering that her mother's bad judgment had caused all four of them, she had to distance herself from it and from everybody involved. She'd bet anything that when he learned her step-father had corroborated her father's story, within a week Schyler would ask her to marry him. And she resented knowing that her future happiness with him had been contingent upon circumstances over which she had no control. She loved Schyler, her father and her stepfather, but as the import of all that she'd learned finally struck like a piercing saber, she wanted to get away from all of them. She didn't phone Schyler the next day nor the next. On Thursday, she left a message on his phone at Branch Signal telling him that she'd be in touch as soon as she sorted out a few things. The next afternoon at five o'clock, she walked out of her office, got into her rental car and headed for the Adirondack Mountains.

Chapter 14

Her cell phone rang before she was out of the Baltimore metropolitan area. "Veronica, this is your father. I thought you'd want to know that Schyler has a court date Monday morning at ten o'clock. He won't tell you. He hasn't been himself this past week, because you haven't shared with him what you learned from Howard. I'm not worried, because I know you're trying to sort things out, but he's in love with you and that's a different matter."

"Thanks for letting me know. I'll be there. It's hard to share what you don't understand, and I'm…well, I'm trying to piece things together. I hope you'll accept that."

"I do. If you need a shoulder, I'm here for you. That's what fathers are for."

"Thanks, Father. It's…it's comforting. I'll stay in touch."

Concerned that her inability to declare that all was well, when it wasn't, might be construed as doubting her father and thus jeopardize the love and trust she and Schyler had built, she drove off Route 95 at Fullerton, about twenty miles north of Baltimore, and parked. She needed desperately to be alone, someplace where nobody knew her name and she could wash the last iota of resentment out of herself. Resentment toward her mother, her stepfather and her father—both of whom could have given her the facts when she first mentioned to them her mother's request—and yes, Schyler. Schyler, the man who would not declare himself, who loved her but couldn't envisage marriage to her until she forgave what she had not accepted and could not understand. Yet, she loved all three of them, in different ways, yes, but it was love all the same.

"Having any problems, lady?"

She pulled herself out of her mental mist and looked toward the voice and into the concerned expression of a Maryland trooper. "Thanks, Officer. I'm all right. I guess I'm just worried. Did you ever feel like damaged goods? Run over by a Mack truck? Or maybe tossed a few hundred miles in the eye of a tornado? I just had my butchered, drawn and quartered life served up to me like a couple of helpings of barbecue."

The officer removed his hat, scratched his head and looked as if he wished he hadn't stopped. "You...uh, feel like driving? I can call somebody to come give you a hand."

"I appreciate the offer, but I'll be fine. You helped me a lot."

He stared at her as though uncertain of her mental state. "I did?"

"Yes, sir. I didn't know I felt like that until I said it aloud to someone, and I know it's safe with you."

"It sure is, ma'am." He tipped his hat and walked back to the squad car, shaking his head as he went.

She continued to Indian Lake in the Adirondack Mountains where she could enjoy nature's last blush before it died into winter. Instead of dealing with what distressed her, she avoided thinking of it. Thus, the weekend passed uneventfully, and Monday morning three minutes before ten o'clock, she stood behind the last row of seats in Criminal Court trying to locate Schyler. She finally found him and, seconds before the judge walked out of his chambers, she took the seat beside Schyler and clasped his left hand with her right one.

Her misgivings about being there uninvited quickly vanished. He turned sharply at her touch, and when he recognized her, his eyes widened and his bottom lip slipped downward. Then, with a smile that projected the warmth of midsummer sunlight, he turned his palm upward and squeezed her hand. But his composure and apparent self-possession belied the moisture on his palms and the way he ground his teeth. She handed him a mint, and sucking on it seemed to relieve some of his tension. After almost two hours of legal wrangling, the judge called a five-minute recess and left the courtroom.

"You don't know how happy I am to see you," Schyler said. "I don't know why you've been so…so silent, this past week, but I'm glad you're here. I suppose my dad told you."

"Yes. He called me. I wouldn't have been anywhere else right now but here with you."

"I… Thanks. Dad wanted to come, but he was with me when I was sentenced, and he…he nearly fainted. I couldn't put him through that again."

She wanted to hold him to her breast, to shield him from the ugliness and the unfairness. "I'm with you no matter what. To me, you'll always be my standard for men."

She saw the love mirrored in his eyes, and her heart leaped as though in celebration.

"In less than five minutes I'll know whether my name will remain tainted, whether my children will have that shame, whether I'll ever practice law."

The piercing stab of his words ripped into her, and she fought back the tears. He needed her, not the weakness of self-pity. As the judge entered, Madison Wright joined them to give Schyler moral support.

"Please stand, Mr. Henderson." She and Madison rose with Schyler. "The court finds that you were falsely accused, that the witnesses against you perjured themselves and that you were unjustly found guilty, sentenced and incarcerated. Mr. Robbins has confessed to having committed similar fraud over a period of thirteen years. I will have this expunged from the records and will recommend to the attorney general that he take appropriate measures to rectify this injustice. Case closed."

Veronica sat down. She had plenty to cry about, she assured herself, but instead she laughed aloud. Then she took her cell phone out of her bag, turned it on and phoned her father.

"Schyler has something to tell you, Father."

As though coming out of a dream, Schyler took the phone from her. "It's all over, Dad. I've been cleared."

She heard the words, and her eyes finally released the water that she had refused to let them spill.

"Let's go, you two," Madison said. "They're turning out the lights."

Schyler embraced his friend. "If you ever need me, just yell."

"I lived in the dark, so to speak, for years, Madison," she said. "It's finally seeing the light that nearly blinds you."

She didn't miss Schyler's quick frown as they left the courtroom together. They faced each other on the bottom step, aware that it was closure time.

"I'm not sure where I stand with you right now," he said. "You froze me out this past week, and I don't know why. Where do we go from here?"

She remembered what it was like to be lonely, thought of the children she wanted with him, but might not have and recalled the many hours of exquisite pleasure he'd given her and nearly faltered.

But she had to tell him the truth. "I love you, Schyler, but I hurt. I didn't know pain could feel like this."

He stepped closer, reached toward her and let his hand fall to his side. "But I'm here for you. Can't you—"

"I had a mountain of decades-old debris heaped on me in the space of less than twenty-four hours. It didn't sink in until the next day and now… Well, I'm trying to deal with it. Both of them could have made it easier for me, could have saved me months of doubt and unhappiness. And you. Though I love you, I have to make myself accept the fact that you refused to take me as I was. You exacted a price: Love you, love your dad. Yet I believed in you and willingly accepted you as you were, cobwebs and all. Can you blame me for harboring resentment against all three of you?"

She couldn't allow his obvious distress at her words to distract her. "What you and I should have together won't flourish in an environment of bitterness, so I have to deal with these feelings. Can you give me time to work it out?"

With the speed of a thoroughbred breaking away, he shuttered his feelings, but his voice betrayed their intensity. "When I felt you touch my hand, looked over and saw you there beside me, I could have withstood any setback, any blow. You were with me, and I knew right then that you were all I'd ever need. This isn't the happy moment I'd hoped for, but if you tell me I have to wait, I have no choice. You'll call me?"

"I'll call you." She reached up and touched his bottom lip with her thumb. "Take g…good care of yourself."

When she got to her office shortly after noon, she closed her door and told her secretary she didn't want any calls or visitors. Her gaze fell on the FEDEX letter at the top of her in-box, and her curiosity peaked when she saw AFTC in the upper left-hand corner. Fearing another complaint against her or CPAA, her fingers trembled almost uncontrollably as she opened it. Her sight blurred, and she squinted as she read:

"Dear Ms. Overton, AFTC is pleased to inform you that because of your efforts to standardize and raise the level of foster home care, AFTC has given you its Annual Award for Distinguished Community Service. We hope you join us at our awards banquet November 29 to accept this honor."

Schyler had certainly engineered it, but that didn't diminish its importance, for his board had to have agreed unanimously.

She telephoned him at both of his offices and his cell phone but couldn't reach him and had to settle for leaving messages asking him to call her. Disheartened, she managed to review the reports of several of her social workers and to draft an article for the features section of *The Maryland Journal.*

I don't want to be without him, she mused. *Much as I welcome that award, it has no luster, because I can't share it with him.* She wished Enid were there, but her friend was still on her honeymoon, and Madison, who had returned only to be with Schyler at the hearing, had already gone back to her.

"I'm a big girl," she reminded herself, packed her briefcase and headed home. But his face as he'd looked seconds before she left him at the courthouse seemed to have staked out a permanent place in her mind's eye. She went to bed early.

Schyler bunched his shoulder against the sudden sting of autumn air and jogged toward his favorite boulder, the big rock his dad named Schyler's thinking stone. Caesar raced ahead of him, with his tail wagging, waited at the stone, certain of his master's habits. The overcast sky, rough water and biting wind struck him as irritants, reminding him of the lonely months of his incarceration. Months of seething anger at the unfairness of it and, finally, an inner peace that seeded in him a determination to put himself in a position to help other victims of social injustice.

He thought of that morning in court when he'd waited to know if he would bear that burden forever. Veronica had not only waited to know whether he had been cleared, but had come to him when he'd felt as if he hadn't a friend and stood with him, declaring to all who would see her fidelity to a man with a criminal record.

He knew she loved him, and she had demonstrated her loyalty, but she seemed to need more than he had given her. Had he been arrogant in his insistence that if she loved him, she also had to love the man who had fathered her, though she didn't know him? He had softened his position on that, but she knew it remained important to him. When Caesar pulled on the leg of his jogging pants, he noticed the encroaching darkness and headed home, dragging his loneliness behind him.

"Why can't you return her call? You said she wants to thank you," Richard said as they finished dinner.

He closed his eyes and shook his head, as though banishing the topic. "I don't need her thanks, and I don't feel like making small talk with her. I need an understanding."

His father's expression was that of an exasperated man. "Don't we all? Listen to me, Son. Veronica believes in straight talk, and she's right. Saves a lot of pain down the road. She's not pretending her relationship with you is what she needs it to be when she knows it's not. You had no right to tell her she had to accept me or else, and I told you so at the time. She didn't tell you she'd love you as soon as the judge exonerated you, did she?"

His thoughts went back to that night on the grass-covered edge of Rock Island when, with only his word for proof, she had believed him innocent, encouraged him to clear his name, and had sworn she'd be there for him no matter what. And like a shaft of light in the darkness, she had been true to her word.

He rubbed his forehead. "It is because she believed in me that I have no criminal record. But she…after the hearing, she walked away and didn't once look back at me."

"And you haven't made it better by not returning her call. I understand what she's going through. How would *you* like to learn that the people closest to you, who'd been responsible for your nurturing and whom you loved most in the world, had misled you for thirty years with a who-struck-John tale about something as important as your father? She had a delayed reaction, and when it sank in, you can bet it wasn't love she felt."

"No, I guess not."

He needed to get away and do his own thinking. After all, he wasn't a boy seeking fatherly advice. He took the dishes to the kitchen, still perfumed with the fragrance of thyme, sage, onions and celery that flavored the roast quail his dad cooked for their dinner. He put the dishes in the dishwasher and stood at the sink, relishing a moment of solitude. He couldn't imagine a better place to gather his thoughts than Rock Island, and while there, he could check the remainder of the architect's changes. He walked into the living room where Richard watched Peter Jennings deliver the evening news.

"This seems a good time for me to check on those lighthouse repairs."

Richard nodded. "Hmmm. How long do you think you'll be there?"

He lifted his left shoulder in a quick shrug. "Maybe a week. I'll leave Baltimore Monday afternoon."

Richard sat back on the soft leather sofa, put his hands together and knocked his thumbs against each other as he sometimes did when mulling over a course of action. "You taking Veronica?"

He stared into eyes so like those of the woman he loved. "Veronica is not mine to take anywhere."

He hadn't meant to communicate his anxiety about her, but he had, and the forlorn tenor of his voice stunned him.

Richard patted his son's shoulder. "Do what you think best. A few weeks from now, you'll wonder what this gloom was all about."

Maybe she'd overdone it when she asked Schyler to wait while she came to terms with her feelings, but she couldn't live a life of pretend. She couldn't imagine why he hadn't returned her call. Perhaps he was ill and hadn't been to that office. She telephoned her father.

"He isn't ill. More than anything else, Schyler is perplexed," Richard said after they'd greeted each other. "He told me what you said, and I agree that I might have straightened it out when you first mentioned it. I have no excuse. All three of us are culpable. I'm positive of that." He cleared his throat several times. "Can you... Will you tell me about Esther. Was she happy?"

She didn't know what he wanted to hear, but she had to speak the truth. "She was happy, Father. Our lives were difficult. My stepfather told me last Sunday that he changed his identity and my last name so that you couldn't find us, because Mama had sworn to die before she'd give me up. He worked as a laborer but, yes, they were both happy."

"I'm glad. I'm so glad. She was the love of my life."

"I understand that now, and I know your own life couldn't have been an easy one."

"No, but I have you now, and that compensates for much of it. Don't let your relationship with Schyler deteriorate. Try to understand that his deep commitment to me is because I was his salvation."

"Oh, I've accepted that." She thought for a moment, and then the words tumbled out of her. Uncontrollable. "I love him so much that sometimes it frightens me."

"And still you have the guts to hold out for what you need. I'm proud of you."

"But it's been a week, and he hasn't returned my call."

"Don't worry about that. He said the only words he wants from your lips right now are that *you want him.*"

"Where is he?"

"At Rock Island. You can fly to Norfolk, hire a shuttle boat for about fifty dollars and be there half an hour later. I'll call his cell number and let him know you're coming."

"Thanks, but I'd rather take a chance. If he's not there, I'll take the boat back to Norfolk. I...I love you, Father."

She listened to the most pregnant silence she'd ever heard. At last, in a voice that trembled, he said, "God answered my prayer. I love you. Always have and always will."

She made the airline reservations, packed and sat down. If he'd gone to her beloved Rock Island without her, knowing how much she loved the place, maybe he didn't want her there. But it was she who had asked for a cooling period, and she was the one who had to bring them back together. When she recalled her self-righteous accusations of her father before hearing his defense, she knew she had no right to judge Schyler. Her father had said that they were all three culpable; so was she.

As the boat neared Rock Island, butterflies battled for space in her belly, goose pimples popped out on her arms and she had to struggle to control her chattering teeth. She must have lost her mind; otherwise, she wouldn't have done such a foolish thing. The boat docked, and she asked the captain to wait while she made certain that Schyler was there. She looked toward the lighthouse door just as he stepped through it, and wild sensations permeated her body. She wanted to jump to shore and scale every barrier that separated them. She turned to the captain, smiled and pointed toward Schyler. The captain tipped his hat, tossed her bag ashore and accelerated the motor.

With the winged grace of Mercury, he raced to meet her, and she jumped from the boat and into his arms. "Baby, you're here. How did you...where did you...?"

As though words had no power to express what he felt, he parted his lips over hers and let his passion roar through her. She clung to him, savoring the feel of him, his strength, his taste and his scent, as frissons of heat skittered along her nerves. He must have doubted his five senses, for he set her away from him and stared into her face. She gazed up at him as tension danced between them like an unharnessed electric current, wild and dangerous. She didn't try to hide from him the love she bore him nor her naked longing to be one with him again, and the answering fire of his smoldering gaze ignited in her a sweet and terrible hunger that only he could assuage.

No words could have sufficed. He lifted her into his arms and carried her into the lighthouse and up the stairs to his room. He stood her beside his bed and looked deeply into her eyes.

"I want you to remember this as long as we live. *I belong to you*. And my love for you is not contingent upon anything or anybody."

She placed a finger on his lips. "It's all right, I under—"

"No, sweetheart. Isn't all right. I have to say it, and you need to hear it. I need you as I need to breathe. You are my life. I know now that nothing—I mean nothing—could have compelled me voluntarily to give you up. You are my life, Veronica. Can you forgive me?"

Tears of joy dribbled over her smile as she saw the scraps of her soul begin to fit themselves together again. "There's nothing to forgive; that's why I'm here. I told my father—"

Quickly, he cut her off. "I don't want to hear about him right now. I want to know if you love me. I need you to love me, because that's all that matters."

"I do. I do. If you only knew how much I love you!"

She watched his eyes darken and his breathing accelerate, knew the telltale signs of his rising passion and rimmed her lips with the tip of her tongue. As if she'd shot fire into him, he had her in his arms and his tongue in her mouth, and her heat began its dance in the seat of her passion. She moved his hand to her left breast to ease the ache that she knew wouldn't cease until she felt his vigorous suckling. Tuned into her needs, now, he dipped his hands into her sweater, freed the treat that awaited him and nourished himself. Needing more of him, she climbed his body and fitted herself to him, undulating, out of control and free to let herself fly.

He pulled the sweater over her head, unhooked her bra and freed her other breast. She unsnapped her slacks and he lifted her to his bed and pulled them from her body. She thought she would incinerate as he stood above her savoring her as a wild beast would savor his catch. Frantic to know once more the feeling of him inside of her, she raised her arms and spread her knees. In seconds he was beside her. She reached for him, greedy for the pleasure he would give her, but he stayed her hand and charted his slow course over the feast before him. Her eyes, ears, neck, nose and face soon knew the torture of his lips, while she felt his fingertips singe her body.

"Schyler, please. Please, I can't stand it."

"Shhh. Let's not chase it, baby. Wait till it finds us. Be patient and let me love you. I want every bit of you." She felt his tongue skim over her mouth and opened to him. He darted inside, but as she opened it for his full kiss, he bent to her breast and began to suckle her. Her cries of passion seemed only to excite him more, to embolden him. His hot fingers skimmed the inside of her thighs, and she tried to trap them, but he was making his own way into a barrel-like roll as she undulated helplessly.

"Honey, I can…I need you inside of me," she moaned.

"I'm going there. I want you to have everything I can give you."

When he hooked her knees over his shoulders, unfolded her love petals and kissed her, she couldn't hold back the screams. Mercilessly, he loved her until she called out his name. "Schyler. Love. I can't stand this."

"All right, sweetheart, it's what we both want."

He made his way up her body, taking his time, kissing and loving every spot that he could reach. Thoroughly unstrung, she reached for him, found him and brought him to her. Then his hand closed over hers, and he gazed down into her eyes. "There's no going back, Veronica."

"I don't want to turn back. I want you."

He moved his hand and let her have him, then sank into her and began to rock. She thought she heard the waves sloshing against the island's banks, and the wind howl as he plunged in and out of her, increasing her headlong dive to insanity. His kiss blocked her scream as heat attacked the soles of her feet and began its upward spiral until the squeezing began. But he denied her the ecstasy for which she reached, dragged her back from the brink, withdrew and let his magic fingers play their tune. She moaned in agony at the sweet torture, until he rejoined them.

"Tell me what you want. Tell me."

She hooked her legs under his knees, let him roll over on his back and loved him. While he suckled and caressed her breast, she moved above him until her passion escalated into wave after wave of rapture. The shutters clanged as the wind blew them open and shut and the salt air swirled about them, but that only heightened her hunger for that last, powerful rupture. She tightened around him, and he took control once more and drove her to ecstasy. Like human quicksand, he sucked her into his body, into his being until she became one with him. She danced beneath him until she exploded in passion.

"Schyler. I love you so."

He gave himself up to the powerful vortex that shook his body, and collapsed in her arms. Shaken nearly out of his senses, he wrapped her tightly to him and pressed a kiss to her lips. When he'd heard the motor of that boat, he'd suspected that his dad had come to keep him company, and then he'd seen her. He'd never known such joy.

"What was happening to us those other times?" she asked him. "I never felt this way before."

He shook his head, still stunned by their coupling. "Neither have I, and I have to imagine it's because nothing stood between us. Free. I felt as though you were mine to love."

She stroked his back. "So did I, as if I had free rein to do as I pleased with you. I thought I'd just fly."

"And I want you to feel that way with me. This past week cemented a few truths. I don't like being away from you. Not one bit. I think we ought to get married."

"Is that so?"

"Uh-huh. And my dad's been after me about grandchildren."

"No kidding!"

"Really." He kissed her nose.

"Well that's tough. I want to be asked."

He knew he had a foolish grin on his face, but he couldn't help it. He was too happy to care. "Will you marry me, Veronica? I'll be a good husband to you and a good father to our children, and I'll love you as long as I breathe."

Her smile lit up everything around him. "There's nothing I want more, Love."

Epilogue

At six-forty-five on Christmas Eve, Richard Henderson and
Howard "Sam" Overton entered the vestibule of the Bethel
AME Church from opposite directions, though they hadn't
planned it.

Richard walked directly to Sam and extended his right
hand, which Sam quickly grasped.

"I hope you can forgive me, and Esther too."

A rueful smile crossed Richard's face. "Perhaps it is I who
should ask *your* forgiveness. I always knew it was you who
Esther loved, but I loved her so much that I thought I could
make her forget you."

Sam braced his back with both hands and let a smile play
around his eyes. "Do you get the feeling we're just as we were
when we started, except that our daughter wouldn't choose
between us, as Esther did?"

"Yeah," Richard said. "I thought about it a lot. She's smart.
You did a good job. Wonder what Esther is thinking about this?"

"Can't say, but I'm sure it's what she wanted, that it's what her last request was all about. Where's Schyler?"

"In the church. Ah! Here comes the bride."

Jenny adjusted the train of Veronica's beaded, white satin gown and the tiara and veil that she'd weighted down with seed pearls. Then Enid stepped ahead of Veronica in a pale blue gown that matched the bride's dress. The organ pealed a signal of the bride's approach, and Enid began the long walk to the altar. Veronica marveled that the pieces fit together almost magically, but she didn't breathe as deeply as she should have until she stepped into the vestibule and saw her father and stepfather standing beside each other waiting for her. As she walked up the aisle with her father on her left and her stepfather on her right, she saw the smile that covered Schyler's face, for he had broken with tradition and turned to face her.

"This is a great day," Sam Overton said.

"More than I could have hoped for," Richard replied.

Standing beside Enid at the altar, facing Madison and Schyler and looking at her father and stepfather, who had refused to sit down and, as though by consent, had remained at the altar, she blinked rapidly to stave off the tears. Somehow, her glance fell on Jenny who, with her usual temerity, shook her finger in a brazen reprimand that said "don't cry," and Veronica couldn't help grinning.

The Reverend Mr. Donald Butcher cleared his throat. "Dearly Beloved…"

Mother Nature has love on her mind…

Temperatures Rising

Book #1 in *Mother Nature Matchmaker*…

New York Times Bestselling Author

BRENDA JACKSON

Radio producer Sherrie Griffin is used to hot, stormy weather. But the chemistry between her and sports DJ Terrence Jeffries is a whole new kind of tempest. Stranded together during a Florida hurricane, they take shelter…in each other's arms.

Mother Nature has something brewing…
and neither man nor woman stands a chance.

Coming the first week of May 2009,
wherever books are sold.

KIMANI™
ROMANCE

REQUEST YOUR FREE BOOKS!

2 FREE NOVELS
PLUS 2 FREE GIFTS!

KIMANI™
ROMANCE

Love's ultimate destination!

KROM08R